CAVE HAEC LEGERE![1]

Inscription by a mediæval monk in a book of magic

1. *Cave haec legere!* Latin, "Beware of reading these," the plural evidently referring to all three books of the planned trilogy. In the 1907 edition of *Román Manfreda Macmillena* (RMM), Karásek places this untranslated epigraph at the beginning of his preface (*úvod*), just under the heading. In the 1924 edition of *RMM*, it comes two pages after the first title page and four blank pages before the preface.

MANFRED MACMILLAN

BOOK ONE OF THE *THREE MAGICIANS* TRILOGY

JIŘÍ KARÁSEK ZE LVOVIC

Translated from the Czech and annotated by Carleton Bulkin
with an introduction by Carleton Bulkin and Brian James Baer

The complete manuscript of this work was subjected to a partly
closed ("single-anonymous") review process. For more information,
visit https://acpress.amherst.edu/peerreview/.

Published in the United States of America by Amherst College Press
Manufactured in the United States of America

Library of Congress Control Number: 2024931296

DOI: https://doi.org/10.3998/mpub.14429180
ISBN 978-1-943208-79-1 (paper)
ISBN 978-1-943208-80-7 (open access)

TABLE OF CONTENTS

INTRODUCTION

"It is essential to disrupt order and consensus in the world."
Jiří Karásek ze Lvovic, *Manfred Macmillan*, LXXIII

A queer novel was a disruptive thing in 1907, when Czech author Jiří Karásek ze Lvovic published *Román Manfreda Macmillena* (Manfred Macmillan's Novel); but then, the 36-year-old Karásek had been making waves for years. He had shaken up the Czech arts scene as cofounder of *Moderní revue* (Moderne Revue, 1894–1925),[1] the first-ever Czech modern arts journal. In its pages in spring 1895, he had vigorously defended Oscar Wilde as an artist and a homosexual—as Wilde was facing the charges of "gross indecency" that would soon destroy him. Opponents branded the journal a purveyor of vice and attempted to block distribution of its "Wilde issue" that June. In September, Karásek scandalized contemporaries with the openly queer verse of his *Sodoma* (Sodom) collection, which the authorities confiscated at the printer's (fig. 1).[2]

While *fin de siècle* Central and Eastern Europeans were increasingly questioning the status quo in the arts, the sciences, and politics, queer artists defied the age's "pettiness and sobriety" at additional personal risk.[3] Homosexual acts

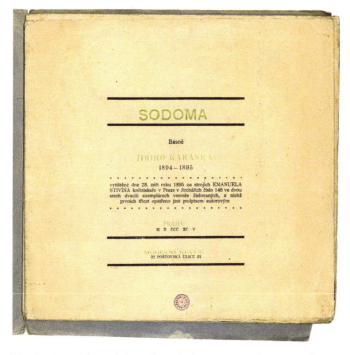

Fig. 1. A rare first edition of Karásek's poetry collection *Sodom* (1895), printed by Emanuel Stivín. Most of the 220 copies were confiscated at the printer's by the Habsburg authorities. Courtesy of the Library of the Museum of Czech Literature (Prague).

were proscribed by law and pathologized by medical opinion in the Austro-Hungarian Empire (which included the Czech lands) and beyond.[4] Nevertheless, Karásek was highly active in Prague's literary scene, where gossip about his sexuality was rife. He not only republished *Sodom* in 1905 but moved forward with *Romány tří magů* (The Three Magicians' Novels, 1907–25), an entire trilogy of queer novels.

The present volume establishes the paradigm for all three books: the romance between an "active" and a "passive" personality, the reinvention of one's life through art, and magic as a powerful antidote to pettiness and sobriety. The hero of *Manfred Macmillan* is a dandy, magician, and "artist of life"[5]—an aristocrat unfettered by convention who finds personal inspiration in the self-reinvention of the historical Sicilian alchemist and celebrity Alessandro di Cagliostro (1743–1795).

Karásek went on to become "unequivocally the most prominent interwar icon of Czech homosexual culture," as Czech queer historian Jan Seidl argues.[6] Recalling *Manfred Macmillan*'s reception for the Czechoslovak gay/lesbian-community journal *Nový hlas pro sexuální reformu* (New Voice for Sexual Reform, 1932–34) years later, the author mused that "for the first time in Czech literature, I removed the veil from the mystery of our [third] sex [...] without normal people throwing my books away in disgust."[7]

On Reading Early Queer Literature

In the first volume of *Histoire de la sexualité* (The History of Sexuality, 1976–84), Michel Foucault (1926–1984) famously situates the "birth" of the modern homosexual in the year 1870,[8] with the publication of a scientific article by German psychiatrist Carl Westphal on "contrary sexual sensations." From then on, Foucault argues, homosexuality ceased to be a sin or a vice and became a totalizing identity, "a species." Since the publication of Foucault's work, many historians have challenged his interpretation of the historical record, offering evidence of individuals and institutions—such as the molly house in eighteenth-century England[9]—that attest to the existence of a queer consciousness or identity well before 1870. Moreover, typologies of sexual pathology had also emerged before then.

Yet after 1870, one can see a distinct shift in literary treatments of homosexuality. Earlier in the century, authors such as Honoré de Balzac and Théophile Gautier had incorporated homosexual characters and homosexuality in their works but not as expressions of their own sexual experience. In the final decades of the nineteenth century, however, works of poetry and prose by queer-identified authors portraying the contemporary homosexual experience emerged. This output began as a trickle of works either pornographic (such as *The Sins of the Cities of the Plains* [1881] by Jack Saul, *Teleny, or The Reverse of the Medal* [1893] by Anonymous, and *La pédérastie passive, ou, mémoires d'un enculé* [Passive pederasty, or, Memoirs of a bottom, 1894–95] by L.B.); or coded (e.g., Walt Whitman's *Calamus* poems [1860, finalized 1881], Karl Heinrich Ulrichs's *Manor: Eine Novelle* [Manor: A Novella, 1882], Pierre Loti's *Mon frère Yves* [My brother Yves, 1883], Oscar Wilde's *The Picture of Dorian Gray* [serial 1890, book 1891], and Howard Sturgis's *Tim: A Story of School Life* [1891]).

After the 1895 prosecution of Oscar Wilde on charges of gross indecency, and particularly after his death, this trickle turned into a steady stream. It now included works both less pornographic and less coy about their characters' sexual desires. The final years of the nineteenth century and the first two decades of the twentieth witnessed the publication of an array of "gay" fiction, some of which would enter the European canon, such as André Gide's *L'immoraliste* (The Immoralist, 1902), Mikhail Kuzmin's *Kryl'ia* (Wings, 1906), Marcel Proust's *À la recherche du temps perdu* (In Search of Lost Time, 1913–22), and E.M. Forster's *Maurice* (1913, though published only in 1971, the year after Forster's death), while others would prove more ephemeral, such as the prose works of Jacques d'Adelswärd-Fersen, Achille Essebac, Georges Eekhoud, and Xavier Mayne.

Since the Stonewall uprising on June 28, 1969, these early literary works by queer-identified authors have attracted increasing attention from scholars working in LGBTQ+ studies and beyond, resulting in major surveys of the history of gay and lesbian literature. Consistently absent in these historical overviews, however, is the Czech author Jiří Karásek ze Lvovic (fig. 2).[10]

In the case of Karásek, it is difficult to attribute this neglect to the usual causes: a life cut short, a small and perhaps unpublished corpus of literary works, or personal obscurity. Karásek lived a long life, published extensively, and was a prominent public figure. His verse collection *Sodom* was read into the record of the Austrian Reichsrat (parliament) in defense of artistic freedom and later reissued in multiple editions. He coedited an important arts journal and was recognized for his literary criticism. He later became a symbol of interwar Czechoslovakia's nascent homosexual rights movement. In 1931, he was awarded the Czechoslovak State Prize for Literature. In short, Karásek was a prominent public figure.

The answer more likely lies in the geopolitics of queer literary history, which has traditionally privileged works written in the major Western European languages and Russian for translation and hence, incorporation into international histories of gay literature. With the possible exception of the modern Greek poet Constantine Cavafy, authors writing in

Fig. 2. Jiří Karásek ze Lvovic as a dandy of a certain age. At the Karásek Gallery (ca.1930). Courtesy of the Literary Archive of the Museum of Czech Literature.

minor languages have generally remained overlooked and their works untranslated.

Yet the justification for this English translation of Karásek's openly queer novel *Manfred Macmillan*,[11] the first in the *Three Magicians* trilogy, is not merely to expand the geographic and linguistic coverage of gay literary histories. In addition, as a writer in a minor European language who spent almost his entire life in his hometown of Prague, Karásek offers a rare vantage point for analysis from a postcolonial perspective: that of a colonial subject. The Czech lands were part of Habsburg holdings from 1620 until the dissolution of the Austro-Hungarian empire in 1918. Combine that with his queer sexuality, and Karásek could be said to inhabit a "triple consciousness."[12]

Indeed, not only are the relationships in the novels openly queer, but colonial marginalization is also invoked directly in *Manfred Macmillan*. At the very outset, Karásek situates his hero's summer villa at the Bílá Hora battle site, where the Bohemian state lost its independence in 1620. As such, it functions as a symbol of the glorious past, of a dream now extinct and beyond the real or the possible, a theme elaborated in chapters LXIV–LXVIII.[13] Karásek further develops such geopolitical considerations by contrasting the imperial capital of Vienna, presented as the nexus of cosmopolitan chic and an international destination, with the seemingly moribund, even necrotic city of Prague.

The Prague of Manfred's adventures in book one of the trilogy, however, is also a city with unique esoteric legacies and a mysterious, vibrant magic all its own. This is most evident in book three, *Ganymedes* (Ganymede, 1925), which draws upon a home-grown golem legend and the alleged kabbalistic conjurations of the city's historical High Rabbi Judah Loew ben Bezalel (ca.1520–1609). Even in Italian Bohemist Angelo Maria Ripellino's survey of the topos of *Praga magica* (Magic Prague, 1973; English transl. 1994) in Czech literature, Karásek's rendering of the city stands out for its complex engagement with the antiprogressivist discourse of decadence and the antira-tionalist discourse of magic and occultism—particularly as it seemed to take on the sober Max Nordau's concept of degeneracy, turning it on its head.[14] Critically, this edition of Karásek's novel seeks to complicate the dominant fram-ing of the author as Czech literature's leading decadent by exploring his pioneering contributions to gay literature. In turn, it should challenge traditional colonialist historiogra-phies, which assume works from the periphery to be neces-sarily belated and derivative.

Before situating Karásek and his novels in the context of his time and place, a few words should be said about reading early queer literature in general, and Karásek's work in particular, in order to avoid succumbing to a number of tempting binaries. First, early gay literature should not be read from today's vantage point as a direct repudiation of, let alone an emancipation from, the medical and legal dis-courses that pathologized and criminalized same-sex desire. These discourses not only shaped but also to some extent enabled the emergence of gay literature, bringing unprece-dented attention to queer lives and queer voices. At the same time, the relationship between early gay literature and the surrounding discourses with which it was entangled was complex and unpredictable. Indeed, these discourses often overlapped.

For example, the French forensic doctor Auguste Ambroise Tardieu (1819–79) published a two-volume study called *Les vices de conformation* (Vices of Conformation, 1874) on genital deformities. Volume one consisted of his scientific analysis, while volume two contained the first-person narrative of the hermaphrodite Herculine Barbin (1838–68), written in a highly emotive and literary style. Or consider German psychologist Richard von Krafft-Ebing's

Psychopathia sexualis: Eine klinisch-forensische Studie (Sexual Psychopathology: A Clinical-Forensic Study, 1886), which underwent numerous editions and was translated into multiple languages in the late nineteenth and early twentieth centuries. It contained a number of first-person narratives or case studies by queer individuals. While these were ostensibly included to confirm his theorization of same-sex desire as nonnormative, their intense affect and literariness—at times invoking the romantic motif of the despised outsider, as expressed in Byron's verse "I stand among them but not of them"[15]—allowed them to transcend their role as data. As the Russian studies scholar Evgenii Bershtein notes with regard to the Russian translation of Krafft-Ebing's work,

> [T]he narrative strategy of allowing patients to tell their own stories often turned "medical cases" into hymns to their sexual peculiarities. These first-person narratives could transcend their initial pragmatics and genre: conceived as clinical illustrations of disease, they transformed into powerful articulations of "difference."[16]

This was also the case with the English study *Sexual Inversion* (1897), "which contained thirty-four new case histories gathered by [the authors] that, unlike other British sexological texts, did not focus exclusively on people from prisons and asylums."[17] Moreover, this volume was a collaboration between the poet and art historian John Addington Symonds and the psychologist and physician Henry Havelock Ellis. In fact, Symonds first reached out to Ellis after finding in the latter's *The New Spirit* (1890) a positive evaluation of American author Walt Whitman's *Calamus* poems (1860).[18] Other literary figures made contributions to the field of sexology. For example, English poet and essayist Edward Carpenter published *The Intermediate Sex: A Study of Some Transitional Types of Men and Women* (1908), and

American writer Xavier Mayne released *The Intersexes: A History of Similisexualism as a Problem in Social Life* (also 1908).[19]

At the same time, works of queer fiction began to include encounters with sexological treatises, typically presented as a defining moment in a character's understanding of their sexuality or sexual identity. See, for example, Mayne's novel *Imre: A Memorandum* (1906), in which the main character comes upon a book about homosexuality by a Dr. D., who argues that it is a curable "malady"; and Radclyffe Hall's *Well of Loneliness* (1928), in which the heroine finds a copy of Krafft-Ebing's *Psychopathia sexualis* in her father's library, with his comments in the margins.[20] Much later, Charlotte von Mahlsdorf would recount in her memoir *Ich bin meine eigene Frau* (I Am My Own Woman, 1992; English transl. 1994) how her Aunt Louise, herself a cross-dresser, finds the teenage von Mahlsdorf trying on her clothes. Louise then presents her niece with a copy of *Die Transvestiten* (The Transvestites, 1910) and instructs her to "read it carefully." From that moment on, von Mahlsdorf would use that term to self-identify.[21]

In late nineteenth-century Britain, the juridical construction of homosexual acts as the criminal effect of a crisis of masculinity afflicting the bourgeoisie intersected spectacularly with the realm of literature during the prosecution of Oscar Wilde in the spring of 1895.[22] For more than a decade after the trial, it was common for works of emerging gay literature to include a Wildean figure—for example, the Malinque character in Gide's *The Immoralist* and Strup in Kuzmin's *Wings*. As noted above, gay literature of the post-Wildean period was both less pornographic and less coded than before, setting the terms for the introduction of gay literature into the mainstream. That said, it would remain a common trope to present the queer seducer as foreign or to situate the act of seduction in a foreign land.[23] Malinque has a Greek name, and the protagonist Michel's first queer experience happens in North Africa. Strup is said to be half-English, and he and Vanya inaugurate their sexual relationship on an artistic pilgrimage to Italy. The hero in d'Adelswärd-Fersen's *Lord Lyllian* (1905; English transl. 2005) is entirely English. In Karásek's *Manfred Macmillan*, the title character is a multinational aristocrat with an English surname. In the trilogy's second volume, *Scarabaeus* (Scarabæus, serial 1908–09, book 1909), the love triangle includes Marcel (French) and Oreste (Italian) and takes place in Venice—as does Thomas Mann's later *Der Tod in Venedig* (Death in Venice, 1912). In James Baldwin's still later *Giovanni's Room* (1956), not only is the American hero's lover Italian, but the novel takes place in Paris as well. And the first post-Soviet collection of gay writing in Russian bears the title *Drugoi* (The Other, 1993), and all the stories take place outside of Russia.[24]

The second binary opposition to avoid—Karásek's literary contrast between Vienna and Prague notwithstanding—is to suppose an actual contrast between an isolated and backward periphery and a cosmopolitan and progressive metropole. Like many colonial subjects, educated Czechs in the Austro-Hungarian Monarchy were typically bilingual. In addition, those who attended *Gymnasien* (university preparatory academies) would not only have been instructed in German but also received exposure to classical Greek and Latin; some knew French and other languages besides. As a result, they had access to a pan-European cultural identity and could keep abreast of developments in the rest of Europe through foreign newspapers, journals, and books—which, in addition, were selectively translated into Czech.[25] The diaries of Kuzmin and the Russian artist Konstantin Somov confirm that they were reading a variety of literary and other works, including those dealing with the topics of illicit sex and queer sexuality, in several European languages. Karásek himself knew German, had reading knowledge of French (he lacked confidence in his accent),[26] and had a few books in English and many in other languages in his library.[27]

Central and Eastern Europeans therefore had access to proto-gay authors such as Lord Byron (1788–1824), either in translation or in the original. The name of Karásek's title character in *Manfred Macmillan* may well be a nod to Byron's hero Manfred[28]—and indirectly, to Byron himself, whose fluid sexuality and romantic nature had made him something of a gay icon by the late nineteenth century. In fact, Karásek's contemporary Xavier Mayne suggests in *The Intersexes* (1908) that Byron's *Manfred* be read as a "homosexual allegory." Proposing that the "burden of Manfred's conscience," "that unspeakable sin," is of a sexual, possibly homosexual nature, Mayne writes:

> we may then argue "Manfred" as, in a sense, an uranian drama, according to the foregoing; a sexual love between Manfred and a youth, or some more mature friend, as the burden on the conscience of Manfred—or rather the loss that oppresses him."[29]

Mayne also claims that Horace Walpole, the creator of the first gothic novel, *The House of Otranto* (1764)— with another main character named Manfred—was homosexual.[30]

All that being said, cultural, medical, and juridical discourses were by no means homogenous across the Global North in the *fin de siècle*. Moreover, individual authors' specific engagement with such discourses was shaped not only by their local literary culture and politics, but also by their life experience and aesthetic orientation. When Karásek was launching his literary career in the 1890s, juridical and medical discourses in Central and Eastern Europe were fanning a powerful obsession with social degeneration and civilizational collapse, of which homosexuality was deemed a prime symptom (see Nordau, *Entartung*

(Degeneration) [1892]; Otto Weininger's specific notions of an androgynous ideal in his study *Geschlecht und Charakter* [Sex and Character, 1903]; and Vasilii Rozanov's treatise *Liudi lunnogo sveta* [People of the Moonlight, 1911]).[31] Homosexuality itself remained exotic for most of the medical community. In 1906, the Hungarian physician Sándor Ferenczi attempted to persuade his Budapest colleagues to accept "uranism" as a natural form of sexuality and to support decriminalization—but reconsidered after encountering Freud's views.[32] In Great Britain, on the other hand, homosexuality was a greater obsession in the legal realm than elsewhere.

In the creative sphere, many Central and Eastern European writers and artists who defended homosexuality did so on aesthetic rather than medical or juridical grounds, perhaps reflecting the political realities of their regions. For example, after the limited constitutional reforms of 1860–61, Habsburg subjects enjoyed few opportunities to influence policy, even at the local (district and municipal) level, and then only on specified matters. For reasons of state, the Habsburgs would not recognize the historical Czech lands (Bohemia, Moravia, and part of Silesia) as a single administrative unit, which limited the significance of the Bohemian Diet. The Diet was anyway controlled by hereditary and ecclesiastical elites often beholden to Vienna. As a result, there was no space for social activism among Prague's "third sex" (homosexual) community until well after World War I. It was therefore natural that Karásek's disruption took place not in the sphere of law or medicine but in the name of individuality and artistic freedom. In the following sections, this Introduction will attempt to outline the social, historical, and cultural context for Karásek's rebellion and to gauge its limits, real and imagined, in personal terms. This is the environment in which Karásek's novels and poetry were produced and received.

Art and Politics under the Habsburgs

The tortured aesthetes of Karásek's *Three Magicians* novels are mavericks who neither seek nor expect recognition from contemporary society for their unconventional tastes, including their same-sex romances. Rather, they find safety behind the veils of individual self-stylization, aristocratic pedigree, occultism, medievalism, and, above all, privacy. In an essential, antirationalist, and magical subtext, these veils serve to insulate and occlude their unnamed sexuality. As the gothic villain Marcel divulges to Gaston in *Scarabæus*, invoking the occult concept of magnetism:

> The moment someone approaches me, how tremulous my anxiety as I search for the first glimmer of his spirit, for the first spark that would show that he too is surrounded by an atmosphere of the same magnetism as I, and together with him I yearn to give vent to all the possibilities and all the energies of my inner self.[33]

The veil of this aestheticist creed offers privacy and protection by separating real life from art, and the trilogy's magicians deliberately stylize their lives in an art all their own. Centered on queer heroes, the novels add up to a statement that remains defiant and disruptive, even if that defiance and disruption are aesthetic rather than political.

In the real world, the Habsburg Monarchy's liberal elites had long asserted a leading role in politics and culture, particularly since the limited constitutional reforms of 1860–61. They claimed a tutelary role and espoused a restricted if continual expansion of the franchise based on a liberal education and the eventual responsibilities of property. Their program invoked science, reason, and progress, and was tightly bound up with prevailing codes of respectability. The franchise remained severely restricted by class and income until the end of the Monarchy, and women were never seriously considered for inclusion. Among Czech nationalists, the liberals of 1848 founded the National Party to pursue similar aims and a vision of Bohemian "state rights" grounded in historical privileges, allying pragmatically with amenable leading nobles and clerics in the Bohemian Diet. They also promoted "respectable" Czech culture and advocated for the official use of the Czech language in Czech-speaking areas of Bohemia, as well as the expansion of Czech financial capital. With limited success, they also sought to increase their leverage through a program of Austro-Slavism and pan-Slavism. Gaining control of the Prague city council (1861), the inauguration of the National Theater (1881), and the reestablishment of a Czech administration alongside the German one for Charles-Ferdinand University (1882) were key milestones.[34]

Although most Germans in Bohemia and the Monarchy as a whole were workers and agriculturalists, German speakers enjoyed privileged access in the fields of government, commerce, and education; Slavs and Magyars usually needed a German-language education to enter the middle class.[35] For their part, German liberals aimed to lead by propagating "German intellection, German science, [and] German humanism."[36] They and their Czech counterparts did not caucus together in the lower house of the Reichsrat in Vienna.

Yet that state of affairs was continually challenged both domestically and from abroad. Having founded the German Confederation at the Congress of Vienna in 1815, the Habsburgs were then forced by military defeat to cede their leadership role to Prussia's Hohenzollerns in 1866. Although Czech liberal elites had begun to assert themselves in local administration, commerce, and education, the 1867 Austro-Hungarian Compromise granted Hungary internal autonomy while leaving the Czech lands under direct rule from Vienna. The Czech elites and their insular vision of Bohemian "state rights" and a respectable national culture looked increasingly ineffectual and out of touch. Many of them defended the authenticity of the dubious Dvůr Králové (Queen's Court, 1817) and Zelená Hora (Green Mountain, 1817) literary hoaxes, both eventually discredited as forgeries in 1886—which further undermined the cultural establishment's authority with educated younger Czechs and the literati among them.[37]

By the mid-1890s, political and artistic tensions were becoming more pronounced. In 1894, a group of young artists flocked around the new *Moderní revue*, the first modern arts journal in Czech.[38] It became a symbol of its generation's dedication to renewal in the national arts scene, but not on their elders' terms. Under the leadership of poet, translator, and publisher Arnošt Procházka (1869–1925, fig. 3), in collaboration with Karásek, it also became the first Czech publication to translate Oscar Wilde and Friedrich Nietzsche.[39]

As the younger critic Karel Sezima recalled Karásek and Procházka's collaboration years later, Karásek was someone with "dependably refined taste and distinction" (fig. 4), while the other, despite his erudition and flair for languages, "was often almost unbelievably tasteless, and not only in the bourgeois or academic sense. He was like a tightrope walker prone to falling off his rope."[40]

One of the new journal's contributors was the Polish decadent writer and critic Stanisław Przybyszewski (fig. 5),[41] remembered today as the friend and champion of Norwegian painter Edvard Munch, particularly of his iconic painting *The Scream* (1893).[42]

Przybyszewski was not a queer writer but a notorious womanizer and advocate of free love. His novel *Androgyne* (1900) is closer to a decadent study of the grotesque than one of intersexuality. Czech literary scholar Jiří Krystýnek asserts that any literary influence by Przybyszewski on Karásek was mainly negative, as allegedly seen in *Gotická duše* (A Gothic

ARNOŠT PROCHÁZKA

Fig. 3. Editor, translator, critic, and author, Procházka was a friend and longtime supporter of Karásek (photo ca.1900). Courtesy of the Literary Archive of the Museum of Czech Literature.

Soul, 1900): "under the strong influence of morbidly perverse delirium and monstrous psychopathological conditions in Przybyszewski's *Totenmesse* [Requiem Mass]."[43] Przybyszewski's self-declared Satanism may also resonate in *Manfred Macmillan*, with its occasional reference to

Fig. 4. From the studio of K. Smolek in Smíchov ca.1900. Courtesy of the Literary Archive of the Museum of Czech Literature.

Fig. 5. Polish decadent author Stanisław Przybyszewski
contributed to *Moderní revue* as a fellow modern. From the
Warsaw studio of Jan Idzikowski (ca.1902) and the collection
of Jan Fiszer. Courtesy of the Adam Mickiewicz Museum of
Literature (Warsaw).

Black Masses and black magic, although such imagery signified rebelliousness in general terms for French decadents
as well as for the Czech poet Stanislav Kostka Neumann in
his *Satanova sláva mezi námi* (The Glory of Satan Among
Us, 1897).

Separately, the 1895 *Manifest České moderny* (Manifesto
of the Czech Moderne), published in the journal *Rozhledy*
(Horizons) at the beginning of 1896, called for both political and artistic renewal: for freedom of speech and social
reform, as well as greater nonconformism in art. To varying
degrees, its signatories distanced themselves from the older
generation that had coalesced around the *Máj* (May) circle
and the journals *Lumír* (the name of a mythical Czech bard)
and *Osvěta* (Enlightenment, or Education). *Lumír* contributors had aspired to raise Czech literature to "European"
levels—but to their critics, they could sometimes seem mired
in eclecticism and imitation (*epigonerie*).

In any event, the manifesto's signatories soon splintered
over the call by critic František Xavier Šalda (1867–1937)
for a complete break with the past, and also over whether
to forge links with the Realist political party of Tomáš
Garrigue Masaryk, who had been instrumental in discredit-
ing the two forged manuscripts; personal squabbles likely
played a part as well. Even so, the modernists continued
to distinguish themselves from their elders. For their part,
the older liberals and their National Party now split into
the "Old Czech" and moderately more progressive "Young
Czech" factions. Czech-German language politics and limi-
tations on the franchise remained vital issues. To varying
degrees, these fissiparous groups might discuss the condition
of workers, students, or—at a stretch—even women. Violent
demonstrations broke out in June 1897. Progressives and
radicals demanded an expanded franchise and greater civil
liberties but were forcefully suppressed by Habsburg troops.
A state of emergency was declared, and it lasted two years.

In Vienna, the Badeni government fell in November. Many in the new generation grew more disenchanted with the old liberal program and its apparent lack of results; a few had even clamored for the monarchy's downfall. But no one was advocating for the toppling of laws or customs that targeted the "third sex."

Against this backdrop, the 24-year-old Karásek—former seminarian, now a fledgling author and postal official living with his widowed mother, and always saving to buy more artwork—dared to take a stand in print to defend Oscar Wilde as an individual artist and a homosexual with the right to be left alone in his private life. Unsurprisingly, Karásek and other participants in the Wilde polemic among Czech journals also invoked the ethos of "science and reason" by citing Krafft-Ebing's studies.[44] Krafft-Ebing's and other studies were increasingly informing legal debate and police practices in Central Europe and beyond.[45] In the continent's rapidly growing cities, where new migrants often could not afford privacy, human sexuality was becoming ever more visible in public spaces (parks and corsos), as well as in press reporting on vice and scandals. Moreover, a range of standards prevailed even among Austria-Hungary's elites—the aristocracy, the military officer corps, and the diplomatic service. Karásek moved within, or at least on the edges of, some of these circles through his "friend from Vienna" (see below), who inspired the character of Manfred-Marcel-Adrian in the *Three Magicians* trilogy.

The Habsburg Monarchy's Queer Elites

Vienna's press censorship prevented public reports that Emperor Franz Joseph's cosseted youngest brother, Archduke Ludwig Viktor, was homosexual. The emperor maintained a protective attitude toward this sibling, whom the family called "Lutziwutzi." Yet word got out. Princess Eleonora (Nora) Fugger von Babenhausen captiously described Ludwig in her memoirs as "unmanly, affected, and of repellent appearance."[46] Furthermore, in the wake of the 1907 Eulenberg affair in Germany (see below), the tabloid weekly *Illustrierte Oesterreichische Kriminal-Zeitung* openly asserted that the potential for homosexual scandals existed "in all social classes up to the highest" in the Habsburg lands.[47]

Still another Habsburg archduke, Wilhelm Franz of Austria, was a practicing homosexual, according to biographer Timothy Snyder.[48] Born on one family estate in the Austrian Littoral (Croatia) and raised on another in Galicia (Austrian Poland), Wilhelm conceived cultural and political sympathies for the Ukrainians—in apparent rebellion against his father's adopted Polish nationalism and identity—and for this, he earned himself the nickname of the "Red Prince." Snyder records that Wilhelm's escapades with men did not, in themselves, bar him from the theoretical "Ukrainian crown" he sought.[49]

Using Viennese archives to research Habsburg military justice in the period 1848–1918, István Deák examined prosecutions of officers for homosexual acts. He found that "the military courts were not preoccupied with sexual crimes," and that such cases as existed tended to involve minors, subordinates, or non-consensual sex.[50] General Oskar Potiorek, whose family was of Czech origin, was generally reputed to be homosexual;[51] nevertheless, he was removed from command not for sexual offenses but after the failure of the Serbian campaign in 1914.

At least some middle-aged officers were discouraged from marrying by the army's requirement for a substantial marriage bond, for example 50,000 krone (crowns) for Habsburg military intelligence chief August Urbański von Ostrymiecz in 1908—"equal to nearly half [his office's] annual budget." In any event, the homosexuality of Urbański's counterintelligence chief, Colonel Alfred Redl, seems to have been "a relatively open secret," as the colonel would appear in society with his "longtime companion" Lieutenant Stefan Horinka as "uncle and nephew" (Schindler 2005, 488). Horinka (sometimes called Hromodka) benefited in his career from Redl's patronage. At the time of Redl's death, Horinka was planning to marry a woman who was expecting his child. After Redl's apparent suicide, he was stripped of his commission and sentenced to three months at hard labor.[52]

During the same period, German counterintelligence tipped off the Austrians that Redl had sold secrets to the Russians, enabling a lavish personal lifestyle. Redl had attended military school in Moravia and from 1910 served as chief of staff for the VIII Corps in Prague.[53] By 1913 his superiors were well aware that the Russians were on to their network, but only the tip from the Germans put them wise to Redl's role. The colonel was interrogated in his room at the Hotel Klomser in Vienna, where he admitted his guilt and was handed a Browning pistol, apparently to allow him to avoid scandal by an honorable suicide—which was most likely the actual cause of his death. In fact, Redl had been selling secrets not only to Russia but also to France and Italy for years.[54]

In presenting the matter to the emperor and the Reichsrat, military brass both underplayed the extent of the intelligence damage and framed the matter as one of a homosexual in financial difficulties[55]—ergo blackmailable on both counts. In so doing, they capitalized on memories of the recent Eulenberg affair (1907–09) in Berlin, where a half-dozen military officers had committed suicide following blackmail attempts, and roughly twenty were convicted by courts-martial, all over homosexual acts.[56] The emphasis on Redl's lifestyle and sexuality therefore deflected attention from the security lapse itself.[57] Leaks to the Austrian press also emphasized Redl's suicide and homosexuality. Among those who took up the story was *der rasende Reporter* ("the roving reporter") Egon Erwin Kisch (1885–1948), from Prague and of Sephardic Jewish heritage.[58] Under pressure from military censorship, Austrian papers reported no salacious details of the case; but Kisch did, in Berlin, and the story then spread. Yet Redl's sexuality as such was evidently not the House of Habsburg's true concern.

Neither did "discreet" homosexuality usually become a career issue for the largely aristocratic Austro-Hungarian diplomatic corps—of which Karásek suggested his "friend from Vienna" was a member[59]—although these might face blackmail attempts and shakedowns. Entrants were expected to be single and remain so until promoted to legation secretary. At the outset of their careers, attachés received no salary and yet had to maintain appearances to ensure social entrée; the cost of maintaining a household abroad could be prohibitive for a married diplomat with children and servants.

The senior Austrian diplomat Count Tadeusz Koziebrodzki, posted to the Württemberg court in Stuttgart as envoy extraordinary and minister plenipotentiary since 1909, was embroiled in potential scandal in 1914, when a waiter he had been involved with pressed him repeatedly for hush money. Koziebrodzki informed the foreign secretary of the situation, instructed his lawyer to refer the matter to the local police, and yet remained at his posting until his death in 1916. His fellow diplomat Baron Leopold von Andrian, who was friends with queer modernist Austrian author Hugo von Hofmannsthal, wrote of his same-sex attractions in diaries and letters, but it seems not to have impacted his career.[60] When Baron Arthur Eisenstein was brought home from Berlin in 1890, however, his recall may have been due to indiscretion.[61]

Yet most queers in Austria-Hungary or Europe more broadly were more exposed to informants and blackmail, arrest and prosecution. In Paris, where sodomy was unmentioned in the law, police raids on public trysting places were even more common than in London, where sodomy was explicitly criminalized.[62] For the vast majority, discretion was therefore the rule, and few queer men and women dared let their inner selves out except in anonymity or sanctuary.

Whether in Vienna or Prague, as Karásek sought his bearings as a young artist and a human being, the notion of homosexual desire as innate and therefore inevitable to some had only begun to filter into public discourse. Acting on such desire continued to be viewed as a moral choice. Although hostile legal and social codes militated against indiscretion, even settled queer urbanites generally lacked privacy;[63] the public shame of an arrest thus remained an additional powerful deterrent to queer behavior, even if actual convictions were few in Prague.[64] As a result, where queer desire surfaced at all in public life, it was deeply associated with the marginal, the illicit, and the criminal.[65] At any rate, the defense of "sexual minorities" was not a public issue for Czech elites or anyone else—yet.

Karásek's Life and Career

Born on January 24, 1871 to a railway conductor and his wife, Jiří Josef Antonín Karásek was a native of Smíchov— at the time, still a village outside Prague's city walls and later a working-class district.[66] He was christened Josef but came to use the name Jiří ("Georg" in German) for civic purposes.[67] His father died in 1890, the same year he completed his secondary studies. Jiří then pursued divinity studies for less than two years before abandoning them, at least partly out of concern for his widowed mother's finances.[68]

Meanwhile, modernity was advancing rapidly, for all in Prague to see. Telephones and electric doorbells had begun ringing in Bohemia prior to 1883, and the number of Prague telephone subscribers surged from 187 in 1883 to 602 by 1888.[69] The city's first electric tramway was launched in 1891. In 1897, the Präsident horseless carriage, steered by handlebars, became the first factory-produced automobile in the Czech lands, and these could be seen on city streets.[70] The Čihák brothers' monoplane, the first Czech-built airplane, came together in 1913.[71] Yet for Karásek, modernity's vehicle would be the arts.

Karásek's first two novels appeared in 1891 and 1893, suggesting literary ambitions even as a divinity student.[72] He may have experienced a spiritual crisis during those years, and like his narrator Francis in *Manfred Macmillan*, modeled after himself, "put God out of my mind and turned away from people."[73] Nevertheless, Karásek the artist held to a "highly aestheticized Catholicism,"[74] like the elder writer Julius Zeyer (1841–1901), whom he emulated.[75] As he wrote his friend Marie Kalašová on Christmas Eve in 1905:

> After all, the beauty of the Catholic rite has no equal: it will manage to outlive the dogma. Even for one who does not believe, it offers the possibility to continue to pray: with the incense, the chanting, the lights, the gold of the altars and vestments.[76]

After a year in Bavaria, Karásek returned to Prague and began a lifelong association with the postal service, at first as a postal official. Over the years, he eventually rose to become the administrator of the postal museum and ministry archives.[77] As a young man, Karásek continued to live with his mother. One immediate neighbor was a retired professor given to late-night fits of religious moralizing, and the other the penurious and now-forgotten writer Václav Bambas;[78] Karásek may have lived with his mother until her death in 1900.

Karásek worked as a postal clerk (*poštovní asistent*) with the railway post from 1896 until at least October 1898.[79] His duties enabled various trips to Vienna. There, he became entranced with the collections at the Albertina Museum, which inspired him to scour the city's art galleries and antiquarian booksellers for treasures. This passion for art permeates the novels *Manfred Macmillan* and *Scarabæus*. As Karásek's young friend and publisher Otakar Štorch-Marien (1897–1974) recalled:

> He would then visit Viennese auctions and antique shops and bring home whole sheaves of items, which were of no particular interest to anyone at the time and the price of which has now risen often more than a hundredfold. Yet Karásek kept only the most important of them and exchanged or sold the rest. In this way, he obtained the funds for further purchases, to which he also devoted every spare crown he could save from his salary or honoraria. He himself became increasingly frugal, did not smoke, drank wine only sparingly, and soon became a vegetarian, so that his personal requirements were minimal.[80]

Vienna is also where Karásek had some of the youthful adventures that inspired the *Three Magicians* trilogy. During the mid-1890s, he had a four-year relationship with a diplomat, perhaps with a Bohemian aristocratic pedigree, whom Karásek later called his "friend from Vienna." The relationship ended when the mysterious friend was posted to the Far East. While Karásek almost certainly fictionalized certain details of his portrayal, he consistently spoke of this friend as a real person. He has never been identified.[81]

In 1894, now back in Prague and 23 years old, he associated himself closely with the founding of *Moderní revue*, which he coedited with Procházka and enriched with criticism and his own works. The very next year, the journal provoked a firestorm with its response to reportage on Oscar Wilde's trial for gross indecency, then under way in

England, in which the "respectable" journal *Čas* (Time) portrayed Wilde as a self-destructive aesthete.[82] The controversy extended into private correspondence as well, as Katherine David-Fox notes:

> [It] struck a chord with [progressive activist and editor] Antonín Pravoslav Veselý, and one can imagine, with others. In contrast to Veselý's somewhat sympathetic contemplation of homosexuality, [Josef Svatopluk] Machar dismissed the discussion of Wilde as 'idiocy' (*pitomosti*) and thought it a sign of naivete that *Moderní revue* wasted its time on such matters.
>
> (Literary Archive, Czech Museum of Literature,
> letter of Machar to Masaryk; May 10, 1895)[83]

In February of that year, the journal launched the *Knihovna Moderní revue* (Moderne Revue Library, 1895–1925?), a series of modern literary titles in bibliophilic editions, as a sideline.[84] Procházka was its managing editor, and it was here that Karásek published his celebrated novel *Gotická duše* (A Gothic Soul, serial 1899–1900, book 1900; English transl. 2015) as well as poetry collections and other prose works.

After the publication of *A Gothic Soul*, Karásek became infatuated with a rugged young man. Yet, as he wrote to Edvard Klas (pseudonym of Vladimíra Jedličková), it was a chaste and deeply unsatisfying bond; not only was the youth unattainable, he may have reminded Karásek of some masculine ideal that his bygone "friend from Vienna" had represented; this ideal would later be revived in the *Three Magicians* trilogy.[85] This seems to have been a low period for Karásek overall, not only personally but also creatively. Four of his six major poetry collections were behind him, and he produced no original books between 1900 (*A Gothic Soul*) and 1907 (*Manfred Macmillan*). Instead, he turned to preparing his collected works and critical essays for republication.

In 1898, *Moderní revue* associate Hugo Kosterka established the Symposion: knihy nové doby imprint (Symposion: Books of the New Era, 1898–1913), which published in larger print runs than *Moderní revue*'s sideline—about 700 copies per title rather than 200.[86] Kosterka did so after an extended sojourn in Scandinavia, where he developed contacts with several authors. He met Karásek and Procházka after graduating from the law faculty in Prague in 1890 and becoming a postal official himself. Under the Symposion imprint, Kosterka published dozens of titles, particularly Scandinavian literature in his own translations—including Ibsen, Strindberg, and Knut Hamsun—as well as books with an occult twist, in addition to Karásek's collected works from 1902 to 1912.[87]

In the first volume of these collected works, Karásek appended the aristocratic-sounding "ze Lvovic" to his surname, complete with a coat of arms, asserting a family connection to the sixteenth-century Bohemian astronomer (and supposed "teacher" of Tycho de Brahe) Cyprián Lvovický ze Lvovic—whose name is gratuitously dropped into the *Three Magicians* trilogy's third volume, *Ganymede*.[88] Contemporary journals suggest Karásek was experimenting with the "ze Lvovic" as early as 1901 (see *Zvon* reference below). He later even claimed Emperor Franz Josef had restored the family title.[89]

From the outset, this genealogical claim evoked skepticism, as for example from the literary weekly *Zvon* (The Bell, 1901),[90] and no actual family connection has been substantiated by researchers.[91] The claim to an aristocratic pedigree is most easily explained as self-stylization in the manner of his three magicians.[92] Yet Karásek's claim was not unique. Other prominent figures in the *fin de siècle* Habsburg Monarchy likewise adopted an aristocratic bearing as a form of self-reinvention, including Zionist Theodor Herzl and author Richard von Schaukal.[93]

The publication of *Manfred Macmillan* (serial May–September 1907 in *Moderní revue*, book July 1907) and *Scarabæus* (serial May 1908–August 1909 also in *Moderní revue*, book 1909) marked Karásek's return to literature.[94] During his dry spell, he seems to have been a habitué of Prague's Café Slavia, meeting there with young writer friends, swimming in the Vltava near the little church of Zlíchov, or setting off from Střelecký Island in a dinghy with fellow poet and writer Josef Müldner. Another companion was author and fellow esotericist Emanuel Lešehrad, who like Karásek affected an aristocratic-sounding name (z Lešehradu). Karásek would also take his dog Harry, a Leonberger, out for walks.[95]

Together with Procházka, Lešehrad, and Kosterka, Karásek was at the Café Union in January 1902 for the inaugural meeting of the Kruh českých spisovatelů (Czech Writers' Circle, 1902–40),[96] where writers of the "1890s generation" continued to distinguish themselves from the establishment in the May circle, and he was promptly elected treasurer. The new formation's members joined forces with Umělecká beseda (Artistic Forum),[97] which itself included authors in addition to musicians and other artists. Together with Jaroslav Kamper, Karásek frequented the literary salon hosted by Anna Lauermannová-Mikschová (pseud. Felix T   é   ver, fig. 6); in addition, he visited those of Gabriela Preissová and others. He maintained an intimate correspondence with Klas and a friendly if more reserved one with Kalašová[98] while continuing to coedit *Moderní revue* with Procházka.

Around 1903, Karásek struck up a friendship with the ephebic young Croatian actor Ivo Raić Lonjski (1881–1931, fig. 7). Raić arrived in Prague that year fresh from a stint at Max Reinhardt's Neues Theater in Berlin[99] to play leading roles at the Czech Národní divadlo (National Theater), among them Romeo and Pierrot.[100] As Karásek's

G.B.UNTERVEGER in TRENTO.

Fig. 6. Karásek confidante and salon host Anna Lauermannová-Mikschová. From the studio of G. B. Unterveger in Trento (Italy), 1886. Courtesy of the Literary Archive of the Museum of Czech Literature.

Fig. 7. The Croatian actor Ivo Raić Lonjski (a.k.a. de Lonja) had an international career, including appearances at the Czech National Theater from 1903 to 1905 (photo 1903). Courtesy of the National Theater Archive (Prague).

correspondence with Kalašová shows, he admired Raić and spent time in his company. He later described the actor as a kind of script consultant on theatrical aesthetics as he composed the verse play *Apollonius z Tyany* (Apollonius of Tyana, 1905). When Raić played Pierrot that year, Karásek gave his performance an enthusiastic notice in *Moderní revue*: "Mr. Raić is one of those few artists who does not [merely] *reproduce* but *creates*."[101]

The actor left Prague abruptly in the spring of 1905, whether under a cloud of scandal after various escapades with the "Šapica" homosexual circle or tensions at the National Theater.[102] Raić later became a stage manager and sometime director at Zagreb's own National Theater.

After Raić's departure from Prague, scholar Karel Kolařík notes a steady decline in the frequency of Karásek's correspondence with Kalašová. Kolařík further observes that Karásek continually lauds his friend and salon host Anna Lauermannová in his letters to Kalašová, possibly to maintain a certain cordial distance; and that Lauermannová's own diaries paint his correspondent as a somewhat lovelorn older woman perhaps jealous of Karásek's other friendships and affections.

At some later date, Karásek burned his letters from both Klas and Kalašová, suggesting a parting of the ways from each; and in the 1940s, when he was ill and in financial straits, he remembered Kalašová as resenting his friendships with others. Although this friendship seems to have come to an unhappy end, Kalašová herself did not destroy Karásek's letters and notes to her.

Years later, Karásek related that he had conceived the idea for the *Three Magicians* trilogy in the mid-1890s and began active work on *Manfred Macmillan* as early as 1904.[103] That work was first serialized in *Moderní revue* and then published in book form under the Čeští autoři imprint (Czech Authors, 1905–19) founded by Kamilla Neumannová (fig. 8), who incorporated several of Karásek's other works

Fig. 8. Over a career spanning decades, Neumannová brought modern and other titles to Czech readers. She was the first to publish *Manfred Macmillan*. Photo 1901/02. Courtesy of the Literary Archive of the Museum of Czech Literature.

into her series as well. (She had married Stanislav Kostka Neumann in January 1899, and they had two children. Neumann abandoned his family in 1904, and the couple formally divorced in 1914.)

The "notorious" book design by Josef Richard Marek for *Manfred Macmillan*'s first (1907) edition, under Neumannová's imprint, provoked powerful reactions. It featured a red velvet cover (evoking one of the novel's motifs) and the title printed in "deep-red gothic typefaces" (fig. 9). For *Čas*'s self-proclaimed "respectable" and anonymous reviewer Jindřich Vodák, the very cover "announced that something cursed, infernal, magic, insane, morbidly chimerical and magnetic will be found inside."[104] Yet in a bookstore, a "beautiful young man" named Otto

> was *tempted* by the red binding and the deep red types, but "went three times around the shop before entering" and buying it. The episode indicates that it took a great deal of courage to buy the book. The reason for that is probably [...] the extraordinary design and [that] Karásek's literary treatment of aberrant sexuality was well known in intellectual circles.[105]

Otto then wrote Karásek to ask where they could meet, as the author later recounted to Anna Lauermannová. Wary of entrapment, Karásek suggested they meet in front of the Basilica of St. Jakub's in Malá Strana, which features in the novel. The young man later became Karásek's lover for a time.[106]

Neumannová also published a separate line of titles called Knihy dobrých autorů (KDA, Books by Worthy Authors, 1905–31), a vital source of foreign decadent and other modern literature in Czech translations. Procházka soon became the managing editor (and occasional translator) for the series, remaining with it until his death in 1925. Karásek's later editor at Štorch-Marien's Aventinum publishing house, Vratislav Hugo Brunner, likewise joined the KDA cohort

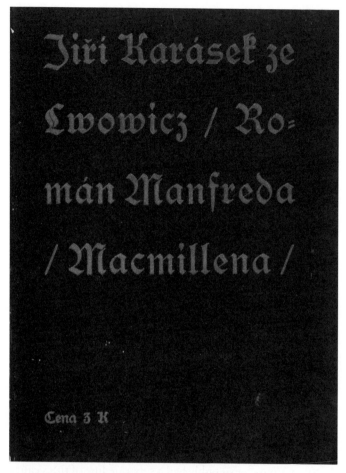

Fig. 9. The notorious cover of the first edition of *Manfred Macmillan* (1907). The author's name, the typeface, and the red velvet bespoke vaguely queer gothic decadence to contemporaries. Courtesy of the Library of the Museum of Czech Literature.

Fig. 10. This portrait of Karásek by artist Rudolf Bém was painted shortly after *Manfred Macmillan*'s publication. Oil on canvas, 1908. Courtesy of the Art Collections of the Museum of Czech Literature.

early on. Yet another Neumannová series, Knihy pro bibli-
ofily (Books for Bibliophiles, 1911–28), included a translation of Wilde's *Ballad of Reading Gaol* and a volume of his
"poems in prose."[107]

In the aftermath of the spring 1895 Wilde polemic,
Karásek self-published his poetry collection *Sodom* (1895),
confiscated by the Austrian authorities at the printer's and
later defended in the Reichsrat in Vienna. He had thus chosen to be a public figure and even courted notoriety—not
only as a writer and polemicist but also as a voice that
brought homosexuality out of the shadows. He was not
always applauded for taking that stand.

In an apparently pivotal episode in Karásek's life, the
1909–12 Affair of the Anonymous Letters, he faced vicious
allegations from rival critic Šalda (fig. 11) and others that
he had sent a series of letters containing literary gossip and
anti-homosexual slurs to various writers.[108] Whereas he
had been quite frank in private with Lauermannová about
acting on his same-sex attractions, his public response to
the new allegations required a subtler position: "I have a
purely *literary* relation to homosexuality: I take up its psychological aspect in some of my works, I apply it as tragic
material in my artistic output."[109] Yet he also declared: "I
have been writing [literary] critiques for eighteen years and
signed them all with my full name! I do not like anonymity
[...]"[110]—and therefore dismissed the charge that he would
write such scurrilous, anonymous letters as inconsistent
with his style of life. The affair seems to have thoroughly
demoralized Karásek. His memoirs refer to an especially
low period around this time, and it may even have deterred
him from completing the *Three Magicians* trilogy sooner, as
Lishaugen speculates. It is at this point that his literary output begins to slow markedly.

Karásek remained in Smíchov until at least January
1907.[111] He moved to a new home in 1916, perhaps finally

Fig. 11. František Xaver Šalda (1912). Karásek's reputation and livelihood were put at risk by rival critic Šalda's dubious claims in the Affair of the Anonymous Letters (1909-12). Courtesy of the Literary Archive of the Museum of Czech Literature.

able to arrange more of his book and artwork collections to his liking. Having visited Karásek there in the mid-1920s after the publication of the novel *Zastřený obraz* (A Veiled Painting, 1923), Štorch-Marien later recalled that the flat was "in the courtyard wing of the palatial building U Textorů at Karmelitská Street no. 12, opposite the Church of Our Lady of Victory."[112] Štorch-Marien continues:

> [it] consisted of three large rooms with a long glass-walled corridor that served as a library. It held thousands of volumes, and except for the windows, there was no wasted space whatsoever. Two of the rooms were furnished with period pieces from the first half of the 19th century, but the third, used as a study and bedroom, had a very different aspect. Karásek came upon the design for the furniture, made of natural polished oak, in an English magazine and had the furnishings made on that model, with one original feature: copper fittings with a motif of bird's heads. It was [...] made to the design of the poet Stanislav Kostka Neumann [...]
>
> The walls of the rooms were filled with paintings of domestic and foreign origin. Among them was a portrait of a girl representing Karásek's mother from his youth, perhaps by Josef Mánes, and a large portrait of Karásek that always seemed to me to have come straight from the walls of an English castle. It was by Rudolf Bém, better known under the pseudonym Vratislav Hlava; it had a very dark background from which a young man's complete figure in the poet's likeness stood out vividly [see fig. 10]. The study room, which contained a tall, narrow cabinet with compartments for albums of engravings and drawings, was truly "paved" with pictures by Polish painters, foremost among whom was Wlastimil Hofman, a close associate of Przybyszewski.[113]

As various "amateur" and bibliophile Czech print shops went under during World War I,[114] Karásek founded his own imprint to continue propagating his works—calling it Thyrsus, after a staff carried by Bacchus and his followers and a name Karásek had proposed in 1894 for *Moderní revue*. In 1915, he established Thyrsus in Smíchov at Palackého třída no. 3, and he set out to distribute unsold copies of his works bought up from other publishers. The operation continued until 1916, perhaps broken off with his move from Smíchov (fig. 12).

Fig. 12. A Karásek portrait by artist Wlastimil Hofman, a longtime friend. Oil on canvas, 1917. Courtesy of the Art Collections of the Museum of Czech Literature.

Karásek also found a still more suitable space for his art collection. In 1924, he allowed the Czechoslovak Sokol, a national-patriotic gymnastics association, to install it at the Tyrš House on Újezd in Prague's Malá Strana (see fig. 13). It opened in May 1925 under the name Karáskova galerie (Karásek Gallery).[115]

Ten years later, as attitudes toward the Soviet Union were changing, the city of Prague organized an exhibition of Russian painters (although the only contemporary ones were exiles). In the exhibition's brochure, the Slavic philologist Matija Murko, a Charles University professor from Slovenia, suggested a permanent gallery of Slavic art that would redound to the greater glory of Prague.

TYRŠŮV DŮM – POHLED Z ÚJEZDA

Fig. 13. The opening of the Karásek Gallery (1925). Tyršův dům (Tyrš House) hosted the Karásek Gallery from 1925 to 1941. Courtesy of the Library of the Museum of Czech Literature.

Donors then began to come forward. But to Marko's disappointment, Karásek spoke up and reminded everyone that Prague already had a Slavic collection in the Karásek Gallery.[116]

In time, Karásek returned to the trilogy project. He found supporters not only in his coeditor Procházka[117] but also in his old friend and fellow decadent Przybyszewski. As a longtime mystic, Przybyszewski had a particular interest in Karásek's use of the golem topos in *Ganymede*, and the two met to discuss it in Prague.[118] At the time, Przybyszewski was managing a bookstore in Gdańsk, where he assembled material on Polish rabbinical experiences with golems and sent it to Karásek[119]—who had conducted some of his own research and had a local golem tradition in Prague to draw upon. On the stylistic level, Krystýnek finds Zeyer's influence in the trilogy clearer—viz. Karásek's lyricism and neoromanticism—than Przybyszewski's, whose prose Krystýnek dismisses as "morbid."

While Karásek continued his association with *Moderní revue* and otherwise indulged his interest in the arts in this period, his literary output now slowed to a trickle of minor works that attracted scant critical attention. Before completing the *Three Magicians* trilogy with *Ganymede* in 1925, he again addressed queer themes in the short story "Legenda o Sodomovi" (Legend of Sodom, 1920) and the novel *A Veiled Painting* (1923), which has been read as a continuation of *Manfred Macmillan* and *Scarabæus*. While Lishaugen finds that it continues and develops motifs from the trilogy's first two books, and "there are elements implying an aesthetic change," he describes it as a "culmination" of earlier motifs rather than the "epilogue" to the trilogy.[120] Alongside art collecting and bibliophilia, another continuing interest of Karásek's was the occult.

Inspirations from the Occult

Contemporary descriptions of *Manfred Macmillan* often cast it as an "occult" (*okkultní*) work as well as an "erotic" or "sensual" (*erotický*) one.[121] As "magicians" in the gothic sense, Manfred (*Manfred Macmillan*), Marcel (*Scarabæus*), and Adrian (*Ganymede*) are all practitioners of applied esotericism ("magic"). Karásek himself was an avid esotericist, and the esoteric arts are integral to the *Three Magicians* trilogy. These ancient currents were alive and well in Europe and in Czech cultural circles during the *fin de siècle*. For Karásek, their mystery may well have resonated with those of the "third sex," aesthetic truth, Catholic ritual, his own genealogy, and (in a Zeyeresque, neoromantic sense) Bohemia's storied medieval past. This section explores these currents and links them to the trilogy. Secret societies and cults have been associated with unorthodox sexual practices (viz. Olga Tokarczuk's thoroughly researched if fictional treatment of the Frankists, an eighteenth- and nineteenth-century Sabbatean Jewish movement, in *Księgi Jakubowe* (The Books of Jacob, 2014; English transl. 2021), although such practices could also be exaggerated or invented by hostile outsiders.

European occultism emerged during the Renaissance. In Italy, a turn away from medieval scholasticism led to interest in "primordial wisdom," and ancient Greek works began to be translated into Latin. Seekers found inspiration in Plato, the Hermetic tradition, and gnosticism, as well as the kabbalah, a Jewish mystical tradition that had originated in thirteenth-century Spain. European authors such as Agrippa von Nettesheim (1486–1535), Paracelsus (Theophrastus von Hohenheim, ca.1493–1541), and Athanasius Kircher (1602–1680)—also explicitly invoked in *Manfred Macmillan*—composed influential syncretic works of mysticism that blended ideas from multiple traditions.[122] It spun off into Christian "cabbalah" and Hermetic "qabbalah"[123] during the Renaissance. In the *Three Magicians* trilogy, Karásek cites works by these and other early esotericists as repositories of secret knowledge and keys to life's omnipresent mysteries.

For centuries, applied esotericism was the science of the day, even if it had its skeptics and was actively suppressed by the Church. It found expression in alchemy, necromancy, transference of souls, and other techniques (as well as in charlatans and hucksters such as Cagliostro—central to *Manfred Macmillan*). Such practices might summon the aid of supernatural beings including angels, demons, and elementals, and practitioners might form secret societies to systematize and advance their knowledge. Later literary works, particularly of decadence and symbolism, drew upon these traditions,[124] which are integral to the plots of all of the *Three Magicians* novels: Masonic magic in *Manfred Macmillan*, Egyptian magic in *Scarabæus*, and kabbalah in *Ganymede*.

The romantic tradition of fantasy had a pulse of its own within Czech literature. The "romanettos" of Karásek's elder literary colleague Jakub Arbes (1840–1914)[125] may have reminded early critics of Edgar Allan Poe, and Arbes even acknowledged himself to Karásek as Poe's "follower" (*stoupenec*).[126] Yet Karásek also insisted on Arbes's originality and authenticity as a specifically Prague writer[127] who deserved recognition for his key role in the development of the Czech novel.[128] Arbes's works occasionally present fantastic events and phenomena, but unlike Karásek, he usually provides mechanical "explanations" or frames these works within dreams.

Since 1989, various esotericist studies and circles have emerged in the Czech lands, and recent Czech scholarship has attempted to reconstruct Karásek's participation in the Czech esotericist scene.[129] In Prague, he was linked to a Christian mystic Martinist order. Other members had included or did include Zeyer and the Austrian banker, translator, and author Gustav Meyrink, who wrote the German-language novel *Der Golem* (The Golem, 1915; English transl. 1977).[130] Member Karel Weinfurter praised *Manfred Macmillan*'s occult qualities in a review.[131] Karásek may have been a member of the Czech hermetic society Volné sdružení pracovníků okultních (Free Association of Occult Practitioners) from its inception in 1920.[132] Even as Karásek continued his rich association with *Moderní revue* until its demise in 1925, he edited the journal *Okultní a spiritualistická revue* (Occult and Spiritualist Revue, 1921–24) from 1923 to 1924. As a contributor, he used the pseudonyms Antonín Frankl, Jiří Tiller, and J. Lvovský.[133] In 1927, the hermetic association's members formed the new grouping Universalia, of which Karásek was likewise a member. Universalia staged lectures and facilitated the publication of a number of hermetic works, including grimoires (books of incantations).[134]

Interest in mysticism and the paranormal spread rapidly in Europe and beyond during the period before World War I, manifesting itself as, for example, spiritualism, mediumism, telepathy, hypnotism, somnambulism, and theosophy, with charismatic figures who, in the English-speaking world, included the Russian-born Helena Blavatsky, founder of the Theosophical Society in New York in 1875; British theosophist and social reformer Annie Besant; and British hermeticist A. E. Waite.[135] It seems to have grown in reaction to the rapid pace of scientific innovation, finding additional inspiration from the conjunction of Mars and Earth in 1877, when Italian astronomer Giovanni Schiaparelli created the first detailed map of the red planet, complete with "channels."

Such interests were shared by—or at least excited the curiosity of—many contemporary scientists, scholars, and cultural figures and did not fall out of fashion until after World War II. The Society for Psychical Research (SPR) was founded in London in 1882, and its membership included both spiritualists and scientists—although few among the latter were outright "partisans" of supernaturalism.[136] An American SPR emerged in 1885, and the popular writer-astronomer Percival Lowell consulted with its leadership.[137] Internationally famed Russian medium and author Vera Ivanovna Kryzhanovskaia (pseud. J. W. Rochester) was married to the head of the SPR in St. Petersburg, founded in 1890.

In Germany and Austria, there was a general revival of occultism between 1880 and 1910.[138] Efforts in 1896 to found the first Czech spiritist association, allegedly to be called the Spiritistická společnost pro psychologická studia (Spiritist Society for Psychological Research), were thwarted by the Prague police as "dangerous to public health," as prominent spiritist Karel Sezemský recalled in a 1930 book; however, this memory may actually relate to the Společnost pro psychická studia (Society for Psychical Studies), its statutes formulated only in 1909.[139]

The Czech SPR's statutes distanced the group from folk spiritism, which members evidently viewed as amateurish—and as competition. The group launched the journal *Occult and Spiritualist Revue*, printed by the prominent spiritist publisher Zmatlík a Palička beginning in 1921. The first issue specifically disavowed "public experiments," perhaps wanting to avoid the nuisance of police interference that Sezemský later recalled. *Manfred Macmillan* and the other *Three Magicians* novels contain numerous references to occult "experiments" and "experimentation," yet Karásek's magicians never engage in public displays.

Against the backdrop of modernism, applied magic in literature could serve as a response to conventional morality, not only in the Habsburg space (e.g., Meyrink's *The Golem*) but beyond. Fictional works with esotericist themes from this period onward are legion but see, for example, Valerii Bryusov's *Ognënnyy angel* (The Fiery Angel; serial 1907-08, book 1908; English transl. 1977) and W. Somerset Maugham's novella *The Magician* (1909), as well as the slew of titles by Kryzhanovskaia translated into various European languages, Hungarian author Mária Szepes's *A vörös oroszlán* (The Red Lion, 1947; English transl. 1997), down to J. K. Rowling's *Harry Potter* series (1997–2007). Karásek depicts his own magicians as outsiders, even reprobates, judged and misunderstood by others. Their same-sex desires, even if unnamed (as "third-sex," "Uranian," "inverted," etc.), are foundational to their self-exclusion from "ordinary" values.

In fact, there was at least some overlap between esotericist and queer circles in Central Europe. Karásek himself described the phenomenon of the "third sex" as a "mystery."[140] He indicates that his lover of the early 1890s, the "friend from Vienna," had an active interest in the esoteric arts. This friend might well have been a member of Vienna's Club der Vernünftigen (Sensible Club), a discreet circle of queer elites, as was German symbolist Stefan George's circle (*George-Kreis*) in Berlin.[141] Between the world wars, prominent Czech businessman and impresario Vácslav Havel—openly rumored to be attracted to men—wrote the enthusiastic introduction to an esotericist novel (using the pseudonym "Atom").[142]

Writer and editor Petr Nagy directly questions Karásek's claim that an isolated queer esotericist was the model for Manfred-Marcel-Adrian:

> The circumstances of the birth of Karásek's trilogy are surrounded by a certain layer of confabulation [*skazky*], fed by the author himself and recounting the living prototype of the main heroes of the novels in question—the mysterious figure of the "Viennese friend," who allegedly became

the inspiration for the trio of "magicians" from his trilogy, i.e., Count Manfred Macmillan from *Manfred Macmillan's Novel*, Marquis Marcel d'Offémont from *Scarabæus* and Adrian Morris from *Ganymede*.[143]

Apart from his "friend from Vienna," it is plausible that Karásek indeed met other individuals who were additional models for his magicians—these queer "outsiders" enabled by status, wealth, and pedigree to transcend conventional morality—in the overlap between queer and esotericist circles.

Publication History and Critical Response

Manfred Macmillan and *Scarabæus* were both initially published in serial form in *Moderní revue*, then by Kamilla Neumannová,[144] and later reissued by Otakar Štorch-Marien under his Aventinum imprint in 1924 and 1925, respectively, among Karásek's collected works. The later editions were carefully edited by Vratislav Hugo Brunner, slightly modernizing some of the syntax, with only occasional semantic or orthographic changes; under Brunner, paragraph indents were added, and the rows of three asterisks that had separated chapters became Roman numerals. Brunner was a man of many talents; see Figure 14 for his caricature of Karásek and Šalda for the promotional journal *Rozpravy Aventina* (The Talk of Aventinum, 1925–34).

The critic Karel Sezima, in his September 1910 review of *Scarabæus* in the literary and cultural journal *Lumír*, finds Karásek's most recent work generally more polished than his earliest ones: "His analytical intellect has become more supple, has gained in dialectical finesse and ironic agility."[145] He considers the characters sharper and less reduced to structural vehicles for abstractions—perhaps (he speculates) because of Karásek's intervening theater work—and yet "they lack three-dimensionality, as it were."[146]

Sezima then lays bare some reservations with aestheticism itself: can art for art's sake honestly produce characters and works as believable and engaging as art based in life?[147] Karásek himself had opined in an 1893 review that Zeyer's exoticized characters tended to be wholly good or wholly wicked, "without cracks, sudden shifts, [or] mysterious recesses in their inner selves."[148] The remark suggests that as an author in his own right, Karásek considered how and whether to endow his own characters with more complex psychologies. Yet even as Sezima praises Karásek's style and artistry, he suggests that *Scarabæus*'s decadence is no longer fresh. While this sympathetic reviewer does not exactly call Karásek a self-absorbed aesthete who has failed to keep pace with the times, he comes close. Czech decadence was no longer in vogue, as Pynsent argues, even if it still produced isolated works.[149]

At age 54 in 1925, Karásek was appointed director of the Postal Museum when his predecessor Václav Dragoun retired. Karásek and his chief archivist undertook a reorganization of files that Dragoun had extracted from Vienna following Czechoslovak independence, separating them into improvised subject-matter files, then further into dependent subject files, rather than by source and chronologically. Karásek was proud to be called *pane řediteli* ("Mr. Director") by his friends.[150]

In Karásek's own telling, Procházka had long been urging him to complete the trilogy. When Karásek did produce the manuscript for *Ganymede*, he was clearly moved by his coeditor's enthusiastic reception.[151] It has been suggested that Karásek's imagined response to Sezima's review, and perhaps to other criticism, helps to explain why he did not finish the *Three Magicians* trilogy until 1925.[152] Karásek was no stranger to critical polemics, however, and period reviews of *Manfred Macmillan*, while varied, had acknowledged its artistry, as Sezima's did of *Scarabæus*. A 1913 Czech literary history had high praise for Karásek's recent verse collections *Endymion* (1909) and *Ostrov vyhnanců* (Island of Exiles, 1912), framing Karásek as "a mature artist who is a particular master of the linguistic instrument."[153] Still, perhaps more significant is the impact of the Affair of the Anonymous Letters (see above), in which Karásek was publicly accused of homosexuality and subjected to a hostile investigation that could have cost him his livelihood with the postal service.[154]

Sezima criticized "the revolting affair" (*nechutná aféra*) in which the acerbic Šalda and his loyalists "had finally devolved into a posse shamelessly hounding an inconvenient

Nakladatel: Pánové se dosud neznají — pan Karásek ze Lvovic — pan F. X. Šalda — —
Oba pánové unisono: Těší mne velice.

Fig. 14. A handshake between rivals (1925). This light-hearted if wry caricature of Karásek and Šalda by artist V. H. Brunner was published in Štorch-Marien's *Rozpravy Aventina* in September 1925. The caption reads: "Publisher: The gentlemen haven't met—Mr. Karásek ze Lvovic, Mr. F. X. Šalda. Both gentlemen in unison: Very pleased to meet you." Courtesy of the Library of the Museum of Czech Literature.

critic."[155] Had Karásek followed through on a threat to take
legal action,[156] he might well have found his literary works
used against him—as had Oscar Wilde—and then faced
sanctions under the penal code's anti-sodomy provision in
Paragraph 129(b) (§129[b]).

Both *Ganymede* and new editions of the trilogy's first two
novels were brought out in 1924–25 by Aventinum, which
sought to raise overall standards in Czech book production,
as well as in the content, editing, and physical quality of its
titles. Yet the winds had shifted in society and culture, and
Karásek never quite opened his sails to them. As Lishaugen
notes of the *Three Magicians* novels' contemporary reviews,
they tended to start from "realism, modernity, progress,
democracy, anticlericalism, contemporary society and the
collective," whereas Karásek now represented "the opposite": "neo-romanticism and decadence, reactionism, aristo-
craticism, Catholicism, the past, and individuality."[157] Even
within the homosexual rights movement, despite his status
as an icon, Karásek likely chafed at emerging "masculinist"
and even integrationist currents as represented by *Nový hlas*
editor Vladimír Vávra.[158]

Karásek's great supporter and colleague Procházka died
the same year that *Ganymede* was published, and his demise
spelled the end for *Moderní revue*. After Procházka's death,
Karásek went on to win the Czechoslovak State Prize for
Literature in 1931. The Prague-based journal *Hlas sexuální
menšiny* (Voice of the Sexual Minority, 1931–32) dedicated its issue no. 12 of that year to the occasion, which
inspired pride in the community.[159] The journal's editors
frequently urged its homosexual readers to step out of the
shadows and become involved in the campaign for liberation and decriminalization. Despite increased arrests under
§129(b) in the 1920s and 1930s, Karásek remained ahead
of his contemporaries as an unusually public homosexual
figure.[160] Efforts at penal code reform that included the

decriminalization of homosexual acts ran aground in the more conservative political climate.[161] Even as Slovak activist and *Hlas* contributor Imrich Matyáš exhorted the community to action, he explained that he was not advocating "that homosexuals should put a sign on their backs saying, 'I am a homosexual.'"[162]

In between these events, Karásek gave an interview to the fledgling literary monthly *Elán* to comment on cultural relations with the Slovaks in the new state: "We thought that they were a backward race, subjugated by the Hungarians, to which we must now bring culture and educate. That was a mistake, and a very thorough one at that."[163]

Karásek retired as Postal Museum director in 1932. A recent archival science article regards his successors with lugubrious sympathy; subsequent efforts to undo the filing improvisations he oversaw remained unfinished even after World War II.[164] Yet the former director now had more time to devote to literature. In 1938, he published his autobiographical novel *Ztracený ráj* (Paradise Lost), in which he describes his childhood and youth in Prague with characteristically exquisite detail and no holds barred, a kind of "coming out" novel. The years of the Nazi Protectorate of Bohemia and Moravia were harsh ones for him and still harsher for many others; in 1941, he defended the Karásek Gallery holdings from Nazi expropriation and placed various items in safe places, even as the collection continued to grow from gifts and bequests.

Meanwhile, he edited a number of older writers' works for republication—including some by Arbes[165]—but had in essence laid down his own pen. The 1941 anthology *Očima lásky* (Through the Eyes of Love), a collection of poems on Prague, included him alongside other urban panegyrists from canonical literature. Even a quisling such as František Zavřel recognized his courage and talent in a 1942 memoir.[166]

Fig. 15. His friendship with the author having endured several changes of regime, artist Wlastimil Hofman captured Karásek at age 75 in this sketch. Pen and ink, 1946. Courtesy Art Collections, Museum of Czech Literature.

He survived the Nazi occupation and also the communist putsch of February 1948, still living on Karmelitská Street.[167] The communist regime withheld space and funds for a widely anticipated reopening of the gallery, and the collection was shunted into inaccessible National Gallery storage spaces. Karásek would likely have been aware of the new regime's forcible ouster of the discalced Carmelites from their monastery on Hradčanské náměstí (Castle Square) in 1950.[168] He died in March 1951, barely a month after his eightieth birthday. After his death, the regime nationalized his artwork collection.

Ten years later, communist Czechoslovakia and Hungary became the only states in the Soviet bloc to decriminalize consenting homosexual acts, inspired by the medico-legal debates begun eighty years before. Had Karásek lived to see that development, he would likely have remained cautious about the future of the "third sex." His life experience had taught him that social attitudes and official policy did not depend on a single law. As he remarked in 1932 when already over the age of 60, §129(b),

> although still in force, has ceased to be a threat, and I can honestly say that I would not consider its eventual demise to be any particular victory or advantage. Those who expect complete freedom after the demise of §129 are terribly mistaken. Decent [*sic*] love will [continue to] be just as protected as it is today. And sexual eccentricities will continue to be penalized under other sections of the law, and there will be nothing left for the sexually eccentric but jail or the sanatorium.[169]

Conclusion

One of early queer literature's most intriguing characteristics is the potential not only for multiple interpretations of a given text but for reading them on various planes: artistic, historical, (post)colonial, and as analogues for the stories of any marginal group (Czech, esotericist, queer). The historical and personal contexts outlined above are meant to inform the reading of *Manfred Macmillan* and the *Three Magicians* trilogy, not to determine it.

Aiming at both a broader audience as well as a queer-identified one, queer authors after Wilde mastered doublespeak including through modes of camp and kitsch. Wilde himself was enormously popular in Central and Eastern Europe: his novel *The Picture of Dorian Gray*, in which art separates the narrator's outer and inner lives, was soon translated into German, Russian, Czech, Hungarian, and Croatian;[170] and his essay "The Decay of Lying" (1891) was translated into Czech in 1895 as "Úpadek lhaní"—to Karásek's great delight, as his context forced him to choose constantly between dissimulation and authenticity in his queerness. Or could he achieve both at once?

Karásek was enthusiastic for Wilde's aesthetics of "lying," as evidenced in his preface to *Manfred Macmillan*: "to say of a genius that he did not lie is tantamount to saying that he lacked creativity."[171] Indeed, as Roar Lishaugen argues in his book on the *Three Magicians* trilogy, Karásek's approach enables "both a *straight* and a *queer* reading."[172] With its potential for analysis on the additional planes of decolonization (national, linguistic, social, personal), Karásek's trilogy plays with the mystical notion that, beneath the facade of reason and enlightenment, and the splendor of imperial power, there lie irrational, unpredictable, magical queer energies; and while these energies may disrupt order and consensus in the world, they also create new beauty in it. It is our hope that the historical and personal contexts outlined above will generate new readings of *Manfred Macmillan* and the *Three Magicians* trilogy (and new readers), and that Karasek will find his rightful place in modern queer history.

Carleton Bulkin
Brian James Baer

Notes

1. On this specifically Central European usage of "moderne," see Dipper, "Moderne" and Procházka, "Význam slova 'moderní'." There is no uncontested English translation of *Moderní revue*; I use the Czech form, as it is readily understandable.

2. For a discussion of the *Sodom* trial, confiscation, and amnesty, see Zach, *Nakladatelská pouť Jiřího Karáska ze Lvovic*, 8–9, 28. In 1902, the censors had also confiscated Karásek's poem "Nad obrazem Marie Magdaleny v Hradčanské Loretě" (Karásek to Klas, letter of August 15, 1902, in Karásek, *Milý příteli...*, 39. On *Moderní revue*'s "Wilde issue," see Pfefferová, "Oscar Wilde a Moderní revue."

3. *malost a střízlivost*. Karásek, *Ganymedes*, 73.

4. Uniquely in the region, the 1852 Austrian penal code's Paragraph 129 (§129) proscribed sexual relations between either men or women; it applied in the Czech lands (Seidl, "Pokus o odtrestnění homosexuality," 16–18). Hungary had its own provisions, and these obtained in Slovakia. The 1852 Croatian code did not formally recognize such acts between men as crimes, but provisions against "gross indecency" left scope for harassment. The German Reich's 1871 code had its Paragraph 175, later broadened and intensified by the Nazis. The 1866 Russian code's Articles 995 and 996 addressed *muzhelozhstvo* (sodomy) (Biedroń, "Historia homoseksualności w Polsce," 62), which was translated into Latvian as *pederastija* (pederasty) (Lipša, *LGBTI People in Latvia*, 1). There were harsher punishments for the rape or seduction of minors or the incompetent. In its harshness, the Russian code drew inspiration from that of Baden-Württemberg (Karlinsky, "Russia's Gay Literature and Culture," 349). It applied in the Baltics, Congress Poland, and the rest of the empire.

   Beyond law, other powerful social hierarchies shaped queer consciousness and behavior. Encouraged by an Orthodox priest, Russian writer Nikolai Gogol effectively committed suicide in 1852 while attempting to purge himself of same-sex desires through fasting and prayer, while doctors prescribed bloodletting with leeches and ice baths (Karlinsky, "Russia's Gay Literature and Culture," 349; Karlinsky, *The Sexual Labyrinth of Nikolai Gogol*).

5. Cf. Nietzsche's use of *Künstler des Lebens* in *Also sprach Zarathustra* (Thus Spake Zarathustra, 1883–85), and the alternative German form *Lebenskünstler*. The philosopher's popularity and influence expanded after his death in 1900.

6. *jednoznačně nejvýraznější meziválečná ikona české homosexuální kultury* (Seidl, "Mužnost jako ctnost," 290).

7. *jsem po prvé v české literatuře snímal závoj ze záhad našeho sexu [...] aniž odhazovali lidé normální s odporem mé knihy.* Karásek, "Feuilleton," 16; cited in Lishaugen, *Speaking with a Forked Tongue*, 11. Karásek was an editor for *Nový hlas* during its run, although Vladimír Vávra (pseudonym of Vladimír Kolátor) was the editor in chief (Seidl, "Mužnost," 289; Lishaugen, *Speaking with a Forked Tongue*, 79).

8. Invented by Vienna-born Hungarian journalist and activist Károly Mária Kertbeny in an 1868 letter to Ulrichs, "homosexual" was easily translated into other European languages and outlasted Ulrichs's "uranian" (see note 29 below).

9. See Norton, *Mother Clap's Molly House*.

10. There is no mention of Karásek in the major anglophone histories and anthologies of gay literature such as *The Gay and Lesbian Literary Companion* (1995), Malinowski and Brelin; *The Gay and Lesbian Literary Heritage* (1995), Summers; *The Penguin Book of International Gay Writing* (1995), Mitchell; *The Columbia Anthology of Gay Literature* (1998), Fone; *A History of Gay Literature: The Male Tradition* (1998), Woods; or in the more recent *Queer: A Collection of LGBTQ Writing from Ancient Times to Yesterday* (2021), Wynne.

11. Previously translated and introduced in Italian by Růžena Hálová as *Il romanzo di Manfred Macmillen*.

12. The concept of double consciousness was developed by W. E. B. Du Bois to describe the experience of Blacks in the United States. See his essay "Of Our Spiritual Strivings." It has since been applied to other minority groups including sexual minorities. Karásek's life and works reflect marginalization not only by circumstance but also by choice: as a member of the "third

sex," as a seminarian who forsook his studies, in his pursuit of a Catholic aesthetics stripped of doctrinal content, as an author of confiscated works, and as one who chose to publish on an "exclusive" basis rather than for mass circulation.

13. For recent essays on the decolonialization of Habsburg studies more broadly, see Beller, *Rethinking Vienna 1900*.

14. Framed in his book *Entartung* (Degeneration, 1892) as the breakdown of Western culture and civilization, manifested in morals, the arts, and contemporary social movements.

15. In "Childe Harold's Pilgrimage," Canto III, stanza CXIII (1816).

16. Bershtein, "Discourse of Sexual Pathology," 165.

17. Crozier, *Sexual Inversion: A Critical Edition*, 2.

18. Norton, *Myth of the Modern Homosexual*.

19. In fact, Mayne dedicates *Intersexes*, a cultural history of homosexuality, to Krafft-Ebing: "To the memory of that pioneer dispassionate, humane, scientific study of similisexualism, Dr. Richard von Krafft-Ebing, I inscribe this book, with humility; remembering that without his suggestion and aid it would never have been begun nor carried on to its close."

20. For an (unfavorable) Czech review see Eisner, "Román z Lesbu."

21. Baer, *Queer Theory and Translation Studies*, 168–69.

22. See Kosofsky Sedgwick, *Between Men*.

23. Robb, *Strangers*; Baer, *Other Russias*, 2–3; and Tobin, *Peripheral Desires*, 203.

24. Baer, *Other Russias*, 2. See Robb, *Strangers*, on (especially Mediterranean) tourism as temporary sanctuary for queer and other European travelers seeking anonymity and privacy. In *Scarabæus*, Karásek's narrator gushes, "Here, only here [in Venice] can one be the same in dreams as in waking. Here, only here can one find mysterious hearts that would remain inaccessible to us elsewhere. Here, only here can one listen to the seductions of intriguingly obscure beings, exorcized demons, the dark seraphs of sin and vice" (Karásek, *Scarabaeus*, 28). Italy was a favorite haunt for both Julius Zeyer (see below) and Byron himself (Stejskalová, "Italská cesta Julia Zeyera 1883–1884").

25. For geographical and geopolitical reasons, German was the natural conduit for much cultural transmission to the Czech-speaking space. See also David-Fox, "Prague-Vienna, Prague-Berlin."

26. Karásek, *Upřímné pozdravy z kraje květů a zapadlých snů*, 10.

27. Kostková, *A chceš-li, vyslov jméno mé.*

28. In Byron's "Manfred: A Dramatic Poem" (1817). Translated into Czech by Jaroslav Vrchlický as *Manfred: dramatická báseň* (1901). Also note Karásek's 1903 *dramatická báseň* on Cesar Borgia, who is mentioned in *Manfred Macmillan* XLVII.

29. Mayne, *The Intersexes*, 359, 360. The term "uranian" (German: *Urning*) was coined by Hanoverian lawyer Karl Heinrich Ulrichs, who launched the five-essay series *über das Rätsel der männmännlichen Liebe* ("on the riddle of male–male love") in 1864.

30. As a genre, the gothic novel is described as "European Romantic pseudomedieval fiction having a prevailing atmosphere of mystery and terror. Its heyday was the 1790s, but it underwent frequent revivals in subsequent centuries" (Matthias, "Gothic novel").

    Walpole's work was translated into Czech only in 1970, but Karásek would have had access to the text in German. In various ways, *Manfred Macmillan* (hereafter *RMM*) draws on the tradition of the gothic novel. For a discussion of the genre in Bohemia, see Neff, *Něco je jinak*, 55–77 and Řezníková, "Gotická duše moderny."

    Mayne opens the section on Byron by declaring: "Lord Byron is a striking example of the literary Dionian[*sic*]-Uranian. During all his life, the great English poet was more or less temperamentally homosexual; an idealistic, Hellenic, romantic homosexual" (Mayne, *The Intersexes*, 355–56).

31. The *Three Magicians* trilogy reflects this discourse with references to *oboupohlavnost* ("bisexuality," in this period-specific sense). In the present volume, see the description of Manfred's beauty as *zpola mužská, zpola dívčí, nebo přesněji, směsovala všechny krásy* ("half-masculine, half-maidenly, or more precisely, all beauties were commingled in it") (Karásek,

RMM 1924, 75. Cf. also Karásek, *Scarabaeus* 1924, 7; and *Ganymedes* 1925, 34–35).

32. Robb, *Strangers*, 54.
33. *S jakou chvějnou úzkostí ve chvíli, kdy se mi blíží někdo, pátrám po prvním záblesku jeho ducha, po první jiskře, jež by svědčila, že také on jest obklopen ovzduším stejného magnetismu jako já, a toužím vybiti s ním všechny možnosti a všechny energie svého nitra* (Karásek, *Scarabaeus* 1924, 112).
34. The university was founded in 1348 by Holy Roman Emperor Charles IV, whose mother was Czech. It became Charles-Ferdinand University in 1654 under Habsburg emperor Ferdinand III and was renamed Charles University (Univerzita Karlova) in 1920. The German-language institution, formerly the German Charles-Ferdinand University in Prague (1882–1919), became the German University in Prague.
35. Czech nationalists agitated for, *inter alia*, greater official use of Czech at the local level in Cisleithania ("Austria"). For a review of language policy in Hungary under the Dual Monarchy, see Berecz, "The Hungarian Nationalities Act."
36. Schorske, *Fin-de-Siècle Vienna*, 117.
37. See Cooper, *Czech Manuscripts*.
38. Archived at Hathi Trust https://catalog.hathitrust.org/Record/100332349 and Jihočeská vědecká knihovna in České Budějovice https://www.digitalniknihovna.cz/cbvk/periodical/uuid:ae75fb18-435d-11dd-b505-00145e5790ea.
39. Kostková, "Kritik-básník," 17.
40. *spolehlivě vytříbeného vkusu a distinkce, Arnošt Procházka býval nezřídka až k nevíře nevkusný; a to nejen v měšťáckém anebo akademickém smyslu. Provazolezec, stále jakoby κ pádu se svého lana náchylný* (Sezima, *Z mého života*, vol. 2, 13–14). Stanislav Kostka Neumann—writer, artist, and cofounder of the Czechoslovak communist party (1921)—dismissed Procházka as a "*Czech* 'decadent': a typical petty bourgeois" (český *'dekadent': typický maloměšťák*, emphasis in original) as opposed to a French one; he was hardly more charitable to Karásek (Neumann, *Vzpomínky*, part 1, 153–54).

41. Jehlička, "Stanisław Przybyszewski."
42. Głuchowska, "Munch, Przybyszewski and *The Scream*"; Jaworska, "Munch i Przybyszewski."
43. *pod silným vlivem chorobně perverzního blouznění a zrůdných psychopatologických stavů v Przybyszewského* Totenmesse [Death Mass, a Przybyszewski work first published in Berlin in 1893] (Krystýnek, "Przybyszewski v české literatuře za války a po válce," 80).
44. See Appendix I, "The Czech Polemic on Oscar Wilde."
45. On legal debates, see Karczewski, "Transnational Flows of Knowledge"; and Seidl, "Pokus o odtrestnění homosexuality" on attempts to reform the penal codes in newly independent Poland and Czechoslovakia respectively. See Kurimay, *Queer Budapest*, 26–34 on Hungarian police consultations with Berlin and Paris counterparts after Budapest's formation in 1873; and Karczewski, "Transnational Flows of Knowledge" on their Warsaw counterparts. Like Budapest, Warsaw maintained a vice registry, but its contents have largely been lost (Karczewski, email message to author Bulkin, October 10, 2022).
46. Mutschlechner, "Ludwig Viktor – 'Archduke Luziwuzi'." See also Snyder, *The Red Prince*, 37, 282.
47. Spector, "Wrath of the 'Countess Merviola'," 34, 44n.
48. By this measure, the *fin de siècle* Romanovs may well have outdone the Habsburgs. According to Nina Berberova, at least seven period Romanov grand dukes were homosexual (Karlinsky, "Russia's Gay Literature and Culture," 351).
49. Today's Ukraine was then divided between the Habsburg and Russian empires. On "Willy's" trysts and ambitions, see Snyder, *The Red Prince*, 3, 117.
50. Deák, *Beyond Nationalism*, 145.
51. Schindler, "Redl—Spy of the Century?" 488. See also Bassett, *For God and Kaiser*.
52. Dynes et al., *Encyclopedia of Homosexuality*, 1101. Schindler, "Redl—Spy of the Century?" 495. Hungarian director István Szabó's Oscar-nominated 1985 film *Oberst Redl* (Colonel Redl) is based on English playwright John Osborne's *A Patriot for Me* (also 1985).
53. A "natural choice for Redl, given his expertise in Russian espionage, and the worrying extent of Tsarist subversion in

Bohemia" (Schindler, "Redl—Spy of the Century?" 484). "[...T]he heavily Czech VIII Corps (Prague) [was] the most politically sensitive command in the army. [It was l]ong suspected by the high command of harbouring Slavophile and even treasonous tendencies" (Schindler, "Disaster on the Drina," 159). On Redl's tenure at the VIII Corps, see also Appendix IV, "A Prague Café"; and Snyder, *The Red Prince*, 66, 81.

54. The official explanation of Redl's suicide as motivated by homosexual shame presumed its own plausibility even if knowingly false, as did hearsay "explaining" Tchaikovsky's suicide (Miller, *Out of the Past*, 201).

55. Schindler, "Redl—Spy of the Century?" 485.

56. The scandal implicated several at the highest levels. Eulenberg referred to Emperor Wilhelm in correspondence as "the little darling" (Snyder, *The Red Prince*, 65).

57. Kronenbitter, "Redl, Alfred." See also Schindler, "Redl—Spy of the Century?"

58. See Appendix IV, "A Prague Café" for Kisch's reportage on a visit to the semi-clandestine gay backroom of a Prague café, placed off-limits to soldiers during Redl's tenure as chief of staff to the VIII Corps.

59. See Appendix V, "Karásek on Creating...."

60. Von Andrian (a.k.a. Andrian-Werburg) is better known for his 1895 novella *Der Garten der Erkenntnis* (The Garden of Knowledge; English transl. 2022).

61. Godsey, *Aristocratic Redoubt*, 90–91.

62. Posthumus, "Oscar Wilde and Decadent Imitations," 48.

63. Aldrich, "Homosexuality and the City."

64. Jan Seidl and Lukáš Nozar found the rate of prosecutions at the Prague Regional Criminal Court to be "relatively moderate" to 1933: 15 arrests (~5 convictions) in 1898–1902; 25–40 arrests (< 10 convictions) in 1903–07, 1908–12, and 1913–17; ~10 arrests (~5 convictions) in 1918–22 (the transition to the new republic); and ~60 arrests (20 convictions) in both 1923–27 and 1928–32 (Seidl, "Legal Imbroglio," 55–56 [figures 5–7]).

Lawyer František Čeřovský—who defended many clients charged under §129(b)—observed greater judicial leniency immediately after Czechoslovak independence in 1918. As he explained, "liberation ideology" (*osvobozo-vací ideologie*) and expectations of liberalization (*liberálně vyčkávací stanovisko*) were widespread, as was a certain level of reserve and mistrust toward the penal code inherited from the Habsburgs. Yet within a few years, the country's supreme court was making examples of "postwar immorality" (*poválečná znemravnělost*) in homosexual conduct cases (Seidl et al., *Od žaláře k oltáři*, 35–37).

The arrest figures for women are much lower: no convictions and 10–20 arrests in 1923–27 and 1928–32 (Seidl, "Legal Imbroglio," 55).

65. In fact, a key topos of the *Three Magicians* trilogy is the parallel between queerness and criminality, homosexual acts ("sodomy," broadly interpreted in practice) having remained illegal throughout the Habsburg era.

In the popular imagination, queerness could even characterize and authenticate criminality itself. The novels of Karásek's contemporaries Raymond Chandler (1888–1959) and Dashiell Hammett (1894–1961)—set in California, where sodomy remained illegal until 1976—were also accented by queerness (Chandler, *The Annotated Big Sleep*, 214n, 226). In Chandler's first novel, *The Big Sleep* (1939), the blackmail note that motivates General Sternwood to summon detective Philip Marlowe comes from an older queer who runs an illicit pornography library out of a Los Angeles bookstore and has a kept boy.

66. Neff, *Něco je jinak*, 62.

67. National Archives of the Czech Republic, Prague Police Directorate residence applications 1850–1914.

68. Štorch-Marien, *Sladko je žít*, 106.

69. Jahoda, email message to author Bulkin, May 2021.

70. Manufactured by the Nesselsdorfer Wagenbau-Fabriks-Gesellschaft A.G.

71. Beneš, "Elegantní jednoplošník Rapid bratří Čiháků."

72. See my attempt at a Karásek bibliography in this volume. The author excluded his juvenilia from his collected works and renounced them as "the excesses of my youth" (*samá alotria*

mého mládí) in *Ženský svět* 29 (1925), no. 3, 25; and no. 4, 34) (cited in Holeček, "Vydávat Karáska...").

73. *zapomněl* [...] *Boha a odvrátil se od lidí* (Karásek, *RMM* 1924, 133).

74. Karásek, *Upřímné pozdravy*, 68.

75. Karásek and other Czech queer artists held Zeyer in special reverence. Putna finds the evidence for Zeyer's alleged homosexuality credible even if inconclusive. Zeyer's correspondence contains references to an "unutterable" secret, and significant circumstantial evidence in his life and works suggests he was queer. After World War I, Czechoslovak president Tomáš Garrigue Masaryk, unsympathetic to homosexuals (see Appendix I, "The Czech Polemic on Oscar Wilde"), told writer Karel Čapek that he had found Zeyer *nemužný* ("unmanly"), coded language for "queer" (Putna, *Dějiny homosexuality v české kultuře*, 88; Pynsent, *Julius Zeyer*, 26n).

76. *Krása katolického ritu je přece jen nepřekonatelná: dovede přežiti i dogma. I tomu, kdo nevěří, dává možnost dále se modliti: kadidlem, zpěvem, světly, zlatem oltářů a rouch* (Karásek, *Upřímné pozdravy*, 51).

77. Lishaugen, *Speaking with a Forked Tongue*, 164.

78. Karásek, *Vzpomínky*, 237.

79. Karásek, *Milý příteli...*, 72.

80. *Navštěvoval pak vídeňské aukce a antikvariáty a odvážel odtamtud do Prahy celé soubory listů, o něž nebyl tehdy ještě zvláštní zájem a jejichž cena je dnes často větší než stonásobná. Karásek si však ponechával z nich jen ty nejvýznamnější, ostatní vyměňoval nebo prodával. Tím získával prostředky na další nákupy, na které věnoval i každou volnou korunu ušetřenou z platu či honorářů. Sám byl čím dál tím skromnější, nekouřil, víno pil jen poskrovnu a brzy se stal i vegetariánem, takže jeho osobní spotřeba byla minimální* (Štorch-Marien, *Sladko je žít*, 107).

81. See Appendix V for Karásek's 1925 article describing the inspiration for the trilogy.

82. For additional discussion, see Beran, "Oscar Wilde and the Czech Decadence," 256–69; and Appendix I, "The Czech Polemic on Oscar Wilde."

83. David-Fox, "1890s Generation," 347–48.

84. Lishaugen, *Speaking with a Forked Tongue*, 165.

85. See Appendix II, "A Double Coming-Out" for Karásek–Klas letter of December 21, 1901. Putna finds that "[i]n Karásek's works, two archetypes for lovers are recurrent: the 'white I' [*bílé já*] and the 'brown you' [*hnědé ty*]. The 'white I' is passive, tender, even effeminate, suffers from loneliness, and longs to be assaulted and raped; we find the 'Sebastian' motif in Karásek's works as well [...] The 'brown you,' on the other hand, is a masculine element, including in the narrower sense of the word—active, aggressive, warlike; this is who is meant to 'stab' the white Sebastian [...] The polarity of 'white' and 'brown,' passive and active in a romantic male couple, will recur several times in Karásek's work [...] (e.g., in the *Three Magicians* novels)" (Putna, *Dějiny homosexuality v české kultuře*, 126). *U Karáska se opakují dva milenecké archetypy: "bílé já" a "hnědé ty." "Bílé já" je pasivní, něžné až zženštilé, trpící samotou a toužící být atakováno a znásilněno; i u Karáska zazní motiv "šebestiánský" [...] "Hnědé ty" je naopak prvek maskulinní i v užším významu slova—aktivní, agresivní, válečnický; je to ten, kdo má bílého Šebestiána "probodnout" [...] Polarita "bílého" a "hnědého," pasivního a aktivního ve dvojici mužských milenců, se v Karáskově díle ještě několikrát vrátí. Avšak, pokud dojde k jejich setkání— nebude to v antickém rouchu, nýbrž v jiných stylizacích (například v Románech tří mágů).*

86. Lishaugen, *Speaking with a Forked Tongue*, 165. See also Opelík, Forst, and Merhaut, "Hugo Kosterka," 872–73.

87. Opelík, Forst, and Merhaut, "Jiří Karásek ze Lvovic," 666–67. Karásek withheld his first two novels from Kosterka's set of his collected works, deeming them subpar.

88. See Appendix V, "Karásek on Creating..."

89. Lishaugen found that Austrian archivists could unearth no evidence for this claim of restoration (*Speaking with a Forked Tongue*, 180). For period research into the family line in Hradec Králové including Cyprián, see Rybička, *Královéhradecké rodiny erbovní*, 24–26.

90. Anonymous, "Literatura," *Zvon* 2 (1902), no. 14, 194–95 (see p. 195).
91. Homolová, Otruba, and Pešat, *Čeští spisovatelé 19. a počátku 20. století*, 126–28.
92. As cited in Lishaugen, *Speaking with a Forked Tongue*, 180.
93. Burri, "Theodor Herzl and Richard von Schaukal."
94. Opelík, Forst, and Merhaut, "Jiří Karásek ze Lvovic," 666–67.
95. The breed is large in size and known for its gentle temperament.
96. Opelík, Forst, and Merhaut, "Kruh českých spisovatelů," 1007–8. Karásek was an active participant. The Circle's founders Jaroslav Kamper, Viktor Dyk, and Hanuš Jelínek are all prominent cultural figures who recur in Karásek's memoirs and correspondence.
97. Karásek and Procházka were both already active in the Artistic Forum (Jelínek, *Padesát let Umělecké besedy 1863–1913*, 159). A *beseda* was a nineteenth-century form of civic club. Its particulars varied by location and circumstance, but it could have a restaurant, newspapers, journals, card tables, and even billiards. It was often a venue for "educational" or cultural events such as topical debates, plays, or concerts.
98. Files of correspondence with Klas (Jedličková) and Kalašová are the two most significant in Karásek's extant letters, per Karásek scholar Karel Kolařík (Karásek, *Upřímné pozdravy*, 75n). Other files contain little beyond brief notes to set meetings (Müldner, Lešehrad), or were lost or destroyed, as were letters to or from Ivo Raić (Karásek, 75).
99. Born in Vienna, Reinhardt was manager of the Neues Theater (today the Theater am Schiffbauerdamm) from 1903 to 1905.
100. Croatian theater historian Antonija Bogner-Šaban observes that a 1905 portrait of Raić by Czech lithographer and painter Viktor Stretti seems to poke fun at his androgynous physique by posing him as Michelangelo's David while dressed in his Pierrot costume (Bogner-Šaban, *Ivo Raić*, 73, 76).
101. *Pan Raić jest jedním z oněch mála umělců, kteří* nereprodukují, *ale* tvoří (emphasis in original; Karásek, "Divadelní kronika," 150).

102. Bogner-Šaban, *Ivo Raić*, 76. "Šapica" is Croatian for "paw." It is unclear whether the name of the group is translated from Czech into Croatian or was originally Croatian. Bogner-Šaban cites Hora-Hořejš, *Toulky českou minulostí* and Kovařík, *Literární mýty, záhady a aféry.*

Czech writer Karel Matěj Čapek-Chod depicted a comically overblown Croatian diva—likewise claiming an aristocratic pedigree—in his novel *Turbina* (The Turbine, 1916). Separately, Pynsent points out a Karásek parody in Čapek-Chod's novel *Antonín Vondrejc* (1917–18): "an ethereally choir-boy-loving aesthete [...] whose novel *Gotická duše* is called *Missa solemnis*" (Pynsent, "Čapek-Chod and the Grotesque," 207).

103. See Appendix V, "Karásek on Creating..."

104. Lishaugen, *Speaking with a Forked Tongue*, 166, 191–92, 213. *Už obálka nepříjemně chlupatá, silně červená, s rudě vpáleným gothickým nadpisem zvěstuje, že uvnitř bude něco prokletého, infernálního, magického, šíleného, neorbidně [sic; morbidně] chimérického a magnetického* (Vodák [anonymously], "Románek infernální"). Lishaugen explains his identification of the reviewer as Vodák at p. 186n.

105. Lishaugen, 169–70; emphasis in original.

106. Lishaugen, 158–59.

107. Lishaugen characterizes Karásek's work with Neumannová as a deliberate association with an "exclusive" publisher of modern literature in limited editions; his steady postal employment afforded him some latitude in this (164). Aventinum later issued Karásek's collected works in 19 volumes from 1921 to 1932 (Opelík, Forst, and Merhaut, "Jiří Karásek ze Lvovic," 666).

108. See Heczková, "Doslov"; Karásek, *Milý příteli...*, 86.

109. *Já mám k homosexualitě vztah ryze literární: zabývám se vážně její psychologickou stránkou v některých svých dílech, užívám ji za tragickou látku ke své umělecké tvorbě* (Karásek, *Anonymní dopisy*, 21–22; emphasis in original).

110. *píši osmnáct let kritiky a* všechny jsem podepsal plným jménem! Nemám rád anonymity (Karásek, *Anonymní dopisy*, 9; emphasis in original). There is a pointed comparison

here with rival critic Šalda's use of pseudonyms and the so-called 1899–1900 "Pseudonym Affair," a polemic between Šalda and *Moderní revue* that turned on the integrity of contemporary literary criticism (Vojtěch, "Polemičnost a strategie," 151).

111. Postmark, Karásek to Klas, letter of January 2, 1907 (Karásek, *Milý příteli...*, 65). Prior letters to Klas specified the address as Palackého třída no. 406, 3rd floor, in Smíchov (Karásek, *Milý příteli...*, 11).

112. Built during the Renaissance and renovated multiple times, this building is an architectural monument today (Národní památkový ústav, "Dům U Textařů: dům U Bílého preclíku").

113. Štorch-Marien, *Sladko je žít*, 106–7.

114. Zach, "Thyrsus."

115. Hynek, "Jiří Karásek ze Lvovic." Karásek's gesture in donating this collection of largely Slavic artwork recalls Zeyer's patriotic endowment of the Památník národního písemnictví (Museum of Czech Literature) within the Academy of Sciences (Pokorná, "Zeyerův fond při České akademii věd a umění"). Karásek served on juries awarding honoraria for the Zeyer Fund (Benešová, *Verše*, 445).

   For a period description of the gallery's holdings, see Volavková, *Pražská muzea*, 29. Today, the Museum of Czech Literature has enabled virtual access to some of Karásek's collection on its website: https://karasek.pamatniknarodniho pisemnictvi.cz/. For a discussion of the gallery's contents, see Petruželková and Kolařík, *Knihovna Karáskovy Galerie*.

116. Murko, *Paměti*, 212.

117. Citing Karásek, "Romány tři magů" (see Appendix V, "Karásek on Creating..."), Lishaugen characterizes Procházka's support as "pressure" (*Speaking with a Forked Tongue*, 86).

118. Krystýnek, "Przybyszewski v české literatuře," 69–70.

119. Lishaugen, *Speaking with a Forked Tongue*, 86–87.

120. Lishaugen, 52.

121. *Ottův slovník naučný*, 744.

122. The monumental kabbalistic work *Sefer HaZohar* (Book of Radiance) emerged in north-central Spain in the late 13th century. Parts were translated from Aramaic and Hebrew

into Latin as early as the 14th century (Huss, "Translations of the Zohar," 83–85).

Per professor of philosophy and esoterica Justin Sledge, the printing of a complete translation of the work into Latin in mid-16th century Italy was a milestone in the development of European philosophy (Sledge, "Safedian Kabbalah," 57:40; Sledge, "Christian and Lurianic Kabbalah," 15:30).

123. Sledge, "Kabbalah and the Contemporary World," 33:05.
124. To cite just a few examples, there are mystical elements in French decadent Joris-Karl Huysmans's novels *À rebours* (Against Nature, 1884) and *Là-bas* (Down There or The Damned, 1891); German symbolist Stefan George's verse collection *Das Jahr der Seele* (The Year of the Soul, 1897); Russian symbolist Valerii Bryusov's *Ognënnyi angel* (The Fiery Angel, serial 1907–08, book 1908); and works by Austrian authors Hugo von Hofmannsthal and Rainer Maria Rilke.
125. In the 1890s, the young critic Karásek first attended the "bohemian" Mahábhárata circle hosted by Arbes in Prague's Malá Strana pub U svatého Tomáše. The group was characterized by "a tendency to the absurd and persiflage, and its principal mode of expression was hyperbole and parody." Member Václav Jans sketched Karásek in miniature, surrounded by grotesque, predatory fish and a red devil (Kolařík, "Raná literární tvorba Jiřího Karáska ze Lvovic," 607).

Karásek felt kinship with the elder writer as "a fellow native of Smíchov" (*smíchovský krajan*) and wrote of him as "a novelist much beloved by me [...] whom I so respected and whose art I had so loved since childhood" (*romanciér mnou tak milovaný [...kterého] jsem si tolik vážil a [jehož] umění jsem miloval od dětství*) (*Vzpomínky*, 51). Arbes was also an outspoken maverick who had run afoul of the authorities as a journalist and served time.

126. Karásek, *Vzpomínky*, 237.
127. Karásek, *Vzpomínky*, 103.
128. Karásek, *Vzpomínky*, 237. See also Lacina, "Jakub Arbes."
129. See Nagy, "Karáskovy Romány tří mágů" for his citations of (a) Papoušek, *Dějiny nové moderny*; and (b) Nakonečný, *Lexikon magie*.

130. Plass, "Historie Martinistického řádu v Čechách," 24–26. Karásek corresponded with Zeyer but never met him in person. Karásek also wrote much of *RMM* and *Scarabaeus* at Zeyer's former villa, purchased from him by Anna Lauermannová-Mikschová in 1881 (Karásek, *Upřímné pozdravy*, 11n).

131. Weinfurter, "Nový román okkultní." Weinfurter would be "a famous popularizer of mystics and occultism" (Lishaugen, *Speaking with a Forked Tongue*, 64, citing Nakonečný, *Novodobý český hermetismus*, 31–36).

132. Lóže U Zeleného Slunce, "Společnost českých hermetiků Universalia."

133. Opelík, Forst, and Merhaut, "Jiří Karásek ze Lvovic," 665.

134. Lóže U Zeleného Slunce, "Společnost českých hermetiků Universalia."

135. In 1910, Waite codesigned the Rider-Waite tarot deck, still sold today.

136. Crossley, *Imagining Mars*, 129–30. Lauermannová had hosted Zeyer at her literary salon.

137. Crossley, *Imagining Mars*, citing Lowell's biographer David Strauss.

138. Goodrick-Clarke, *The Occult Roots of Nazism*.

139. Hudáková, "Organizace československého spiritistického hnutí," 49–50.

140. Lishaugen, *Speaking with a Forked Tongue*, 82. While Karásek does not use the term "third sex" in *RMM*, he provides a circumlocution: "there are those who are outside of both sexes" (*Existují však, kdo jsou mimo obě pohlaví*, *RMM* X).

141. Poet and critic Stefan George shared many affinities with decadence, and his works often feature homoerotic themes. The George-Kreis had "almost cult-like rituals and symbolism," emphasizing the renewal of culture through the power of youth and beauty. Within his "aestheticized view of human sexuality," he described the capacity for same-sex attraction as *übergeschlechtliche Liebe* ("suprasexual love") (Thuleen, "*Dichterstreit:* Homoeroticism"). See also Rieckmann, "(Anti-)Semitism and Homoeroticism."

142. The volume was the first novel in the spiritist hexalogy *V koloběhu světů* (As Worlds Circulate, 1920–22) by Emilie Procházková (Putna, *Václav Havel*, 34–35. Václav Havel's grandson Václav Havel was the first postcommunist Czechoslovak president.

143. Nagy, "Karáskovy Romány tří mágů," 6. See note 85 above for Putna's analysis of Karásek's "white I" and "brown you." Yet some contemporaries read Manfred and Francis in *RMM* rather as *dvojníci* (doubles or *Doppelgänger*) (*Ottův slovník naučný*, 744).

144. Adamovič, Neff, and Olša, *Slovník české literární fantastiky*, 112.

145. *Analytický intellekt* [sic] *zpružněl, nabyl dialektické finessy a ironické pohotovosti* (Sezima, "Z nové české belletrie [sic]").

146. *schází jim takořka třírozměrná prostornost*

147. Sezima, "Z nové české belletrie," 482–85.

148. *bez trhlin, skoků, záhadných prohlubní ve svém nitru* (Karásek, "Julius Zeyer," 116.

149. Pynsent, *Julius Zeyer*, 157n.

150. Špiritová, "Spisy bývalého Poštovní muzea v Praze"; Karásek, *Vzpomínky*.

151. See Appendix V, "Karásek on Creating...

152. Adamovič, Neff, and Olša, *Slovník české literární fantastiky*, 112.

153. *Einen gereiften Künstler, der besonders das sprachliche Instrument meisterhaft handhabt* (Jakubec, *Geschichte der čechischen* [sic] *Litteratur*, 425–26).

154. Lishaugen, *Speaking with a Forked Tongue*, 74–75.

155. *naposled se příliš okatě zvrhla ve štvanici na nepohodlného kritika* (Sezima, *Z mého života*, 227); cited in Heczková, "Doslov," 86. Slight paraphrase for clarity.

156. Lishaugen, *Speaking with a Forked Tongue*, 75–76.

157. Lishaugen, 194.

158. See note 7 on editorial roles at *Nový hlas*. On masculinism and integrationism, see Seidl, "Mužnost," which cites Vávra, "Slovo čtenářům" and "Od Hlaváčka k Nestroyovi."

159. Seidl, Nozar, and Wintr, *Od žaláře k oltáři*, 86. *Hlas sexuální menšiny* vol. 1, nos. 1–16 (1931) is archived at Česká digitální knihovna but with limited access as of January 4, 2024. For issue no. 12, see https://www.digitalniknihovna.cz/cdk/uuid/uuid:2b20b3d0-ed30-11ed-9b5a-0050568d9066. For

additional discussion of *Hlas* and its contents, see Lishaugen, "Nejistá sezóna," 33–35; for an analysis of personals ads in *Hlas*, see Seidl, "'Najdu mladého přítele, přírodu milujícího?'"; for a review of the journal's representations of the queer individual, see Kazbalová, "Obraz homosexuálního jedince v časopisu *Hlas*."

160. See note 64. Between 1932 and 1934, Čeřovský found prosecutors of those charged under §129(b) "generally very prudent, professional, and humane" (*poměrně velmi prozřetelně, vědecky rozumně a lidsky shovívavě*), with courts often issuing suspended sentences instead of jail terms—especially in Prague. Even so, higher courts tended to take a harsher approach. By 1938, he reported a generally stricter line by authorities and the courts (Seidl, Nozar, and Wintr, *Od žaláře k oltáři*, 35–37). See Karczewski, "Call Me by My Name" for an analysis of the correspondence between two men prosecuted for homosexual acts in Poland in 1925.

161. For a detailed analysis of this decriminalization effort, see Seidl, "Úsilí o odtrestnění homosexuality."

162. *že by homosexuálni na chrbát si vyvesili tabulu s nadpisom "som homosexuálnym"*; cited in Jablonická-Zezulová, "Matyášove práce."

163. *domnívali jsme se, že je to zaostalá, Maďary porobená rasa, již musíme teprve vychovávati ke kultuře. To byl omyl, a sice velmi důkladný* (Karásek, "O kvalitách slovenského duchu").

164. Špiritová, "Spisy bývalého Poštovní muzea v Praze," 100–101.

165. In his introduction to a new edition of the Czech gothic novel *Pekla zplozenci* (Hellspawn, serial 1853 in *Lumír*, book 1862) by Josef Jiří Kolár, Karásek explicitly traced a line of development from Kolár's gothic fantasy through Arbes to himself. See Lang, "Josef Jiří Kolár," 71. *Hellspawn* was the first title in the series *Obnovený obraz* ("restored picture" or recreations of the past), which would include others by Arbes, edited by Štorch-Marien. Under the Nazi occupation, reviewer Lang's reference to "renewed interest" in the Czech literary past seems natural.

166. Zavřel, *Za živa pohřben*, 25, 73, 81–82. Zavřel was an "ambitious" author and playwright "of little talent," as Karel Čapek's widow Olga Scheinpflugová recalled in her memoir *Byla jsem na světě* (I Was in the World, 1988).

His "politico-pornographic" (Blažek, "Comment") novel *Fortinbras* (1930) portrayed then-Foreign Minister Edvard Beneš, thinly disguised, as a monster who must be destroyed for the good of the nation. Zavřel was tried as a Nazi collaborator after World War II.

167. See Klas to Karásek, letter of April 19, 1941 (Karásek, *Milý příteli...*, 69).

168. This church ("U Jezulátka") features in Karásek's novel *A Gothic Soul* (1900) (Lodge, email message to author Bulkin, December 23, 2023). It was a favorite place of meditation for the author (see Appendix II for Karásek to Klas, letter of December 7, 1901; and Karásek, *Milý příteli...*, 11–12).

169. *byť neodstraněný, přestává býti hrůzou a řeknu upřímně, že jeho konečný pád nebudu pokládati za žádné zvláštní vítězství a za žádnou zvláštní výhodu. Ti, kteří očekávají po pádu tohoto §129 úplnou svobodu, mýlí se strašně. Decentní láska bude stejně chráněna jako dnes. A sexuální výstřednosti budou se i dále trestati podle ostatních paragrafů a nezbude těm, kdo jsou sexuálně výstřední, než žalář nebo sanatorium* (Karásek, "Morální záchvat Německa," 12–13). This proved to be the case, since the communist regime did not take decriminalization seriously in practice. Even after 1961, the Czechoslovak medical community continued to use forced conversion therapy, a national "specialty" of the 1950s. Public discussion of homosexuality was confined to media crime reporting (Seidl, Nozar, and Wintr, *Od žaláře k oltáři*, 285, 290; Seidl, email to author Bulkin, January 10, 2024).

170. Translated into Czech in 1905 by Antonín Tille. Despite Wilde's regional popularity, only the exceptional critic was capable of separating the author's life from his works until long after his death (Mayer, *Oscar Wilde in Vienna*, 76–78). See also Bershtein, "Next to Christ."

171. *říci o géniovi* [sic]*, že nelhal, je tolik, jako říci o něm, že byl bez invence* (Karásek, *RMM 1924*, 61).

172. Lishaugen, *Speaking with a Forked Tongue*, 11.

TRANSLATOR'S NOTE

All translators aim to adapt their texts into different frame-works of language, meaning, and culture, and often for a new generation of readers. In this translation of *Manfred Macmillan*, I have tried to maintain the readability and flow of the original language while preserving a few of the text's characteristic quirks (e.g., the alternation of "irreality" and "unreality"). I have also inserted a few archaic and less com-mon spellings ("mediæval," "œuvre," "æthereal," "grey," and "façade") to reflect Karásek's gothicism, *fin de siècle* aestheticism, and defamiliarization strategy.

Translators from Slavic languages into English face certain peculiar challenges. These include different systems of verb tenses, particularly when it comes to English perfect tenses and Slavic verbal aspect, which more carefully distinguishes a completed action from an ongoing or iterative one.

In addition, Czech narrative prose employs different conventions from English in shifting between the past and present tenses. The normal purpose of a shift to present tense is to heighten the reader's sense of immediacy and involvement, even tension. In this text, I have maintained these shifts as they occur in the original narrative. Where these considerations do not apply, I have tended to follow English practice in preserving the sequence of tenses.

Slavic languages also lack specific definite or indefinite articles. Czech *ten* may sometimes function as a definite article, a demonstrative pronoun, or a demonstrative adjective; and the adjective *nějaký* can mark a noun as "indefinite," but this distinction is otherwise almost always clear from context.

While *Manfred Macmillan* and the *Three Magicians* trilogy as a whole are prose works, their author was an accomplished poet, and contemporary readers were likely to approach even his prose with this in mind. In *Manfred Macmillan*, Karásek employs rhythm, sound patterning, varied syntax, parallelisms, and poetic language to frame an image or establish the mood of a scene.[1] With rare exceptions, I have preserved the structure of his sentences (sometimes elaborate, sometimes terse) in their original length as units. On occasion, I have reduced the number of modifiers within a sentence for readability while trying to preserve as much information as possible. As in Karásek's original text, my attempts at alliteration and sonority are intended to mark poetic language.

Lexically, the texts of Karásek's *Three Magicians* trilogy evoke a rich sensory palette of light, sound, fragrance, and texture. Landscapes, artworks, and couture all inspire the author's poetic imagination. In places, Karásek brings his knowledge of art history, esoteric literature, or the practice of magic to bear.

A frequency analysis of *Manfred Macmillan*'s text finds that words related to mystery (*tajemný, tajemství, tajný*, etc., 106 occurrences), riddle or enigma (*záhada, záhadný*, etc., 32+), and secrecy (*tajný, tajnost*, 11+) present the largest single thematic category. These concepts stem from magic (*magie, magický*, 65; but also *kouzlo, kouzelný, kouzelník*, etc., 25) and the supernatural as in, for example, the ghostly, spectral, and phantasmagorical (*přízrak, duch, zjev, fantasmagorie*, and related words, 65), and the demonic (*démon, démonický*, 27) or diabolical (*ďábel, ďábelský*, 16; *satan*, 2). A frequent metaphor for unseen forces is the magnet, which has historically fascinated occultists (*magnet, magnetický*, etc., 14). Magical forces are associated with the medieval (*středověk, středověký*, 19) and less often with the Baroque (*barokový*, 5). They may be cunning or sinister (*pošetilý, pošetilost*, 11) and evoke a sense of the absurd (*absurdní, absurdnost*, 10).

Destiny (*osud, osudový*, etc., 58) and futility (*marnost, marný*, etc., 29) also represent powerful forces in the universe of *Manfred Macmillan*. Death, and what is dead, deathly, or deadly (*smrt, mrtvý, smrtelný*, 63+), and darkness (*tmavost, tmavý*, etc., 32) or blackness (*černý, čerň*, etc., 34) hang heavily over the narrative. The grave or the gravelike (*hrob, hrobní, hrobný* [*sic*], 18) is often underfoot.

To grapple with these forces, psychology and identity are defined in terms of soul (*duše*, though sometimes "mind"; and *duševní*, 93), but also the heart (*srdce*, etc., 47), the psyche (*psycha, psychický*, 15), and the imagination (*imaginace, imaginární*, 9).[2] The idea of a private core, inner depths, or inner(most) self hidden from the world (*nitro*, 51) is prominent and contrasts with the outer self, personality, persona (*osobnost*, 22), appearance, and manifestation (*zjev, zjevení*, etc., 25). An occult form of "initiation" (*zasvěcení, zasvěcený*, etc., 25) is necessary to achieve private knowledge of another self, or a true understanding of life's deepest mysteries.

Key states and emotions in Karásek's ghost-storytelling are madness (*šílený*, *šílenost*, etc., 64) and sorrow (*smutek*, *smutný*, *smuteční*, etc., 19), and no less potently, terror, horror, and dread (*děs*, *hrozba*, *bázeň*, and related words, 65+).

These states are alleviated by love (*láska*, 47), friendship (which can be queer-coded language for intimacy; *přítel*, *přátelství*, etc., 40), and beauty (*krásný*, 39+). Since beauty is so central an idea to aestheticism and decadence, I have consistently translated *krásný* as "beautiful" even when referring to a male character such as the magician Manfred.

Naturally, a magician performs occult experiments (*pokus*, 31; *experiment*, *experimentovati*, 6) in a laboratory (*laboratoř*, 11), often using alchemy (*alchymie*, *alchymický*, 9) to achieve his ends.

Karásek is a fine and deliberate stylist who is as clear as he wants to be—but a degree of obscurity sometimes serves his purpose. As he states in his preface to *Manfred Macmillan*, a "good stylist" can always achieve "the necessary obscurity." For example, the ellipsis (...) may leave something unsaid either in dialogue or in narration, or it may rather suggest apprehension or wistfulness. As the Introduction above suggests, euphemism and discretion were not only useful but necessary for queer Central Europeans in the *fin de siècle*— as well as a source of wit—and so they remained for decades to come. The style of esoteric literature through the ages was often similarly deliberate in its obscurity, whether to prevent the uninitiated from penetrating and misusing privileged information while still affording useful knowledge to insiders, or to maintain deniability before hostile authorities, an outraged public, or disappointed clients.

Karásek occasionally uses italics for emphasis and small caps for invocations with an oracular quality. I have preserved that typography here. On occasion, where the Czech adds important emphasis solely through syntax, I have selectively italicized a word or two in the translation, since the emphasis would otherwise be lost in written English. Also in a very few instances, I have inserted paragraph breaks into a character's extended speeches, since period Czech punctuation had no easy way to do so. (A dash would set off the beginning of an utterance, which ended with a period, and a new dash indicated a new speaker.) Lastly, I have set off Manfred's disquisition on Cagliostro's life and its meaning in quote marks to maintain the distinction from Francis's narration.

This translation is based on the 1924 edition of *Román Manfreda Macmillena* prepared by contributing editor Vratislav Hugo Brunner for Dr. Otakar Štorch-Marien's Aventinum imprint. While Karásek's style and syntax are notably more modern than the previous generation's often were, Brunner's edits further reflect an emerging consensus on modern Czech syntax and orthography. There are minor orthographic, syntactical, and other textual differences between the 1907 Kamilla Neumannová edition and the 1924 Aventinum edition of *Manfred Macmillan*, including the substitution of Roman numerals for section dividers as chapter headings. Scans of these editions, and many other wonderful titles besides, are available on the website of Národní knihovna České republiky (National Library of the Czech Republic) at Kramerius5.nkp.cz.

Modern literary translators often avoid annotation in order not to distract or alienate the casual reader. The *Three Magicians* novels can indeed be read and enjoyed casually. At the same time, their combination of *fin de siècle* esotericism, art history, and queer self-reinvention presents useful opportunities for cultural discovery. These would elude most contemporary readers without some explanation. The undergraduate can use the notes to place the works in a wider cultural context. The graduate student may find useful avenues of inquiry to explore, with enough sources in the bibliography to start from.

This translation has benefited greatly from the support of several friends and colleagues. My particular thanks go to Jan Krč, who read all of the translation and offered many constructive comments. Fellow translators at Czechlist on Facebook have been unfailingly gracious in sharing their insights on particular passages. Friends Melvyn Clarke, Maija French, Garry Richards, and Linda Wallace Bartow read part or all of the English manuscript and offered helpful comments and questions. Michael Biggins at the University of Washington Libraries went above and beyond in helping to locate individual items of Karáskiana. The reference teams at the National Library of the Czech Republic and the Seattle Public Library gave invaluable advice and assistance. Tomáš Mařík at Antikvariát Valentinská in Prague helped to obtain titles on the secondary book market when otherwise unavailable. Kateřina Bečková at Muzeum hlavního města Prahy (the Prague City Museum) fielded several questions particular to the history, artwork, and legends of Prague. Any errors that remain are entirely my responsibility.

Particular thanks are also due to curator Dr. Jakub Hauser at Památník národního písemnictví (the Museum of Czech Literature), Dr. Konrad Niemira at Warsaw's Muzeum Literatury im. Adama Mickiewicza (Adam Mickiewicz Museum of Literature), Josefina Panenková at Prague's Archiv Národního divadla (National Theater Archive), the theater archive of Hrvatska akademija znanosti i umjetnosti (the Croatian Academy of Sciences and Arts), and Martin Zoul for their kind assistance in locating, contextualizing, and facilitating the images reproduced in this volume.

For more on Czech LGBTQ+ literature past and present, the reader may wish to consult the 2011 study *Dějiny homosexuality v české kultuře* (The History of Homosexuality in Czech Culture) by Martin C. Putna and his colleagues, particularly pages 83–181. The website Odnaproti.cz offers selected author profiles. Jan Seidl and several of his colleagues have done the most to record and preserve Czech queer history. Most of the work of Seidl, Putna, and their colleagues has yet to be translated into English.

Notes

1. For an analysis of certain aspects of Karásek's prose style relative to Zeyer's, see Pynsent, *Julius Zeyer*.
2. In Karásek's usage, *psyche* and *psychic(al)* have paranormal associations common in the *fin de siècle*; viz. the names of the societies for "Psychical Research" based in London and elsewhere.

MANFRED MACMILLAN

PREFACE

So begins the remarkable tale of my friend Manfred Macmillan.[1] Must I also reassure you that from start to finish, this novel is utterly preposterous, the only reason I think its story worth the telling? But if others bother to write stories that cost them no effort whatsoever and leave their imaginations entirely inert, why shouldn't I then tell a tale that, though invented, has demanded such psychic courage as to drive me nearly mad? Why should the lies I've so purposely constructed be thought less true than the tales others have so offhandedly transcribed from reality?

There is no art without falsehood, with one qualification: that what is invented must have a deeper meaning than mere fact. In making up events that have never happened, our soul approaches the essence of everything more vigorously than when it merely ascertains that things exist. For it is of no great import whether a thing is or not: what matters is the vigor of the soul we invent a thing for, and not its inertia, which may lead us to settle for the outward, incidental appearance of things.

I do not thereby exclude truth from art. On the contrary, in cases where it is utterly irrelevant whether a thing is true or not, it is apropos to tell the truth. But of course, only as a last resort. The great, divine CAGLIOSTRO[2] himself—may the shade of his imagination be a kind companion to my hero throughout this tale!—never confined himself to metaphor in creating his style of life. In heightening a contrast somehow or other, he would uncover much that was true.

I pondered for quite some time how to take this story, already absurd in and of itself, and make it as absurd as possible. At last, I resolved to move it to Prague, a device that may appear perfectly mad. Indeed, I have heard objections that no setting could be more unseemly, though only from that city's poets, utterly self-infatuated and blind to anything outside themselves, and so this is natural coming from them.

I should like this tale to be read as it is written: in absolute capitulation to what is preposterous in it.

But do not imagine that this preposterousness masks any profound truths. It is only first-rank writers who lend themselves to such baseness. Far be it from me to create such madness only to conceal some good example therein. Nothing is so scandalous as a good example when we believe in it, and nothing so uplifting as one when we hold it up to ridicule.

*Yet I display such candor in this tale that had I written it
under my own name, I should have felt compelled to burn
it the next day. Among the advantages of art is that we can
cloak ourselves best by unmasking ourselves. The only difference is that while one person may cloak what is preposterous
about himself in art, another will do so in the preposterous.
Though the former genre is taken quite seriously by literary
historians, I decidedly prefer the latter. As to the method, it
is only a matter of remaining incomprehensible. But that is
merely a question of style. If a good stylist should care to, he
can always achieve the necessary obscurity.*

THE TALE

I

Count Manfred Macmillan was from one of those noble
families that, in the past five centuries, had moved from
one country to another and one nation to another so often
that no territory or race could claim them.[3] He was everywhere and nowhere at home. He lived alternately in the
various capitals of Europe but returned regularly to only
two: Vienna and Prague. In Vienna, he owned a large palace
that he loved to enliven with a retinue of friends who had
attached themselves to him during his world travels: they
were themselves original and the most varied of men. No
woman ever had access to Manfred. He was consistent in
his scorn for them.[4] In Prague, he had a deserted palace near
the Church of St. Jindřich,[5] a Baroque pile with perpetually
covered windows, as well as a château in the vicinity of Bílá
Hora as a summer residence.[6] If he were sad or wanted to
be alone, he would say he was going "to a monastery" and
without giving his destination, make off for Prague.

Anyone would have been astonished to see what Manfred
was like in Vienna and what he was like in Prague. In Vienna

a dandy, in Prague a dreamer. In Vienna the center of society, in Prague a recluse adrift among its churches. It was as if he alternated between two souls. I know not whether he was different still in Paris, Rome, or London—I saw and observed him only in Vienna and Prague.

Once when I had told him of my observations, he said to me with irony:

"I have but one occupation anywhere: tedium."[7]

II

Manfred captivated me from the moment I laid eyes on him. All my life, conversation with ordinary people has been an ordeal. I love only those who hold some danger for me. I particularly enjoy the contact with their core selves, much as we play with a dagger though it may wound us. I love to teeter over shadowy depths, and for my friends I choose only those who harbor a demon that, given the opportunity, might pounce on me.

I felt this demonic quality luring me to Manfred. Vienna became my destiny from that moment on. It came alive. It spoke to me. I was suddenly transformed into a being whose own existence leaves some trace amid the cacophony of strangers.[8] From all around, something ingratiatingly soft, warm, and velvety was enfolding me, an atmosphere of smooth, naked bodies with slow, supple movements, feline. I suddenly understood all the pleasure-seekers previously alien to me, and I also understood the bizarre desires that came spouting from their grey-green eyes, longings to experience life in their own way, to burst forth in a cheerless crimson flame only to peter out into disgust.

Manfred was one of that kind.

He was the perfect dandy. Arresting as his appearance was, there was nothing eccentric about it; and yet at the same time one felt that he shunned eccentricity not out of a sense of propriety but merely because it was not his genre. His dress was fashionable and distinguished, but nothing about him could have been called the *dernier cri*[9] or purchased in any establishment on the Kärntner Straße.[10] He was not quite young, but he did his utmost to look perfectly so. He regarded youthfulness as the only acceptable way to appear in public. By eternal youth, he meant to distinguish himself from those oblivious to the indecency of being old.

Nor did he ever choose old people for friends. He gave them a wide berth, as wide as possible. The only thing that lifted his spirits was the company of young friends. For he regarded old age as contagious, as though it could spread to a person and make him old in turn. Nor did he bother with unattractive people. For the mere sight of the ugly can cause one's own looks to go. He bore his own inbred and cultivated beauty lightly, spiritually, as if it were the most precious of ideas.

Most of the dissatisfaction in the world stems from people's incapacity for tedium, and they therefore wither away. The philosophy of dandyism teaches one to be capable of tedium as a way of experiencing life.[11] The dandy should not be inspired by anything. But since that is too tall an order, he may sometimes be permitted inspiration, except in one instance: never may he marvel at perfection, which is only for snobs. As it happens, the dandy is inspired only by mediocrity. Bad theater supplies him with illusion, and bad romance with the feeling of falling in love. The dandy should neither love nor despise people. He has only to be convinced that the world contains people who are either interesting or useless, and that the useless ones are everyone else.

These were the rules by which Manfred lived. Knowing life is only worth experiencing if we don't take it seriously, he would put off great matters and concern himself with trivialities. Knowing that one is made stupid only by positive knowledge, he would try his utmost to master all of mediæval magic and nothing of the claims of modern science.[12] If he read a good many of the latest books, he did so only to confirm his conviction of the utter nonsense of all modern literature.

His eroticism had no room for the commonplace. Women did not exist for him. His soul was content only in the company of the beautiful personæ of his friends. He would invest these friendships with every outward sign of love. But he would subordinate himself to none. He would first seduce himself with his own desire and only then choose an object suitable to it.[13] Such was the model for his friendships. And if he did love anyone, it was more for that person's winsome shortcomings than for his genuine merits. For he could hardly have exalted anyone else above himself, and he appreciated tender inexperience in others but not in himself.

He lived life as a dream. Action made him disconsolate and was not to his liking. He was only ever hopeful for what could not be and sulky over what did not concern him. He spoke with everyone as if he himself were uninteresting, and everyone therefore raved about him as if he were the opposite.

He led a quiet and sensitive life. He disliked commotion, even on the stage, and was still less given to acting out his life in dramatic poses. But he genuinely savored a delicate mood, and his soul would be all aquiver were anyone to make some remark to him that he thought choice.

He was much sought after. This was of no consequence to him. He was courteous to people only insofar as they could be considered fools with manners. He would speak to them about anything but sensible matters, for he could not be ordinary even out of politeness; and he would deliberately be on good behavior with them, but only so he should not have to be decent. People respected him, perhaps because he mocked them so. But they sensed that he deemed them unworthy even to be of service to him in his tedium.

One thing alone interested Manfred: when he found the real to be insupportable, he would enter into the artificial. He felt that only when we dare everything can we feel everything. Neither extremes nor violence frightened him. He delighted in working himself up over impossibilities, in plunging his soul into an artifice of madness. He was intoxicated by all we find terrifying today in the books of the Middle Ages. But whereas those who lived in that age were possessed by the devil, Manfred sought mastery over that devil and command over what was diabolical in himself. He wanted to mechanize his soul, to use it as an instrument to feel something of the terror of someone who believed in the devil ages ago. What was then seen as fate ought to be a game for him.

Manfred felt that in this way, he could break free from the vulgarity of his own day, thereby joining his soul to the esoteric and occult movements of mediæval mysticism, which had come to life for himself alone and to which he alone was privy. He would magnify the horror within himself as if it were some secret power, but only for the sake of his private experiments and not to become its tool.[14]

III

Max Duniecki had introduced me to Manfred. But it was a long while before I clearly sensed how enigmatic he was.

I liked to stroll to his Baroque palace in its narrow, quiet street near the imperial palace. This entire quarter is steeped in a kind of ceremonial severity, the grandiloquent aloofness of the Spanish court.[15] The palaces are forbiddingly sealed up, and the carriages depart in such secrecy. Everything here is sublime, from the coats of arms on the façades to the antique door knockers, from the solemn poses of the emperors and warriors on the monuments to the white marble of Canova's Maria Christina in St. Augustine's Church.[16] Even the denizens of this quarter reflect this style.

On Manfred's invitation, I would sometimes go out for a drive in his carriage to the Prater, full of pink flowers.[17] He sat opposite me, graceful and mannered, his figure precise and careless in its line, while I tried now and then to take in the charm of it, to feel myself Viennese, with no desire to occupy me other than to be attractive and alive. But I was a mere dilettante in such things.

Max Duniecki, of the Polish aristocracy but not of the Slavic mold, a Parisian, introduced me to all that Vienna society could offer. His pale, slender face had the beauty of one from a long-cultivated, dying race. He would solicit my friendship using all manner of refined politesse; but the only thing I loved about him was the scent of his cigarettes and his altogether novel perfume, unknown to anyone else and which he was the first to use. In vain, however, did I attempt to force myself into intimacy with his being, sometimes melancholy but never surprising, and like the Viennese waltz, nothing but a blend of confection and commonness.

As Max and I wandered through the Schönbrunn Palace gardens or took a drive out to Laxenburg[18] when the lilac scent was giving way to that of the acacias, my sole purpose would be to talk of Manfred. At last seeing the futility of my longing to achieve intimacy with Manfred, I came to understand Max Duniecki's grey-green eyes and became the friend he wished me to be—but my thoughts were of Manfred Macmillan, whom I earnestly wished would love me the way that Max did—Manfred, who certainly lived life to the full and who would surely then relegate me to the ranks of those whom he had used for his pleasure, while Max adored me and reserved his friendship for me alone, at the same time violating my freedom.

But I continued to call on Manfred. There was never an evening when the various nuances of his persona failed to surprise me. Change—that was the only constant about him. The more I observed him, the more he perplexed me. When he fixed his look upon me, I felt myself transforming. I was not even myself under his gaze. He controls his eyes well, I thought to myself. I would have given anything for them to show interest in me personally. But it was no use.

Until one evening, as I was about to leave for the opening of a play with a hero who intrigued me (it was about Cagliostro), a servant brought me a note. It contained just one sentence: "Manfred Macmillan requests the honor of Mr. Francis Galston's company at the theater this evening."

At first, I had no intention of complying. But something was telling me to go and accept Manfred's invitation. Perhaps there was also a little curiosity as to why he wished to arrange for my presence that evening.

IV

He was already in the loge, alone, overly severe somehow.

"I do hope," he greeted me, "that we shall have no visitors. I would like to have you all to myself tonight."

I was unaccustomed to such strong desire on his part for my company.

"This *Cagliostro* interests me; who is the author of the play?"

"I haven't read the name anywhere before: Walter Mora."

"It sounds like a pseudonym... I thought you might have divined his real name."

"I have absolutely no idea."

"A name like a portent; it gives me a black feeling. I've never heard it before in my life. Has it ever struck you what mystique there is in a name? How much a few syllables can tell us! The name of one's next lover, of some destiny, of the next hope, or of a sudden death... Small wonder that Cagliostro personally could not stand the names given him at birth. He would never have created such style from his life had he remained Giuseppe Balsamo. That name might have sufficed for the seminary of St. Rocco in Palermo, but for his exploits in the Masonic lodges and at the courts of royalty, he could be none other than 'divo Cagliostro...'[19] Walter Mora... The name sends a slight shiver down my spine. You're not laughing at me, are you? No... You're a fantasist in your own right, which is why I want you all to myself this evening. The stylized reality of the stage may be more dangerous to me tonight than you suppose. I sometimes experience dreams as if they were genuinely true. But the only effect real life has on me is to make me ridicule it."

V

The theater was packed. The mood of the audience, nervous, restless, and yet somehow bracing, took hold of me.

I love nights like this at the theater, when you expect something startling to come from the stage. All those we love, who appeal to us, are more beautiful in these hours. I am not thinking of women, though there is also some fleeting allure in their perfumes, in the rustling of their gowns, in the glitter of their jewels, in the snowy whiteness of their exposed bosoms, even for one such as I, who take no interest in them. But that would not suffice to sustain this mood tonight. The attitudes women strike are all the same, and one knows there is nothing more behind them than the miserably ordinary. But the men, the young men with hearts of mystery and contrived in their outward appearance, our encounters with them seemingly at destiny's command, who have a psychic charm about them that women lack; refined and cosmopolitan, they live life as a play of impressions and artifice, and poets, unintelligible to others, speak to them in veiled symbols.

Yet they are expressive of their very innermost selves, and at just such moments, the soul that has been merely casual in its flirtations seems to fill with enthusiasm. Otherwise so disdainful, tonight they are in a fever, keenly observant, sparking fire in one another. Their eyes grow lustrous, their complexions pale, their lips crimson.[20] A desire as if for something they have never heard, for things they have not seen, for all that others do not understand; once grasped, it can belong to none but them, overpowering them. They feel themselves in thrall to a poet and his interpreters. I love such evenings. The intoxication of great life, great art, is alive in them. Something like the celebration of a playwright as a personality. Even the actors shed their ordinary appearances, for they now *become* who they otherwise only play at being.

VI

Such was the première of Walter Mora's *Cagliostro*. So caught up was I in the play that I had quite forgotten Manfred's presence beside me. Turning to him some time later, I was horrorstruck by the change that had come over him. His face, which otherwise gave the impression of a curious darkness, with cheeks smooth though with a touch of bluish-black shadow from his too-hard, constantly shaved beard, with something apparently untamed in his helm of thick black hair, with demonic mockery in his cold, coal-black pupils—his pallor had intensified to a sickly, ashen tone; his eyes were now round with terror.

He was watching the stage. Instinctively, I sensed how the performance astounded him. Manfred's entire being seemed utterly transformed. As the last lines of the *pièce* rang out, Manfred seized me by the arm with a brutality positively fevered and peremptory, and dragged me out of the theater, grinding out these words between his teeth:

"Come along! Come along! I couldn't bear to speak to anyone now! Quickly! Quickly!"

VII

He pulled me into his carriage, sat down in the corner, and pressed his body to mine, his excitement suddenly communicated to every nervous fiber of my being. His breath, heavy, panting, fanned and flooded my face. I felt utterly powerless, passive, in his arms. I cannot say whether he was having a fit such as one has on seeing a phantom, when you begin to doubt yourself and want a living person in your arms to convince yourself you are real. But I sensed Manfred needed someone like me, and though I could not say why, my intuition was nevertheless telling me that our friendship was beginning at that very moment, that we were now marking off a new intimacy to last the rest of our lives. I felt as if his being, now afire, were incinerating and consuming my own. I had become an instrument for the entire surfeit of his fervor. He was attaining calm and balance through me.

In a fragrant white chamber where he never hosted guests, he had the tapers lit on all the candelabra, ordered food, wine, fruit, and confections, and without touching any of it himself, urged me to eat and drink. Unable to think of food in my excitement, it was all I could do to sample them. He implored me to stay with him in the palace till morning, and I knew this was my obligation to him.

The chamber where we stayed that night was his late mother's boudoir. Lovely rococo ladies, enwreathed in

seeming waves of muslin and garlands of roses, eyed us
from their portraits and miniatures. Yet all their coquettish attitudes appeared to scoff at our distress: for one, it
was the book she held in her hand, unread, that expressed
her disdain; for another, it was the fan concealing her
bosom, though in such a way as to emphasize its snowy
whiteness; for yet another, it was the articles of her toilette
table, where she sat dusting her complexion with a moist,
scented powder. Something of Old Vienna lingered in the
air of that chamber. There was a cheerful lilt to its dead-
ness, such as the jesting in one portrait of a lady pluck-
ing the feathers from a captive Cupid's wings. The two of
us, however, must have made a simply cadaverous impression in this place. Everything else, inanimate, was cheerful,
coquettish, and engaging. Fragrances were wafting from the
clouds of the ladies' veils, their filigreed lacework flutter-
ing, the violet tones of their bodices deepening to magenta,
a topaz radiance bursting golden through the yellow hues
of their sleeves. All was aglitter: their rings, tiaras, brace-
lets, the strings of pearls upon their necks, the fabrics.
All was aglow: their bouffant white hair, keenly vivacious
eyes, powdered complexions, and above all, the roses, the
painted roses in their coiffures, on their bosoms, at their
sides, in their plaits as they hung over the balustrades, in
the clusters blooming over the walls, in the bouquets spilling from the vases. Old Vienna was alive here... a beautiful,
long-gone age... the sweet, white mystery of its light-filled
cheer, undimmed even by death... an age that saw smiling
eyes, flowers, lips, and scents... now shut up in a dead lady's
forgotten chamber, like the last breath of its essence...

Little by little, this chamber brought Manfred back to
life. No shadow, no horror, could make its way in here. He
held my hands in his and pressed himself to me. I felt happy
in this intimacy with him. I had the friend I had always
wished for.

Outside, a hard rain began to fall. One could hear its tor-
rents battering the palace façade and windows. At moments,
the wind rose like a scourge that whipped the rain against
the panes of glass, howling in the arcades. Amid the wild
abandon of that element, the sweetness of our refuge in this
white, well-heated chamber only intensified, the soft ticking
of an old porcelain clock slipping into its fragrance like a
silvery lather, like the reflection of water shooting up from a
fountain and returning to the surface as mist, with an inflec-
tion of weary poignancy.

VIII

We said not a word about that evening's performance,
though I sensed that Manfred's excitement had to do with
the play we had seen. Suddenly he asked me:

"Dear Francis, have you ever had anything mysterious
happen to you in Prague? You're my only friend who stays
there on occasion. It's a city that can attract a foreigner such
as yourself only on some particular business. Why do you go
there? What is it that draws you?"

"What draws me to Prague?" said I, surprised at the
abruptness of his question. "There are certain psychic states
for which we must have a suitable environment. I don't
understand the language spoken there. I know nothing of the
present life of the city. All I seek there is the past. If I want
to know, in life, how the dead would feel if stored in crystal cases in temples,[21] if I want to look at life as if through
the glass of my own coffin, I go to Prague. Its atmosphere is
heavy and oppressive with the tragedy of all that has happened there. Looking upon the Castle, Malá Strana below,
and the Old Town Square across the river, I feel that the Past
alone is present in Prague. I need know nothing of its history.
Once I am there, it all comes to me as if I were watching it

all unfold before my very eyes. I need know nothing of the executions that followed the Battle of Bílá Hora. One cannot help but pause on a certain small patch of ground in view of the ancient houses, where the dark thunder of drums dampened with black cloth seems still to echo off their walls. In Prague, all is over and done with. It is a matter of indifference who lives there now, just like the matter of who occupies the ruin of an old palace when its owners have died off. I love to walk through Prague at night. At such times, I seem to discern its soul's every breath. In its rare moments of sudden brightness, I seem to feel the dead, glorious city awakening, steeping its mind once again in the dark and sorrowful mirror of its fateful vainglory."

"You are right, Francis. There is a visionary beauty to Prague. A beauty that passes through dreams and thence into death. She smiles not, she weeps not: she neither flourishes nor languishes. She is but a reflection of herself. The mornings there have a lifeless grey to them, while the night is black and still. Her existence is an impression, an illusion. Should I wish to live life as if it were a dream, I go to Prague. Should I wish to live life without purpose and behave as if it were a dream, Prague is the one place where I can have such an existence. Everything there is a phantom. Everything has its particular look, as a fictitious thing does its illusion. Death and life signify the same thing there. Prague belongs to the mystics. Have you ever noticed that it's the only city where you have the feeling you might meet someone so strange, so fateful for you, that you should be standing suddenly helpless before his power, his influence? Death is the ultimate beauty there. Could mysticism not be the ultimate power there as well?"

"You speak as if you were shackled to Prague by some unresolved mystery."

"We sometimes imagine that we create our own destiny. Suddenly we realize we're in a struggle not with ourselves

alone, but also with some other opposing force. Our entitle-
ment to existence consists in our individual belief that *we
ourselves exist.*"

"I don't follow you, Manfred."

"Wouldn't it devastate you, Francis, to discover all of a
sudden that nature, creating ever newer and different species, might one day... *repeat* an experiment and create two
absolutely identical human existences? Wouldn't it slightly
terrify you if your image in the mirror suddenly stepped
forth from it, came to life, and you had to share your future
existence with it?"

I intuited at once that concealed in Manfred's words was
the secret of what had happened to him. My imagination
grew suddenly turbulent. Manfred had given me the broad
outlines of this mysterious event, and I instantly began to fill
them in with the most outlandish forms of my cruel, elegant
invention.

Pausing, Manfred looked at me even more firmly and
searchingly, as though considering whether to involve me in
his inner adventures. Suddenly he said, in a tone that quite
startled and confused me, the shadow of his eyelashes seeming to cast a darkness into my core:

"Do you trust me?"

Seeing me about to express ready devotion to entering
into his destiny, to sharing it with him, he quickly went on:

"I recognized your interest in me long ago. But it has
amused me to make myself inscrutable to you. Even now,
I hesitate to say anything that might allow you to see inside
me. Yet it is a necessity... for in making you my confidant,
I rid myself of a burden that has been suffocating me.

"Do you wish to experience my turmoil and distress as
the price of being my friend? See now, my egotism is greatly
reassured. You shall share my burden and give me your
friendship besides. But I know that by nature you fare best
when in a state of devotion. I desire your passivity now, for

the same reason that an analogous man might desire a woman. All of you is in harmony, your eyes, your lips, your soul, and I think God must love you as much as anything else so in balance. You shall reserve your beauty and your warmth for none but me now, Francis. For me shall your desirous, scarlet lips burn. For me shall your eyes darken like emeralds. And your arms so pale, with their hint of the white rosebush's sweet fragrance, shall encompass me with a magic circle to keep the shadows that terrify me at bay. You will give yourself to me whole. You will sacrifice yourself to my destiny rather than your own…"

Manfred spoke these outlandish words like an incantation. I felt myself completely surrendering to him. I was becoming a cat's-paw in his hands, a mere object. He was taking away my will and my reason.

"We shall be friends," he continued, his features kindled with a passion unknown to me till then. "Why give yourself to a mere mediocrity like your dear, sweet, ordinary Max Duniecki? Better to cast your lot with me: you shall keep someone poised on the edge of an abyss and madness from falling headlong into them.

"And now—I can tell you all, without fear that some stranger shall penetrate my secrets. Nevermore shall you leave me once you acquire this knowledge. You shall not be *able* to. Let Max Duniecki find himself some other friend for his amusement. For I wish to live with you now as I have lived alone, secretively and apart from other people: *eccentrically, senselessly, with relish and desperation.*

"When I speak with other people, I tell them whatever I like, but my soul is altogether elsewhere. With you, with you, I shall speak only of things where my soul is also. At the same time, you shall lighten the sorrow that weighs upon me with a power greater than you yourself can believe. Instead of misery, there shall be only suffering; instead of grief, only sadness, for we shall now pass through the world like shadows in intimacy. It is revolting, what we can experience in this world. For in being in contact with people, by the very act of speaking with them of *their* affairs, we ourselves are lowered. But in our solitude, Francis, we shall feel deeply the maddest and therefore the deepest and most genuine things. We shall live in a kingdom of remarkable flashes of light: other eyes shall see nothing of the secrets that envelop us in a magical cloud."

IX

Where was Manfred Macmillan now, the dandy, the scoffer who treated everyone with mortifying insouciance, with elegant impudence, with impertinent chic? He was so well versed in the art of "snubbing" his fellow men, of making them feel that even if they were of the best sort, they were less than nothing to him. His method of dealing with people was to employ insults of every nuance against them, to take graceful swipes at their smug pretenses. But the sole reason this technique succeeded was that he was not only absurd but also original.

I recalled how once, having casually remarked that I didn't always consider such conduct evidence of strength in a personality, he said with a smile:

"From the moment I cease to look down on people, I shall be nothing. The only stupid thing is that people submit to me, not that I have put their stupidity to work for me."

And now—what a difference! I could feel the enchanting, tranquil pulse of human sociability in him. Manfred was a completely changed person. Or was I simply mistaken? Was he experimenting on me? He was so enigmatic. Could he be trusted?

But—whoever he was!—I was destined to surrender to him. I'd always dreamt of a being who moved with singular grace, to whom I might offer myself for one absurd and unthinkable night, a night of experiences I could find no name for to the end of my days. Here he was. We had found each other and united our souls. It may have been mad and futile. But it was as imperative as any destiny...

X

We had been looking at each other in silence for a long while. Manfred's commanding, pridefully powerful gaze spread over me, his eyes widening until they looked enormous. At last I said, if only to disrupt his way of controlling me like this, so very magically dominating:

"Manfred, can you be satisfied with me? I remain always on the surface of life, where you roam its depths. But I have a sense for the imponderable, for the miraculous in every form. Will you be content if I want to hear these things from *you*?"

Manfred gave a smile. But that smile sent a wave of feverishness over me. Something in it was draining my soul to the dregs.

"Without knowing it, Francis, you have a double being within you, and I need them both. You possess imagination and perceptivity.[22] You are a poet and a woman. Those who are only women revolt me. They are creatures without imagination. They reduce a man to physical reality, they drag him down to earth. No matter what you do, a woman can't become anything more profound than a woman.[23] You call a dog by one name all its life, and that's good enough for it. A woman's love is the same. It gets by on a single idea: that you belong to her. All her life she says nothing, answering to a single name.

"I despise beings who exist only as women. They cannot interest anyone with what they understand, and only out of cleverness, to be interesting, they talk about what they don't understand. But I'm also indifferent to those who can only be men. They have intellect but no emotion. But there are those who are outside of both sexes. Like you, Francis, so beautiful and pale as if because of some secret crime that's been hushed up…[24] You can be a companion to me because of your intelligence and your ability to follow my thoughts. But you can also be for me what a woman is for others, a mysterious kind of intimacy, a delightfully vague shading of the emotions. Skeptical of everyone as I now am, you are a being I happily turn to behold, that my stagnant heart be gladdened. A kind of æthereal breath wafts from your every movement. You are as inspired by tenderness as by melancholy.

"You can be strong enough to bear the weight of an idea with me, an attempt to plumb as deeply as possible the mysteries that surround us. But when it's time for lyricism, you can also become so much like a woman, late at night, that you become receptive to everything that stirs the soul. You become the instrument on which I can play my moods.

"You can go head-to-head with an idea and stand up to me in the realm of the intellect. But you can also yield to me, passive in the realm of emotion…"

XI

Manfred broke off.

His hands, alive with a psychic pulse, were now twitching slightly in a play of light and shadow. By themselves, they looked like a sovereign work of sensitive beauty. One wore an ancient ring with a gleaming beryl stone, its shine prominent in its tarnished gold setting.

As soon as these delicate hands laid themselves upon me, I was glad to let them take me as their prey. I opened my soul outward, like a flower its calyx, to receive all that came washing over me from Manfred. My life now seemed to have multiplied with dizzying rapidity. Manfred was giving me the illusion that I possessed a beauty I had only yearned for till then.

XII

"I don't know whether you in Prague share my love for the temple of St. Jakub.[25] But when I was there some time ago, I had a unique experience that has proven fateful for me.

"Do you remember? There on the high altar is a miraculous Madonna, a statue encircled by a golden halo. An ancient legend tells how one night, Mary seized the arm of an adventurer come to rob her of her strings of gold and pearls in the night.[26] There has always been something irresistible to me in these miraculous statues, arrayed in their golden fabrics, weighed down with gemstones, and enveloped in fragrances. This one here is especially remarkable in its tarnished golden glow, its crystal case like a fairy-tale cavern, surrounded by the most exquisite silence, the lips of the attendant faithful moving but timidly in prayer. A tearful dew lies upon the white lilies blooming in her presence. But the Madonna's face glows with a light all its own, the sole source of luster for the lamps that illuminate her and the gems that adorn her...

"This grandiosely somber temple possesses something feudally glorious, something of Spanish Catholicism about it. How it pervades and sanctifies the very air enclosed within these timeworn walls! As you enter, the specter of the Middle Ages seems to seize and inundate you with its dark, ancient shadows. The entire living world behind you fades away all at once and vanishes. And there is nothing left but this fantastic temple. Yes, fantastic: just look at how grandiose the lines of its height and length are!

And the outlandish excess! Altar upon altar, statue upon statue. The famous paintings by Brandl and Reiner[27] are fading to darkness within the glinting gold of their frames. The work of all these artists of yore—goldsmiths, jewelers, gem cutters—shines with their chased metalwork and crystalline translucence from the altars, from the caskets of remains. The marble of the pillars glows. The golden statues flood everything with their luster, elevating it all to mediæval pathos.

"Below the flagstones are deep tombs with myriad dead bodies, their remains housed in reliquaries beneath the stone slabs of the altars: the dead, nothing but the dead, and you think that not for you but for them is vespers sung here. For them does the organ swell with somber music, the taper give off its mournful scent, the incense burn white, the golden treasure glitter, and the miniature gardens of artificial roses smile atop the altar.

"To appreciate the mystery of these objects, you must emulate the dead. Often have I wandered through this temple and spent hours daydreaming here. I have found myself captivated by a cloth of deep blue, the color of ripe grapes, embroidered with arabesques, as if strewn with a rustling of silver leaves astir and covering the altar, draped in white linen redolent of purity... Then there is the mighty pulpit, perched upon an upright lion. Or I have lingered before the magnificent grille separating the chapel of St. Francis from the chancel. On other occasions, I have experienced a little of the Inquisition's terror before the scourged Savior in the glass case. There was a kind of anguished sorrow, a dolorous beauty in all these objects, in all these implements from centuries past. The pall of an ancient time seemed to lie upon everything.

"But most radiant of all was this Marian statue. As I stood there before it, awash in colored lights, I thought of all the confessions made to it over so many years, all the sorrows, the guilt, the hardships, the peculiar motives and longings that afflict a person. But among these confessions, might there not have been some extraordinary crime, the secret horror of something beyond human understanding? The tears of people sick and tired of life had flowed here. But hadn't there also been the despair of some dark abomination, the destitute misery of a life turned upside down? Hadn't there ever been some mysterious rain of bitter, black tears on this holy statue?

"An endless succession of candles has been lit, day after day, for this Feast of Sorrow. Fruitless, mediæval griefs had once come alive here, unavailing despair. At certain moments even now, you might still catch the specter of a remnant from an ancient time, a hooded figure in an ashen grey cloak, a coarse horsehair scarf round its neck and sandals on its feet as it pours out its penitent moaning to the Madonna.

"Isn't walking into this temple just like some visionary's stroll through the Middle Ages, dear Francis? A remarkable space! Here, what is dead is alive, and what is alive is dead. But don't wander blithely about this temple! Don't imagine yourself perfectly safe and taking nothing but a pleasant dip into some lovely ancient style! So I used to do, until the Mysterious One unexpectedly appeared to me.

"Mind you, I thought none of this has anything to do with me, who only stops in to pass the time. And suddenly something starts to choke me. I have the sense that something is lying in wait for me behind every pillar. It feels like someone is hiding behind every altar, secretly watching me.

"All at once, I'm terrified. All these brooding objects, which I've been looking over like an antique collector, now sport mocking grimaces. The Christ in the glass case is eyeing me closely. Some cadavers' faces come to life inside their reliquary frames. Some bony hands threaten to strangle me in their clutches. It's all become cruel and grotesque. It all seems like the twisted invention of some madman. It's all like the grim remnant of some stranger's devious desperation.

"I flee the temple in horror. It's quite some time before my wildly beating heart calms down and I can once again see the indifference of the world outside..."

XIII

"Until one day... one day I was trapped there, and Francis, I shall forever shudder to think of it. Come to me, put your hand in mine! There—now I feel your warmth, and I can tell you everything.

"You surely recall that famous marble crypt for the Vratislavs of Mitrovice,[28] before the altar of the Holy Cross that gleams into the temple's dimness with the whiteness of its statuary. I have often stood next to it, looking at the figures. The hands of Glory wreathe a fallen warrior, behind whom stands Death with its scythe. But down below, the huddled figure of Grief is weeping, its head buried in its lap, so melancholy and inconsolable that it has always drawn me.

"One day when I was daydreaming here, watching a shadow stray from one wall to another, like the final vestige of some being that had exhaled the last of its sorrows here, I had the sudden feeling that someone was behind me. I turn, and a shudder of horror passes through me.

"It was nearly evening. The temple was completely empty. When I entered, there was not a living soul in sight. Nor, as I stood over by the Vratislav crypt, was there even the slightest sound of anyone else's footsteps coming in. But then I find myself face to face with a *living person*.

"He eyes me closely. Then he stirs. He comes towards me. Alarmed, I step back. He stops. He looks at me. Is this a specter? Suddenly, I can see and recognize… *myself* in this inscrutable being facing me.

"I struggled to contain my alarm.

"I averted my eyes.

"Then I earnestly begin trying to convince myself that there is absolutely no one else in the temple, and that what I saw was a hallucination that has quickly vanished away again.

"Yes, it was a hallucination, I repeat.

"But then why do I suddenly lack the courage to take another look? Another shudder of horror went through me. I listen. Behind me, the distinct sound of breathing. So, there *is* someone here. Some skulking being that has been following me as if on some strange mission.

"I fall prey to a terror that makes every object seem larger. The space has become unrecognizably enormous. The high altar is as black as some grandiose catafalque. The shadows are deeper. It's all dreadful. I'm put in mind of Swedenborg's words that even as our bodies still live, our spirits commune with other spirits, though our transient self is unaware of this.

"I turn and look toward the Vratislav crypt. Right by the sculpture of prostrated Grief, someone is standing there, almost touching it. All I can see of him is the glow of his brooding, melancholy eyes. The rest is lost in shadow. Then I can make out the turn of the stranger's mouth. His lips are moving, as if he were reciting something to himself.

"I feel insanity close at hand. I suspect that the stranger has come from the crypt. I remember a legend that a Count Vratislav came back to life, left his coffin, and years later was found as a skeleton huddling on the stairs beneath the stone slab of the crypt, unable to raise it.[29] The most absurd and horrible things come to mind. Yet I remain, despite an overwhelming desire to flee."

XIV

"I look once more upon the stranger. I can see him quite distinctly.

"His posture suggests that he doesn't notice my presence. Nevertheless, I sense that I'm the reason he is there, looking at me.

"Suddenly I see his fingers starting to twitch. There is a kind of ghastly languor in his movements.

"All at once, I have an inkling of the mysterious relationship between him and myself. Here in this solitude, in the deep silence of these gloomy objects, it suddenly seems to me that with his form identical to mine, the stranger has been standing here for entire ages, and that he has been waiting for me..."

XV

"I felt feverish. My eyes were burning, heat fanning over my cheeks. The figure now lifted slightly. Something milky, white, transparent, I don't know what to call it, was glowing around the outline of this strange apparition, something that made it even more spectral than it was. It was shining with a pale mysterium[30] that faded to transparency. A kind of enervation was radiating from it, enveloping my senses like a veil. I was steeped in its profoundly captivating influence. I think I could never find a word for the state of mind that seized me then—not in human language, which has terms only for real emotions and not for transcendental states. Horrified, I confirmed my realization that the stranger was none other than *I myself*.

"Yes, this was another self of mine. I could recognize myself as plainly as could be. I was assuredly not alone in breathing the air of this sorry planet, for here was someone else exactly like me, completely identical to me, who would raise his eyes to the stars at night and think the same thoughts as I myself. And now I was seeing this mysterious being before me. It had come to apprise me of its existence, to tell me it was part of my every breath, my every movement. I felt the terror of knowing I was not alone in this world, that there was another being who was *simultaneously* me and shared my existence with me. I could not help feeling now that it was myself I was walking toward. Nor could I help knowing that were I to investigate the system of secret forces concealed deep in the core of my being, there is someone else looking within my secrets along with me, that every passion, every struggle, every temptation that flares within me is but an echo of the passions, struggles, and temptations that have flared at the same time in the core of this other.

"You cannot imagine how necessary you are to me just now, Francis, how precious the greenish gold[31] of your eyes. If I go forth with you now, I shall not lack for courage to face this other again. In your eyes, I can read the strange answers to my even stranger questions. For you don't merely listen to me... you also *respond* to me with your gaze... You tell me you want to come with me, that you understand my addled soul, that you accept its madness as your own. Now I need the reality of your body, your breath, your hands, the touch of your being, I who have asked nothing but fiction of any object or being till now... This bond with you must give me the strength to prevail over this other one: your love shall fortify me and at the same time weaken the other one's influence... For I sense that it lacks love, as it is only a curse on my being, draining and depleting it.

"Francis, you sweet madman with a delirious, infatuated heart, pale as your tortured name: you alone are sacred to me. In your fragility and empathy, only with you can I cool my fevered brow, I who once sought solace at every altar. There is a bit of madness in every soul, and it sometimes bursts out. Yet my soul is now nothing but constant madness, a constant sparking of trembling emotions, of monstrous transmogrifications deep within. Yes, such is my being, in the inner life I live, I who have the look of a dandy and the smile of one who's never heard of destiny, and lives only to dally with the greatest profundities. Shall I be your happiness, my good friend? Shall I not bring you to ruin? Ought I to warn you to shun me? No, you cannot, you *must* not go away. If we can't be happy together the way others are, we can at least be in love with our madness. And as destiny leaves the shadow of our sorrows behind us in the blue, we shall renew, with a redoubled secret strength, all the words, thoughts, and ideas of the magical sciences, preserved in forgotten books by those who lived and thought in the Middle Ages, and who succumbed to death in the weariness of those paths that led them deepest, to the very heart of the Mystery. In all that we live, we shall spread this mystic shadow of dead knowledge, of forsaken, esoteric cults. We will immerse ourselves in everything, explore everything, and be intoxicated by everything.

"We shall pass heedlessly by all ordinary things, made for daylight and for anyone who walks by to gaze upon. We shall love what is exceptional, what comes alive at night in the moonlight, made just for us and for our moments, for eyes filled with hallucinations by mystical forces.

"The Romans believed that a secret mark carved into an emerald would blind any who looked upon the stone. We shall strip the emerald of its power, overcome the spell with the empowered force of our vision, and gaze into the mysteries as others do into the ordinary and immutable. Over a fragile bridge built only for our imaginary footsteps, we shall cross together into the secret realm, O adept of mine with your head pale and beautiful, the head of one who has lived in times of decay, a head from an old cameo that has been raving only to itself thus far and shall now be able to rave just as well for me. With tender melancholy, we shall together enter into the shadow plays of mysterious ages past.

"Though reality is of the utmost importance to everyone else, for us it shall be but a passageway. We shall be the brooding Levites[32] of the Kingdom of Darkness, sinister red flames of recognition on our brows. Knowing we have no way to pray, we shall at least hope for a way to blaspheme. We shall be beautiful, Francis, *completely* beautiful, and that shall be all. We shall conceive and desire every dream and longing, and taste deeply of knowledge the mere inkling of which would crush anyone else. Just as Peter keeps the keys of heaven, so shall we the keys of the inferno. We will hate the Divinity but love what is divine, and our inner riches shall outshine the complacent fatuity of the unwitting angels. And though we may have lived in the world of everyone else, the secret instinct within us shall continue to work in our other world.[33]

"Indifferent to the greatest sorrows of this earthly world, we shall stand fast, turned to stone. We shall give rein to our desperation, our torment, only in the dark peripheries. The Unknown, where we take refuge with our love, impossible in the tangible world but a brute fact in those outposts of irreality where every footstep is deeper and every sorrow more wrenching. We shall keep silent before mankind about our love as if withholding our names and our nobility from the throng. For our lips—strange to say!— though seemingly not made to kiss, shall indeed kiss, and our souls, though their being in love is seemingly impossible, shall indeed reel, light and golden, between love and beauty. Such love is only for those who, in spite of every other heart, can tread with a disdainful step, for they were at each other's side before they met, and shall remain so even if they part. We shall adorn their hair with a bonfire of flaming red flowers. On every lip shall desire ignite with the color of red wine: and we shall be more beautiful than the shadows wherein angels are reflected.

"So do I see our future, when all the hidden potentialities of our life shall blossom, transposed into forgotten fictions from this world of living pettiness, of middling pleasures, of dubious happiness. Francis, it is you I believe in. Never forget those moments when we merge forever into a single strong and beautiful being, capable of defying anything... even the greatest, most malevolent forces of magic..."

XVI

"For we have an *enemy*, Francis. You may be certain: the one I beheld in the temple of St. Jakub is *not* a phantom. He does exist. He is myself in every breath of his mind, in every beat of his heart. But whatever this other one lives, he does so at the expense of my own strength, my own being. I have been keeping him at bay until now. But once he manages to become stronger than I, I am lost. I shall be a mere cat's-paw under his magical influence. Do you know what it is to be under someone else's power? I don't know what the core of a man living bestially, driven by instinct, is like. But I do know that even the core of a man who's reached the apex of the intellectual world is, in and of itself, a hideous thing. Imagine if I were to fall under the power of a man with such a core, capriciously experimenting on me in my helplessness!

"I know you want to tell me that the one I saw in St. Jakub's temple doesn't exist, that he's a mere figment of my overheated imagination. But you haven't heard all of it yet. For if at first the stranger I saw at the Vratislav tomb had something phantasmagorical about his appearance, he then changed all at once into a very real person, though without losing any of his character as the Mystery-Inspired One. Yes, that is the most curious part of my entire novel."[34]

XVII

"I can see him clearly, his face dark as my own, his eyes as brooding as mine when I'm alone.

"There's something uneasy, restless, about him when he knows I'm watching him. Suddenly his arm comes up to rest against his forehead for a moment. He cocks his head and then takes me in with a somehow hateful look, as if angry that I'm studying him. And off he goes. Indeed. Off he goes. I can hear his footsteps distinctly. I see him pause for a moment at the altar nearest the entrance, where there is a small painting of a Madonna between two bushes of white flowers. And I hear the clank of the glass door at the entrance as it opens.

"Likewise hurrying, I exit the temple in pursuit of the unknown one. I'm not agitated as I do this but quite mechanical, determined simply to find out who he is. I catch up to this stranger as he goes inside the Týn courtyard. Alone, we walk through the deserted space. I see nothing that would look out of the ordinary to anyone else. Suddenly, the unknown one pauses. So do I. He gives me a look, a mocking, mischievous one. Then he strides out of the courtyard and into the Týn alleyway and vanishes all at once from my sight... Where did he go? Into a house? The Týn temple?[35] Ought I to search every entrance to see whether he's hidden there? Ought I to pursue him into the church?

"I feel how grotesque the situation has become. What now? Should I detain the stranger? By what right? On what grounds?

"I didn't know what to do next. I had a feeling that the unknown one was in hiding somewhere, and that he would leave as soon as I went into any of the houses.

"I decided to pick someplace and go inside: so, I went into the Týn temple. At the tomb of Tycho de Brahe,[36] I thought I saw the stranger. A feverish shiver came over me. But this was the trick of some shadow cast by a pillar.

"I went out the same way I had come in. On the altar at the entrance, on the golden floor, is a likeness of St. Anthony. Suddenly I thought the unknown one was looking at me from the saint's face and mocking me.

"I ran out into the street, but no one was there. The unknown one, if he'd been hiding anywhere here, must have left long ago. I went out onto the Old Town Square and looked in every direction but saw no one. The square was deserted and had an atmosphere of death under a sky of lapis lazuli darkening to black. The Marian Column loomed in its midst, mute and solitary.[37] The shuttered houses towered gloomily, like brooding tombstones. Only the pealing of the bells, the dark clang of bronze, like a message from another age, went sailing over the rooftops of the city, which listened in funereal silence, shadows sweeping over everything like mourning veils, shadows beneath which one cannot help but sense death. I could no longer see the one I was looking for. There was only something that was also shadowlike left of him in the air. But what the soul could still sense, the eye could no longer see…"

XVIII

"Ever since, I've been relentlessly visiting the church of St. Jakub. I've spent long hours at the Vratislav tomb. But the unknown one appeared no more. I would wander the streets in the twilight of the waning day, when everyone takes on an extraordinary, inscrutable aspect. I studied the physiognomies of those I passed. But it was futile. He'd vanished without a trace.

"And yet I sensed he was hidden here somewhere. Up and down the gloomy streets. In and out of the temples that nowhere affect one so deeply as in Prague. The only place for him is here in this city of death, caught in the embrace of silence and slumber. Only here does the air suit his secret existence, where the antiquated buildings' every wall is roamed by the flickers of creatures who once exhaled the last of all their life's sorrows here, as if they had sent their souls on ahead into the distant reaches of time.

"The soul of the Middle Ages is swirling around every object. Its presence is as palpable here as the sea's is elsewhere. Every spot is infused with the breath of the past. It's always cropping up before you from everywhere. From the verdant shade of the deep gardens with their spreading trees, its breath is upon you. From a dark portal, from the depths of a palace entrance, it wafts over you. You're in an ancient city here, one that harbors the soul of its bygone populace, the stifling sepulchral nearness of those who lived here in ages past.

"In the luminous blue twilight, I've always felt as if I had forever receded from everything of the present. I would get the sense that something extraordinary could happen to one at that moment. At such times, I'd constantly be expecting to see the face of that unknown one somewhere, springing out of the gloom. Then there'd be a chance to grab hold of him and never let go, on any pretext.

"Thoughts of the most fantastic, Romanesque adventures would tumble through my mind.[38] I would sometimes go into houses that struck me as mysterious. I would climb the rickety wooden stairs to the first floor and step inside the dark corridors and passageways of these outlandish edifices.[39] But I'd leave with my head spinning, maddened by the impossibility of gaining certainty about that apparition at St. Jakub's temple, my movements a little somnambulistic, my eyes wide and feverish, my nerves all indescribably atremble."

XIX

"I could think of nothing else at that time. My terror of that unknown one hounded me from pillar to post. My heart would pound wildly. I would feel like I was teetering over abysses of horrible phantoms. A demon was trying to drag me in after them. Its shadow was heavy as lead upon me. Everything seemed futile, all my efforts ephemeral.

"That unknown one kept standing over me, within me, draining me of all my strength, all my blood, and he drank off my last ounce of courage. All was disrupted, destabilized. I did not experience but only *sensed* this weight upon me. That other being, ah, he was real enough to torment me cruelly, yet not spectral enough that I could merge with him, a shadow within a shadow! I can't even describe the state I was in. My very inability to find the unknown one intensified my maddened agitation. A specter will vanish if you show it that it's real. But the unknown one maintained its unreality and so couldn't vanish from my distraught imagination.

"At that time, I got the sense of how little it takes to induce the madness to summon up a demon. I lived in a state of terror then, not for days, for hours, but every second. And only then did I see how little control we can have over our own psychic apparatus. Upon the stage of our psyche, the imagination can enact the most bizarre scenes, while we remain no more than helpless spectators.

"How often I told myself it was all an illusion! There's nothing there!

"But it takes at least a little reality to make us believe in the unreal. My specter, however, did not abandon his irreality. He refused to incarnate himself into anyone with an existence."

XX

Manfred broke off.

I dared not look into his eyes, for such was the magnetism they exerted over my entire core. I was fearful lest I discover some new secret in them. But though Manfred's eyes were upon me, so absorbed was he in his innermost thoughts that his confession seemed directed to himself rather than to me. Transfixed, I listened on.

"All who have approached the riddle of being, the misunderstood oracles who've foretold mysteries, the forgotten poets who've intuited them, the star-crossed lovers who've lived them, all who have been stricken, from near or far, by their shadow and the darkness beneath their outstretched wings, have each been felled by a single shot, a single blow: the recognition of the futility of everything. We can't know ourselves if we're ourselves alone and not someone else as well: all the mysticism of the Middle Ages intuited this.

"I haven't been only myself these days. I've also been that other one. With the other one's eyes, I've looked into him, and he has looked from my perspective into my depths. I feel like I've actually reached the peripheries where human existence begins. I've now become a person, whereas before I was only a caricature of myself. Make no mistake: only when we acknowledge that we're futile do we have the right to exist... You once accused me of being contemptuous of people and mocking them. But are they at all human when they experience their entire lives the same way as any everyday event? Never have they touched the mysterious, never have they despaired over their existence— at most, over the loss of their comfort. Never have they felt the joys of madness, only satisfaction at some effect they've created.

"There are also poets, philosophers, and artists whose inanities have filled acclaimed books and celebrated galleries, and never once have they felt what it is to be human. They've never drunk the poison that is the recognition of their true existence, of their destiny. They've attained glory despite never having been human for a single hour of their lives. Those bitter, desperate souls like Chatterton, Poe, Baudelaire, Gérard de Nerval—who died of hunger, alcohol, madness, or suicide on the window grilles of a brothel[40]— were all people born to *live* their art, not merely to produce it like everyone else. In their art, beautiful in form, they had a terrifying ability to blaspheme desperately against the triviality of everything, in music and rhythm to confess that all the greatness of existence is nothing but a staggering vacuum of futility.

"*That* is why I have contempt for people and their small art, you see. *That* is why I don't acknowledge as my equal anyone who gets close to me. It's preposterous to believe in human equality: how could I take satisfaction in having anyone share in my unlikeliness! I'd rather have a heart full of pride and bitterness. I'd rather be completely sheared off from life, like a dead flower from a living stem.

"Now do you understand the reason for my mockery? It's not just a pose. You can appreciate how what others call superficial dandyism is rooted in one's very core. I have no love for people. I give them all the go-by, like clouds. I don't think of them when they vanish for good. No one means anything to me.

"And yet I surround myself with them and live among them; but they're of no consequence to me, those whose mission it is to bore me, and whom I bore as a pastime. Believe me, life is nothing but contact with people who are either irrelevant or a nuisance. If there's anyone you care for, rest assured that wily destiny shall whisk them away and leave you with someone who's a true pest. Shall destiny take you from me as well, Francis? It is you alone I care for, you alone I love.

"I might be happier if I knew how to mock myself as I do others. But I take myself profoundly seriously. So then, my dear, drain the bitter phial of my existence to the bottom! I need another soul to share in my sufferings. Into the dark, mournful flowering scabiosa that wreathe my days, weave the passionate, blood-red anthuriums of your love for me! Plait their purple flames into your every word! Let them flare from your every look, your every gesture, your every smile! Through these flames, I desire you to be my herald, my light, all along the future path of our friendship. With you at my side, the burden of the shadow that has fallen so inescapably over the whole of my existence shall be lighter..."

XXI

How mysterious Manfred had become! These words, spouting from these lips, were all of scarlet and glory. They were mine, for me alone. Anyone else would have thought them mad and senseless. With the abyss of this fateful love in my heart, mine was the only soul they touched, I alone understood them, for I knew they had the intensity of a supreme desire. Never had I heard words like these, nor seen any being so transformed as Manfred's.

Was this still his face, swarthy, with a helm of thick, magnetic hair[41] rather than a rippling, freely flowing coiffure? Its expression was altogether different. Under the breath of his emotion, the shadow of his eyelashes seemed to dim and brighten. Under the accents of the words tumbling from his lips, his eyes were widening and narrowing. They were like the pulsating feelings at his very core. I had the sense that with a single wave of his hand, a magical gesture by this initiate, Manfred could call to life a being slumbering within my own core, secreted there.

I myself had become someone different. Manfred was giving me new feelings, emotions that lay beyond life and yet revealed its mysteries to me more profoundly than anything I had ever lived.

Manfred! A name that could be spoken only in solitude and shadow. Like a demon shrouded in darkness, he gave me the exquisite gift of his friendship. I was both thrilled and terrified. For I felt that his destiny was unlike that of anyone else in the world. The refinements of his being would have been absurd in anyone else, so deeply had he submitted to the chimæra.

Had anyone merely told me about Manfred, I would have denied his existence. I'd never have believed that such super-human defiance could ever shine through a human face, that any could dare offer battle to the very vortex of eternity. But here he was before me. He was offering me his friend-ship. With his mystery, he baptized my being, which now began to live something quite different than ever before. Everything he said to me felt like a torment. But because it was Manfred saying it, I felt no pain. My soul said only: do with me what you will… I am yours alone.

I seemed to have lost my will, my reason.

Manfred's magical influence had taken complete control of me. I myself was turning pitch black from his shadow. This mysterious being of dark and cynical countenance— whom I had once yearned for, eager to know the passions that roused, that clutched at his heart—held me in the grip of a love that seeks either salvation or destruction. Manfred now represented a path, a goal. All I had lived until now was as nothing. This dark dream was everything. Once manifested, Manfred's will was a command that brooked no opposition. All else was forgotten under his words, out of which bygone ages spoke to me of all their secret liturgies.

How manifold was that life at Manfred's core! How passionately he felt everything, how he struggled and suffered! How this profound sense of fatality exalted him over the ordinariness of life! Within this body through which the night coursed and eddied, within these eyes extended by their lashes, so alive in their play and flutter, within this voice that a shadow seemed to have spilled through, demoniacal states were roused and visions feverishly ripened. Manfred lived life like some mysterious rite. He would consecrate it with the depths of his anguish.

Now I could grasp what he once said to me as I was ridiculing the tastelessness of the century in which we live:

"Why allow our times to violate us? Any prejudice such as the date of our birth must be overcome. No one can be born at the wrong time if they do not wish it. We have the power to choose the time of birth that we need for ourselves..."

Manfred was born in the Middle Ages and had lived then. This flirtatious dandy would open the books of Paracelsus,[42] Agrippa von Nettesheim,[43] and Athanasius Kircher[44] like those of his contemporaries. He had interests in mediæval alchemy, magic, psychurgy, and theurgy while being utterly unconcerned with modern science.

He paid no attention to the noise of the streets. But sitting alone in his chamber, surrounded by the ancient books of dead men, he would hear bells echoing in the distance, lose himself in their sound, and come upon an age when he was truly alive... while the present was as mere unreality for him...

XXII

"Did you ever meet that mysterious stranger, Manfred?"

Manfred's eyes cast a kind of perverse light upon me like a reflection of painful agitation.

"I never did catch sight of him, though I stayed in Prague for some time looking for him. Then I had to tear myself away from these morbid notions. I left Prague to sojourn in London and Paris.

"What has my life been like since then? When it was possible to suppress the memory that the other one existed, that I was sundered into two beings who would never be united but now pose a constant threat to each other, I indulged in whatever dulled and intoxicated the senses. No one would have expected me to give in so profoundly to the mysticism of knowing that I inhabit two beings: I had hidden all my core secrets beneath a mask of dandyism.

"But don't imagine that I could ever entirely *forget*. Often in the midst of the wildest revelries, those whom I was entertaining, making fun of them, would suddenly notice a shadow crossing my brow. But they could not guess what had shaken and provoked me: I could see the white tombstone of the Vratislav crypt, and standing near it, the shadow of the other one, staring at me with those dreadful eyes of his as if rebuking me for the gall to laugh when my being lay completely in his power. And all at once, I felt a sudden madness threaten to hurl me into the darkness of the deepest abysses."

XXIII

"The other one *did exist*… but those all around me felt less than nonexistent. The best method of being alone is to surround oneself with people. In solitude, we think of others; in company, of ourselves. And so, with laughter ringing out on every side, I felt how different a being I was from those who can laugh, I who am incapable of laughing: for the thought of the other one's secret existence was always hovering over me. It threw a shadow over me, as impending death does over the visage of a dying man.

"My imagination would be constantly scuttling around that one torment like a beast in a cage. When I arrived towering, vibrant, radiant in my affected languor, none would suspect that I harbored an entire inferno of doubt at my core.

"In desperation, I would sometimes seek out a being to confide in. I'd suddenly make friends of people I'd taken a liking to for any reason, whether because they knew how to keep quiet for long stretches or choose the right perfume, while at other times I'd take to someone because he scoffed constantly at everything, or to another because he had an eccentric way of powdering his face—but no such friendship ever lasted. The more interesting the person, the briefer my relationship with him. I kept in with only a few people, treating them like amulets we have no faith in but keep at hand in case there should be something to them after all.

"I continued to sparkle at gatherings and to ramble from town to town, with heartfelt contempt for all who admired me. How easy to be thought a wit! You need only consider how idiotic the world around you is and wax ironic about its mediocrity, and you are thought witty—that is, you gain the latitude to be rude to people. But we keep company with others solely to inspire our aversion to people. For it is unpleasant to have anyone standing above us. The only reason to talk to people is to find them loathsome."

XXIV

"If we sense that our strength lies in eternal solitude, we may surround ourselves with company. To foster contradiction with other people, I would seek out only those who understood me, and with whom agreement was therefore out of the question. For only those who don't understand you will ever concur with you, and to find consensus is just as embarrassing as to have faith in something that goes without saying.

"In the end, I found myself thoroughly disgusted with this way of life. I was disgusted with London, where gentlemen smell of nothing but morality and corylopsis,[45] neither of which is anything but the perfume of sweat and the stable. I yearned for something else. Had you asked me what, I would not have known. I hardly knew whether I wished to start something new or simply put an end to what already was. Should I crave gloom or gaiety? I wished for only one thing: to rid my life of all irresolution, semi-anxiety, and semi-tedium. I felt that life had only one pleasure: to play it *va banque!*[46] That is, that life's a pleasure when it quickens a being's dynamism but not when it stifles it.

"It never entered my mind to devote myself to any object or to take up any steady work. Only a man of little will can work. A man of great will can't help but dream. For a man of great will scorns all that can be done easily, and if he did want to accomplish anything, he could only reach for something he dreaded doing.

"I've had some remarkable fixations and indulged in the preposterous like the perfect dandy, for the dandy is continually putting off important matters and never carrying through with them. I have longed to experience everything and to sample life in all its forms and possibilities, for believe me, Francis, life makes sense only if we accumulate as much madness in it as we can lay our hands on. Life per se is worth nothing, but it's everything once transposed. Find a style for life and you'll make it into a miracle. But my life at that time? A decent moment here and there, a little opium for my cigarettes and a few friends for my tedium, a constant stream of the firmest pledges and never any action, and also the occasional interest in someone I might even have fallen in love with if I'd had the time. Am I going to be cured of this, my Francis? Of a life that's all tomorrows and no todays? Oh, to escape oneself, to flee far, far away, to experience some intense sorrows, some cruel passions, just to know that all this is to some purpose and not merely a desperate self-parody…"

XXV

He hesitated, looking at me with unseeing eyes, perceiving not real objects but a dream.

He was in mortal anguish. I wondered how to comfort him, though to no avail. The perfect storm within him was back: his love of paradox was locked in a struggle with his deep longing for life, the demon of his revulsion with his inexhaustible desire to achieve serenity.

Manfred looked into all the mysteries of existence too solemnly to live blithely on its surface. No depth of the soul remained occluded to him. No psychic subtlety withheld its meaning. His transcendental self was too victorious over his corporeal persona, he lived too much in visions rather than reality. You can escape reality if you change your location. But an apparition goes with you. No amount of space can alienate it from your imagination, any more than a sorcerer can alienate himself from a spell he has fallen under.

That was why Manfred would swing so desperately from one extreme to the other. First drained of hope, utterly despondent, then suddenly ecstatic, full of lyricism; now doubting, then believing; now preposterous, then initiated into the deepest truths of existence.

I thought of what I would be to him now: a beneficent power that can relieve him of some of these anxieties? Or would I myself ultimately succumb to horror and leave him forever?

My sadness was ineffable: I begged fate to grant me the strength for the task it had set me at Manfred's side, so that together with him I might bear the passions and illusions consuming his life. I sought no other happiness than my delirious love for the enigmatic grief rocking this exquisite, broken man's core.

I prayed to fate that were any to deal my heart a fatal blow, let it be none but Manfred. Death by his hand seemed a beautiful gift to me, for all he touched took on the allure of the impossible. Ah! What strength there was in him who now seemed so perplexed by his destiny. I knew that he possessed the courage to take hold of any madness, since my love for him had begun to break wildly and furiously free of the rest of life's banality.

I swathed my entire future with him in a tragic blackness, in a profound coexistence full of grandiose, shattering passion. Yet am I of the same mysterious lineage? Would I be able to speak to him in words that would be his, and not merely in the mindless sounds that others address to him? Would my silence ever be more eloquent to him than the speech of others? Would he hear the secret beating of my loving heart as he does the voices of ages long past? Would he understand the flashes of my eyes, now tender, now passionate, now faltering, and quickly encouraging once again, he whose own eyes burn bright like two black ebony mirrors with the pure vitriol of his fires and the portents of his dreams?

XXVI

At midnight, I shall lead him forth just as if we were walking by day. We shall wrap our heads in dreams as if in the veils of our imaginations. In trance and twilight shall we live, lest we see that to be free from pain, our entire life must never be made conscious. I shall dispel the shadows of monsters from him, and with a soft, fragile hand lift the dark burden from his forehead. Thus did I envision my future at Manfred's side, the only style for my life ahead one of elegant poignancy, like that of a wingless angel, of someone heaven-sent but lacking sanctity, his breast filled not with God but solely with the desire to keep this grim man's heart, dealt such a terrible blow, from the abyss, and to redeem his mute curse, even at the price of my own happiness.

For Manfred—as I now sensed—was the sort who could inspire all manner of mad adoration at a stroke. No longer was there life for me in all that preceded the shadow of this night: only now was life beginning. How fierce and insistent it was, how wildly it ignited when his eyes took up the luster of mystic stones, the shooting flames that spurt from his troubled and afflicted core! What heroism this genteel dandy possessed, surely a great deal of his noble forefathers' martial instincts as their sabers furiously clave enemy faces below their ancestral fortress: but even more boldly had this scion stood off against the Mysterious Enemy, wrestled and done battle with him in the precarity of darkness.

Ever deeper was the hue of his black eyes, ever starker on his arched forehead the beautiful blue line of the vein between his brows as it advanced toward his hairline: all his courage and defiance was concentrated there. Gazing upon it, I felt myself caught up in its tempo. All my emotions were ebbing and flowing in time with its pulse. Thus did Manfred's love stigmatize me, inflict upon me the very wounds that caused its own suffering, brand me with the keenest of the horror beneath which it was itself sinking.

Creases now furrowed Manfred's brow, a brow Neronian, full of sternness. A provocative defiance had run amok inside his steely head, helmeted in hair so black as to have a bluish tinge.

My sole emotion was the delight of secret complicity. Never did I find Manfred more beautiful than in such despondency, with this portentous scowl. His fascinating allure had set me aquiver with unaccustomed gratitude. The brutality of his terror summoned a pallor to my cheeks that bespoke a love in utter thrall to him.

Tremblingly, I now peered into his heart, as if from the heights of a castle tower into the terrifying depths of a well.

XXVII

But suddenly, Manfred rose sharply from the chair where he had slumped into these black thoughts. As impulsive as his every experience was, I instantly divined that a new anguish had sprung within his core. But the only words he spoke to me were a question:

"Can you guess, Francis, what room lies just above the chamber where we now converse?"

When I gazed up at him without answering, mutely, he continued, affecting a mocking note in his voice:

"On the second floor is the *secret* of this palace, its ghost. Every old family house has its lady presence, a benign spirit that haunts the ancient rooms at midnight. Here, too, there is a specter. Would you care to pay it a call? The eighteenth century will come back to life for a moment if we take a candle to the second story and look inside. But I assure you that my ghost is of an *extraordinary* nature. Otherwise, we would not disturb it for no reason."

There was the outlandishness of a jest in these words from Manfred. Yet only a man going to rack and ruin can scoff like that. This was the capriciousness of a man who is facing disaster, jaunty before turning deadly serious over what he is laughing at...

XXVIII

I rose to my feet, game for anything. For it was Manfred's prerogative to crush my life and pierce my heart with any sort of horror, now that we belonged so completely to each other.

Yet I felt shivers not only in my face but also in my chilling heart. Only Manfred's presence held me erect. His every approach, his every touch held for me the thrill of peril. He was subtly tantalizing me, as if with a slowly approaching sword-tip that reserves the potential to wound.

We started down the corridor. Up the stairs we went, to the second story. I was breathless, less from dread at Manfred's plan to resume my initiation into the mysteries than in anticipation of them, in my uncertainty over them.

At moments, I came to a dead stop. The candle I held cast but a dim light on the stairs, and in time the flame began to gutter to the point that I felt warm drops of wax trickling down my hand. From outside, there came the sound of howling wind and a driving rain, dashing against the trees in the garden, against the wall of the façade. Vainly, I tried to rid myself of this dark, haunting image filled with terror, as in a black dream when we attempt to lose a heavy burden.

XXIX

Long uninhabited, the second story showed signs of neglect. The silence here was deeper, the deathly stillness deathlier. Everything bore the stamp of oblivion: even the grillwork door that barred the corridor from the staircase gave the impression that it had not turned on its hinges for an entire century. It gave a piteous screak as Manfred was opening it. But this sound died away as suddenly as if the grille itself had taken fright at this disruption to the prevailing calm.

Immense terror swept over me from the interminable corridor as if from the depths of a bottomless cellar. Amid the darkness, close to Manfred's side, this entire palace was like an enchanted castle in slumber, where anything that had disturbed its tranquility, but for the two of us, seemed long ago to have been turned to stone.

In the corridor, between the windows on the wall facing them, there hung a series of paintings, indistinguishable from one another, having blackened with age. Here and there was a forgotten piece of furniture, shunted away here years ago. As I looked out one of the hallway windows into the garden below, the view seemed to be of a cemetery, of cypresses and cedars,[47] of the trees of the Dead.

One door was fitted with a lock. Manfred took out the key, which he apparently carried with him at all times, and opened it.

We entered a small anteroom that contained nothing but the entrance to the chamber beyond. Manfred went in, asking me to wait in the anteroom while he lit the tapers on the candelabra.

I suspected Manfred's secret to be hidden in that chamber. A terror somehow corporeal, tangible, touched me. I felt the blood running cold in my veins. Yet I mastered the trembling in my flesh, for I felt shame at being less of a man just then, a thing that at other times would fill me with pleasure in my awareness of the passivity and vulnerability that set me apart from all other men.

But by the mastery of his absolute sovereignty over my being, Manfred now put such courage into my mind: I *had* to feel safe when near him, *had* to be strong under his power.

I glanced into the room where Manfred was still lighting the candles. The chamber was gradually growing brighter. It was indeed identical to the room where we had been sitting on the first floor. The same shape, the same windows.

The locked shutters struck me as odd. Then I recalled that all the palace's second-story windows were always closed up like that.

On entering at Manfred's summons, my first impression of the room was one of a family museum or archive. It could be seen straightaway that this was not a chamber anyone lived in. But the harmonious orderliness in its outlandish excess showed that it was curated by the steady hand of a frequent visitor who tended to matters with great care.

At first, I could not make out what the individual items accumulated here actually were. The books, the paintings, the various bric-a-brac all blended into an impression of an antique collection. But in the unfamiliar instruments, the crucibles, miniature scales, microscopes, fluids in fragile phials, for a moment there swept over me the vision of a scientific laboratory. Before I could reach any more definite conclusion, however, Manfred took me up to a portrait on the wall that dominated the entire setting with its proportions and its prominence.

"Do you recognize this man?"

"This is your likeness, Manfred, in eighteenth-century dress..." said I, caught off guard but sure of myself.

"You are mistaken," replied Manfred, a cool smile in his eyes.

"Then it is the likeness of some ancestor of yours. But the family resemblance is all too striking: particularly the bearing of one who moves through life with the proud serenity of a born infante."[48]

Manfred's eyes then flashed cryptically scintillant, enkindled. They poured out a sudden stream of the ravening intensity of fire and the profounder darkness of shadow.

"He is no relation of ours whatsoever, Francis, despite that expressive bearing. Look down here, in the corner of the frame: can you see?"

I read the legend: *Divo Cagliostro.*

There are visions that can instill terror in our souls, like a lightning strike that leaves us speechless... This inscription below the mysterious portrait, the name of this daring personage, had just such an effect. I could not say anything. In supreme consternation, I could only repeat, as if to myself:

"Cagliostro... 'divo Cagliostro...'"

"Yes, Cagliostro... All these objects you see around you once belonged to him or have some connection to him. Cagliostro once stayed in this chamber as a guest of my great-grandfather... I have gathered together in this room everything that can serve as a memento of him..."

XXX

"But the uncanny resemblance of this portrait to you, Manfred?"

"Cagliostro was as dark as I, as dark as anyone in league with the forces of darkness. I shall tell you the secret of this portrait and this chamber, which no latter-day passerby could guess was hidden behind the palace façade, risen up like a mute shadow in the depths of night. Without a second thought, I can now lay this mystery in the pale, translucent, suffering beauty of your hands, Francis... I know you shall receive it with the compassion, the tenderness, that turns your gaze into a green ray of light, a star, gold.[49]

"You shall now ponder the mystery of my being, tantamount to sharing in my madness. We shall have sanity enough if we do not think of ourselves. Should we choose to plumb our own depths, it is no great matter to us. Only through madness like a wing of flame can we touch the bottom of our very selves: the ancient Greeks knew it well, this *sacred* madness. Plato possessed this madness. It is when what lies within the soul is quite distinct from what is in reality, when the disparity between the internal and the existent is most absolute.

"Madness is all that enables us not to be like everyone else. The world of the sane is always the same. It gives the same responses to the same stimuli. Only one who is mad has a world all his own, shared with no one, where he sees everything differently, feels everything as no one else does. Well then, my madness has but one inspiration, one agent... Cagliostro, the divine Cagliostro..."

XXXI

"Years ago in Venice, I walked into an antique dealer's shop. By chance. Or did a mysterious impulse lead me there? Who had wanted me to lay eyes on the thing there that was to become my destiny? God or the devil? Chance is to the devil what design is to God. When the devil wants access to someone, he sends chance his way. God does not surprise. God directs. The devil surprises. The devil tempts.

"I love old things, not only for their beauty but for the marvelous legends they tell of those who touched them and kept them nearby. Such storehouses of antiques appeal to me. You find a great many religious articles there, eternal lamps that no one lights, Madonnas that no one prays to, and chasubles that no one puts on for Mass. And yet everything still breathes of sanctity and incense.

"You also find family belongings there, delightfully floriated Meissen porcelains, cups of opalescent glass, inlaid furniture, and graceful portraits. In a corner full of cobwebs, from some château or other, from the estate of a defunct family, there hangs the portrait of a young aristocrat of whom all is forgotten, even his name, except for the beautiful smile on his face as he stands erect, now just a prince from the land of the Chimæra, his hair faintly powdered, his complexion radiant, his mouth a fragrant blossom. A Rococo marquis in a pearl-grey coat with rose-colored lapels, whip in hand, and a lean greyhound at his side, while behind him shimmers a plane of air and water like a band of turquoise blue infused with silver, lulling us into infinity rather like the vapid drifting of thoughts. Why am I so taken with these images of people who don't exist, why do I find such life in the silvery greys of eyes once painted by a brush on a canvas, in the smiles of beings in whom there is also something composed, like a moonlit nocturne of grey and silver, with the deadly stillness of a ship resting at anchor? All the belongings of those long dead possess this charm. Do you not also, Francis, sometimes hear the fairy tales told by faded chaises longues, covered in old fabric of golden hue, to the shepherds on Viennese porcelains, coquettishly inclining their ears to listen when they think no one is watching them?"

XXXII

"From the shop's shadowy depths, stirred by my approach, an aged Jew with a bent back came out to meet me. At first, he spoke without looking at me, his gaze fixed on the ground. Then all at once, when he'd lifted his eyes to my face, he cried out in amazement. As if I were some kind of phantom, his arms outstretched against me in the stance of one warding off a ghost, he retreated, horrified, to the rear of the shop, past the ramparts of antique furnishings.

"I had no idea why the old man took such a fright. Only after I'd convinced him I wasn't a ghost, that I did exist, did he lead me into a side room of his shop, where I was struck dumb with astonishment.

"There I beheld a portrait of myself—the likeness of a man from the eighteenth century utterly identical to my own.

"And so the old man's first thought as soon as he looked at me was that some demon had brought the portrait hanging in the storehouse to life."

XXXIII

"I bought the painting. It was so irresistibly enticing to me that I had to have it. I carried it from town to town. I also began to take an interest in the man it depicted, in Cagliostro. I procured all the literature about him. I started to collect all his memorabilia.

"Would that I'd never set foot in that Venetian second-hand shop! What a crimson mantle of fire and torment the demon threw over my shoulders as the man showed me this portrait: Astaroth[50] himself undid his accursed wings to attach them to my body. You can't imagine my torments, Francis: all the aching in your soul, inspirited by luminous silver spells, fades gently away as if drifting tearfully off to sleep. But my life is being consumed by an infernal flame. I cannot even say what the cause of my suffering is.

"Cagliostro has become my demon. Imagine my surprise when, in our own family archives, I found evidence that my ancestor Count Evelyn Macmillan, famous in the Masonic lodges of the eighteenth century, had congress with him and hosted him at our palace in Vienna.

"Look here, these are Cagliostro's letters. Do you find them surprising? Their penmanship is identical to mine, and were not their paper yellowed and the ink faded with age, you might think them written by myself. No, they are authentic, these letters. The similarity between Cagliostro's handwriting and my own is no mere happenstance: this resemblance contains a deeper connection that shall be clear once you know all.

"I shall be succinct, Francis. On the night when I read in the family archives, in a letter from Cagliostro to my ancestor, the sentence: THE DISCIPLES OF ELIJAH, SHOULD THEY SET FOOT IN THE SHADOW OF BLACK MAGIC, ARE IMMORTAL, BUT ERE THEY CAN ATTAIN THE HIGHEST PERFECTION OF THE TWELVE WHO COMPRISE THE FIFTH DEGREE OF THE ORDER, THEY MUST TWELVE TIMES BE PURIFIED BY OSTENSIBLE DEATH AND A TWELVEFOLD EXISTENCE UNDERGO ERE THEY BECOME ETERNALLY ONE, it was clear to me that my life was nothing more than *one of the twelve existences of Cagliostro*…"

XXXIV

"Do you find this so implausible, Francis?

"Bear in mind that our birth date is but the date of our *body's birth*. But no one knows when the soul is born. No one knows when the body's antecedent was born. No one knows what existences the soul lived through before taking its present form, of which we know only that it is happenstance and transitory.

"These questions remain unresolved. The hypothesis that we transfer our soul's existence from one body to another remains unrefuted.

"Cagliostro claimed that one of his existences was as Apollonius of Tyana.[51] Could I not then be another of them?

"I am sometimes astounded at the echoes that speak to me from my core. I know they are not from my present life. They must be a voice from some earlier one of mine. They are a reverberation of what I experienced in it, of which I no longer know anything.

"In vain would we look to science to fathom the mysteries of our existences. Science will never tell us anything. All it can do is tell us that we are a nervous apparatus called a person. But magic can instruct us in our secrets. Its hypotheses readily explain what baffles the whole of empirical science."

XXXV

"While retracing Cagliostro's footsteps across Europe, I happened to have—it was in The Hague—a strange dream. I dreamt that I paid a call on him, and that he came out to meet me. I was standing quite close to him, eye to eye.

"A moment later, Cagliostro vanished. I was alone in the chamber. It contained the portrait of a proud, white-haired man that caught my eye: a nobleman in some kind of strange costume, beautifully embroidered and bejeweled, and underneath it a smaller likeness, that of a fetching youth with a cap on his curly hair, a cord flowing far below his chin on either side. Behind his waist was a plethora of short-barreled blunderbusses, and in his right hand he held a rapier, flexing its thin tip with his other hand.

"If the old man looked like a rebellious prince from somewhere in Lithuania or Tartary,[52] the youth had the aristocratic beauty of a prince from a realm of decay: for all his armor and martial bearing, one sensed that he was projecting his weakness into a grey, stagnant atmosphere, underlaid with aged, faded gold as a mere stylization of vigor. Drawing on tradition based on family legends, one would simulate a courage one no longer had. The contrast, of vigor in the family founder and decay in the later grandson, impressed itself deeply into my memory, lodging itself there as definitely as a thing does only rarely in our dreams. The old man seemed to possess a masterful authority, every inch a brute; while the boy was left only with something in his hands capable of mastery, along with the despotism of a cruel, passionate, even insensible will.

"Just then, I had a jolt of terror in my dream. Cagliostro reappeared, with an aspect so grotesque that he looked like a phantom of hell. He drew so close to me that he began to fade into me. I screamed and woke up.

"But from this dream, I could recall the old man and the youth in the portraits so vividly that they were unforgettable.

"As you know, I am also a bit of a painter. I took sketches of both likenesses—and in time forgot the matter altogether.

"A year later, when I arrived in Warsaw, I was introduced to Count Eugène Mosczyński, whose ancestor had been acquainted with Cagliostro, in whose laboratory he used to make gold and produce tinctures to enlarge pearls and precious stones.

"I then expressed a wish to see the portrait of this acquaintance of Cagliostro. His great-grandson showed me into the family gallery. Imagine my astonishment! As I was about to leave there, I suddenly see a likeness of the old man from my dream—and underneath it, that of a boy flexing a slender rapier. I scramble for my portfolio and take out my sketch. Indeed, a perfect likeness, down to the smallest detail.

"How do you explain this uncanny dream? I had never been in in Warsaw before, or the Mosczyński gallery. So I must have seen these two portraits in an existence other than my present one. I beheld them as Cagliostro, as my dream had recently brought them to me. How else to explain my ability to remember these paintings that I had never seen before?"

XXXVI

"In the entire eighteenth century, I know of no one greater than Cagliostro, whom everyone calls an adventurer and a swindler. To me, he is the supreme *Artist of Life.*[53]

"Had Cagliostro been dependent solely on local mediocrity, he might have achieved fame. Yet for the remarkable
way he composed a scheme and style for his life by sheer
invention, seeking by his *uniqueness* to distinguish himself
from those wanting only to imitate these qualities, he is taken
for a charlatan. History does not recognize him, though he is
the greatest artist of life, greater than Napoleon, whom history presumably finds so toothsome only because he was a
horrendous consumer of human flesh, and where he should
have shown some spirit, he could manage only a crass imitation of the old monarchical style. History may not recognize
Cagliostro, but that is of no consequence when we consider
whom it does recognize…

"Are you taken aback by my opinion of Napoleon?
I have not always thought so harshly of him. I even found
him amusing, so long as his imperial epic poetry did not
include ambitions to become a parvenu sovereign, so long
as the dominant story was of a native Ajaccien's[54] concili-
ated banditry combined with the naturalized Frenchman's
acquired capacity for prostitution. In time, a magnificent
style might have developed out of these two elements had
not Napoleon, in deferential awe of history's judgment,
so utterly spoiled everything with his respectable bourgeois character that he became 'the Great' only for the
French bourgeoisie, and at most for German professors
as well.

"The Judgment of History! How ludicrous it is!
A supreme Philistine sits on his throne and confers the
rewards of virtue upon poor mediocrities, as at the annual
entrance examinations for the Pensionnat du Sacré-Cœur.[55]
And should he confer glory upon one of greater worth,
it is always because the said genius has pretended to be
poor in spirit, never because he truly is a genius. History's
approval, its favor, is an insult, its disregard an honor.
Therefore, Francis, make no mistake: there are no geniuses

in history. History romanticizes and beatifies only milksops and dilettantes. The only Genius of Style, Cagliostro, *divo Cagliostro*, has been expunged from it. History reveres not the Creators, the Hierophants, the Poets. It reveres dynasties of ignoramuses and the vulgarity of usurpers. It reveres the greatness of what is real, of what can be substantiated: murder, war, conspiracy, conflagration, the greatness of whatever reeks of vulgarity and bloodshed. But what of the greatness of the fabrication, the invention, the imaginary, what has no reality? The greatness of the Chimæra? The fantasy? The lie?

"So long as history remains in its present form, it can accommodate no name such as Cagliostro's except by prostituting it. To do this brow sufficient reverence with a golden laurel, all other heads should have to be stripped of their crowns and tiaras.

"It is *plebiscites* that create history. And one can therefore only despise them from the depths of one's soul. History does not revere personality. It does not admire the Dream. The howling rabble, the herd that is called the nation, inscribes history with its revolutions. But revolution does not exist unless it can be agitated by a single man of the Dream, his utterances unrefuted. Cagliostro's world of the spirits is a greater reality than the executions of Robespierre and Marat.

"History is one of state officials and not stories of powerful individuals. The instant Dante inscribed his parchment with the terrible word *Inferno* is greater than all the tales of kings' wars since that day. All the famous men history acknowledges won fame by using their mediocrity to buy public agreement. Cagliostro made a mockery of his age, parodying and ridiculing it. If all the great men are deemed so in others' eyes, Cagliostro was great *in and of himself.*"

XXXVII

"This was his style of life: *the greatness of invention.*
Cagliostro lied. Naturally. But to say of a genius that he
didn't lie is tantamount to saying that he lacked creativity.

"Cagliostro had a masterful imagination. He invented his
youth, as he did his name. It is true that the Paris police,
the Roman Inquisition, and a whole swarm of authors led
by Goethe himself[56] have set out to demolish these charming inventions with their sober, grey documentation. But
fortunately, his advocate Thilorier[57] preserved all that was
his client's beautiful, original biographical creation in his
*Mémoire pour le comte de Cagliostro, accusé; contre M. le
Procureur-Général, accusateur,*[58] a memorandum addressed
to the Parlement of Paris in 1786, after Cagliostro's incarcer-
ation in the Bastille. Otherwise—had it ever become worth
the trouble—we should know only of a certain Giuseppe
Balsamo of Palermo, son of Pietro Balsamo, of Jewish origin, who lived in humble, squalid surroundings and aspiring
to become a priest, entered the seminary of San Rocco and
then lived on the charity of a monastery in Carthage.

"I do not disparage Cagliostro's miserable father, for
Pietro Balsamo was not, as it seems, wholly lacking in talent;
word is that at least he went bankrupt. But as to the style of
Cagliostro's later life, such humble, frugal beginnings as the
baptized son of a Jew who took the brethren's compassionate
charity would not do. If he was not to be Giuseppe Balsamo,
Cagliostro had to have been brought up in princely splendor in the Mufti Salahayyam's court in Medina by the wise
Althotas,[59] attended by bevies of slaves. He could not have
been initiated into chemistry and botany by a kind-hearted
friar-apothecary in Carthage: only the exotic Althotas could
have initiated him into magic. Nor could Cagliostro have
gone out into the world just to misbehave, though there is
also stylized humor here, as when he reads martyrologies

aloud for the good monastics at evening meals but substitutes the names of bandits and harlots for those of the saints; or when he lures the miserly goldsmith Marano to a seaside cave on the pretext of showing him a treasure, only to have his companions tan his hide while made up as devils.

"Cagliostro stylizes his life in still other ways for public consumption: with his host of servants, he decamps to Mecca, to a sharif's palace, where he is received so warmly by the prince that he comes to regard the prince as his father.

"He lives there for three years, but at last he is impelled onward, out into the world. As Cagliostro says his goodbyes to the sharif, the prince embraces him with tears in his eyes, saying only:

"'Happiness, O misbegotten son!'

"Cagliostro sets off for Egypt, and from its priests he learns the secrets of the temples and the pyramids. He then spends three years doing nothing but travel through Africa and Asia, until finally reaching Malta, where he is received and fêted with full honors by the Johannites' grandmaster, Manuel Pinto da Fonseca.[60] Here he suddenly discovers that some kind of Trapezuntine princess was his mother.[61] Althotas enters the order at this time. They also try to force Cagliostro to take the monastic habit, but accompanied by the Chevalier d'Aquino, he then retires to Rome, whence he begins his public career.

"This life, this youth, though fictitious, is truer to the style of Cagliostro's later life than the youth of which official registers and biographical detectives could tell.

"In fact, any genius's youth is of next to no interest: they unfold not of their own volition but that of others. The spirit has still not awakened so that it can stylize a life. Happy the man who commits at least some absurdities along the way. Failing that, youth is like a cliché from which any requisite number of stenciled imprints can be produced. Consequently, except for perhaps a few details, the opening pages of celebrity biographies are identical with those of drab people. Indeed, it is precisely this insignificance that ensures interest in the youth of geniuses on the part of every literary historian, whose rational mind is always a mésalliance between his own stupidity and someone else's ordinariness. But I believe it ought to remain the prerogative of geniuses to keep their lives secret, insofar as these infringe on the style of their œuvre, or to invent them, insofar as these may burnish their individuality as artists.

"Suppose that as a man of outrageously stylized good taste, of swashbuckling mystery, Cagliostro should have to tell stupid biographers, prying into his parentage, about relatives with whom he has nothing in common, vulgar people living in some nook in a seedy alley off Palermo's main avenue il Càssaro![62] That he, a prince of the dark realm of magic whose revelations make people's nerves burst into flames of hellfire, should have to acknowledge some grubby old deaf woman, gobbling down her rice gruel with her fingers, as his mother!

"In his *Italienische Reise*, Goethe, who disgraced himself by stooping to Eckermann's natterings,[63] had the audacity to visit Cagliostro's family home and question his sisters and brothers, ignorant creatures incapable of grasping that one of their own flesh and blood could be as complete a stranger to them as anyone else. It was unworthy of Goethe to spoil another life's style in this manner, to upend the fictions of a genius who'd made his own life into a grandiose work of art.

"I can understand why Cagliostro resented even those facts from his own life that were otherwise consistent with his style, simply because they were true and not of his own making. I myself hate the particulars of my actual life, so much so that if anyone asks me whether I know London, I prefer to say that I was brought up in Berlin; and if anyone wants to know how my father died, I say that it was of a stomach ailment, though he was killed in a duel. Even in my youth, during my tutor's history lessons, if I had to recount historical facts, so strong was my aversion to telling of things that had actually happened that though I had perfect command of the material, I would suddenly begin to invent historical details, astonishing my tutor, who didn't know whether I was playing a joke on him or, in fact, so utterly unversed in his paltry science of events that had actually happened.

"Cagliostro's adepts would naturally have us perceive abomination in all that exists, simply because it exists. Of course, this is beyond the grasp of one such as Goethe, who improvises cloying love letters for some stupid Frau von Stein and allows himself to be rewarded with her sponge cakes.

"Cagliostro found the courage to strike through all his actual experience, and to replace the real with make-believe. In those situations where life had compelled him to live the norm, he could invent the exceptionalities he coveted. That is why his birthplace is Trebizond and not Palermo. That is why his name is Count Cagliostro and not Giuseppe Balsamo. The style of his life demands that his youth not be what biographers natter on about or what writers like Goethe find out, but what he himself relates."

XXXVIII

"Cagliostro is a *genius of fantasy*. He had the madness to build a Tower of Babel. But he built it in such a way that his ravings surpassed the rational edifices of all other men.

"Truth was something so vulgar to him that he had a horror of descending to its level. He was an artist, or so I should say were that word not abused by all manner of people nowadays. Who is truly an artist nowadays? If anyone affects a convoluted and impassioned existence in books and lives the same life as any other old stuffed shirt, he is an artist. But show me a single artistic personality in whom what he wants to live and what he does live are in such harmony as in Cagliostro! An occasional phosphorescence of chic does not make one an artist. But to glow, to sparkle constantly— that is the whole thing.

"Cagliostro knew how to live, while others can only grow old. He knew how to take charge of people, while others can only take orders cravenly. If in time his life became a farce, it was still distinctive. For there's a difference between acting in a farce that others have penned for us and acting in one of our own making. Should it be necessary to do preposterous things, then even there, better to be preposterous in a grandiose way rather than only in a middling one like everyone else. Cagliostro proved his genius in his very life, while others do so only in their works: it gave him the luster of *breathtaking preposterousness*, whereby he made fun of others and took himself seriously. Of course, his celebrity seemed more humbug than glory. Glory is enduring. But that's not always an advantage. The good part about humbug is precisely that it doesn't last forever. It is only the sudden flash of a comet that makes it so intensely terrifying.

"In Rome, where Cagliostro appears all at once like an exotic, enigmatic personality, he takes everyone's breath away. He disturbs people's imagination as if etching it with poisons. Baron Bretueil introduces him to Cardinal Orsini, who engages Pope Clement XIII's interest in him. Cagliostro becomes a cause célèbre everywhere through his conjurations and miracle potions. He mocks people's stupidity and is trailed by crowds. In Spain, in England, in France, in Holland, in Germany, he creates a stir everywhere. He flits through Palermo as the Marquis Pellegrini. In Spain, he lives as the German physician Thiscia, turning hemp into silk, mercury into gold, and making diamonds and pearls miraculously larger. He becomes the master of London's Masonic lodges. He then leads a princely life, surrounded by splendor and servants. The women all follow him in droves, though he scorns them. All the men rave about him, though he cons them. Cagliostro's portrait can be seen on fans, rings, and in the lockets of highborn ladies. Marble statues of him with the inscription 'Divo Cagliostro' adorn the chambers of the aristocracy. Cagliostro allows no deeper acquaintances with anyone. Once he bedazzles someone, he abandons them. Once his reputation collapses somewhere, he vanishes. He turns up in mystery and disappears in mystery. Nor does he give his enemies any opportunity for all of them to persecute him. Even in this, he preserves his freedom of choice, and in the choice of those who dare attack him, he always conducts himself in good taste. He knows that even in the hatred we inspire, it matters that there be style."

XXXIX

"There are plenty of anecdotes about him, both superb and scandalous. Yet not all of them tally fully with his individuality and style.

"It's true that at the Carnival in St. Mark's Square in Venice, in a mask, he approached a German prince to tell him that his father had just died. This news was confirmed a few days later by a letter under a black seal, brought by a court messenger. Equally true are the stories of Cagliostro's divinatory arts, whether in reference to hydromancy, gastromancy, catoptromancy, or crystallomancy. At a gathering, Cagliostro would ask someone to say of whom he was thinking. On receiving an evasive reply, he would pull a mirror out from under his cloak and say:

"'Perhaps this is that person?'

"And in the mirror, off at a distance, the respondent would see the object of his thoughts, whom Cagliostro could not possibly have known.

"But along with such plausible particularities, there are also a good many tales that are hoaxes and calumnies. Cagliostro had a knowledge of ancient magic. His experiments, which seem farcical charlatanism to those whose knowledge of the occult is scant, adhere precisely to the principles laid down in *Disquisitionum magicarum* by Martin Delrio,[64] among others. Present-day mediums continue to invoke them in their own practice of spiritism.

"But in addition, so that he not profane magical knowledge, Cagliostro probably took pleasure in turning away the importunate and unworthy. Yet in his magical pranks, there was never any of the ineptitude attributed to him by the authors of the most inane anecdotes. Their sources are rather murky. Cagliostro had the misfortune to be accompanied on his travels by a woman, Lorenza Feliciani, necessary to him as a servant. He himself so detested women that he wouldn't even kiss Catherine the Great's hand, since she was a 'femelle.'[65] To complete the mockery, he founded female Masonic lodges and had his servant woman, drenched in perfume and arrayed in silks, preside over them. When he later dismissed her in Switzerland, Lorenza, whom some writers have wrongly adjudged to be Cagliostro's wife, did what every spurned woman from the duchess to the washerwoman does. She heaped such calumnies on Cagliostro that a whole host of his biographers feeds on them to this day, except that Lorenza later recanted the slanders; but writers continue to repeat them.

"In Holland, the Masons hail Cagliostro with great festivities. The occult sciences undergo a revival. Passing himself off as an emissary of the prophet Elijah, when he is questioned as to his origin, at first Cagliostro says that he sprang from the love of an angel for a mortal woman, and that he descended to earth to aid the faithful in fulfilling their quest for the highest perfection, through physical and moral rebirth. He instructed others in how to overcome evil magical forces and harness them. He gave initiations into the production of red powder, the *materiæ primæ*[66] able to turn metals into gold, and he made rejuvenating potions. As one who had made sense of the magical symbols, he then did so with the three chapters excised from the Bible by the priests,[67] which contain the supreme mysteries of existence. As one who had attained to the highest perfection, he then entered into communion with the seven angels whom God first created—whose names are Anael, Michael, Raphael, Gabriel, Uriel, Zobiachel, and Anachiel[68]—and became immortal.

"When questioned as to his origin, Cagliostro would now reply with but a single sentence:

"'I am who I am!'[69]

"On another occasion, he drew a snake with an apple in its mouth rather than answer. But when his listeners impertinently insisted that he explain further, their curiosity unsatisfied by these symbols, he laughed them off by launching the construction of a sort of Tower of Babel on the heights, claiming that this edifice should unite heaven and earth and bring all worshipers of the sacred symbols into direct communion with the angels.

"Cagliostro conned the seekers after eternal youth with even more savage mockery, pulling their strings in time with his own grotesque rhythms. For it was not his will to initiate all manner of people into the occult sciences—he deliberately travestied and parodied divinatory practices, just as he did mediumship and clairvoyance. Yet he himself was an absolute master in the realm of the occult. For not even when up against the Roman Inquisition afterwards did he deny these abilities, though they got him thrown into prison.

"The general faith in Cagliostro had reached such a pitch that the mere touching of his garments was believed to confer miraculous powers. In the Psalm 'Memento Domine David et omnis mansuetudinis eius,'[70] the word 'Cagliostro' was now sung instead of 'David' in the Masonic lodges."

XL

"In Berlin, Cagliostro tells the Germans that he has spoken to Alexander the Great, living on in Egypt as head of a society of warrior magicians.

"In Mitau, he charms Elisa von der Recke, née Countess von Medem, an admirer of Lavater,[71] and all her relatives. Elisa's six-year-old nephew serves as a medium for Cagliostro's divinatory practices. Cagliostro uses his breath to invest the boy with magical powers and anoints his head with the 'oil of wisdom.' Cagliostro then commands him to enter a tabernacle—where three candles are positioned on a small table within its white interior—and to communicate what he sees. With Arabic incantations, the visitor summons spirits whom the boy describes. When an old man appears in a red cloak with a white cross on it,[72] the earth trembles, and a hollow comes into view.

"At moments, however, an incantation misfires. Instead of ghosts, the boy sees only monkeys. At other times, there are attempts at clairvoyance, facilitated by the boy's first gazing into the water's reflection, into its shimmering surface, then by his autohypnosis. Cagliostro places a basin of water on a table, and as the boy looks into it, he spies his uncle approaching the castle. Those present declare this impossible, knowing that the boy's uncle is journeying far from there. But in short order, this genuinely unanticipated relative indeed turns up, having returned against all expectations.

"All this illumines Cagliostro with an infernal aureole. His stunned adepts are left reeling. Some even clearly see the demon Astaroth hunching over Cagliostro, caressing his face with his black paw, its claws retracted.

"At Count von Medem's estate, Cagliostro marks the spot where a treasure lies hidden, buried there six hundred years before by a magician. Sorcerers have repeatedly attempted to lay hold of it, but something has always worked such havoc on their spells that they couldn't find the treasure's precise hiding place. Yet had they succeeded in seizing it and the books the magician had buried there, terrible calamity would have been visited upon the land.

"Cagliostro began to dig, but before he could unearth the treasure, he was compelled to withdraw to St. Petersburg. He therefore bade some of the spirits in his thrall to keep watch over the treasure until he could return.

"In St. Petersburg, Cagliostro turns up in the guise of a Spanish count as a wonder-working physician. Prince Potemkin, lover to Catherine the Great, is dazzled by him and introduces him at court. There, this terrifying genius creates a sensation. Everyone is curious, eager to penetrate his dark mystique. Adept at stirring up anxiety, Cagliostro also knows to keep to the shadows himself, making his existence uncertain. He would cast a mighty darkness over the people if ever the vigorous sparkle of his phosphorescence might illuminate his inner workings.

"Cagliostro treats all who have been declared incurable by the doctors, using poisons to restore them to health. He returns a countess's deathly ill child to its mother, having completely cured it of disease. Yet this countess soon realizes she has been given a different child in place of her own. Cagliostro disappears from St. Petersburg, leaving behind him only a series of cryptic rumors, like an eerily phosphorescent pageant of will-o'-the-wisps. Catherine, whom Cagliostro has offended several times, takes her revenge in purely feminine fashion: she calumniates him in a pair of theatrical pieces performed at one of the imperial palaces, and it is unclear whether she also devised scurrilous anecdotes about him, such as the deception with the child, just as Elisa von der Recke would later do, likely also purely from offended vanity, with stupid and, moreover, similarly feminine inventions about Cagliostro's stay in Mitau.

"In Warsaw, Cagliostro keeps company with Count Mosczyński. He conducts alchemical experiments in the count's laboratory and summons spirits, uttering unintelligible words while brandishing a rapier, but the count himself comes to view his guest with skepticism.

"On his return to Germany, Cagliostro is again greeted everywhere with the same general enthusiasm for this man so filled with the passion of infernal ideas. Fires are stoked afresh in alchemical crucibles, and experiments resume in secret laboratories. Cagliostro is ubiquitous, his glory now ablaze with the most intense flames, the most astonishing flares, yet at the same time they are terrifying, like the unleashed, all-consuming element of someone universally taken for the devil incarnate."

XLI

"Having made the acquaintance of Cardinal de Rohan, Cagliostro settles in Paris. Seventy Masonic lodges give him ovations. Cardinal de Rohan publicly kisses his hand. Likenesses of Cagliostro again grace every ring and locket.

"He gives soirées and summons the spirits of Diderot, Voltaire, Henri IV, and Montesquieu to dine with him. But he has a setback in which feminine intrigue again ensnares him. He is implicated in the affair of Comtesse de la Motte's necklace,[73] imprisoned for half a year in the Bastille, and eventually banished from France.

"As he leaves prison, his followers set lights in their windows and hail him with great festivities. Cagliostro issues a manifesto prophesying the imminent outbreak of revolution and the demolition of the Bastille."

XLII

"In London, he meets the erratic Lord George Gordon[74] and wields influence over the Swedenborgians in their Theosophical Society as well.[75] He again projects the horror and madness of one who has made a pact with the devil. He works the people up to a fever pitch, rousing them to unholy indignation. But none can stand up to him despite how he disturbs the general peace, fraying everyone's nerves like some diabolical improviser playing a violin pizzicato.

"At his seances, the pathos only deepens. Cagliostro has all the furniture cleared out of his house, the shutters closed, the fires in the fireplaces and the candles in the candelabra extinguished. At a black-draped altar upon a red carpet, wearing a miraculous amulet round his neck and a robe embroidered with arcane symbols, he conjures up spirits and questions them about the past, for of eternity the dead may never tell the living.

"Cagliostro now claims to have attained immortality. No sword can pierce him, no poison kill him, no fire incinerate him. He has no need of rest. And so, he never sleeps. There is but one hour when he is idle: at midnight. Then his spirit leaves his body, which becomes as stiff as a cadaver, and it retires to the underworld. What his spirit does there, it may not tell. Once the hour is over, his spirit returns to his body, and he resumes his activities on earth.

"Some friends of Cagliostro once decided to test the truth of this assertion. They deliberately set his clock so that it ran behind. But at the appointed hour of midnight, Cagliostro indeed fell into the rigid state that made him resemble a diabolical corpse. Yet when he awoke, he declared that, were such snares to be laid for him, he would leave London at once."

XLIII

"He returns to Germany, continuing on to Austria.

"Emperor Joseph II[76] is hostile to him, despite my great-grandfather Evelyn Macmillan's putting in a good word.

"Family lore has preserved the secret history of how my great-grandfather met Cagliostro. After the two become acquainted in Venice, Cagliostro turns up in Vienna one day. My great-grandfather hosts him here in the family palace and presents him to the Emperor himself, recounting the stories of this mysterious occultist to the sovereign. In the royal palace itself, experiments are conducted, spirits summoned, auguries taken, and truths divined. The Emperor tries in vain to expose the fraud.

"One day, Cagliostro begins to claim that he exists in two persons. One is here in the imperial château, the other a prisoner in the Bastille. To ascertain the truth of this, the Emperor Joseph II lodges Cagliostro in a well-guarded chamber and immediately dispatches an envoy to Paris with an inquiry to the French government. The governor of the Bastille, the Marquis de Launay, does in fact give official confirmation that Cagliostro is in his custody.

"Yet the Emperor Joseph remained unconvinced of Cagliostro's magic ability. Around this time, when Cagliostro expressed a desire to settle in Roveredo,[77] the Emperor turned him out, despite my great-grandfather's renewed intercession, nor would he allow him to settle in Trento.[78]

"Cagliostro goes to Rome. He resumes his activities in the local Masonic lodges. He musters adepts for seances like a demon plotting hellish pageants. He engages people, has them all marveling, smites them with fevers, and views their inflammation with delight, like an arsonist at the fire he has started.

"Fearing arrest, he sends out a circular to all the world's lodges, urging his friends to spare no effort to free him if he is thrown back in prison, to set the prison on fire, if need be, for fire cannot harm him and he shall emerge unscathed. Yet he was betrayed and imprisoned in the Castel Sant'Angelo.[79] The Roman Inquisition sentences him to death. Pius VI commutes the sentence to life imprisonment and puts Cagliostro's work on Egyptian Freemasonry[80] on the Index of Forbidden Books.

"Cagliostro is now wasting away in the Forte di San Leo.[81] Some say he tried to throttle his confessor for clothes to escape in. Others say he himself was strangled by his inquisitors. Still others claim that the devil took possession of Cagliostro's body under the terms of their contract. What is certain is that no one knows how he met his end. This sorcerer, beyond human in so many respects if not one of the devils himself, and if he did not depart for the underworld at the end of his earthly *simulation of humanness* as if for home, he surely didn't deserve that his every trace should completely vanish from the world, but rather that in another existence, his spirit continue to be active on this planet of doubt and turmoil.

"Was not my own existence borne of this corpse buried somewhere on the grounds of the Forte di San Leo prison? I was weary of living in the banality that is outward appearances, in the mundanity that is life. What mysterious force compelled me to plumb the depths of the Mystery in search of Cagliostro's shadow? Was it just a desire for paradox and perversity? Was it infirmity, was it madness? Or is there some higher purpose in my living as none has ever lived, in dreaming what none has ever dreamt?

"I know you won't dismiss me, Francis, as anyone *uninitiated* would. I am in a struggle, but I know not what with. If human existences come from God, surely only the devil can use them as mirrors that reflect his own face.

"Is my existence just such a mirror, where Satan takes satisfaction in his semblance? I know that evil alone gives me pleasure. Even if I do love you, Francis, the mere knowledge that I can torment you is testament to how indispensable you are to me. My love intensifies my desire to torment the one I adore. What fate awaits me? Can I survive the struggle I've undertaken? Can your love sustain me? Only the prospect of injury, the vulnerability of my limbs, spurs me to battle. I have no wish for the impenetrable armor that is the battle-gear of the seraphim:[82] there would be no charm to such a contest. I yearn for destruction as much as for victory..."

XLIV

Manfred broke off.

I looked over at the portrait of Cagliostro. Whether under the effect of Manfred's words or a sudden brightening of the candles, Cagliostro seemed all at once to come to life.

It was a marvelous portrait, full of morbidity and mystery, the face's tone translucent, the eyes expressive of some elusive magical power in slumber. One had the impression that these eyes could peer into depths where no one else would dare look. They were the eyes of one who saw nothing of reality and everything of irreality.

The slender figure was wrapped in a long coat of dark blue silk. The waistcoat, dove-grey and unbuttoned at the top, revealed a snowy pleated muslin jabot at the opening. Cagliostro stood erect, in a kind of commanding pose.

It was remarkable how the eyes changed as one took a closer look at them. It was like gazing into the eyes of a living person. They were now beacons of irony rather than organs of sight, while the body seemed to consist of nerves rather than flesh. The entire portrait had something sphinxlike about it. Mockery. In the corners of the eyes, then lower, at the corners of the mouth. No... the mockery was in the entire body, in every twitch, every contour, and in his stance. Indeed, the eyes. They were cunning. They knew all your secrets. They bared your soul. A mysterious and evil perplexity passed from these eyes to yours. You had a sudden sense of the falseness and tawdriness of everything you had ever lived and felt.

And yet, this is *Manfred*, this imaginary Cagliostro. This individual both fictitious and alive suddenly merged into one for me. I could not have said which was speaking to me then, whether my friend or the specter in the portrait: the two were a single being, almost disembodied, vanishing as soon as one tried to touch it: a being beyond everyday life, perceived more by dream and desire than by the senses.

"Manfred!" I exclaimed, as if to make myself conscious of the reality. Other eyes now opened into mine, black as an abyss—were they the portrait's, or my friend's? I do not know. But then I felt a jet of light breaking through to me from them, and suddenly I had a living person's hands in my own.

"Manfred!" I whispered, in awe of the passionate body that pressed itself against me, as I felt the breath of these lips abloom with the damp of blood and roses, and the perfume from this lily-pale complexion, veined with blue threads at the brow and temples, and the scent from this hair's dark mysterious night.

I saw that I was now everything to this being, laden with a fateful mystery, a terrible curse—was this in reality or in a vision? No, it was reality, even if fragmented into such bizarre lights and shadows that it gave the impression of a phantasmagoria. Words of a mad, impossible love were passing over Manfred's lips, over their scarlet dark and heavy. Desire spoke from them distinctly, a desire that had until then only hung in the air, intoxicating me with its veiled, shimmering flashes. But now it was the breath of those lips dazing me with a purple nectar, spilling as if from the calyx of a magnificent poisonous flower.[83] I could detect the onset of an exquisite, sybaritic pleasure. I sensed that even the morbidity of this overcultivated body knew the throes of sensuality when suddenly casting the being it loves into a warm bath of smoldering blood.

Then I could clearly distinguish the reality of Manfred's body from the fiction of Cagliostro's portrait. Cagliostro blanched, turned grey, and vanished. Was it still he? No, it was a kind of phantom, the phantom of a beautiful young man from the eighteenth century. Perhaps it could not even be called that of a man. Its beauty was now half masculine, half maidenly, or more precisely, all beauties were commingled in it. His posture retained its bristling severity. But on the other hand, there was something vulnerable, enervated, coursing through his body at the same time.

Before, this portrait had the power to enthrall, but now it seemed itself in thrall. I had thought Cagliostro to be experiencing our secret along with us: and now that he understood it, he was withdrawing into a dead age, into ancient dreams, in order to leave us to our solitude…

XLV

"Not even this portrait of Cagliostro is real. It is the stuff of imagination. Look now, Francis, here is another portrait, just as real as Goethe's narratives, a portrait by Bartholozzi.[84] Yet it's no less an insult to Cagliostro's personage than his biographers' anecdotes. Look at the staginess of this pose, at the vapidity of this high forehead, at the base sensuality of this vulgar mouth, at the conventional delusion in the eyes, at the foppish coquetry in the fur tossed around his neck, at the theatricality of the crossed arms! How could anyone see Cagliostro like *that*? Yet all concur that this is a faithful likeness. But that's no wonder: everyone was merely looking at Cagliostro through the conventionality of their own eyes. The way we look to other people, this arbitrary outer appearance of our personæ, is usually an insult to our souls. Only the *initiated* can see us as we are, peering within and intuiting our external appearance from our inner self alone.

"That's why I believe in the authenticity not of Bartholozzi's portrait, but of the one I found in a secondhand shop in Venice. I have no idea who painted it. But he was certainly a being who had penetrated Cagliostro's enigma. In painting this portrait, he could already intuit the form of Cagliostro's next existence, and in transferring Cagliostro's features to the canvas, he unwittingly foresaw my own. Or, for this initiate's sake, did Cagliostro himself momentarily assume my form when he sat for the artist? This portrait was created in ecstasy, while others are worked out with sober, grey accuracy. This is a conjuration by a spirit kindled with love, whose enthusiasm could see a form of beauty where others saw only the ordinary.

"This transformation explains his love. We can love only if we see someone as improbable. If the enchantment is broken and we see our love's object just as others do, that's the end of love. But that doesn't prove that it's everyone else and not the one soul we've enchanted who sees us as we are: on the contrary. That's why we're so taken by this portrait that we deem fictive, and so cool to likenesses verified as authentic: the artistry of this portrait lies precisely in its love for Cagliostro's personage. Art and love, these are the soul's two wondrous states in which we can best see things as they are not."

XLVI

"Following in Cagliostro's footsteps across Europe, I embraced everything this artist of life had once experienced in its various cities. Yet I found nothing to surprise me as I visited the places where Cagliostro had once made an impression. Everything was so familiar, so recognizable. I felt as if I'd merely *forgotten* the look of those places. Wherever objects with some link to Cagliostro could be found, I procured them, and I've brought them all together here in this chamber. I felt like I was collecting the mementos of a life that I myself had once lived. The things I'd been able to feel and experience as the fictional Cagliostro in the eighteenth century were vivid and enduring. The things I had to live as Manfred Macmillan in the present were as vague and insipid as a memory.

"This Cagliostro chamber has become my refuge. No one else has ever set foot in it. It is the secret of this palace. You're the first apart from me to enter it. A mysterious existence casts a shadow over all these things.

"Legend has it that my great-grandfather, long after the Roman Inquisition had thrown Cagliostro into prison, came home at midnight one night to find the windows of this chamber brightly lit. He was alarmed, for he knew that no one lived on the palace's second floor. In the window, the shadow of someone pacing the chamber would appear at intervals. The stranger came to a sudden stop there. He could be seen to be reading a book. Then, as if divining that he was being watched, he lay the book on the windowsill and leaned out into the night air. At that very moment, my great-grandfather knew for a certainty that the mysterious late-night guest at his palace was none other than Cagliostro. He roused the servants, and they rushed up to the second floor to see what the matter was: yet the chamber was dark and deserted. Except there was a book on the windowsill that had never been there before. It was a volume by Paracelsus.

"Ever since, this chamber has sustained the palace's reputation as haunted. A mysterious light could often be seen glimmering through the corridor and footsteps heard from someone pacing here at midnight.

"No one wanted to live on this second floor, and so it's been abandoned for decades. I am the only one who ventures up here, eager to discover Cagliostro's ghost and to speak with his imaginary shadow. When I stay in Vienna, I come here every night after midnight. I think of this chamber when I'm away from Vienna, and I visit it at least in spirit.

"Were it not for this fiction, my life would be unbearable. There are days when I despair over how drab and grey everything is. Nothing interests me. Worrisomely futile and bleak, everything seems to lack magnetism. I don't mean the feeling of everything's *transience*, which is even agreeable at times; for in the end, only what is transient is beautiful. What I mean are the moments when we feel like we're in our own and everyone else's way, when everything within and without is a wasteland, when the only thing we can expect of life is tedium. We are exhausted and utterly spent. We lose all sense of light and color. We feel we've seen it all and done it all. Life is always the same. We strive to fill that void we feel at our core. We seek people out but find their company loathsome; we go to the theater, but the tedium is stifling; we go out in the carriage and know not why, nor why we return home, nor what we'll do there. We have only one *certainty*: that no thing or being can seize our attention and cure us of our malady.

"At such moments, I always come to Cagliostro's chamber: here alone can I find the meaning of my existence. Day after day, I open my diary and write my dreams in it. And so over the years, a record has emerged not of what I've lived but of what I imagined myself to have lived. Here is my fictive biography, Francis: you'll find it contains nothing of the reality of our lives. In telling you of Cagliostro's life a moment ago, I was in fact telling you of my own. This diary is only a different form, a different possibility for my life.

"Cagliostro claimed to have lived before the Flood and to have been present at the wedding in Cana of Galilee.[85] How absurd is it then for me to suppose that one of his marvelous spirit's sparks has flown into this century and ignited my existence? If the chimæra and the sphinx are the essence of all existence, then I am *alive*: for the chimæric and the sphinxian alone justify the fact of my existence. All else, the real and material, is a line too lowly placed to serve as a guide for my own life.

"I adore all that is absurd and impossible, feelings that have no stimulus, and things that have no shadow. For only possible things can kill the soul, and only impossible things rally our nerves to continue our existence. This diary recounts all the fiction that has ever happened to me in my life. Under invented names, characters one could meet only in dreams flit in and out like passing shadows.

"I lead a double life: one in reality, and that one I never call to mind. The other in irreality, and that one I record in every detail, for it alone is mine, created by and therefore lived by me."

XLVII

Manfred opened his diary to me. I beheld it in awe.

"You may peruse my entries, Francis. I have no more secrets from you."

I took the diary in my hands not with curiosity but with a hesitant, turbulent heart.

It was a book full of feelings and sensations, but nothing in that subjective form relished by most autobiographers. The uninitiated would have supposed he was reading a purely literary work, for Manfred spoke of himself as if of someone else, of one suffering and doubting as if he himself were not. He was perfectly candid about himself but gave the sense of wanting to conceal all that filled his soul to overflowing.

I read a few of the prefatory sentences. It was indeed difficult to tell whether the book's contents were the ecstasy of a mediæval mystic or the nervous morbidity of a modern. Within this volume, between its covers of yellow silk damask,[86] the subtle music of these rhythmic sentences recounted the reveries of an extraordinary soul, living in the unreal as others do in the real, telling of passions and vices peculiar to ages past, and experienced only in a fevered imagination.

As if behind pale veils, something that signified Manfred's imaginary life was passing before my eyes in obscure symbols. But all this was nevertheless tied to specific dates and specific persons. A medley of the lived and the imagined, the real and the irreal, the existent and the nightmarish, such were the contents of this fictional diary, but it was all finely wrought, as if chased in silver and precious stones.

Life and reality alike gazed with wide-open eyes here, like a fabulous serpent looking out from a jacinth. The people and beings Manfred met here spoke in words that breathed of opal and gold. Their every movement bespoke magic, and within the shadow of their every intrigue, there lurked the cunning of demons. It was as if Manfred had daily beheld his existence in some wondrous chrysolite looking glass and then described his impressions, bathed in an eerie light, awash in luxury.

The same opulence, the same embellishments of imagination, marked the descriptions of Manfred's consorts and lovers in this outlandish diary. One interesting boy whose eyes would sometimes darken like agate—though in real life, scarcely an hour's conversation with him would bring

on the doldrums—was here transformed into a being outwardly resembling the Earl of Somerset, or the "sweet and
dear Steny" of James I,[87] in a coat of woven gold studded
with diamonds, a smile on his face, telling of beautiful and
wonderful things. Manfred would ponder them, gazing
into the eyes of the young man whose only real interest for
him lay in the twinkling of his eyes. Vice's beauty burned
here with its darkest fires: every kiss Manfred might give
in life was here deadly and saturated with scarlet poison.
And every parting from his beloved, every betrayal in love,
scattered bleeding roses over the being he turned his back
on in life.

Every magnificent and dissolute Renaissance youth found
a panegyrist in him: to the very climax of their passions,
he would relate scenes where he cast himself as a spectator,
stunningly fetching in garments rattling with gems and silver, flanked by greyhounds or peacocks, attended by boys
with heads of golden curls and cheeks like ivory and rose
petals. In so doing, he would hobnob with Ezzelino da
Romano[88] or Cesare Borgia,[89] smitten with them, with their
curse and their glory. Like an adept of Guidon Bonatti,[90]
he would read Ezzelino's destiny in the stars so that he
might approach him at an auspicious moment. He would
accompany Cesare Borgia on his nocturnal peregrinations
through Rome, where after magnificent orgies, they would
leave corpses in ransacked bedrooms to wreak terror in the
morning. If he saw beautiful hands that enchanted him,
they were the hands of Galeazzo Maria,[91] proudly reflecting a sickly pallor from his purple cloak. And if he came
home from a gathering, intoxicated with someone's fetching
looks, he would transpose his image to the centuries of the
House of Medici's glorious tournaments, sheathing his bold,
sturdy body in the armor of a mediæval knight on a rearing
charger, its caparison festooned with gold. He would tryst
with whomever he loved exclusively in Florentine palace

chambers, there to inhale the scent, heavy as that of roses, hovering over his lips, there to be dazzled by the other's gaze as if by the glitter of precious stones.

With no greater mystery had the Marquise de Brinvilliers imbued her peculiar poison, more notorious than the Borgias' Acqua Tofana,[92] than Manfred did his words, so profoundly transformative of all I had thought being's essence till then.

Reverent was my hand upon the pages of Manfred's diary, as if I were touching his very core. I wondered how the excerpts I had been reading could transport me into so completely different a psychic state, as if everything around me were giving off the heady, poisonous scent of some arcane perfume: there was a violently overpowering passion to it, a madly heightened pleasure.

XLVIII

At last, the long-awaited name appeared: *Cagliostro*.

The fiction was transforming into reality. I am on the verge of my initiation. I too shall now play my phantasmagoric role as an entity in this diary. What fiction will Manfred choose for me? To what century will he transport me, and in what costume will he drape me?

All that Manfred had been telling of himself accorded with what Cagliostro might have said had he found himself suddenly shunted from the eighteenth century to the present, his soul full of dead questions but still mocking and skeptical. A rueful smile passed over Manfred's pale and careworn face as I reached these chapters, written as if from real life and yet as incredible as accounts from the brink of the most extreme madness.

"Here is where the story begins," said Manfred. "All that came before was mere child's play."

"You are an artist of your own life, Manfred. You embellish your experiences with arabesques and encrust them with jewels. Yet your artistry is less assured at this point. Now that Cagliostro has appeared in your life, you yield to him."

"I yield to Cagliostro because there is but one style I can live by. To experience life in his way means I must leave my own life behind. The extraordinary became ordinary to him, the ordinary exceptional in his presence. The lies he invented were electrified by his style, that is, by his *greatness*. The great problem of his life was precisely that he was disposing of materiality's hypnotism so he could transition to that of fiction. Should he have denied all he saw, just because the common people couldn't see it? Could he help it if those around him suffered from myopia? For Cagliostro, people were nothing but a musical keyboard that his fingers roamed over until they coaxed a particular note from it. Cagliostro would experiment on people. Was that lying? Granted! Depending on the circumstances, the style of an average life may be true or false, but it is always meager. The common people's geniuses have been fanatics for truth. Why shouldn't there also be a genius someday who's a fanatic for lies? Every one of the common people's geniuses has had a purpose. They were humanity's workmen, and that is vulgar. Cagliostro was absolutely without purpose. Therein lies his greatness. Superfluity is a condition of great style. Everybody was after something. Cagliostro was after nothing but his own self, and that is what makes him the greatest."

I sensed that by these words, Manfred meant to conceal some sudden embarrassment. I saw that his eyes were fixed on my hands as they turned the pages of his diary. He grew increasingly restless, as if recalling something whose dissonance rankled him. His finely shaped lips, where all the sensuality of his being seemed concentrated, were trembling and their scarlet was paling.

There was silence all around us, a silence so sepulchral that the slow patter of the dying rain outside was now audible. I had the feeling that time had stopped for a moment.

Our eyes met. Manfred's gaze spoke of such acute suffering that I shuddered to the depths of my soul as if it had been struck by a sudden blow. I guessed that the profound change in Manfred had to do with what I was about to read.

I read one sentence... Then another, a third, and I nearly stopped in amazement... Hadn't someone already said these words to me today? It all sounded so familiar... A thought suddenly emerged in my mind, and it frightened me. I tried to remember. Could this be? Yes...now it came to me...

Manfred and I are sitting together in a loge. The theater lights have been lowered to a deep crimson twilight, the spectators' faces distinguishable within it only as vague whitish smudges. Onstage, an actor is playing Cagliostro. The atmosphere is that of a smoky, dreary, dankly yellowish day. Cagliostro, as disgusted with people as a clown in a fit of spleen, has fled to scoff in privacy at life, death, and the irreal quality of everything. That monologue—of a sharpened aversion to everything, when the soul perceives corporeality as contagion, life's bitterness mounting within it like some monstrous artisanal work that scatters ashes upon the withered heart—became so firmly lodged in my mind as to be unforgettable.

In Manfred's diary, I was now reading all I had heard at the theater. There could be no question of any delusion. I was only hesitant to voice the irrefutable certainty that had taken root in my mind.

Manfred seemed to read my inmost thoughts. His eyes had the look of one trying to catch hold of the elusiveness that is a dream.

"Well, Francis, now do you understand?"

"I'm confused, Manfred. Could this really be possible?"

"Didn't you find those words familiar? Didn't you recognize the fateful coincidence in them?"

I did not understand what Manfred meant. But though the words were wrenched from my lips against my will, I said:

"Manfred, are you—Walter Mora?"

Manfred merely lifted his eyebrows, surprised at the question. For a second, a slight flush colored his pale cheeks. He stood stock still for a moment, his eyes alone glinting brighter. Something seemed to be at work within him, something with which he was struggling mightily. My conjecture had given him a sudden shock. Something hidden was resonating within those depths, a feeling that made him shiver wildly. But then, regaining his self-control, he said firmly and with emphasis:

"You are mistaken, Francis. I am not Walter Mora. Were I he, had his play been nothing but a dramatization of this diary, there would be no mystery. Nor would having an identical thought have meant anything. Is of no importance if two personalities have the same thought. For the same idea can produce virtue or vice, a saint or a criminal. The same idea doesn't preclude distinctions. Remember life as we live it in the average way. We never actually do what we want. We want things and do the opposite. Do you know how that looks to me? As if someone were foisting our life upon us, as if it'd been predetermined before we started to live it. Just think of how we talk to people! There's such a disparity between what we say and what we feel that at times, if we stop and listen to ourselves, we may think someone else is speaking. We possess a craven instinct not to seem different than other people, and so we say and do things we otherwise would not. Only when we're alone, with no one watching, do our own personalities come out. Our similarity to others fades away, and we're each preposterous or mad in our own way. If Walter Mora were to say the things I say when I'm around people, that wouldn't frighten me. But Walter Mora does say things I say to myself when I'm alone, things I confess from the most secret depths of my core. Now tell me how there can exist another being as inspired by Cagliostro as I? This is a mystery, as harrowing as the precipice of a terrible danger. The apparition at the temple of St. Jakub cast the first shadow across my path. But this second one, this second specter, is ghastlier still. For if previously I'd been able to remain alone, today I must ask you, Francis, to share my burden..."

"Couldn't one take the same path to reach the same outcome without there necessarily being anything ghastly about it? It should be possible. We can live our lives whether we're either completely indifferent or oblivious. Once we reflect on life, all we can see is how shabby it is. And we then seek refuge in fictions. It's entirely possible that another soul could have been as inspired by Cagliostro as you, Manfred."

"Of course it is. Cagliostro's tale, however exceedingly grotesque it may seem, is in essence a tale like anyone else's. It contains an *actuated* humanity. Each of us harbors something of Cagliostro within us, but we don't each have his audacious genius to make our dreams reality. We don't each have the audacity to exchange an inferior life for a glorious illusion, the way alchemy changes base metal into gold. It is certain that the tales of Cagliostro, the great lies of his life, are worth more than all the petty and miserable truths of sober folk who wish to create the impression of gravitas, enormous gravitas, especially when they're being absolutely narrow-minded as they explain the truth of some matter, when they have no idea what they're talking about. If we dwell upon these zealots of petty truths, we shall learn to despise the truth more than is unavoidably necessary. For even in and of itself, the truth wouldn't be as trite as it becomes in the grip of these narrow minds. But to think that, since the time I assumed Cagliostro's style of life as the successor to it, someone else's enigmatic existence has been getting in my way as if to threaten me and scare me off, and showing me not his *resemblance*, which would merely humble my pride, but his *identicality*, which is a terrifying thing—I can only conclude that I have an enemy bent on the destruction of my being, of my life's work. I saw him in St. Jakub's. Isn't he also concealed beneath the mask of Walter Mora? Why does he not only have my face but even say my own words to me now? Look at how I've altered in a single evening, Francis! My enemy is glorying over me in triumph. Yesterday I could still laugh at least outwardly, if no longer inwardly. But today... what storms in my soul, and what gloom in my eyes...! As I left the theater where I'd listened to Walter Mora's play, I brought the influence of this enigmatic poetic fiction away with me, as powerful and injurious as a mortal wound we bear from the tumult of battle. I suspect the end is near, the inevitable end of everything."

XLIX

It was nearly morning when we returned from Cagliostro's room to the chambers on the first floor. What a night it had been! Never in entire years had I experienced so much as in those few hours.

The servant was already awaiting Manfred's orders and bringing in coffee and cigarettes. His calm mask signified only that he was used to his master's caprices.

With a final star in the cold, chill amethyst sky, a cloudless, silvery, liquid morning was breaking outside, and things were revealing themselves in forms somehow dreary and wan. Amid the garden foliage, the birds were chirping insistently on a single note, and this solitary sound seemed only to intensify the deathly silence inside the house, where the mirrors, turbid as if from a dream, were wakening their surfaces, and where the tapers lit late last night were guttering on the candelabra.

From night's unreality, all was now coming back to sober life. There was a growing sense of urgency to resume the daytime activities interrupted by yesterday's nighttime. But for me, all I had lived until now seemed forgotten. It felt like years since I'd had contact with Max Duniecki. And yet I had been his friend only yesterday...

L

That same day, Manfred had my things moved to his palace. Since that night's strange events, he had utterly changed his way of life.

He remained in seclusion with me for the first week. The servant informed all visitors that Manfred was ill.

After that, we started to ride out into the streets in a closed carriage. At my urging, Manfred began to appear in public again, but he made himself unapproachable and no longer received anyone at the palace.

The change in his behavior gave rise to a veritable swarm of bizarre tales. Everyone was trying to fathom Manfred's secret. Whenever he turned up somewhere with me at his side, I could feel the stares directed at us and the whispering in the corners that gave off an air of malice and jeering. Yet Manfred took no notice of any of those things that annoyed me. His pale face showed no engagement whatsoever with the one he was looking at, or with those trying to look at him.

A dangerously dark spell accompanied Manfred. Even the most superficial people who once boasted of intimacy with him could sense it, though Manfred had only mockery for them before. Their eyes would turn toward me as well. I strove to face them down with the most malicious smile I could muster. Manfred had the reputation of a man whose friendship held fateful consequences for young men. They all now looked at me as his new victim, a cat's-paw for his fancies. Yet within their scorn was a quivering curiosity eager to fathom me as well. So I made myself as interesting as possible to justify my career as a lover. I enhanced my presence with a certain wicked perfume. I would provoke them with preposterous outfits and attitudes of distinguished refinement to suggest that, seduced by Manfred, I had lost all sense of respect or esteem for anyone else.

Manfred now became perfectly indifferent to everything that had annoyed him previously. While he had been scornful of people before as well, at least he was interested in their appearance. He had needed people, handsome young men, for the same reason he did perfumes and flowers: for pleasure, for something to stimulate the senses. Now he lost interest in everything. Once so superbly capable in his treatment of people, beaming with happiness and delight at their expense, he was now nervous should anyone approach him.

"How intolerable they are!" he would sigh when we were left alone. "They show not a single flaw: their tedium is consummate, and as a result, they can be serious only in the face of tedium, for this is their sole form of social intercourse. They make no effort to live, they don't interfere in their destiny: they let chance do all the work for them. They deem our friendship a scandal, they whose passions are nothing more than animal: for our love is a subtle essence, something entirely beyond this world, a deity with inscrutable eyes. I understand that to Cagliostro they were nothing but raw material for contemptuous jests. This farceur of other people also had his melancholia, gnawing away at his life, moments when, alone and far from people, he would sneer at how ludicrous existence was: if he did go among people, this was only an instant of raging vengeance to make fools of humanity. They've spoiled everything, even the grandiosity of the lie. They permit falsehood, but in small increments, as they employ poisons, only up to a certain dosage. They have spoiled vice. They permit it in every form from fornication to murder, but only if perpetrated in cowardice, that is, furtively and without causing offense. Their morality is all greyness. But by the devil! let them show some integrity; what I can't stand is that they make a show of their integrity. Integrity should be hidden away like a bodily infirmity. For integrity tolerates only mediocrity and values only boredom. Integrity adores greyness. It sees whatever has color, fire, passion, as a transgression. To deal with people is to surrender one's individuality. To associate with them is a sacrifice in itself: to conform, for their sake, to their prejudices about us, we become who we're not. In fact, there are hardly five people we might care for: and we never actually meet them. All our lives, we talk to people we find unpleasant and who oblige us to amuse them. All our lives, we corrupt only our own morals instead of anyone else's, which is the only sensible thing to do."

LI

How many dreams I now wove around Manfred's being, beautiful, hopeless dreams—for they were born of dread that my fevered eyes should one day see their miserable end: I was dazzled by Manfred, by his every look, his every gesture, the dark splendor of his inner rhythm. But though Manfred loved me, he could still keep his misgivings about me: he never allowed me any *dominance* over himself. He nourished only my sweet adoration and his own being's enchanting charms. He enclosed me in a magic circle that left no escape, and within it, he racked my heart with cruel grace, as if on some torture device, with all his caprices. But so passive was I that I bore my destiny with devotion.

A single personality now preoccupied us both, emerging from the powdery grey background of its spectrality: Walter Mora. A sinister, magical star, a terrifying specter that we longed to comprehend, but it was no use. The real Walter Mora would never step forward from his fictionality. We made attempts to strip away his pseudonym. But in the theater where the mysterious *Cagliostro* was staged, we were told that the author had forbidden any betrayal of his identity.

He remained a chimæra. Like a cloud, he hovered over all our conjectures. We could never latch onto even the least ephemeral fact about him. Our imagination would work all the more furiously. Something red, infernally red, shrouded him in dusky shadows. His eyes had a look never found in any human gaze, and his heart was filled with a madness hitherto unknown to any.

"Does he even exist?" I wondered, as time went on.

"He does indeed!" Manfred would reply. "And should he exert such intense influence on us from afar with that sphinxlike expression of his, should he have such power to nourish flames within us, think what an inferno he could unleash at our core if he came near, overpowered us, and experimented on us! He is surely one of the pirates on the Sea of Dreams,[33] black as the rock whereon errant ships are dashed, brute and beautiful as if pale candles had traced his form at midnight in a darkly ebony mirror. He is surely as contemptuous of everything as Cagliostro, despising glory, reveling in others' mockery, haughtily dismissive of them."

I could sense that Manfred was bent on apprehending and overpowering him using this idea, the way others use their arms. Manfred had been inspired by Walter Mora but now sought to inspire *him* across the distance. Though the fire was consuming him, Manfred strove to hurl its flames to that distant being's depths, to spark there the same madness tearing at himself.

LII

Without Manfred's knowledge, I attempted to contact Walter Mora. I wrote him a letter that I left at the theater, requesting that it be forwarded.

Never had I known greater turmoil than while waiting for his reply. Would he respond? Or would he keep silent? Would he remain an impassive enigma, an impenetrable terror?

The thing was done... I had screamed into the darkness, waiting for some echo. I was so tense and preoccupied that even Manfred noticed my uneasiness. He found my skin suddenly dull and noticed grey bags under my eyes. He questioned me as to what was worrying me and suspected I was up to something peculiar. But he did not know what a risky step I had taken...

Many days went by... and still no response. I spent long, forlorn hours in waiting. As if on a misty horizon, I could now make out something new in Manfred's eyes. The black brutality of their bonfires was shading into languid tones, opalescent with weariness and yearning. He was steadily weakening, and I had to nurse and coddle him like a child.

We had ceased to speak of what once alarmed us, what used to fill us with terror. A bleak silence, a desolate apathy and indifference had overcome us.

Finally, one morning the letter I had almost ceased to hope for arrived. Yet it caught my eye at once in the mail that the servant always brought in, and I took it out before Manfred could notice.

I locked myself in my room. Violent chills ran through me as I held the letter in my hand. I could not explain why I was so agitated. Was there anything so mad, so bold, in writing to an author whose work had interested me? And yet... the very sight of this letter inspired horror and awe.

I seemed to be holding some kind of grotesque mask. My name on the envelope seemed the syllabary of something terrible.[94]

The letter in my hand felt like the testament to some terrible fate.

Shall I open and read it? I was gripped by the temptation to cast the letter unread into the fireplace. But I could not bring myself to do it. From inside the envelope, as if from out of the letter, Walter Mora forbade me to destroy it, with the gesture of one created, like Manfred, to rule over the souls of others. Could I resist that magical injunction?

Only after some moments did I notice the return address on the letter. It was from Prague. I was stricken with horror, as if presented with some terrifying, tangible portent of all that was to come.

So then, Walter Mora lives in Prague... in Prague, home to the towering temple of St. Jakub, where Manfred saw his specter. Roiled by this strange new fact, my imagination began to run wild with the most bizarre conjectures. Was Walter Mora not the very apparition Manfred had seen at the tomb of the Counts Vratislav? Like anyone addled by things beyond his ken, I instantly took my conjecture for fact. My horror now all the greater, I stared at the mysterious letter I held, at the paper where that shadowy hand had written my name, as if thus pronouncing a sentence of the most agonizing, desperate torment upon it. The inferno now in store for Manfred and me had tickled me with the first of its flames. It had hurled the first heat of its furnace in my face, as if to mock the destiny I had called upon myself.

I now knew I ought not to read the letter alone and must take Manfred into my confidence. I felt too weak, too vulnerable, before the magical influence Walter Mora had begun to exert upon me.

Grieved, almost anguished, I went into Manfred's room. I was overwhelmed with remorse that I had presumed to act without consulting him. Yet once I laid the letter before Manfred's eyes, there was no need for me to apologize or explain anything. Manfred instantly guessed everything.

An expression of horror dawned on his features. His hand clenched in convulsive defiance. But he immediately regained his composure, mastering the stormy flush of blood that had surged to his cheeks. His usual pallor restored, he was nevertheless trembling with anxiety, as if some mysterious fluidum's[95] violently flickering sparks were coursing through him.

"Walter Mora—and in Prague! I was not mistaken. He's the one! The one who came to me at the Vratislav tomb!"

The pupils of his eyes flared like a fire banked in ashes.

"Walter Mora *does exist*. With this letter, he puts some part of his being within our grasp. What a wonderful stratagem you've devised without knowing it, Francis! We have a piece of paper where his hand has rested and with the traces of letters he has written, trapping his thoughts therein. The tables have turned. My courage is coming back to me. My every undertaking shall now possess the fiery depth I've always craved, the savage audacity that shall thwart Walter Mora's schemes and frustrate his insidious, clandestine ploys."

A blazing pallor lit Manfred's face with a terrible, deathly beauty. His eyes flared like two fierce forges of suddenly ignited fire. What an inferno raged within his forehead's fragile vessel! What plots had his exquisitely afflicted mind hatched! Was it a tabernacle where some idea lay hidden like a profane Host, the symbol of a Black Mass, where none other than Satan had ensconced himself in all his accursed glory? An infernal Pentecost had brought its flame down upon this inspired head. Illumined by a fiery tongue of sudden, magical power, with burning joy in his heart, Manfred suddenly spoke the terrible and glorious words:

"*Francis, I shall hunt down Walter Mora and capture him...*"

LIII

He fiercely tore the letter's envelope open and took out a page with three letters at the top: *L. P. D.*

"Cagliostro's motto!" Manfred exclaimed in surprise. "*Lilium pedibus distrue!*"[96]

Here is what Walter Mora wrote:

"I write you from a city watched over at night by stars that seem to yearn for another Wallenstein[97] to ask them to tell his future. But in vain! None wants to know his destiny. The lineage of astronomers has died out, and the alchemical fires in the houses of the Golden Lane behind the Dalibor Tower burn no more. And neither Tycho de Brahe nor Kepler now prepares horoscopes for the melancholy Rudolf II.[98] Magic has become a science that some study and ridicule, while others ridicule it in ignorance.

"Here I live, a miserable adept in a kind of exile. And yet, I feel there is nowhere else I could live. Only here do the past and all I have experienced in other existences speak to me. Here do I dream my faded dreams and suffer my bygone torments anew. I read what is written in my heart and in myself, as if in some terrifying book of sorrows. I read my former destinies and temptations. And confounded by all this, my soul trembles, and my head is bowed down with an impalpable heaviness and anguish.

"So too did Cagliostro one day arrive: the resplendent Cagliostro, all in tragic black and infernal scarlet, with all the passion of his being, loving only the extraordinary and the accursed. He appeared against the dark background of my dreams, and in his shadow, I recognized a brother. I followed him and walked through the mysterious realm where he reigns. But then I saw that he was no phantom, that he was human like me: that his heart was full of suffering, and that his silence is as much a burden to him as it is upon my own lips. He neither spoke nor discoursed with me. He only looked at me. And in the abysses of his eyes, on the mirrors of their darkness, I could read the silent answers to my unspoken questions.

"And all at once, his secret became my own.

"For the one walking at my side was no longer Cagliostro.

"He was—I myself..."

LIV

When we finished reading this letter, I looked up at Manfred. I shall never forget the expression that Walter Mora's words produced in those eyes. They were suddenly gushing with a hatred no will could vanquish.

"How I loathe him! Do you understand, Francis? Walter Mora is robbing me of my style of life, of the sole reason for my existence... If he becomes the successor to the style of Cagliostro's life, my own life is an absurdity. It can only come to battle between us. We cannot but inflict terrible blows upon each other, under which one or the other must fall. For our gazes strike deep into each other's core, penetrating the most hidden recesses. One of us must therefore stand down. I shall go to Prague, Francis, and force Walter Mora out from the shadows..."

I began to shudder as I saw this surge of unexpected madness in Manfred's soul. As for me, for whom all that mattered was Manfred's tender, loving heart, and who now watched that splendid nature hurl its devastating fulminations against some distant, mysterious foe, my consciousness was wrenched by the certainty that Manfred was lost to me, irretrievably lost. I was helpless in my love, stupefied with fealty to my friend: his hatred of Walter Mora was stronger than his sympathy for me, whose fascinating idol he was smashing, and whose aching lips he was poisoning with the rancor he harbored for his enemy.

Seeing the excruciating pain in my eyes, Manfred might have grasped something of the abyss that had opened in my heart. With one of those grim embraces he was so fond of choking me with, he clenched me to himself to calm the storm within him.

I began to implore Manfred to think no more of Walter Mora or his vendetta to force his rival out from his mysterious obscurity. But it was no use. Manfred was aflame with unquenchable hate. Darkly but firmly, he said:

"I shall overwhelm him as Cagliostro did the magician Schröpfer. When Schröpfer began to denigrate the Egyptian rite, Cagliostro predicted death would take him within a month. He induced suicidal thoughts in his adversary—and before a month was out, Schröpfer had taken his own life under that inexorable magical pressure."[99]

"You are destroying me, Manfred, by exposing yourself to the danger of these devious magical influences. I love you more than you can imagine; I love you outlandishly, senselessly, in a way no one could understand. From the moment you permitted me to be your friend, the world became a place of wonder for me. Even were there no God in such mad loves, even were it only a demon stoking and guiding it—I want to experience this love for you, Manfred, like a ray of enraptured divinity, like something white and sacred even in profane hands. Ah, laugh at me, for I know how senseless my ecstasy must look to your cold, overly skeptical heart, so practiced in cynicism! ... But don't destroy yourself, at least; I would willingly become a mere object of your scorn, to be despised and cast aside..."

"It would be weak of for me to back down in this, Francis. Your place is at my side, to fortify me with your love. Have you lost the nerve to do so? Without you, I'd be weaker than Walter Mora. With you, I'm capable of overpowering him. But whether you stay or go, I'll tell you one thing: you are the only person I've ever loved in all my absurd life. For you I lay aside all poses, for you whose poignant charm makes me stand erect and for whose every word of love that ripples across your sweetly turned lips, for you I wait with longing. You are meant to be the element of light to my darkness. You are to be the flora in my deserts, the ecstasy in my skepticism. Don't deny the magic of intimate coexistence: let bloom what should flower, let flame what should flame!"

I could not resist these words of passion. Manfred was one of those natures we belong to forever once we have succumbed to them for a single instant. I was in his thrall. He thrilled me to the core, entering into my mind and obscuring the clarity of my emotions there.

I sensed that something staggering lay in store for Manfred and me. His personality subsumed my entire being. I thought of him even when alone. My autonomy faded still further when he was with me, when he touched me and intoxicated me with his breath. I saw everything differently. I thought entirely different thoughts. I experienced a life I had never known.

Manfred was constantly within me. Constant was the flow of his influence's magnetic current into my body. But I sensed at the same time that before my friendship with Manfred, what I had been living was not life. I sensed that my memory of life would be this alone, what my youthfulness was now living with Manfred. That I would only ever recall what his passion was now hurling into my heart like crimson flames. And for that reason, I longed to enchant him with fiery beauty, to be as intoxicating to him as light and fragrance.

I could not help but feel now that each passing day brought me closer to a thing so grimly terrifying, a thing that would make me suffer: that never would a smile return to this easy heart plunging me so passionately into mere existence, as if into some wondrously flowering pleasure. Yet I wanted to banish this though as well. What I wanted was to be alive again, to live empowered, to squander all I held dearest, to scatter all my magenta star-blossoms into Manfred's path for him, and to strew as many outlandish blood-red anthuriums over it as he wished for, the anthuriums of extreme passions.

Then let dark fate come! Everything chosen is linked to tragedy. As we pass through life in the infernally crimson glow of evil magical forces, coloring our deepest selves as if with the smoke of the underworld's censers, we shall multiply glorious youth's passion surrounded by the scent of ominous, dizzying pleasure, making things others never dream of come true. I wanted to be Manfred's fair-haired boy, with eyes darkening like malachite and lips succulent as the juice of grapes: a being who blended the physical with the psychical, a marvelous instrument he could use to play mad variations on pleasure and sin. I wanted to inhabit his fictional realm with him, with Cagliostro's shadow keeping time, in a life lived by no one else, giving form to his dreams and substance to his phantoms.

LV

I wrote several more times to Walter Mora. Yet he never responded again. Perhaps he sensed a trap.

In black magic, if we concentrate our thoughts on a being, even a complete stranger, there is a familiar ritual whereby we lay claim to a particular word that instantly empowers us to learn our object's secrets. My own questions were of a similar sort. Was Walter Mora worried lest one of his imprudently handwritten words should enable me to peer into his inner depths? Or had he guessed that my inquiries were not mine alone but also from his secret nemesis, standing in my shadow?

Manfred would often take Walter Mora's letter from a dark, scented wooden box with a nacreous inlay, where he kept all his secrets. He read it over and over again.

But once he was sure Walter Mora would make no further reply, he announced that we would be taking a trip. There was no question of where. I knew perfectly well we were going to Prague.

LVI

Manfred's palace in Prague, near the temple of St. Jindřich,[100] returned to life from under its spell yet retained the sorrowful air that reigns over all the things and buildings of this city.

The very next day after our arrival, still tired from the journey and the move, we went wandering about Prague, through its dark and hushed streets, entering the melancholy and deserted churches. We even went to the temple of St. Jakub, approaching it by way of the Týn courtyard. Manfred's heart was palpitating sharply as we neared the black façade in all its enormous bulk: but the temple was utterly empty, and the Madonna was dozing away in the shadows, unillumined, bleak, distant. In the church's emptiness, it seemed even vaster. The only sound inside was that of our footsteps. There was something of the isolation of an abandoned cemetery no longer visited by any aching hearts to make confession.

At moments, we would come to a stop. Manfred's excitement was so great that I pleaded for us to leave. I could feel how he was reliving all the apparitions he had ever seen here. Though invisible, Walter Mora was with us. It occurred to me that we were like his prisoners, with him continually mocking our anxieties from the safety of his hiding place.

We walked the length of the cloister courtyard, strolling along its ambulatories. In the diminished light of that cloudy day, I had the sense that we were lost in the shadows of the dreadful Escorial[101] as we wandered the vast edifice's desolate corridors. Silent and dejected, we left by way of Templar Lane.[102] When I glanced into Manfred's face, he seemed to have suddenly aged, oppressed by this atmosphere of gloom.

We made such outings day after day. For the most part, we wandered the streets at twilight and late at night, when everything expands to grandiose proportions in the illusive light of the moon. From the embankment, we would gaze down at the river flowing through the city with a wistful, funereal solemnity, and at the brooding silhouette of the Castle, whence blew a melancholy breeze as from a ruin. The long, bare building, dark as a prison, made a dispiriting impression on us. It seemed to symbolize all the vanity of this land that had outlived its glory.

LVII

Yet we felt that nowhere were our souls more intensely alive than right here in this tragic city, with its towers where the heads of lordly rebels were once impaled, and its square that ran with noble blood from the gallows.[103] Here alone has the past's painful beauty been so richly concentrated that it will last a lifetime for one who lives in dreams and is dead in reality.

None listened more ardently to the soul of this glorious city than Manfred. He saw so many things, so many invisible powers here in every location, more than those who looked only at the present could guess at.

The past here spoke things to Manfred that the present told no one. Walking through the Temple, he was aware that he was crossing the sepulcher of the mysterious Commandery[104] of the Knights Templar, who once gathered here in the underground vaults for forbidden rites. He could hear the echo of their chants and the somber droning of their prayers, and he could see the altar, the accursed altar where the Templars performed their rites. And elsewhere, in dead, outlying streets, he showed me houses marked with cryptic signs over their doorways. Everyone walking past was completely indifferent, but Manfred knew the meaning of the heptagon, triangle, spoon, compass, hammer, or globe on the ancient building's escutcheon. He told me of how he would often enter such places at twilight, at that moment when mysterious things are able to speak to us, put his forehead to the wall, and think of all that these brooding surfaces had seen and heard. And he would then see and hear such things as no one had ever imagined. Of these houses, the records in the old archives told how Masonic lodges had been based there, but this was a designation for the outside world, and only the initiated knew the secrets they harbored.

This was how Manfred lived here, and he would impart ancient confidences. He could hear the passions, struggles, temptations, and despair of those who had lived before him. And he would hear them unendingly, day and night—and consort with powers that shook his existence and yet had no voice except through him.

It was in Prague where Manfred grasped his own mystery, Prague where he intuited that he could see signs in the sky at night, in stars heralding extraordinary things that were to come, unforeseen by any. He possessed the eyes of Tycho de Brahe and Kepler, the force of the stars' superior authority that, in the words of Paracelsus, is the mark of a magician.

He would come to a stop at the Castle at midnight and gaze at the sky and out over the city. He would see the phenomena passing over Prague in cloudlike veils, in shades of darkness, green stars quivering in terror, and phantoms wailing and moaning as if calling to something that is no more. He would ride on the winds that blew from the plains of Bílá Hora, and on them would graze the ancient palaces' cornices and pantile roofs, and weep and keen in the crowns of the old trees. And he would sense that there is a deeper darkness than that of night, and a profounder grief than that in the human heart...

LVIII

In time, I grew accustomed to Manfred's palace, where from the start I felt how cold it was in this long-unoccupied, gloomy building. It was a magnificent structure, its portal with the ornamental capitals of its pilasters, Baroque garlands, crenelated dentil cornices over the windows, cartouches, infills, vases, stone busts, and other details of the façade making it a work of pure style. But the most graceful touch of all was the cantilevered eaves running the entire length of the façade, above which the pantile rooftop's dormers projected. Within the courtyard, there sighed the melancholy of oblivion, and the same air of sorrow pervaded the vast gardens behind the palace, long since untended and left to grow wild, with their huge old trees, strewn with springtime snow flowers as if with white stars.

A wistful mood would lay hold of me as I walked through the house where Manfred's forebears had lived and died. The mysteriousness of their beings now also held sway in my own soul that had become intimate with their latter-day descendant and shouldered his destiny together with him.

From every object here, long-dead eyes would stare at me. From every rustle in the extensive corridors, I could hear the echo of a sigh exhaled long ago. I felt sorrowful in these chambers, where the walls and ceilings seemed still to see all that used to go on here years before, and the dream of some ancient family tragedies still seemed to haunt them. Throwing a door open, I always felt an oppressive fear that I would come upon some lingering specter wandering about here, sighing over a family relic, or glimpse the shadow of a cloak and hear the clanking spur of a cavalier briefly abandoning his portrait frame to disturb the chamber's deathly stillness with footsteps on the cracked and creaky parquet.

Yet the palace's most outlandish room of all was the library. In addition to the usual works of eighteenth- and early nineteenth-century belles lettres, it had a special section containing the biographies of madmen, criminals, and suicides, their breasts once aflame with some passionate destiny. It was the private collection of Manfred's uncle, who had died by his own hand.

LIX

It was Manfred's and my custom to sit in his study, decorated with melancholy old yellow Chinese wallpaper. The room was hung with Oriental fabrics embroidered with gorgeously feathered exotic birds. There was a mélange of Chinese and Japanese antiques, vases, models, and weapons, all looking lifeless and fit for a museum.

I tried to be a calming influence on Manfred, attempting to guide his life into routines of peace and quiet. I would offer him mental diversion. Sometimes I succeeded so well that I had hopes of dissociating Manfred from his morbid notions. We would start to live again and discover life's charms.

Yet Manfred would have none of it. We would not live but only look on at life, letting all the world's sins and pleasures pass us by as if in mute symbols. Our life would become purely the stuff of dreams, vague and indecipherable, of what comes upon the soul only at the close of day, at twilight, with the creeping shadows.

Despite this, I intuited some continual inner struggle in Manfred. We would speak every so often of Paracelsus, his arcane knowledge of the hidden powers of plants and the healing magic of metals. Paracelsus' demon Archeus took hold in Manfred's mind.[105] The notion of a kindred demon dwelling deep within someone, practicing all the arts of alchemy and turning nutrients into blood, resonated deeply with Manfred. But at times, an enemy comes and ousts that person's Archeus, taking its place, intending there to practice his experiments. Had some hostile demon likewise taken possession of Manfred's inner self, there to ply the artifices that had caused his illness? But there is no physician who can expel a malefic demon and thus secure Archeus' return. What remains for him? To wander about this life a gloomy, cursed shade that endures its ultimate fate in this immutable malediction.

He would stand up, restless, his movements sluggish and fitful, as if all the despair and torpor of his soul had passed into them. His head, so exhausted by the blazes of hell, had no hope of ever finding another soul to cool its searing pain. Then I too would be overcome with despair. Manfred's pain would wound me like a poisoned dagger.

There are moments in life when we cannot distinguish our fantasies from the phantoms that frighten us. We hear confused voices either from within ourselves or from a mysterious someone outside us; we do not know. Such a time was now upon us. There was someone else with us, at times so blended with our presences that we could not tell his existences apart. Yet exist he did, terrifyingly real, though we would not even speak his name: Walter Mora. There was no trace of him in the streets, churches, or houses that we passed through. Yet he was always near. He never left us for a second.

Manfred often felt remorse at having dragged me into this fate of his. He loved me with all the goodness of his soul, he whom evil alone charmed and fascinated. But having forsaken religiosity and its notions of good and evil, in black magic he rediscovered that ray of humanity he had meant to smother in himself. He was tender even when tormenting me. I suppose he prayed, too, scorning the saints but solicitous of demons and their damnation. As he poured the grace of faith into his disbelief, so would he mingle the ecstasy of tenderness with brutality as he dragged my being into the abyss. As he practiced religion without God, saturating his defiance of Him with mystical enthusiasm, so too would he practice love without affection, showing his pleasure not with caresses but with crushing embraces.

Manfred often wondered whether I would ever love another besides him. In his curiosity, there was a note of sorrow: after someone else did come into my life, whether I would look with indifference, or reproach, on the one who had taught me what love and friendship are. I tried to dispel this conjecture, assuring him that I wanted him to remain the sole passion of my existence. But he would only implore me to understand his passion and forgive him his wickedness. In this way, he would waver and vacillate, a neverending medley of opposites. He would stir my love and then try to suppress it. Half his life was spent building up what the other would tear down. What the one would avow, the other would gainsay.

But I could no longer be without Manfred. Even when apart from him, I never considered whether my life was imaginable without him. For I had grown accustomed to acting solely under his stimulus. Passive by nature, forever meant to be a clinging plant in the foliage of life, by now I was more bewildered than ever. I had developed an understanding of how all this might end. My posture and bearing alike evidenced sluggish resignation. The magnetism of constant close contact, of constant coexistence, were making me into a mere reflection of Manfred. He was the dominant element in our friendship, whereas I was becoming ever more womanishly servile by the day. When I did find myself alone, however much I wanted to imagine myself a more distinct person and intervene in Manfred's destiny—he needed only come near and fix his eyes on me, and I would be powerless to act except as he wished; he, one of a kind, having nothing in common with others and living a destiny lived by no one else. I believed his power to captivate me was the very magnetism Cagliostro had exerted on people. Even if his revelations initially struck me as absurd, his paradoxes seeming forced and unnatural, when I was later alone and reflecting on things Manfred had told me, all the seeds he had planted within me suddenly blossomed into intense, poisonous purple flowers from the inscrutable foliage of his words.

He was cultivating me, igniting a magical consciousness in me. I had become his adept. For I felt that to possess Manfred's friendship was to grow, and to lose it was to be deprived of something. That to be together with him meant boldness and strength, and to be without him, weakness and ignorance. In Paracelsian terms, I had become his satellite, for he had acquired an absolute influence over me. My entire imagination was occupied with him alone. Like a destiny, he drew me to himself. He steered me as a magnet does the pointer in a compass. He mesmerized all my emotions save one: the instinct to assimilate myself to him. A weak, tiny pointer, I was no longer able to turn away from my despotic North.

LX

Walter Mora did not turn up anywhere. We did not speak his name—but we searched for him all the more intensively. We would dodge the word like a drawn saber but wanted to meet the specter head on, however inscrutable and injurious he might be. Deep within myself, this yearning was beginning to tilt sharply toward madness. I knew Manfred could no longer help but aggravate this urge within my soul.

I had no desire for gratification, which could not have been anything more than a dispiriting emptiness. But at the least, I wanted our anxiety, our passion, to advance from this tortured anguish to definite, full-fledged pain. I was tormented by this enemy who was only a menace and never materialized anywhere. I craved the magical thrill of the first battle with him as I would the magic of one's first adventure.

Manfred became more spiritual now, as if recalling Swedenborg's dictum that "we are all spirits inwardly," at our core.[106] His elemental body was subjugated to his sidereal one.[107] He gained that *clarity of vision in the darkness* that Agrippa von Nettesheim describes, in which the spirit is less fettered by the senses and sheds its subjection to the body, its dependence on it, and sees what the corporeal eye could not.

Often, I would tremble as I sensed some part of what was passing through Manfred's mind. I knew that though with me in body, he was with Walter Mora in spirit, keeping his eye on him, conscious of his every movement. Manfred would tell me such specific things about Walter Mora that I thought the latter was in the room with us. Even if Manfred could see his enemy so plainly, some magical power kept him from knowing just *where* Walter Mora was living. Manfred could describe the chamber, the laboratory where Walter Mora worked. But its direction he did not know. He would often dash out of the palace only to return in perplexity a moment later. I would watch Manfred with a mixture of wonder and awe.

Sometimes he nearly terrified me. Something like a shadow might flicker in the street below, past our windows.

"Walter Mora!" Manfred would exclaim.

But before he could get outside, the apparition, if it existed at all, had vanished.

LXI

Manfred often wished to go out alone, without my company. He would leave in the evening and to return to the palace late at night. He had some secret purpose. There was a secrecy to his doings.

I was not offended at not being taken into his confidence, only fearing for his safety. I knew every magician must work in perfect solitude. I suspected Manfred was making attempts to capture the person of Walter Mora with magic. Instinctively, I sensed how dangerous this experimentation was, though I had never been initiated into esoteric truths. But I asked no questions of Manfred. Nor did I ever dare touch on these matters with him. I only suspected that they were Hermetic truths[108] like those mysterious eternal lamps in Memphis' ancient underground tombs, found burning after fifteen centuries, that would be instantly extinguished if *desecrated*.[109] And would my own curiosity not likewise desecrate them?

Sometimes I also thought about Manfred's hatred for Walter Mora. Hatred for him who had taken *our style of life* from us, hatred for this identical figure—how inscrutable it all was to me! But my love for Manfred was like a slope where my soul was scudding heedlessly downhill.

I could feel his emotions and his malice because he felt them so keenly. Magnetized toward him by love, I also had to keep up this enmity toward Walter Mora, since Manfred hated him so madly, so inextinguishably.

Inside, I was filled with perpetual anxiety for Manfred. The darknesses where he worked to achieve his adversary's capture, so that with these arcane magical powers he might draw him in and destroy him, filled me with dread. Even as Manfred returned to me from them, there would always be something different about his face. I knew then—he had beheld the mysteries. But the dejection in his eyes betrayed the utter failure of all his efforts till then. Walter Mora remained untouchable and unassailable despite all Manfred's magical manipulations.

LXII

As time went on, Manfred's outings worried me more and more. For when night would fall and the palace stood solitary in the darkness, I was scared to death in there. A deep shiver of dread would run through me, especially when Manfred was very late in returning.

Then I would stay up waiting for him, alarmed by every sound from the street. This worrying over his destiny left me shaken. I would get the notion that he'd never come back at all, as if he had meanwhile fallen into Walter Mora's secret clutches in some mysterious way.

Walter Mora! He seemed to be constantly hemming us in with various snares. He had us where he wanted us and was merely toying with us. He was the most terrifying of enemies. He was near us and yet invisible. He could wound us, while our magical influence could not touch him. There was a wall between us, but a wall that set him apart from us without preventing him from getting at us.

Feverishly, I quivered with impatience and dread if Manfred was late in coming home. I often wanted to leave the palace and find him, but I could not venture far, unsure whether he would return in the meantime and be alarmed at my absence. The palace and its silence, so deep and grave-like, would all close in upon me like a dismal pall. No sound was now mere sound but the sign of a sinister presence, nor any silence mere silence but a deathly quiet that set the stage for Walter Mora, invisible and yet present, to speak some fateful words to me.

I would sometimes rush into the deserted corridors, if only for my footsteps to make a little noise in the stagnation of this slumbering edifice. Sometimes I would give a shout inside the chamber as if to show Walter Mora I was ready for him. But then—I would get the sudden sense that the shout had come not from me but from someone else. My own voice would be so inexplicably alien to me that I went rigid with horror. The thought struck me: do I really know what kind of past has me surrounded here? Do I know the significance of the face in this portrait staring so sternly down at me from the wall? Do I know who that is, leaning against the edge of that table over there, in the grip of madness? Do I know who has trod this parquet, weighed down by destiny? And does not all that Manfred's ancestors experienced in these chambers come alive here?

It is awful to be frightened by a specter. But this horror, without anything showing itself, is simply madness. I know of nothing more haunting. Something speaks to me, yet I don't actually hear anything, something appears to me yet I don't actually see anything. I am terrified for no reason. I am terrified not by a specter, but by an emptiness.

LXIII

One evening in Manfred's absence, as the dusk gathered and made objects indistinct and the shadows deeper, this state of anxiety and torment reached such a powerful pitch that I could endure it no longer and had to go outside.

My love for Manfred was now more madness than a feeling of pleasure, however tormenting. We can suffer and yet be happy—sensing our desire's imminent fulfillment like the breath of a fragrance from afar. But my future with Manfred appeared to me as a constant, unrelenting hike against a tempestuous wind in black darkness, on the edge of an abyss. But the greater the mad torment, the fiercer my love for this enigmatic friend, so beautiful, with a complexion like pale ambergris and black clouds in his eyes. Manfred's likeness hovered continually before me like some inescapable fate. I felt I could never bear to part from him again. Even though he chose me as miserable as he was, spiteful toward everything for the torments he suffered, I could not help but go on loving him.

Manfred had brief moments when, all his pleasures spent, he found the rest of my friendship's offerings simply lackluster. Then he would vex me with his caprices. But I bore this torment with patience. For in the next moment, he would again take possession of me with savage affection. His love would ignite with a power I could at best ascribe to some spells, some sorcery. In all his dark beauty, I knew he was suffering. He might therefore cause me any torment save this one—the torment of uncertainty.

That, I could no longer endure. And so, out I went that evening to find him. I made for the tower of St. Jindřich, and I don't think I even noticed the people passing by—except for the impression of a phantasmagoria. I chanced to look at the row of ancient tombstones bricked up in the church walls. Suddenly I felt myself being drawn toward this blackened building, half sunken into the surrounding earth as if burrowed into the distant past.

There are places that retain their former appearance no matter how you alter them. The space around the temple of St. Jindřich remains like a cemetery to this day—though there are no more graves here. When the doleful temple bells ring out as if in summons to funerals—at dusk, when shadows rise from the pavement, and in the park surrounding the church, the breath of the white-flowering trees falls through the air to the ground like a rain of honeyed fragrance, the ancient cemetery here springs to life. A breeze of solemn sanctity touches everything. An atmosphere of coffins, incense, wreaths, rises from the desolate earth. You have a sense that the tower door will open and a procession emerge with a corpse on a black-draped bier. And should you fall back to very near the temple, you feel the former graves in your path, full of flowers. Moist upon them is the bright yellow of roses, and twixt your fingertips the fragrance of violets with tiny, fleeting petals of dark purple.

Into the church I went. A midnight darkness seemed to immerse me in this chilly space, dank as a cellar.

Above the high altar, an overhanging piece of stained-glass window now shone with an orange glare like a stencil of the setting sun. Now and then, the frame of the altar painting glinted golden, the altar cloth dappled with white, or the light in the lamp bled weakly.

Sorrowfully and silently, I set foot on the flagstones, which seemed saturated by the sepulchral air of the knights' cells situated underneath the temple.

The golden statues at the altar by the entrance, on low pedestals, seemed to be standing directly on the tiling. They gave the impression of being petrified phantoms, risen from the tombs and now given heavy material forms by a spell. I gave a shudder, struck by their horrifically grotesque ghoulishness. My visceral sensitivity to morbid horror sparked mysterious kinships with the beings turned to dust beneath the flagstones inside the temple, and around it in the long-defunct cemetery.

I felt a sudden pang of grief for those who had lived out the futility of their lives and were gone forever—grief that they had all passed and gone, and nothing was left. I thought of the people's forgotten faces, pale, with reproachful expressions. They do not exist: and I do. I have my ardent yearnings, my joys, my despair. But I suddenly feel as if I myself were dead, and as if those who had died were alive. There is a sussuration around me like the fall of rushing waters, like the stream of time, one figure after another passing me by, one of the dead after another, each moving in solemnity and silence.

The feeling comes to me that I am not alone here. There is also a host of still other beings, invisible ones, living a secret, hidden life in the forms of their prior existences, as if nearing the end of a dream they had once begun, the end of a longing unfulfilled for them. They are now becoming visible, now that my eyes have become sensitive to them, to their more delicate light and their subtler shadow, quivering in the alcoves and recesses of this ancient temple...

I wrenched myself from this reverie. Slowly I looked around the temple, and as my eyes seized on the cross hanging on the wall, I suddenly felt someone's living presence behind me. A shudder of horror ran through me—for even the cross I was gazing upon had taken on a spectral look. It was not hanging on the wall but hovering in the darkness. I averted my eyes sharply, as we do when we want to end a nightmare.

Seated in a pew near the chapel at the entrance was a stranger with the look of someone lost in dreams.

All at once, I thought I recognized him.

"Manfred!" I was about to call to him.

But my throat clenched with that feeling from our dreams when we want to scream. There was something so terrible in the way he looked at me that I became frightened.

What is he doing here, and who is he waiting for? His form, though identical to Manfred's, seemed nevertheless altered. But why isn't he getting up and coming over to me? He must have seen me when I came in.

I took a step toward him. Is this some hallucination at this late evening hour? No, it is Manfred, but he's gazing at me as if he didn't recognize me. His eyes are plunged into mine but aren't engaging with me. He is lost in thought, as if unburdening himself of the entire weight of his being at the steps of some altar, as if submerging that weight in the darkness pervading the space of this ancient temple.

I was consumed with anxiety. I went toward him—and the shadow suddenly stood erect. Something greater than crime, more horrifying than terror, was staring at me from his face. I could see now that this was not Manfred but someone resembling him, sent mysteriously into my path by fate.

I had uncovered the enemy. "Walter Mora!" flashed through my mind. Yes, it's he! I've come upon him here in the shadows of this temple. I can see his dark, pensive brow. I can watch the flame smoldering with hatred in the night of his eyes.

A hostile impulse also rose up within me. I now felt so strong that I was ready to face all the cunning of this mysterious personality confronting me. Let him come at me! For on my breast I wore the indestructible armor of my love for Manfred.

I felt that Walter Mora could not withstand my gaze. He tried in vain to fix his eyes upon me. His look shriveled.

But just then, there came the sharp sound of a bell from the depths of the temple. A priest came out from the sacristy. Walking over to the ailing man, he came near the portal with the Host.

I turned. The priest's appearance in the darkness was startling. An air like that from a scene out of legend wafted over me. But as the priest was leaving the temple, I looked back at the pew where Walter Mora had been standing so tall. My vision suddenly went dark, as if cast into a deeper blackness.

When it grew light again around me, there was no longer anyone there. Walter Mora had vanished, as if he had retreated before me into the darkness of his mystery.

LXIV

Manfred was waiting for me at home, worried by my absence. On my return, I could not bring myself to tell him right away that I had seen Walter Mora in the Jindřich temple. But then I told him the whole story.

"Yes, he is always near me," Manfred shouted with emotion. "I'm keeping him tied down. Something's been keeping me from getting a hold on him. But there's no more getting away for Walter Mora."

Manfred never left home now. He spent most of his time with me. He seemed unconcerned. But I suspected he was so calm only because he was watching for what was yet to come.

Were we chasing Walter Mora, or was he chasing us?

There were times when I was confident of Manfred's power as a magician. But at other times, I was terrified that we ourselves were going to be ambushed. A gust of wind against the windows at night came to seem like a mysterious threat. I would not have even dared leave my bed to look through the window. So certain was I that beyond its panes, I would see Walter Mora's form, mocking my anxiety.

The dreadful shapes of what the coming days impended loomed constantly before my eyes. There was something chaotic about this and yet certain at the same time. I knew Manfred had carried out a magic experiment to bewitch Walter Mora and bind him to himself. But in my imaginings, every fantastic possibility would start up and unleash a maelstrom. Are Manfred's reasons for trying to overpower Walter Mora so justifiable, so compelling as to be worth any repercussions? We are hurtling to our doom, I thought time and again. But I no longer dared beg Manfred to leave off his magic experiments and get away from Prague.

One morning the footman notified us that he had discovered strange footprints in the palace corridors. So it was: it was determined that someone had climbed over the garden wall, forced his way through the thickets of shrubbery, and then opened the French doors. The footprints continued on up the stairs, and some items in the corridors showed signs of having been disturbed. One of the windows was even open.

"Walter Mora..." said Manfred and I to each other quietly, and I felt a freezing chill in my heart, as if someone had brushed it with icy fingers.

From that moment on, the atmosphere in the palace was freighted with the fear of this phantom that had come creeping all the way inside. I thought I should go mad as dusk came back on. Manfred and I then kept vigil all that night, and we heard the dogs howling at midnight as well. But there was not the slightest rustle inside the palace. Vainly did we stare into the darkness, our senses as taut as if we meant to tear them to shreds with our madness. The phantom of darkness and scarlet, of night and hell, did not come. Walter Mora never appeared.

By morning, Manfred and I were both so exhausted that we thought we would die of this suspense if it went on any longer. On Manfred's brow, I read a sudden resolve to put an end to all this misery with the kind of courage that risks everything. And I myself wished for an end to our torture.

The feeling that something awful would happen once Manfred dared one final attempt frightened me less than the awareness of this fearful uncertainty, this mad indecision, lasting any longer. I could endure no more of this burden. I would sooner give way under it. And I observed similar feelings in Manfred. He took me by surprise with his decision that we would relocate the next day to the château on Bílá Hora.

LXV

Manfred's château on Bílá Hora had all the charm of an edifice abandoned and left to the elements. Beyond the high walls of the garden gone wild, only the pantile roof and tower were visible, and it was otherwise impervious to the gaze of any who might come wandering up to it. Now, in the autumn, it was at its loveliest, for all was awash in melancholy and seemingly glutted with fallen leaves, which completely blanketed the staircase leading up to the portal.

When the wind gusted against the shutters, the old house seemed to start from its slumbers, and to echo with memories of events from long ago. Dark tales of the past swirled all around it. Count Evelyn Macmillan had loaned it out for the secret sessions of a Masonic lodge, and Manfred's own father had left his last tragic memory there. Having quarreled with a friend over a mistress, he challenged him to a duel, carried out near the gazebo. Manfred's father bled to death upon the fallen leaves in the garden. The friend disappeared—and many years later, his name surfaced for the last time when he died a forgotten Beuronese monk in the Emmaus Monastery.[110]

As Manfred and I settled into the château, an oppressive foreboding gripped me within those mute, mysterious walls, where the sorrows of all who had ever lived out their destiny here seemed to have been discarded. Not the slightest echo from the outside world filtered through. So lifeless was it here that one's own heartbeat was constantly in one's ears.

Within the garden, there was an artificial cavern and a pool of water and some old pagan sculptures, mostly amorous in nature but so weathered that one could scarcely make out what they represented. Only the shabby Venus on the low knoll, inside an odd little colonnaded temple, still had the features given her by the sculptor, and otherwise one could hardly have recognized Diana and Actæon or Perseus and Andromeda in the waves of stone whipped by the wind and savaged by the elements. And the little boy who was Eros had neither nose, nor hands, nor wings, nor bow and arrow—but in his eyes, where the rains had left damp traces, the brightness of a smile still gleamed, and his feet still turned jauntily in mid-step, though their toes were gone. When the autumn leaves began to scatter over the stony imp, it looked as if he were strewing this russet and amber finery all over himself. And as the wind flung it off again, he seemed to be wriggling out of it himself, and thus whiling away long, endlessly long hours in this forgotten garden where his lowered bow no longer had anything to do. For no woman had set foot here in years: and love seemed but an old, forgotten myth.

If the garden was a tribute to the pagan cult, the interior of the Baroque château, the chapel's pyramid-like steeple protruding from its mansard roof had an air of eighteenth-century Catholicism. As in a monastery, likenesses of Jesuit saints lined the corridors, and the chapel had all the trappings of a church, though Mass had not been said there for ages. On the vault, in Baroque style, was a fresco of the beheading of St. John the Baptist. On the cartouche, supported by an angel, a chronogram proclaimed the chapel's renovation and consecration to John the Baptist by Count Evelyn Macmillan. The altarpiece, too, depicted John the Baptist. In the posture of that young, naked boy, as painted by Andrea del Sarto[111]—in his pale, perfumed beauty, there was something that recalled the portrait of Cagliostro in the Viennese palace. Or was this just my imagination? I myself was already in such a hallucinatory state over Cagliostro that like Manfred, I saw his image everywhere. After all, the chapel's consecration was significant. John the Baptist is the patron saint of Masons, and the motto on the coat of arms affixed over the doorway by Evelyn Macmillan was: *Aut vincere, aut mori.*[112]

"Cagliostro's motto," Manfred remarked, and he told me how one of the priests had ultimately refused to say any further Masses there, having guessed that the chapel was actually a Masonic lodge.

An actual secret door led to an alchemical laboratory that also contained a library of the esoteric sciences. It was a unique piece of work, this door. One had to press a hidden lever in the altarpiece, and the picture would turn; one could then enter this secret space. On closer examination, I noticed something else as well: all the emblems and trimmings bore Cagliostro's acronym L.P.D. Even the altar lamp, with its appliquéd cartouches and leaf handles, had these letters, stylized in a Baroque design.

The château's chambers were crammed with furniture and mementos. In the dining room were oil portraits of some of the Counts Macmillan, surrounded by a profusion of hunting and war trophies, rifles inlaid with nacre and ivory, and Turkish blunderbusses. An Italian fireplace, brimming with stucco flourishes, bore the Macmillan coat of arms at the center. Like lips that had not spoken for years, all these objects were thickly coated with poignancy and silence. For there was a feeling that no Count Macmillan was ever coming to live in these chambers again. This was a place where none would come except to die. The twilights here were more bloodless, the nights blacker, and the sorrows more ravening. There was no life and no present here, only death and the past.

The Empire salon with its Venetian mirrors, full of majolica and crystal goblets, evoked the same poignancy of a splendor no longer appreciated.[113] Everything in it still shimmered with gleams of gold and silver when the daylight poured over the furniture's flourishes, the mirrors' surfaces, and the goblets' glass, as if trying to revive some glorious past. But at dusk, the shadows would emerge like specters and wander from one mirror to another, as if to survey their forlorn obsolescence within them.

From the bedroom, we had a view of the back of the park. When I opened the window in the morning, an entire faerie vision of autumn vegetation looked into the chamber from trees now golden yellow or covered in magenta leaves, while others still remained coolly green. Below, the park grounds were completely obliterated with lifeless leaves. When the sharp morning sunlight hit them, it ignited inside the leaves like gold afire, while in other patches the ground seemed to fester in rusty blood. Moss had grown

over all the tree trunks and even taken hold on bits of the
garden sculptures.

The sorrow of Bílá Hora, of its rows of trees and smat-
tering of outdoor shrines, was traced on the distant horizon, with something tragic in its infinitely extending line.
A mute silence was natural here, for the soul sensed that any
attempt to speak must end in hopelessness and despair.

LXVI

I know of no melancholier landscape. Something is locked
away there, like a mysterious ancient curse, and it evinces
an uneasy mood in autumn, when howling tempests rage
unleashed. Even those come out to stroll are silent, as if
stricken with fear. They steer clear of each other, making
off into the fields, and when they do meet, they exchange
glances only from the side and as if bereft of hope.

When first I wandered into these peripheries, unaware
that I was entering the site of a battle, I sensed at once
that I was on the terrain of some historical catastrophe.
All at once, unavenged ghosts would rear their heads from
this soil. As I regarded the passersby who came my way,
their steps felt like those of pariahs walking over graves of
bygone glory.

How many generations it has taken for the voice violently
silenced here to speak again, for the arm fallen here to raise
itself! But valor is no more, in either word or deed. Every
call to action is faint and timorous. The present generation
remains hampered by the curse of this calamity, which has
left Bohemia unfree for three centuries.

Enter the field of Bílá Hora, and never will death have felt
closer to you than here. In the distance you see a dying city,
a tragic queen, Prague. She is perishing from exhaustion,
wasting away, and the agony that has oppressed her for

three centuries is a wound that can never be healed. When here on Bílá Hora the scarlet sunsets bleed long and melancholy, and Prague sets all her bells pealing in the blue twilight depths below, it is like attending a grandiosely scaled requiem.

Behold: the night is slowly unfolding, the darkness is gathering, but the sunset's glow still lights the row of trees, casting crimson reflections on the Bílá Hora church cloisters,[114] its rays glinting on the apex of the hexagonal summer palace at Hvězda.[115] Is not the spring at the Vojtěška monastery again spurting blood?[116] Are not the walls of the game preserve and the summer palace stained with the blood of the Moravians who, led by Count Schlick, were the last to hurl themselves against the Neapolitan hordes here?[117]

A land of blood, a field of blood... Hakeldama...[118]

But the gathering dusk has begun to settle, the preserve is darkening, the roads paling. All the bright pools of blood are extinguished, and a vast pall of unspoken grief is lowering onto the desolate highroad. Silence overtakes the lonely courtyards, with only a dog's occasional plaintive howl. The profiles of the pilgrimage shrines are traced in the fields like phantoms, forsaken, lamenting as if shackled to the futility of the prayers offered before them in genuflection.

The visionary Carmelite Dominic à Jesu Maria,[119] having raised a desecrated Marian image as a military standard, now traipses over the battleground. The lips that once bayed here for the troops to charge, lips that gave a wail of agony before dying, have stilled. There is no sound of trumpets, no thundering of drums. Dead and more dead everywhere. Dominic à Jesu Maria sighs. Mary hath vanquished the revolt that did here rear its head. Our Lady Victorious... its altar cloth fashioned from Frederick's own royal pennant as a peace offering.[120] But it is not only Frederick and the blood of his blood[121] who are dead. Even the Habsburgs no longer rule by the spear side.[122] Lost in the past, a gaunt black phantom in the darkness, Dominic à Jesu Maria whispers: "Our Lady Victorious..." But no longer does he whisper this name with confidence, as before. He now pronounces it as if touched by doubt.

Here fell Christian of Anhalt...[123] He was twenty years old, but together with his arquebusiers he repelled the Spanish cuirassiers en masse before, thrown from his horse, he released his own soul on a heap of the fallen... Twenty years old.

Father Dominic's thoughts now turn to that youth in flower, to the trim, fierce frame of that boy so mad with courage and passionate in all his knightly magnificence. Christian... How his eyes, wild onyx gemstones, had blazed in a surge of passion, overflowing with a longing to smite the foe when everyone else had taken flight. In a frenzy, he clave the faces of those who struck at him to unseat him from his horse. His veins swelled with rage; his face, that fair face over which maidens had sighed to no avail, for no thought had ever illumined it but a yearning for the glory of the sword, was suffused with a profound, deathly pallor, and his cap having slipped off, his hair, disheveled by the wind, stood utterly and menacingly black. Felled, he breathed his last and was cast into a common grave.

A lost soul and a heretic, but no coward. Dominic à Jesu Maria contemplates him now with pure indulgence. Three centuries settle every dispute. Futility and pointlessness bring all things to reconciliation.

Toward midnight, when an invisible hand heaves the moon like a pallid monstrance from the tabernacle of the heavens, and phosphorescent light spills over everything, Christian also rises from his grave and roams over the land. He takes the road to the summer palace and walks round its walls. And if he chances to meet a monk-victor, he does not shrink from him, he, the vanquished. For no less dead are the trophies of the victorious now. Faded is the Marian standard, eroded are the walls of its little church, and they exhale damp and dilapidation. Within the Servite monastery,[124] the late-night coachmen quaff their beer, and the Chapel of St. Martin gives the poor a bed for the night. And who can say what the shrines stretching from the plain of Bílá Hora to Hájek[125] represent... Hvězda is like a cemetery. The dead leaves rustle in the treetops and rain down on the ground as if felled onto graves, as if to obliterate not just what has fallen into futility, but also the memory of those who triumphed here...

LXVII

Bílá Hora and Manfred, the past and the present—the mournfulness of the deserted château, the line of trees in the distance, and this friend with the mysterious blackness in his eyes, all this blended together with the contours of my life, giving it tempo and fire. It felt as if I were living in the days of Dominic à Jesu Maria, and Manfred were a contemporary of the beautiful Prince Christian of Anhalt. The past was alive, and the present's charms had lost all their vitality.

The life Manfred and I knew here now was otherwise much like life as we had lived it in the Prague palace.[126] Manfred was initiating me into occultism, not systematically but haphazardly, as various bits came to mind or books to hand. He would rattle off all sorts of outlandish things that I found impossible to unravel, inflaming my imagination to the wildest fantasies.

Sometimes he would sequester himself in his laboratory behind the altarpiece.

I knew he was conducting experiments there that he kept secret from me, but I made no attempt to pry into them, nor did I so much as hint to Manfred that I gave any thought to his investigations in the secret chamber.

I was absorbed in the study of Agrippa von Nettesheim's *On the Uncertainty and Vanity of the Arts and Sciences*, as well as reading Glauber's alchemical treatises, Johann Isaac Hollandus's works *Minerals Opera or the Philosopher's Stone* and *The Art of Gold or the Assembly of the Philosophers* in the Paul Hildenbrandt von Hildenbrandseck edition, various *Sibylline Oracles*,[127] and treatises on whether animals are devils, and on how the titles of forgotten books of black magic from the sixteenth to the eighteenth centuries continued to inspire. This study so fascinated me that to recall my life in the present century often felt like an anachronism. But when betimes I noticed Manfred leaving the bed, even in the middle of the night, to retire to the chapel as I surmised from the echo of his footsteps in the château's deathly quiet, I would be overcome with horror of his experiments.

One night, I dared speak to him at last. Awoken yet again by the sound of his footsteps on the bedroom's parquet floor, I sat upright and said softly:

"Manfred..."

But he did not respond. He remained standing still for a moment, and all I could see was his figure's black silhouette.

As I weighed whether I ought to get up and beg him not to go, Manfred gently opened the door and left.

I am not sure why I did not rise and go after him—for he might have come back. But I stayed behind in the bedroom, trembling all over in terror at my abandonment.

Returning to me only the next morning, Manfred came to my side in a kind of fever. He doted on me all day long but said not a word about the night before. I lacked the nerve to ask where he was always going at night, or to plead for him to leave off these experiments with the mysterious, cunning forces of magic.

LXVIII

We had quite forgotten about the rest of the world in our seclusion. A sepulchral silence had set in all around us, occasionally broken only by the piteous wailing gales of autumn, which on the plains of Bílá Hora strike an especially despairing note. A gust of wind would sometimes batter the château with such fury, and bluster through the rustling leaves in the garden with such ferocity, that it seemed intent on whisking us into a ditch for all time. All the doors and shutters would give a long moan whenever the wind came driving in.

Yet at other times, it was so deathly still that we fell to hearing things.

One evening when as usual, Manfred and I were in conversation, all at once he broke off and raptly cocked an ear.

"Do you hear those footsteps in the garden, Francis?"

I raised my head and began to listen. I really did think I could hear someone walking on the carpet of dried leaves outside. The footsteps were coming closer and closer.

All of a sudden, there was a sound like a branch snapping—and then, silence. Nothing more.

Manfred was deathly pale. I was about to get up and open the window to look out into the garden. But Manfred stopped me, saying in a mere whisper:

"Don't go to the window, Francis! I think we're about to have a visit we are not yet ready for."

We awaited the sound of footsteps on the staircase, the door opening downstairs, and our late-night visitor's arrival inside the château. My heart began to thump so wildly that I thought I was done for. Had there been even a faint knock at the door now, I think Manfred and I should both have gone mad. We were that distraught.

But there were no more noises, only the taper slightly crackling as it burned in the candelabrum...

We scoured the gardens in the light of day. But there was not the slightest sign of any stranger having broken in overnight.

LXIX

The next night, when Manfred again left the bed to make off for his laboratory, and when, awoken by his departure just before midnight, I was nearly half-asleep, I was suddenly disturbed by the crash of some object sharply hitting the floor in the corridor.

I raised my head and listened. There was silence, everywhere a silence like the grave—only the anguished keening of the wind now and then.

All at once, I thought I heard footsteps in the corridor. Is Manfred coming back from the chapel? The footsteps came to a stop—then started up again, and suddenly something sped past the bedroom door at full tilt, and something else struck the floor.

I wanted to get up and go out into the corridor, but I was gripped by such fear that I did not dare. My imagination was so worked up that I thought the noise was coming not from one being, but from several. For something would drop at the same time as someone jumped to the floor, the two sounds coming from opposite ends of the corridor.

Are these some elementals[128] passing the time by frightening me out of my wits? The house has surely been full of them ever since Manfred started in with his magical exploits, ever since the devil himself had imprinted his accursed black stigma on Manfred's soul.

At any rate, I lit a lamp to shoo them off a little. But what's that? I can distinctly hear someone pushing at the door.

Just then, the clock began to strike midnight, with blows that pierced the soul like the stabbing of a sword.

I shouted:

"Who's there?"

But the answer I got was a quite firm pounding on the door that kept up until the handle started to rattle—immediately followed by someone's hasty retreat from it.

I threw the door open and lit the corridor with a candle. It was utterly deserted...

I was overcome with horror. Terror so deluged my soul that I could not bear to remain alone. I began calling out to Manfred. Mad with fear, I opened the chapel door to flee to him.

"Manfred! Manfred!" my voice resounded within that terrifyingly black space.

And my shouts seemed to carry through the entire house, slumping with age, rot, and decay, and prey to the cunning of elementals. The light of my candle filtered through the darkening air of the chapel. But I could not see Manfred.

Yet just then the altarpiece swiveled sharply, and within its frame stood Manfred, astonished at my arrival.

We said nothing for some seconds, our eyes never leaving each other. Manfred had a severe look, like one who is himself turning into a cryptic, unfathomable enigma. His eyes were glinting with the flame of something supernatural. He was gazing at me as if he saw me not in reality but in a dream. In almost spastic terror, I fell back, my body wracked and contorted. But then Manfred called to me in a voice that seemed not his own, though it came from his mouth. Seeing me now, he doubtless thought himself face to face with a phantom, its likeness that of a wan funerary statue.

I described the terrifying experience I'd had to Manfred. Loth to send me off to the bedroom alone, he bade me follow him into the laboratory. And so I found myself inside that mysterious space for the first time.

It was so choked with incense that smoke came billowing out when the entryway was opened. A fire had been stoked in the alchemical crucible. An altar stood draped in black, and it was covered with an array of magical objects for a rite honoring the devil with the same ecstasy as other rites do God. In the center lay a magnetized divining rod in the form of a forked twig whose inclination enabled any magician to find the spot to cast a spell; next to it was a magic wand wrapped in silk, with a gold and silver ring at the center. Then there were pieces of parchment covered with incantations, a leather pouch containing a covenant with the black powers, talismans, wax to create volts,[129] a mandrake in the shape of a shriveled homunculus, precious stones, perfumes, incense, aloes, pepper, saffron, sandalwood, and sulfur. Mounted on the wall was a shelf of occult works from the Middle Ages. The room was lit by a magic lantern. Its panes were each a different color, and the light it gave off was eerily subdued.

With a magic sword, Manfred traced a circle around us to protect us from elementals. He cast perfumes into the crucible, creating an atmosphere that drew psychic powers from the body. He poured water into a vessel. The water suddenly began to cloud, and bubbles rose from the bottom to the surface. At that instant, Manfred placed the vessel over the fire in the crucible, and as the water reached a rolling boil, he explained to me that at that very moment, Walter Mora was afflicted with restlessness and torments like the seething of the water in the vessel.

Then he took up a magic mirror and amid the dim light and the smoke, he peered inside it. He soon began to tell me exactly where Walter Mora was and what he was up to, for the mirror told him of his enemy's every movement; within it, he could see Walter Mora entering all the black and terrible places where only he could breathe; within it, Manfred could look directly into his eyes, as filled with murderous hatred as if they were fully loaded pistols aimed at Manfred.

"He's in agony, scuttling about his lodgings. I see a painting on the wall, and now I recognize it: Cagliostro's portrait. Now Walter Mora's sitting on a chair, opening a book as big as a psalter. Now he's getting up again, tracing a circle around himself with a magic sword. He wants to drive away the elements so they don't spoil his work. But he can't concentrate. He sees that nothing's going right, and he's clutching his forehead. There's apprehension in his face, building to the point of madness."

Manfred suddenly cried out. Then he put the mirror aside.

"That will be all for tonight. Walter Mora has broken the fluidum bond. I can no longer see anything."

He had gone deathly pale, his eyes sunken, his lips feverish. It cost him great effort to exhale.

I now had a sense as if he had been struck by some blow from afar. He seized my hand. He was shivering with chill, and I could feel how icy cold his palm was.

In that instant, I could not say whether I was awake or dreaming. All these black magic rites had set me shivering so. I gazed in awe at Manfred, at that supremely proud head of his, clenched with hatred for this mysterious foe as if by some indestructible helmet.

"Walter Mora has intuited what I had in mind for him. At the final instant, he placed a crown of metal spikes on his forehead—and there was an instantaneous recoil from the force I was applying to him. I could still see him as he was putting the crown to his head—when suddenly, my eyes went dark, and the image in the mirror disappeared. Walter Mora has foiled all my experimentations thus far."

LXX

I took part in Manfred's experiments every night now. But Walter Mora continued to thwart his efforts. He was also watching us in a magic mirror, and at the approach of any force trying to lay hold of him, he would repel it with some new trick. He would use not only his crown of spikes but various anti-incantatory agents. At the last possible moment, he would sometimes thrust his head into a hemp turban, in the technique of the ancient priests of the black arts, and Manfred's attack would be repulsed.

Manfred was growing weaker from these failed experiments. Was this a ruse by Walter Mora to bring him down? For he himself had done nothing to make Manfred suffer—by all indications, he was conserving his psychic strength for the end, for a single, all the more powerful assault on Manfred. Yet Manfred did not lose his head. Now that he had initiated me into his magic experiments as well, using me as an adept, he seemed to be in perfect mental balance. He tenderly caressed and doted upon me, as attentive as if to a child.

He used to go through several moods in a day: tender and temperamental, affectionate and abrasive, sweet and scornful. He was like those queer Chinese roses I read of in Athanasius Kircher[130] that display a succession of all their colors in a single day. Now, however, Manfred was always tender, affectionate, and sweet. He said nothing of his love for me. But I knew he would be mine to the final beat of his heart. A morbid passion came burning through his lips, like two deeply crimson rose petals plucked and curled up by the autumn. But he would tell me none of what I could read in his eyes. They alone would say clearly: you shall be a martyr, Francis. A martyr not for God, but for this one devil whom you have loved, and for whose sake you have chosen unhappiness, for whose sake you have gladly let a bloodied wreath of hellish thorns be pressed upon your pale brow.

But neither was my own love spoken aloud. With my eyes alone, I would watch over Manfred's being, with despairing eyes that sensed utter ruin ahead.

Manfred was beautiful, beautiful with the beauty of those we are bound to lose. I saw him now just as I pictured

Cagliostro at the height of his glory, instilling fear in men and in league with hell.

Believing himself the successor to the style of that glorious life, will Manfred win similarly ecstatic accolades from his contemporaries? Is this not hubris, his desire to gain control of Walter Mora? His experiments were aimed at hypnotizing his adversary and then exteriorizing his sensitivity.[131] Having thus linked with his victim telepathically, he would attempt to lay hold of him. He began to prepare a volt, a small wax figurine, and to distill Walter Mora's astral into it.[132] The volt then became Manfred's adversary for him, and he transferred his torments to it as if to the actual person. Using the magic mirror, he verified the outcomes of his experiments.

All Manfred's exertions were bent on a single purpose: to bring the figurine he had fashioned into so close a bond with the object of his hex that the two become identical. He was applying every possible method to manipulate Walter Mora, to enhance his suggestibility, to induce a particular hypnotic state in him, thus enabling Manfred to implant whatever suggestions he wished in his victim.

This occult crime horrified me, for I was confident of its success. Was this not the analogue of any psychic state when we hypnotize someone near us to bend him to our will? Is there not something entirely parallel to this in love? Of course, in that case the subject does not resist but rather goes along with our experiment.

In Walter Mora, Manfred was dealing with an adversary and acted from afar. He strove to alter the psychic disposition of his intended prey by degrees, so that he could ultimately direct him in this newfound receptivity. He had to induce lethargy, catalepsy, then a state like somnambulism, before his object was sufficiently magnetized to succumb to Manfred's mercies.

That moment was at hand in Manfred's estimation, though Walter Mora would no longer even go to sleep at night lest he fall into his adversary's clutches.

LXXI

In all this, I had one worry. I found Walter Mora's calm terrifying. There was an awful cunning hidden within him. In his ostensible impotence, was this adversary truly unaware that by his own experiments, Manfred was leading himself down the road to ruin?

Every obsession has its price. And for Manfred, Walter Mora was an *idée fixe*. So strenuous an application of personal psychic power to a single purpose can only weaken the rest of one's mental faculties. Once all vigilance has gone, will Walter Mora not rise up and repel the forces Manfred has unleashed against him, hurling them back with redoubled might against his foe? Without defenses, could Manfred not be killed by the very scourge he had unleashed against Walter Mora? For he cannot be certain he is stronger than his adversary. And even if that is so, he cannot be assured that having put all his strength into a single magical assault, he has not thereby weakened the rest of his psychic powers…

LXXII

It was one of the most dismal days of that autumn on Bílá Hora. Since morning, the wind had been beating furiously against the château walls, blustering against the leafless trees and blowing a veritable tempest of fallen leaves over all the garden sculptures, obliterating the arbors. When it paused briefly in this frenzied dance, it could be heard howling in the distance, like a wounded predator slunk into its lair. But it would renew the attack, renew its battering of the roof tiles, renew its assault on the windows and doors with the most terrifying scudding.

I had felt melancholy all day, as though stricken by some evil portent at its outset. But not even the greatest calamity could be as oppressive as the void that reigned in my soul. I took refuge in Manfred. Gazing into his eyes, I tried to think of nothing but his love. But my anxiety persisted. I could no longer distinguish the futility of all the objects around me from that of my own heart's sorrow.

Manfred sensed the chill I now felt in my heart.

"Poor Francis," he said to me in a bitter, gloomy rush. "How I've destroyed all the happiness in you and wiped your cheeks of all their color, all their fragrance! You were once so adorably bashful. Today, you are entirely despondent."

I demurred in response. Never had I felt happier, I assured him.

"I would commit any sin, Manfred, to be as impeccably dark as you. I wish I had your sheer strength of will, a will I believe can ravish even a preordained destiny."

An undercurrent of emotion, something like the moisture of suppressed tears, sprang into Manfred's eyes, eyes that till then had known only command, how to be the overlord one must obey.

"Are you happy, Francis? Poor child, pale as a candle for a funeral service! This is no happiness that I've created for you and imprinted upon your features, now so fatally exhausted. The gift of my friendship can be no happiness, not today, when my every belated smile that might trickle its way into your tender, enchanted heart is redeemed at such cruel cost…"

I sensed that Manfred's misery, brought on by these misbegotten attempts in magic, was reaching a fever pitch.

His thoughts now seemed darker than ever. I feared for Manfred, since I could not imagine the day would come in my life when this friend was not there, when his nebulously rueful smile would not come afire for me as it crossed his sweet, beloved lips, casting hope like a ray of light into my soul, and quietly, like a dream, touching all my being. For this reason, I pleaded with Manfred to abandon his magical exploits, at least for a time. I tried to talk him into our taking a trip somewhere, anywhere, if only to tear ourselves away from this treacherous, stultifying atmosphere of dark and sinister forces.

But gripped in a stasis of despond, Manfred leveled a gaze of pure incomprehension at me in a seemingly somnambulant trance, one that slowly opened out into a static beam of light. My pleas fell on ears deaf to all but his own obsession.

LXXIII

Night descended, a terrifying night, after an evening when the sky, briefly orange from the setting sun, became suddenly a black, a desolate void with neither moon nor stars. Under the effect of a dream state, one taciturn and overly dark, Manfred rose abruptly to repair to the laboratory behind the chapel. At that moment, his being seemed almost detached from anything of this world.

I begged Manfred not to go on weakening himself, at least for tonight, with his magical attempts. But he would have none of it. There could be no discussion of any loss of his magnetic powers, for these were one and the same as his firm belief in them. His faith in the success of his experiments remained unwavering. Do I find that so incomprehensible? If I believed in the devil as I do in God, he would explain this riddle to me. Then I should believe that evil is the only power, and that nothing that lives can be regenerated except by destruction.

"Imagine, for an instant, a world free of crime, a world of absolute good. Do you believe it could last a single day? Imagine if the earth were filled with constant light! I think humanity would go mad if the darkness never did fall. That is the sense of the riddle, that only by evil can the world come to good. So, fear not the audacity or madness in my efforts, Francis! It is essential to disrupt order and consensus in the world—to be a demon in the sense of Ramon Llull.[133] In this way, I am counterbalancing something higher than the mere outward rhythm of things. I have the tenacity of one from hell. I persevere, and nothing shall turn me from my purpose. I fear not even destruction."

LXXIV

I no longer tried to restrain Manfred. I knew it would be pointless. But I resolved never to leave him, to accompany him to his laboratory today as well, even if he tried to send me to bed.

I surrendered myself to fate. I knew that even if I tried to restrain him, that might be the very thing that drove him to his appointed destiny. What a riddle is fate! You can go to the ends of the earth, or come home and forego traveling altogether, and still you have no idea that your destiny is right there, lying in wait for you in the dark, in the very place you sought refuge, waiting to crush your heart and pierce it with a fatal blow.

Manfred traced a circle with his magic sword. I grasped his hand, and a sudden thought flashed through my fevered brain. I offered myself up to him as an intermediary for tonight's attempt. In Manfred's place, I intended to bear the brunt of any repercussions, so that no mishap should weaken his power.

But Manfred would not allow this. He did not wish to exploit my love to such ends. My mere presence would serve as an intensifier for his psychic power, since he was strengthened by the magnetism of my eyes, the magnetism of my whole being that loved him so strongly.

It was near midnight when all at once, Manfred stood erect, his gaze into the magic mirror almost solemn. The sensation of a grandiose kind of power, streaming into his veins, all but lifted him off the floor. At that very instant, it felt as if Manfred were no longer of this earth but of hell. Fire flared from his eyes, the fire of victory.

"The attempt is succeeding," he cheered. "Today at last, Francis, today I gain the upper hand over Walter Mora. He is scuttling about his chamber, all but mad with restlessness. It does him no good to put on his spikes. No good to put his head inside his hemp turban. Now... now he's leaving the chamber. He's walking downstairs. Opening the front door. Now he's outside. There's empty space all around him. He's clutching his hands in the darkness. He keeps walking, not knowing where, aimlessly, under the impulse of an unconscious command. Under the impulse of *my* command. Now he's crossing the bridge. Below, the river rushes on. The light is shimmering on the black waves. And now... now he's near a cemetery. I recognize it. It's the cemetery in Malá Strana. Francis, Walter Mora is walking toward our château. He's already on the path that leads up to it. Now hear this: Walter Mora is here..."

All hell could have no fiercer heat than what now began to rage in my breast. I shot a look into Manfred's eyes. And I seemed to see that madness peculiar to wide-open eyes gaping at their destruction, not grasping that this was the end for them.

And quite plainly, I heard a heavy knock on the château gates... then another, a third... followed directly by a mighty, relentless pounding.

There was no denying it, someone was at the château entrance, determined to get inside despite the late hour...

LXXV

"Walter Mora!" Manfred exclaimed.

At that instant, his forehead came ablaze with hell, with all the flames of its furnaces. Manfred, Manfred triumphant, saw the success of his experiment, saw his rival broken, helpless, at the very gates of his house.

His nerves tensed with frantic courage. He took hold of his lantern, ready to go outside.

My fear for Manfred overshadowed all the other emotions in my soul. The heartrending struggle he had waged with Walter Mora was about to climax in a terrifying scene. I embraced Manfred and begged him not to go outside. But his being was seized with indomitable passion. He wrapped himself in his cloak and then looked up at me. What I read in that stare! Was it a plea to forgive him for the wrong he was doing me, the grief he was plunging me into? Was it the final flash of his proud love, sacrificing itself to destiny?

Gently, he pushed me aside and abruptly made his exit.

Total darkness swept over me. I heard Manfred's footsteps receding, then their echo dying away within the chapel. Then the sound continued down the corridor and onto the stairs, and then I heard the door open down below and close again. A grave-like silence set in.

I felt my heart pounding in my chest. I was on the brink of madness. Putting my hands to my forehead, I wished that everything I was now experiencing were just a dream. But it was no dream, though I stood up and took several steps, though I tried by every possible means to wake myself in case I was dreaming.

Death's horrors could be no more terrifying. Instinctively, I sensed something horrible was happening in the darkness below...

LXXVI

Gripped with sudden resolve, I dashed down to the chapel. I ran through its darkness and came out into the corridor.

I set off fumbling along the walls as I tried to reach the stairs to follow them down. I wanted to go to Manfred's aid if he launched into a battle with someone for his very existence.

There was silence, dead silence throughout the house. All I could hear was the creaking of the weathervanes as they turned in the wind outside.

What was happening to Manfred? What had gotten into this place under its gloomy rooftop? The entire house had fallen prey to cunning elementals. My heart was pounding wildly, and my feet were staggering as if I'd been dealt a mortal blow.

How long can this uncertainty go on? Ah, to tremble for what we love so madly, to be huddled in its darkness, to despair under its burden as if under a heavy tombstone! Blood seemed to be cascading into my brain. Would Manfred's struggle with Walter Mora end in victory? I was praying—but to whom? To God? To Satan? I was praying to some black, ominous star, some guardian of evil, to stand by Manfred. I was engulfed by deadly anxiety.

I thought I heard a muffled cry for help, calling for me. No, I was imagining things. No one was calling. The sound—brooding, lugubrious, like a funeral march—was only in my mind.

I again began groping about for the exit to the stairs. But I was coming up against bare walls in a continual muddle, as if some demon playing tricks on me had rearranged the entire house and summarily walled up the doorways in the château.

I began to call out to Manfred. The echo brought my cries back to me in seeming mockery. My head was awhirl in such chaos that I deemed myself most certainly mad.

I was sinking in a kind of swoon—when all at once my foot slipped, and I went tumbling down the stairs. I reached the bottom. There was pain. But I paid it no mind. To the exit I tottered. I opened the door and stepped out onto the grounds.

LXXVII

So dazed and deafened with fear for Manfred was I that at first I could make out nothing at all. Darkness, darkness all around. This is where Manfred ought to be. I was straining my eyes to find him. Is he over there by the tree? No—that's merely the shadow cast by the trunk. I called out. No one answered. He must be at the entrance to the park.

The garden feels suddenly riddled with madness and death. The grotesque trees with branches like the tentacles of monsters, and the hauntingly shabby and crumbling statuary, so ghostlike, eyeing me maliciously, with impudent, hateful mockery.

Getting a hold of myself, I stride hastily toward the exit from the grounds to the door where Walter Mora had been knocking. It is wide open. "Manfred!" I try to shout—but my voice cracks.

Black darkness as far as the eye can see, my horizon a fathomless chasm steeped in night. Distant lightning streaks the sky, flailing in ominous flashes. With every flare, the darkness seems darker and the night deeper. The atmosphere, so stiflingly heavy with magnetism, is equally thick with the breath of the infernal abyss, its gaping maw ready to swallow any here who would dare trifle with it...

Manfred was no longer anywhere to be seen. He had vanished without a trace... forever... I sank, and in despair, I buried my head in the earth.

LXXVIII

Manfred, my friend, my lover, who hath plunged into the pit, arms stoutly crossed, seeing that all was lost and spurning the fight, madly do I long to see the folds of thy cloak, the dark cloud of thy hair, the flash of thine eyes, to see thee for one second more, so beautiful, who wert mine, and whom hell hath sundered from me. Thou art swallowed up in a gloom too murky, too dense for mine eyes, too poor, weak, human, to penetrate. But thou alone, even now that thou art no more, shalt yet rule my soul. I shall sense thee in every breath of the night, hear thee in every breath of the wind. Greater depths shall I plumb in life itself, by the power of an indomitable passion, by the accursed love of a renegade cherub who forsook God to weep for the demon he loved...

My heart was shattered that night that entombed my love. But my thoughts are only of that supernal being who brought his soul's crimson lips to mine to claim my kisses—and who, aflame with thirst, pulled me to himself and received me whole, my life whole, as a sacrifice. Thou hast willed it, Manfred: and there was aught but thou thyself, whencesoever thou didst come and whatsoever fate or madness thou didst bring. I have put God out of my mind and turned away from people. Believing in nothing, I have crossed the temple threshold, and blaspheming the world, I have scorned people. For thou hast said: "I am Love, I am Destiny."

Darker than this planet's blackest chasms, our sorrows have merged, sorrows that cannot be healed, spreading their wings to their utmost afore our frail bodies ebb into eternity... More demon than lover, and yet dear, so dear, my Manfred, is it madness to wish that thou wouldst again rise from the darkness for one brief moment, for my despairing, suffering eyes to behold thee one last time?

LXXIX

I gave a cry in a voice that scarcely seemed my own. I was crying out Manfred's name into the darkness, then perhaps not even that, though sounds were still coming from my mouth, the insistent, beseeching sounds of the shock and awe of this creature glutted with hot waves of rebellious blood, its froth roiling with all the eruptive despair driving him to madness. Horror hoisted me aloft like a phantom, an oracular warning to all the conniving powers of hell that had taken Manfred from me, that had laid the snares for his destruction.

This psychic tension, this atmosphere of outrage, was drawing my eyes shut in a swoon. But my soul remained ever desperate for this magnificent, vanished shadow. Had it ever existed? Had it been only the product of my imagination?

Nothing was left of the dark happiness Manfred had given me. Had it been real? Was it wholly the fruit of my fevered mind, sick from the blaze of hell?

Abruptly, I opened my eyes wide, as if to hurl a thunderbolt of hatred into heaven itself: but I was seized with the futility of everything, and the mystery of the power that crushes all—and as for the heroic blasphemy I had wanted to send soaring up to the skies, that now became the mere gesticulation of a madness that delivered up one final wail for the phantom, the fiction, that had been my friend:

"Manfred! Manfred!———"

Notes

1. Among *fin de siècle* Czech members of the "third sex," *přítel* (friend) was often coded language for a partner or love interest, as it remains today.
2. Alessandro di Cagliostro (1743–1795) was a prominent, widely traveled Italian magician, alchemist, occultist, and huckster.
3. *Race* (Czech *rasa*, [dated] *rača* < French *race*). In this period sense, the word may refer to a family line or pedigree but also, for example, to "Germans" or "Slavs." It refers to a group that shares certain inherited physical and mental attributes. In other words, Manfred and other worldly aristocrats are not constrained by paradigms. For Karásek, aristocracy therefore represents the capacity to define oneself independently. See Introduction at p. 29 on Karásek's evident invention of an aristocratic pedigree, which was hardly unique in the *fin de siècle* Habsburg monarchy.
4. Karásek's life, work, and criticism reflect a broad and complex range of social relations to women: there is admiration and cordiality, sublimation and rivalry. He corresponded for several years with authors Vladimíra Jedličková (pseud. Edvard Klas) and Marie Kalašová (see Karásek, *Milý příteli…*; Karásek, *Upřímné pozdravy z kraje květů a zapadlých snů*). He frequented Anna Lauermannová-Mikschová's literary salon, discussed his sexuality with her in frank private conversations (Lishaugen, *Speaking with a Forked Tongue*, 72), and drafted parts of the *Three Magicians* trilogy at her villa. His disputes with the older critic Eliška Krásnohorská were generational rather than gender-driven.

   Karásek's fictional dandies may express misogynistic views. For an analysis by Czech literary scholar Libuše Heczková, see "Doslov," 88–90; and see Appendix II for Karásek–Klas letters of December 11 and 21, 1901 (Karásek, *Milý příteli…*, 12–13, 15–17). Lishaugen finds this misogyny an "aspect of dandyism […] related to a notion of an aberrant eroticism" (*Speaking with a Forked Tongue*, 50; cf. Pynsent, *Julius Zeyer*,

174–82). Karásek's male aesthetes also sublimate same-sex desire and aspirations into larger-than-life women, per Czech queer theorist Martin C. Putna (*Dějiny homosexuality v české kultuře*, 127). In a further twist, Karásek subscribed to the contemporary theory of gay males as a "third sex" or "inverts," i.e., female souls in male bodies (see Karásek, *Scarabæus* III; *Ganymede* X). Early German queer activist Ulrichs discusses the concept in *Incubus* (1869). German sexology pioneer Magnus Hirschfeld "kept all the main categories Ulrichs had developed" (Tobin, *Peripheral Desires*, 12, 93).

Women's power is further acknowledged in rivalry: consider Marie Madeleine's portrayal in *Scarabæus* and Radovan's (almost comic) rivalry with his sister for Adrian's affections in *Ganymede* V, as well as the unfavorable comparison of effeminate men with women in *Scarabæus* CXXVII.

Less ambiguous misogyny is prevalent in Schopenhauer's and Nietzsche's writings, where the will to live and the sex drive are unavoidable, and love is their consequence. Marriage is a snare and constancy a prison that breeds triviality and disappointment, in turn blunting thought and spirituality—for men, at least (Pynsent, *Julius Zeyer*, 174–82).

For yet another period perspective on gender roles, see Lang, *Sexual Politics and Feminist Science* on German feminists' interaction with contemporary sexologists.

5. Founded in the 14th century and built in the Gothic style. In the late medieval period, the Church of St. Jindřich and St. Kunhuta (St. Henry, after Holy Roman Emperor Henry II [r. 1014–24] and his wife Kunhuta) was taken over by Hussites (Czech Reformationists). During the Habsburg-led Counter-Reformation, several chapels were added to the structure.

6. In traditional Czech historiography, the 1620 Battle of Bílá Hora (White Mountain) was the nation's greatest tragedy. See Karásek, *RMM*, LXV–LXVI; and "Bílá hora" (poem) in *Kniha aristokratická* (The Aristocratic Book, 1896); as well as *Ganymede* VIII on a village ruined in the Thirty Years War (1618–48). Karásek's wistful musings on such sites mark a neoromantic aesthetic. For a more recent perspective on Bílá Hora and its significance, see Agnew, *The Czechs*, 64–74, especially p. 67.

7. The French decadents often invoked the idea of *tedium vitae* (Latin, "life-weariness"). Certain late 19th-century social critics ascribed widespread "neurasthenia" to moral decay (e.g., Nietzsche, the American philosopher and psychologist William James; see Sabo, "William James and Friedrich Nietzsche," 7, 13, 16–17).

8. "Homosexuality began to speak on its own behalf" in this period, asserts Foucault, and used the emergent medico-legal framework to do so (Foucault, *History of Sexuality*, 101, cited in Spector, "The Wrath of the 'Countess Merviola'," 32–33; but see also Appendix I for Karásek's essentially aestheticist defense of Wilde.

9. French, "the latest thing" (literally, "the last cry").

10. *Fin de siècle* Vienna was the empire's "fashion capital," and Viennese women were known for the elegance and taste of their dress. See Wagener, "Fashion and Feminism," 29. Then as now, Kärntner Straße (Carinthian Street) was a high-end shopping street.

11. For more on dandyism and the Czech decadents, and theorist of dandyism Arthur Breisky, see Bláhová, *Arthur Breisky a Oscar Wilde*. For a literary biography of Breisky including some of Karásek's memories, see Podroužek, *Fragment zastřeného osudu*; NB acknowledgments, 124. For two Breisky stories in English, see Chew, *And My Head Exploded*. Breisky contributed to *Moderní revue* beginning in 1908, and Karásek wrote the introduction to Breisky's 1910 *Triumf zla* (Podroužek, *Fragment zastřeného osudu*, 102). Breisky died working as an elevator operator in New York City.

12. "Positive knowledge" refers to empirical science derived from sensory experience through reason (q.v. positivism).

13. The principle of form following function in the applied arts was then in vogue in Vienna.

14. During the Renaissance, the Latin *experimentum* (Czech *pokus*) might be used to describe "magical spells" (Sledge, "Sefir Yeztirah and Bahir," 7:30).

15. The Habsburgs' senior line reigned over the Spanish empire from 1516 to 1700. From the point of view of some Bohemians, the prestige of the Spanish Habsburgs was tempered by their partisan Catholicism.

16. Completed in 1805 by Venetian neoclassical sculptor Antonio Canova, this pyramidal (Masonic) tomb was commissioned by Maria Christina's husband Albert of Saxe-Teschen. See also Karásek, *Scarabæus*, LIX.

17. A former royal hunting ground made into a park by Emperor Joseph II in 1766, the Prater boasted a "mini-Venice" by the *fin de siècle*. It was frequented by nobles in carriages as well as by the humbler classes, including lovers meeting for assignations.

18. Site of Habsburg castles and a market town 20 km (12 mi) south of Vienna.

19. Italian, "[the] divine Cagliostro."

20. Karásek's idealized male youth has a "pale" (*bledý*) and "translucent" (*průzračný*) complexion, with lips a crimson color suggesting passion. This ephebic ideal is depicted elsewhere in period Czech literature, e.g., in the narrative description of Hégr in Vilém Mrštík's novel *Santa Lucia* (1893).

21. Karásek uses "temple" (Czech *chrám*) rather than "church" (*kostel*) as a way of evoking dark and heavy mystery. See Kubínová, "Prostory víry a transcendence."

22. *Perceptivity.* This primary sense of *smyslnost* seems to have later given way to "sensuality," in the erotic sense; Karásek may be playing with its double meaning here.

23. Views that were prevalent not only in period philosophy but also in (masculine) late-Habsburg liberal political culture. Traditional liberals, who tended to oppose any expansion of the franchise (even while holding that the less-enlightened could be prepared for eventual civic responsibility through liberal education), viewed women as a permanently dependent class and resisted equal educational opportunities for them (Judson, "Rethinking the Liberal Legacy," 65–66).

24. A key theme of the *Three Magicians* is the parallel between queerness and criminality, homosexual acts ("sodomy," broadly interpreted in practice) being illegal throughout the Habsburg era. The crime novels of Karásek's contemporaries Raymond Chandler and Dashiell Hammett—set in California, where sodomy remained illegal until 1976—were also accented by queerness (Chandler, *The Annotated Big Sleep*, 214n, 226).

25. Formally the "Basilica" of St. Jakub (James the Great), in the Old Town. It was originally a 12th-century Gothic structure and later rebuilt in Baroque style. See note 21 on Karásek's use of "temple."

26. The faithful would leave gifts including jewelry in homage to the miracle-working statue. In this Prague legend, a would-be thief had himself locked in the church overnight to steal these gifts, but the statue seized his arm and held him there until morning, when he was discovered.

27. The basilica's portrait of St. Jakub is by Václav Vavřinec (Wenzel Lorenz) Reiner (1689–1743). Four other altars in it feature paintings by Petr Brandl (1668–1735), who had a German father and a Czech mother. Both are among Bohemia's most celebrated late Baroque painters.

28. Count Jan Václav Vratislav z Mitrovic (1670–1712), of the Czech noble family Vratislavů z Mitrovic (Vratislavs of Mitrovice), became High Chancellor of the Kingdom of Bohemia in 1711 under Habsburg ruler and Holy Roman Emperor Charles VI. He died of dropsy (edema) while in office. His monumental crypt is by the wall of St. Jakub's north aisle.

29. According to legend, the count dreamed that he died but then came back to life. After waking, he ordered that on his death, his heart be pierced with a bodkin to ensure that he stayed dead. Unfortunately, the barber-surgeon botched the job. As a result, the count revived in his tomb and took to knocking on his coffin lid. When the monks eventually lifted the slab of the tomb, they found his body outside the coffin, its face frozen in a mask of horror.

30. In alchemy, an unknown element, a building block of matter.

31. Green gold is an alloy with silver, sometimes adding cadmium or zinc, known to the ancient Egyptians and valued by occultists.

32. That is, the priests. The Levites were the Israelite tribe chosen by God to serve Him in the Temple.

33. Cf. John 17:14–15, in which Jesus prays not that His flock be taken from the world but rather that it be uncorrupted by this world's evil until reaching the next existence.

34. The work's Czech title (*Román Manfreda Macmillena*, Manfred Macmillan's Novel) thus refers in part to Manfred's narrative.

35. Formally, the "Church" of Our Lady before Týn (*Kostel*) but sometimes called *Týnský chrám* (temple, church). A 14th-century Gothic structure and the main church in the Old Town.

36. An accomplished Danish astronomer (1546–1601) who received the support of Habsburg ruler and Holy Roman Emperor Rudolf II (r. 1576–1612) and moved to Bohemia. He is buried in the Týn church. His body was first exhumed in 1901.

37. The Marian Column (*Mariánský sloup*) was erected in honor of Prague volunteers, led by university students, who held the Stone Bridge (later Charles Bridge) against the invading Swedes in 1648—notably, fighting for the Catholic Habsburgs against the Protestant Swedes. It became a symbol of the Habsburg Counter-Reformation among later Czech patriots and was torn down by a mob in 1918, when Czechoslovakia became independent (Agnew, *The Czechs*, 71).

38. In architecture, the Romanesque style (10th–12th c.) preceded the Gothic and is coterminous with the foundations of the Bohemian state. For Czech (neo)romantics, that period could evoke visions of ancient national glory.

39. *First floor.* That is, the first floor above the ground level per European usage.

40. English poet Thomas Chatterton (1752–1770) committed suicide by taking arsenic. Contemporaries attributed the death of American writer Edgar Allan Poe (1809–1849) to alcohol, but the truth is unknown. French poet Charles Baudelaire (1821–1867) smoked opium and drank heavily before a stroke left him paralyzed. French writer Gérard de Nerval (1808–1855) committed suicide by hanging while living in poverty.

41. Here, magnetism's occult connotation may suggest both a mesmerizing quality and an affirmation of Manfred's power and insight.

42. Paracelsus (Theophrastus von Hohenheim, ca.1493–1541) was a colorful Swiss-born physician, alchemist, and occultist. A self-styled monarch of medicine, he opposed long-held theories (see note 105) and was sought after by royalty.

43. Despite condemnation for heresy by the Inquisition in Cologne, the occultist and polymath von Nettesheim (1486–1535) continued to fascinate esotericists into the late 19th century.

44. The "Master of a Hundred Arts" and a Jesuit, Athanasius Kircher (1602–1680) interpreted Egyptian hieroglyphs as occult symbols.

45. A genus in the witch hazel family, that is, an astringent.

46. *Va banque* (French, lit. "go bank," i.e., go for broke, all or nothing).

47. The cypress, a symbol of grief, takes its name from Cyparissus, a boy beloved of Apollo in Greek myth. In Ovid's telling, the boy accidentally kills his pet deer while hunting. Apollo grants his request to be made into a cypress so that he may weep forever; the tree's sap beads like tears on its trunk. In the ancient Near East, the long-lived cedar tree was associated with longevity and immortality; the Egyptians used cedar to mummify pharaohs.

48. Any but the eldest son of a Spanish or Portuguese monarch.

49. *Green ray*. An optical effect occurring just after sunset or before sunrise. In Jules Verne's novel *Le rayon vert* (The Green Ray, 1882), it is believed to give observers heightened perception.

50. *Astaroth*. The Duke of Hell; with Beelzebub and Lucifer, one of the three highest-ranking demons.

51. Apollonius of Tyana was a charismatic philosopher-sage born in Cappadocia (ca.3 BCE) who died in ca.97 CE. As a Neopythagorean, he would have accepted the idea of the soul and its desire for union with the divine. Later critics of Christianity upheld him as a more authentic miracle-working sage than Jesus, while the Church portrayed him as a demonic magician. Karásek wrote a play about him circa 1905 that was also set to music (!)

52. *Tartary*. The realm of the Tartars (Tatars); a medieval European concept of the Central Eurasian lands of the Mongols and their Turkic allies.

53. *Artist of Life* (Czech *umělec života*; cf. German *Lebenskünstler*). For a discussion of this characteristically aestheticist term, see Szott, "Lebenskünstler." It dates to at least 1800, when the Romantic German writer Novalis used it in

his novel *Heinrich von Ofterdingen* (published posthumously in 1802), and by Goethe in his autobiography *Dichtung und Wahrheit* (Poetry and Truth, 1811–33). In English, it seems to have become more widespread only during the *fin de siècle*; cf. also Wilde's essay "The Critic as Artist" (1890) and his general approach to style.

54. A native of Ajaccio, Napoleon's birthplace and capital of Corsica.

55. The Société du Sacré-Cœur de Jésus (Society of the Sacred Heart of Jesus) was founded in Paris in 1800 to provide girls with an education and spread to many countries. A *pensionnat* is a boarding school.

56. Goethe based his comedy *Der Groß-Coptha* (The Great Coptha, 1791) on Cagliostro's life.

57. Advocate and inventor Jean-Charles Thilorier (1750–1818) won acquittal for Cagliostro in the Affair of the Queen's Necklace, in which a French cardinal bought a diamond necklace for Marie Antoinette through fraudsters. Cagliostro was suspected of complicity with the intermediaries.

58. French, "Brief for the accused Count Cagliostro, defendant, vs. the Attorney General, plaintiff."

59. Besides Thilorier, who mentions the Mufti, another source for this detail may be Saxon-born author and historian Friedrich von Bülau, whose compendium *Geheime Geschichten und rätselhafte Menschen* (Secret Stories and Mysterious People, 1850–60) includes a chapter on Cagliostro and mentions an "Althatas" (chapter 14), a.k.a. Althotas.

60. Soon after their founding (1118), the Knights Templar absorbed an existing gnostic Johannite tradition claiming continuity with the primitive Christianity of John the Baptist and the apostle John. The Johannite order has an almost equally long history in Bohemia (Buben, "The Order of Malta in the Czech Lands"). Pinto da Fonseca (1681–1773) was a Portuguese nobleman Grand Master of the Order of St. John from his election in 1741 to his death. His court was flashy and filled with intrigue. He introduced the Baroque to Malta.

61. A princess of the Trebizond Eyalet (1598–1867), an Ottoman territory. In medieval times, it had been an empire on the Black Sea coast.

62. *Càssaro*. Palermo's oldest street. From Sicilian *càssaru* (< Arabic *qaṣr*, "citadel").

63. *Italienische Reise* (Italian Journey, 1816–17; Czech transl. 1982) is based on Goethe's 1786–88 travel diaries. Johann Peter Eckermann is known for his *Gespräche mit Goethe* (Conversations with Goethe, 1836–48; Czech transl. 1955).

64. Born in Antwerp, Martin Delrio (1551–1608) became a Jesuit in 1580. His scholarly multivolume *Disquisitionum magicarum* (Magical Investigations, 1599–1600) probed witchcraft practices and was allegedly a key tool of the Flemish Counter-Reformation (Trevor-Roper, *Crisis of the Seventeenth Century*).

65. French, "woman, female" (pejorative).

66. In alchemy, the "first materials" necessary to the *magnum opus* of creating the philosopher's stone.

67. Byzantine Emperor Justinian (r. 527–565) argued that these chapters encouraged the Monophysite heresy that Christ's nature was purely divine. The chapters are: "the [...] writings of Theodore of Mopsuestia; the letter of Ibas of Edessa to Mari the Persian; and writings by Theodoret of Cyrrhus against Cyril of Alexandria" (Hoskin, "Review: *On the Person of Christ*").

68. Angelology and demonology, each with various and conflicting lists of names, are areas of focus in kabbalah and later European mysticism (Sledge, "Witchcraft Skepticism," 32:27).

    Various traditions assign names to seven archangels. The Protestant Bible mentions two angels by name: Michael and Gabriel. The Book of Tobit (canonical to Catholics) names Raphael. 2 Esdras (canonical in some Orthodox churches) names Uriel (a fallen archangel in the pre-5th-century *Temple of Solomon* grimoire; Sledge, "Testament of Solomon," 14:20). The apocryphal Book of Enoch gives three other names not in Manfred's list.

69. As God identifies Himself to Moses from the burning bush (Exodus 3:14).
70. Psalm 131, "O Lord, remember David and all his meekness."
71. Today Jelgava, Latvia, Mitau was the capital of the Duchy of Courland and Semigallia, part of the Polish-Lithuanian Commonwealth until Russian annexation in 1795 in the Third Partition of Poland. Elisa von Medem (1754–1833) was a Baltic German poet and writer. Johann Kaspar Lavater (1741–1801) was a Swiss physiognomist who claimed that a person's cranial and facial features revealed specific character traits.
72. The colors are reversed in the symbol of the Knights Templar.
73. The Affair of the Queen's Necklace (see *RMM* XXXVII). The countess's claim to nobility was dubious.
74. The "quixotic" Lord Gordon (1751–1793) was a Scotsman and British parliamentarian associated with the anti-Catholic Gordon Riots (1780), on which Dickens' novel *Barnaby Rudge* (1841) is based. He was convicted and ultimately imprisoned for defamation (Schuchard, "Lord George Gordon and Cabalistic Freemasonry").
75. Founded in London (1784), a precursor to that city's Swedenborg House (1810). Both aimed to translate and promulgate the works of Swedish theologian-seer Emanuel Swedenborg (1688–1772) (Lines, "Swedenborg Society," 1).
76. Joseph II (1741–1790) was both Habsburg ruler and Holy Roman Emperor from his mother Maria Theresa's death (1780) to his own in 1790. Under a policy of enlightened absolutism, he promulgated centralization, religious tolerance, and reforms to both serfdom and the legal code.
77. Evidently Roveredo in Piano, within the Habsburg lands at the time.
78. Also then part of Habsburg holdings in northern Italy.
79. Built 134–139 CE as a tomb for the Roman emperor Hadrian, the Castel was connected to St. Peter's Basilica in the 13th century and used for a time by the Papal States (756–1870) as a prison. (See *Scarabæus* CXXXVII and related note on Hadrian's male favorite Antinous.)

80. An English translation is included in Faulks and Cooper, *The Masonic Magician*.
81. Site of a fortification since Roman times. The fort was rebuilt in the 15th century and granted to the Papal States in 1631.
82. The fiery, six-winged guardians of God's throne in Isaiah 6:2–3.
83. Poison and concocters of poisons have been closely associated with illicit magic in translations of the Hebrew bible (Sledge, "Witchcraft Skepticism," 14:50).
84. Likely Francesco Bartolozzi (1727–1815), an Italian engraver, a London resident from the mid-1760s, known for his skill at stipple engraving.
85. Where Jesus turned water into wine before the start of His ministry; the first of His miracles (John 2:1–12).
86. The 1907 edition of *RMM* inserts "speckled with the colorful splendor of stylized peacocks" here. That first edition had a showy red velvet cover (Zach, *Nakladatelská pout Jiřího Karáska ze Lvovic*, 22), "notorious for its originality" (Lishaugen, *Speaking with a Forked Tongue*, 168) and befitting *RMM*'s broader theme of defiantly preposterous self-stylization (see Figure 9 in Introduction).
87. On King James I's (r. 1603–25) male favorites including the Earl of Somerset (the handsome Robert Carr) and the Duke of Buckingham (George Villiers or "Steny"), see Young, "James VI and I."
88. *Ezzelino da Romano* (1194–1259). Tyrannical Italian feudal lord, mentioned in Dante's *Inferno* and in Wilde's *Dorian Gray*, chapter 10 ("whose melancholy could be cured only by the spectacle of death").
89. *Cesare Borgia* (1475–1507). Italian cardinal, *condottiero*, and an inspiration for Machiavelli's *The Prince*; "the sins [...] of Caesar [*sic*] Borgia" are mentioned by Wilde in *De Profundis*, the letter he wrote to Lord Alfred Douglas while in Reading Gaol in 1897. Karásek's 1908 Borgia poem was a "dramatic poem" like Byron's *Manfred*.
90. *Guidon Bonatti* (d. 1296–1300). Italian mathematician, astronomer, and astrologer; an advisor to Ezzelino da Romano.

91. *Galeazzo Maria Sforza* (1444–1476). Fifth Duke of Milan, with a reputation for cruelty.

92. *Marquise de Brinvilliers* (1630–1676) will be central to this trilogy's book two, *Scarabæus*. French aristocrat executed under Louis XIV for poisoning family members to gain an inheritance, inspiring a *drame lyrique* opera (1831) and an essay in Alexandre Dumas *père*'s *Crimes célèbres* (Celebrated Crimes, 1839–40), and perhaps also the character Milady in his *Les trois mousquetaires* (The Three Musketeers, 1844).

   Acqua Tofana [Toffana]. A strong poison first mentioned in 1632; Mozart alleged that it was used to poison him.

93. Decadent and symbolist poets used the sea as a metaphor for the unconscious, sometimes specifically invoking the Sea of Dreams as in, for instance, symbolist Stéphane Mallarmé's poem "La mer" (The Sea), from his collection *Poésies* (Poems, 1899) or Belgian symbolist Georges Rodenbach's poem "La voix de l'eau" (The Voice of Water, 1886). The cave of Hypnos, Greek god of sleep and dreams, is the source of the river Lethe in the underworld.

94. *Syllabary.* Here, undeciphered cryptograms. Ancient Egyptian hieroglyphs captivated medieval occultists as secret symbols. Kircher (see note 44) was the first early modern scholar to propose that these signs might represent sounds or syllables.

95. A theosophical concept akin to *prāṇa* ("life force, spiritual energy") in various forms of Indian thought. This image seems to recall efforts by European scientists to capture lightning in a jar.

96. The letters *L.P.D.* were used among Freemasons and on a seal belonging to Cagliostro. The Latin phrase is roughly "trample the lily" (i.e., of the Bourbon dynasty), though that is possibly a later interpretation of the three letters. See this possible source for Karásek: *Kurzer Inbegriff von dem Leben und den Thaten des Joseph Balsami*, 139. It also appears with the plural form *lilia*.

97. Albrecht von Wallenstein (1583–1634, a.k.a. von Waldstein, Waldštejn), is invoked here in the sense of a great native son. Born a poor Protestant and later converted to Catholicism, he fought as a mercenary for the Catholic side during the Thirty

Years War, then went on to become a prominent military man and statesman for the Habsburgs. He built the Baroque Wallenstein Palace (1623–30) in Prague's Malá Strana. In 1625, he had court mathematician Johannes Kepler (1571–1630) cast his horoscope in Prague. The Habsburgs grew suspicious of Wallenstein's loyalties and ambitions, and he was assassinated by imperial officers in 1634 (Agnew, *The Czechs*, 69–70).

98. The Prague Castle's Golden Lane was first built for Rudolf II's castle guards and occupied by goldsmiths in the 17th century. The Dalibor Tower or Daliborka (1496) was used as a prison until 1781. Its first inmate, the Czech knight Dalibor, was said to have rebelled on behalf of the common people and inspired an 1868 opera by Smetana.

99. Johann Georg Schröpfer (also Schrepfer; ca.1738–1774) was a German charlatan, Freemason, and illusionist. Though an apparent suicide, his cause of death is disputed (Geffarth, "The Masonic Necromancer").

100. Formally the "Church" of St. Jindřich and St. Kunhuta, a 13th-century Gothic structure built as Prague's New Town was founded (see notes 5, 25).

101. Located in central Spain, El Escorial is the largest Renaissance building in the world. It houses a monastery, basilica, the royal crypt for 26 Spanish kings and queens of the Habsburg and Bourbon dynasties, and more.

102. *Templar Lane* (Czech *Templová ulička*) was named after the Knights Templar.

103. In 1620, near the start of the Thirty Years War, a Habsburg-led Catholic coalition defeated Protestant Bohemian nobles and their allies outside Prague. Twenty-seven rebels (seventeen burghers, seven knights, and three nobles) were executed on the Old Town Square and twelve of their heads suspended from hooks on the Bridge Tower (see also note 7).

104. *Commandery*. Here, the office of a lodge commander.

105. Paracelsus challenged traditional pathology by arguing that each organ had an *archeus* (a sort of spirit or principle) that filtered out impurities as an "inner alchemist." Disrupting the *archeus* caused illness (Moran, "Paracelsus [1493–1541]").

106. An unsourced quote by or paraphrase from Swedenborg (see note 75), which sometimes includes the language "God created us in such a way that our inner self is in the spiritual world and our outer self is in the physical world" (Swedenborg, *True Christianity* [§14], 20). This divide between inner and outer selves parallels what for Karásek was the "mystery" of the third sex (see note 4).

107. The "sidereal body" or "astral body" is an esoteric concept that originated in Neoplatonism and found new expression in Renaissance-era magic, as well as in later occultism and Madame Blavatsky's theosophy (see note 132).

108. Truths derived from the supposed writings of the legendary Hermes Trismegistus. Hermetics was revived during the Renaissance. Here, the meaning is of a primordial, universal wisdom contained in all religions.

109. The story of an eternal flame that fascinated esotericist thinkers including Kircher (see notes 44, 94).

110. Founded in 1863, the Beuronese Congregation is a major house in the Benedictine Order, its black garb symbolic of penitence and death to the world. As an art collector, Karásek was likely acquainted with the Beuron School of art, which departed from the Romantic aesthetic then prevalent in Catholic religious painting. The Emmaus Monastery was built in Prague in the 14th century as a Benedictine outpost in Slavic Europe; the first Benedictine monastery in Prague was Břevnov (see note 116).

111. *Andrea del Sarto* (1486–1530). A High Renaissance Florentine painter renowned for his frescos and altarpieces. His work *Saint John the Baptist as a Boy* (ca.1526) hangs in the Palatine Gallery in Florence. The National Gallery in Prague holds del Sarto's canvas *Madonna and Child*, recovered from the eastern Bohemian noble family Colloredo-Mansfeld's residence at Opočno.

112. Latin, "conquer or die," a motto used in various military, heraldic, and Masonic contexts.

113. Already bygone styles by then: the showy Empire style is associated with Napoleon I's tenure as emperor (1809–15). Imitations of Renaissance Italian majolica had their heyday in the 19th century.

114. Bílá Hora's Baroque Church of Our Lady Victorious, built on the site of a post-conflict memorial chapel, was completed in 1730 as a pilgrimage site. Closed by Habsburg ruler Joseph II in 1785, it reopened around 1800.

115. Hvězda ("Star") is the site of this geometric Renaissance hunting lodge, completed in 1555 by Holy Roman Emperor Ferdinand II (r. 1619–37). Anna Lauermannová sometimes hosted Karásek at the nearby villa she had bought from Zeyer.

116. A natural spring (*studánka*) at Břevnov Monastery feeds a stream called Brusnice. According to legend, on February 25, 1416, the spring ran red as blood for an entire night and morning; this was taken as a harbinger of the bloodshed to come in the Hussite wars (Břevnovský klášter, "Historia fundationis monasterii Brzewnoviensis"). The text's reference to the Vojtěška therefore seems misplaced, as this section is about later events at Bílá Hora; it is possible that others later reinterpreted the legend to refer to Bílá Hora, or that Karásek is doing so for rhetorical effect.

   Břevnov was founded as a Benedictine monastery in 993 by Bohemian king Boleslav II of the Přemyslid family and the cleric Vojtěch of the powerful Slavník family; Vojtěch was canonized as St. Adalbert soon after his death in 997 (Agnew, *The Czechs*, 14, 16, 24).

117. A formation of Neapolitans fought for the Catholic Habsburgs at Bílá Hora. Bohemian nobleman Count Heinrich von Schlick (1580–1650) was captured in battle and then pardoned; he later returned to imperial service.

118. A field in Jerusalem linked to Judas Iscariot (Matthew 27:1–10, Acts 1:18–19).

119. Famously, Dominic (1559–1630) recovered a painting of the Virgin Mary (Our Lady of the Bowed Head) at a Roman monastery church in 1610. Pope Paul V sent him to support Ferdinand II. Dominic was present at the Battle of Bílá Hora. He died in Vienna and received the title Venerable in 1907 (Hermann, "Thomas a Jesu").

120. Elector Palatine of the Rhine, Frederick V had accepted the rebellious estates' offer of the Bohemian crown in 1619

(Parker, "Battle of White Mountain"). The brevity of his royal career won him the epithet "The Winter King" (Agnew, *The Czechs*, 69).

121. An apparent allusion to Creon's speech in Sophocles' play *Oedipus Rex* (420s BCE). In the play, Creon is commanded by the oracle to drive out the "pollution" (Oedipus' incest) from the kingdom of Thebes.

122. *By the spear side.* By the male side. The Pragmatic Sanction (1713) allowed Habsburg Emperor Charles VI's (r. 1711–40) daughters to inherit the family lands.

123. Prince Christian II was the son of Christian I of Anhalt-Bernburg (1568–1630), a minor German Protestant prince but a key figure in the conflict. He chaired the military council of the Protestant Union (1608), the formation of which provoked the counteralliance of the Catholic League (1609). He urged the Bohemian estates to resist Catholic Habsburg rule. He survived the Battle of Bílá Hora, reconciled with the dynasty, and returned to his estates (Parker, "Christian of Anhalt").

124. The Order of the Servants of Mary (Servites) is an order of mendicant friars, founded in 1233 in Florence. Construction of the monastery in Bílá Hora began in 1628. By Karásek's time, it had a late Baroque exterior and had been repurposed as flats and an inn.

125. Hájek ("Grove"), 17 km (10.6 mi) from Prague's western edge, is the site of a Franciscan monastery built in the 17th century. A line of glassed-in "chapels" (shrines) ran along the road leading to it.

126. Bílá Hora was not formally annexed to Prague until the 1960s.

127. All texts of alchemy and esoteric knowledge popular with occultists. Karásek gives their titles in Latin.

   For more on von Nettesheim's work, see Compagni, "Heinrich Cornelius Agrippa von Nettesheim." On Hollandus, see "Johann Isaac Hollandus." On the von Hildenbrandseck edition, see van Gijsen, "Isaac Hollandus Revisited," 327 n47. On the *Sibylline Oracles*, see Gruen, "Sibylline Oracles."

128. For Paracelsus and his followers, the four types of elementals are gnomes, undines, sylphs, and salamanders,

corresponding to earth, water, air, and fire. Paul mentions them in Colossians 2:8.

129. *Volts.* As used below, these appear to be wax receptacles for spiritual effigies.

130. One of Kircher's many major works is an encyclopedia about China.

131. A voodoo-like practice described by prominent French parapsychologist and hypnologist Paul Joire in the 1890s. The subject's sensitivity (for instance, to pain) could be transferred to an effigy.

132. *Astral.* Apparently, a kind of duplicate body as postulated by Neoplatonists and later invoked in theosophy (see note 107). British theosophist Annie Besant used the terms "Etheric Double" for the physical body's ethereal counterpart and "Astral Body" for the so-called emotional body.

133. "Doctor Illuminatus" to Franciscans, Ramon Llull (ca.1232–ca.1315) was a Catalan philosopher, poet, and theologian. His *Ars demonstrativa* apparatus attempted to codify all knowledge in an elegant system of concentric and counterbalancing wheels. Though his "rationalistic mysticism" led to papal condemnation in 1376, he was later beatified (Priani, "Ramon Llull"; Encyclopaedia Britannica Online, "Ramon Llull").

Various alchemical works have been falsely attributed to Llull (Hillgarth, *Ramon Lull and Lullism*, 297).

Karásek later wrote the novel *Obrácení Raymonda Lulla* (The Conversion of Raymond Llull, 1919), in which a man of the world reinvents himself as a man of God.

APPENDICES

I. THE CZECH POLEMIC ON OSCAR WILDE (1895)

Oscar Wilde's works began to circulate in Europe in the 1890s, beginning in France and spreading from there. The author's fame grew quickly in German-speaking Europe, including Habsburg Vienna. In 1892, the Hungarian-born physician, thinker, and Zionist Max Nordau issued a scathing critique of the aestheticist credo of "art for art's sake" in his two-volume social critique *Entartung* (Degeneration), where he painted decadence and symbolism in criminological terms, as expressions of an underlying pathology.[1] That view, linking aestheticism to moral corruption, resonated both in Wilde's trials in England and in the Czech and Central European polemics over the trials in the spring of 1895.

Coverage of the trials was widespread. It sparked commentary on public morality and British justice. In many contexts, words were minced to obscure the nub of the charges: Wilde's homosexual behavior. In that respect, the Czech polemic is rather frank.

The sentencing turned Wilde into a "literary celebrity," stimulating new translations of his works, productions of his plays, criticism, and mythology, at least outside England.[2] In the Czech sphere, the still-new modern arts journal *Moderní revue* (Moderne Revue) dedicated its June 1895 issue to Wilde. "Wilde fever" peaked in Central and Eastern Europe after the author's death in November 1900.

This appendix includes all the substantive journalistic interpolations that I am aware of in the Czech polemic on Oscar Wilde in May and June 1895, with entries from the journals *Čas*, *Moderní revue*, *Studentský sborník*, and *Naše doba*; the journals themselves represent some of the new ferment of Czech public life in the 1890s, and the polemic offers a case study in public discourse.[3]

. . .

The Crown Prosecution Service formally charged Oscar Wilde with "gross indecency" on April 6, 1895. Even before the trial opened, the Czech weekly *Duch času* (Spirit of the Time, 1898–1938) was reporting on April 14 that Wilde, "the famous English aesthete and herald of morality" had been "convicted" (*usvědčen*) of "an unnatural crime that cannot even be written of in the newspaper."[4] On April 20, the Czech émigré *Dělnické listy* (Workers' Paper) inveighed against Wilde at length in class terms ("the 'poet' and 'aesthete' of the wealthy English and American rabble") and on moral grounds ("a criminal against humanity and nature"). "What does the Bible say about Sodom and Gomorrah?"[5] The April 21 edition of the Opava-based, German-language *Troppauer Zeitung* in Moravia briefly noted the launch of proceedings.[6]

. . .

The weekly journal *Čas: list věnovaný veřejným otázkám* (Time: A Journal Dedicated to Public Questions, 1886–89 biweekly, 1889–1901 weekly, 1901–15 daily) was published by publicist Jan Herben.[7] With its mix of social, political, and cultural coverage, it was aimed at a broader reading public and followed a liberal, anticlerical line.

Herben began his journalism career in 1885–86 at the Young Czech-affiliated daily *Národní listy* (National News) but was fired for his defense of the academic Tomáš Garrigue Masaryk (1850–1937) in the simmering manuscripts controversy (see below). Herben then founded *Čas* in cooperation with the Realist political grouping led by Masaryk and others.

Raised a strict Catholic, by 1880 Masaryk had entered a reformed Calvinist church. His intellectual reputation was bolstered in 1886, when he led a dogged and ultimately persuasive challenge to the authenticity of the Queen's Court and Green Mountain literary manuscripts, touted as national treasures since their "discoveries" in 1817 but persistently suspect.[8] Just as uncompromisingly as Masaryk judged national mythmaking and utilitarian relativity (see note 33 below), he opposed aestheticism's "beautiful lies" and aberrant sexuality. As Czech queer historian Jan Seidl notes, the *Čas* piece is anonymous (2012, 80). Its lighter tone does not jibe with that of "Sursum" (Masaryk) in *Naše doba* (Our Age) below, but its captious approach does; and Herben was an admirer of Masaryk.

Čas, May 4, 1895[9]
Anonymous

A great talent has run forever aground; it has destroyed its own future. The decadent Oscar Wilde has been a public figure for a number of years; he is 41 years old. His plays *A Woman of No Importance* and *An Ideal Husband* have been ranked among the relative best of what today's England has so precious little to offer. Of his essays, we are most familiar with the one recently translated in Vienna's *Die Zeit*[10]—"The Decay of Lying"—in which he protests that lying is in decline, particularly in the arts. This essay, much debated in England years ago, is symptomatic of his intellectual tendency: while reading in a newspaper (*The Weekly Scotsman*[11]) of the trial in which certain unnatural, ancient Greek perversions of his have come to light, we are reminded of how in that essay, he holds forth against all that is natural, finds nature's sunset as disagreeable as the color reproduction of a garish painting, and scoffs at nature with all its sod, praising divans as much more comfortable. This decadent has risen to a level whence he can "set the tone" in his own country. Meanwhile, however, he has been host to an inner beast. This entire catastrophe is of his own making. For it was he who brought suit against the Marquis of Queensberry for libel. The Marquis had been concerned with his son, Lord Douglas,[12] whom he sought to extricate from Wilde's dubious friendship. But at the trial, the defense brought out so much evidence and so many flagrant instances of Wilde's ancient Greek or, if you prefer, French "moral insanity," wherein a young man substitutes, so to speak, for a woman, that the defendant Marquis was vindicated and released, while the plaintiff, Wilde, was arrested.

During the proceedings, Wilde engaged in his subtle badinage and reassessments of moral values. He spoke in paradoxes and answered questions with impudent quips. A few characteristic examples:

Wilde wrote to Lord Douglas: "My dear boy, your sonnet was delightful, and it is a wonder those red, rose-leaved lips of yours should have been made for the music of singing rather than the madness of chitchat." ("Abominable immorality!" cried the judge.)

Q: Have you had this feeling of "mad adoration" for a young man several years younger than yourself?

Wilde: I have never adored anyone but myself.

Q: Why is your friendship so fatal to young men?

Wilde: I don't think any grown man can influence another grown man.

Q: You say, "Your long, gilded soul walks between passion and poetry?"

Wilde: That's a magnificent locution. That letter of mine is unique!

Q: Here is another letter which I believe you also wrote to Lord Alfred Douglas. [March 1893, Savoy Hotel]

Dearest of All Boys,

Your letter was delightful, red and yellow wine to me; but I am sad and out of sorts. Bosie, you must not make scenes with me. They kill me, they wreck the loveliness of life. I cannot see you, so Greek and gracious, distorted with passion. I cannot listen to your curved lips saying hideous things to me. I would sooner be blackmailed by every renter in London than to have you bitter, unjust, hating. You are the divine thing I want, the thing of grace and beauty; but I don't know how to do it. Shall I come to Salisbury? My bill here is 49 pounds for a week. I have also got a new sitting-room over the Thames [*Čas* adds "for you"]. Why are you not here, my dear, my wonderful boy? I fear I must leave; no money, no credit, and a heart of lead.

Your own,

Oscar[13]

[Marquis of Queensberry's defense attorney Edward Carson]: Is that an extraordinary letter?

Wilde: I think everything I write is extraordinary. [I think that is an extraordinary letter. Yes, I don't pose as being ordinary—good heavens!—I don't pose as ordinary. Ask me any questions you like about it.]

[Carson]: [I am afraid I have a good deal to ask you.] Isn't that a love letter?

Wilde: It is a letter expressive of love.[14]

Prior to the trial, Wilde managed to buy back several important letters from a third person, who managed to exploit this fateful case for material gain. However, this did not change matters one bit, since there came to light instances with other young men, of various stations (for example, with [Walter Grainger,] one street newspaper vendor), in which a certain Taylor was also his intermediary. Even during that part of the interrogation, Wilde was banteringly bold:

[Carson]: Did you ever kiss [Grainger]?

Wilde: Oh, no, [never in my life;] he was a peculiarly plain boy.[15]

Wilde sometimes made the excuse of friendship with the young men, of his own literary position. That is why the judge [*sic*] asked him in one instance:

[Carson]: Was Alfonso [Conway's conversation] literary?

[Wilde: No, it was, on the contrary, quite simple and easy to be understood.

(*Laughter.*)

Carson: He was an uneducated lad, wasn't he?]

W: Oh, he was a pleasant, nice creature.[16] [He was not cultivated. (*Laughter.*) Don't sneer at that. He was a pleasant nice creature. His ambition was to be a sailor.][17]

And this bantering gallows humor kept up throughout the days of the trial. In the process, Wilde justified his views on morality, or rather, defended his exaltation above the world's opinions on morality. This is related to his literary views that a thing is neither good nor bad but rather well or badly written,[18] and that he shall be the judge of this.

The plaintiff Wilde, who even absented himself from the final day, was, as noted, arrested at the end of the proceedings, and one thing is clear: that his literary talents will never be heard from again. There is as yet no majority in England capable of separating an individual's art from his morality, in clear consequence of which Wilde's plays and writings are swiftly being boycotted. The newspapers carry telegrams from places where his works have been excluded from repertories and his books banned from particular libraries. Indeed, the case seems even to have generally undercut decadent literature's influence in England, or at least for the "moral insanity" within it to become still more evident.

. . .

Moderní revue (Moderne Revue, 1894–1925) was the first Czech modern arts journal, founded and published by Arnošt Procházka in collaboration with Jiří Karásek ze Lvovic. In the manuscripts dispute mentioned above, lyric poet Jaroslav Vrchlický and others of the Parnassian literary school had dismissed the younger literati among their opponents as "moderns."[19] A separate group of "moderns" including the young critic F. X. Šalda (1867–1937) signed the Manifesto of the Czech Moderne in 1895, calling for greater individualism in the arts and beyond.

In the Czech polemic on Oscar Wilde, Karásek and Procházka were the only figures to defend their English artistic counterpart publicly. Procházka, who did not identify as a member of the "third sex," defended Wilde by citing contemporary psychology.

Moderní revue, May 1895[20]
–C– [Arnošt Procházka and Jiří Karásek ze Lvovic]

Respectable prudes are once again up in arms. The great artist Oscar Wilde has fallen prey to England's notorious "morality." As if this were anything more than a case of psychopathology. And the guardians of "public order and morality" have arrived. Among them, to our surprise, is the journal *Čas*. It says straight out that Wilde had "an inner beast." He spoke in "impudent quips." "He destroyed his own future." As if anyone had the right to ask the author about his private life. Does his work not speak for him? Does anyone ask about Goethe's private life?[21] And what is it that's so immoral? One act is as good as another. Perhaps the herd will join hands and cry out: immorality, sin! How can one speak of immorality in such a case? In [the Parisian journal] *La Plume*,[22] L[ouis] Lormel rightly points out that for those of us who believe in Reason alone, there is no immorality, that Wilde's "crime" is rather ridiculous and grotesque. For he who does not believe in God cannot recognize moral laws, since these have no authority. The act in question should be no more criminal than a normal one. We are even glad that old, conventional morality has had another little shake-up. Such cases are not cured by prison. I recall Verlaine's words in the Introduction to [Henri] d'Argis's novel *Sodome* (Sodom, 1888),[23] in which the very pious hero commits the same sexual "perversions" as Wilde, words declaring the novel to be pure and moral. The "ugly quintessence of the bourgeoisie" is naturally up in arms, but that is of no account to the artist.

. . .

The May 6 issue of the Moravian paper *Mährisches Tagblatt* carried a light anecdote from a garden party that mentioned Wilde, alluding to him as "the now living dead" (*der jetzt Lebendigtodte*).[24]

. . .

The journal *Studentský sborník strany neodvislé* (Student Digest of the Independent Party) may have been founded during the popular protests and street clashes of 1894 in Prague. It was published in the city's Vinohrady quarter and lasted until at least 1907, judging from available volumes on the secondary book market. Augustin (Gusta) Žalud (1872–1928) also wrote under the pseudonyms Gustav Mach and Spektator. In 1902 he cofounded the Realist Party-affiliated weekly *Přehled* (Survey). He is identified as the author of the editorial column below.[25]

Žalud was part of the Prague generation of the 1890s, which included newly visible progressives and radicals, as well as students and workers. Through journalism, political debates, and underground societies, many of these actors agitated for greater civil liberties and universal manhood suffrage. They received at least some inspiration and energy from members of the contemporary progressive Serbian youth movement Omladina. In addition, they received encouragement from the middle-class Young Czech party, which expected an expanded franchise to increase its share of seats relative to their Old Czech rivals in the lower house of the Reichsrat (Imperial Council) in Vienna. In the same Reichsrat, the Young Czechs therefore introduced a bill to expand voting rights, meeting with firm resistance from the established parties.

Demonstrations in Prague led to a state of emergency. In 1894, the year before the Wilde polemic, the Omladina trials resulted in a collective ninety years in prison for sixty-two defendants. By the end of this episode, the Young Czech leadership had distanced itself from progressive and radical youth. Masaryk's progressive Realist Party broke with the Young Czechs.

At the time of the Wilde polemic, Žalud had not yet published his first book, a study of the patriotic journalist Karel Havlíček Borovský (1821–1856). He continued to pursue his interests in ethnography and later became a librarian.

Studentský sborník, May 15, 1895[26]
Augustin Žalud

The first duty of any decent journal is the absolute morality of its reporting. That means not only to distort nothing, but also to keep silent about nothing. As to the forthrightness of our own Czech reporting, we have a new case in point: on April 24, a trial was held in the interesting and instructive case of the broker *Mr. Lion vs. Dr. Nejedlý, V. Stech, and Mr. and Mrs. Schiech*. The Czech dailies generally carried items about the case. Only *Hlas národa* (Voice of the Nation),[27] though at other times the willing purveyor of "amusing" news from the courtroom, was silent. Mr. Lion continues to print his *Český merkur* (Czech Mercury) at the National Printing and Publishing House.[28] So much for [morality in] practice.

And now something about morality in theory. In opposition to *Čas*, *Moderní revue* has taken the side of Oscar Wilde, whose sexual perversity and immorality *Čas* has rightly denounced in its issue number 18. The theory that our "moderns" proclaim here is interesting for its frankness.[29] Even instructive, for the many in our country who have, justifiably, yet to understand decadentism [*sic*]. I suspect that *Naše doba* shall now see its error of judgment with respect to [Arnošt] Procházka's *Prostibolo duše* (Brothel of the Soul, 1894).[30] A few excerpted citations shall suffice: "As if anyone had the right to ask an author about his private life." "One act is as good as another"—"For he who does not believe in God cannot recognize moral laws—" Indeed, as to the latter, we can stand with our decadents. Where there is no religion, there can be no morality. "If there is no God, everything is permitted" (Dostoevsky: Ivan Karamazov).[31] But as for the former, we are happy to count ourselves "in the ugly quintessence of the bourgeoisie." We are still a little out of date in our views. We consider morality indispensable to the development of society, and that "morality must not be merely a matter of taste, and

must not forsake eternal principles, or adhere to acciden-
tal circumstances" (Macaulay).[32] That is why we can show
no enthusiasm for a kind of "morality of higher egoism."[33]
What *Moderní revue* is moving towards is the exclusive and
sheer worship of faculty and skill, which Parker rightly says
are "the attributes rather than the nature of man."[34] And the
aim of it all—complete intellectual anarchy. As for whether
the public has a right to ask about an author's private life,
Čas answered this two years ago. We merely reiterate: not
only the right, but also the duty.

Unless an author be moral, he cannot produce a moral,
i.e., a singularly good work. For his view and understanding of things shall not be correct. We therefore reject both
immorality and affectation in the work of the artist. For that
matter—as I am convinced—not even our decadents are as
terrible as they pretend to be. They are only affected (as far
as I have been able to determine from their writings and their
lives). In reality, they are equally good and peaceable citizens
who do not transgress against morality any more or any differently than the rest of the "ugly quintessence of the bourgeoisie." We have mentioned *Moderní revue*'s theory only in
view of the danger posed by the proclamation of such a thing.

. . .

Čas, May 18, 1895[35]
Anonymous

Oscar Wilde, the English decadent of whom we wrote
last time, has been provisionally released. *Moderní revue* is
astonished to see that our own journal has stood with the
guardians of public morality and order. It itself judges the
matter differently: "The high and mighty prudes (they say)
are once again up in arms... As if this were anything more
than a case of psychopathology... *And what is it that is so
immoral? One act is as good as another.* [emphasis in original]

Perhaps the herd shall join hands and cry out: immorality, sin! … *La Plume* rightly points out that for those of us who believe in Reason alone, there is no immorality, that Wilde's 'crime' is 'rather ridiculous and grotesque.'"—If the *crime* is ridiculous and grotesque, and does not rattle decadents, why should *Moderní revue* be upset by the *sentence* passed against a lecher? From its point of view, the court should also be ridiculous and grotesque, and there is nothing to be upset about. How can decadents, believing in Reason alone, be upset by anything at all?!

. . .

The journal *Naše doba: revue pro vědu, umění a život sociální* (Our Age: A Revue for Science, Art, and Society, 1894–1944, 1946–49) had a sober, academic tone and polemicized both broadly and vigorously with other Czech journals. As did its predecessor *Athenaeum* (1883–93), founded by faculty from the newly independent Czech university in Prague,[36] *Naše doba* carried articles on social, economic, and pedagogical topics, as well as on religion from a Lutheran-Calvinist perspective (the only Protestant churches recognized under the Habsburgs). The journal was based in Prague's Vinohrady suburb. Publisher Jan Laichter was known primarily for philosophical, sociological, and economic titles.[37]

At the time of the Wilde polemic, Masaryk was its editor. Seidl identifies the author "Sursum" below as Masaryk (2012, 82), the future first president of Czechoslovakia.

Naše doba, May 20, 1895[38]
"Sursum" (Masaryk)

[…] In England, they have an "artistic question" of their own. Oscar Wilde, the decadent writer, was put on trial for paederasty [*sic*]. There is consternation among the public and the writers in their respective professional capacities.[39]

This illustrious public is always the same. (And is everywhere the same.) It has read Wilde's books, sometimes in secret, but it has read them; it has circulated his more ribald quips ("Oscarisms") with the piety reserved for those about the stock-market—but paederasty, this is "after all," simply beyond the pale. Oscar Wilde has been put on the social equivalent of the Index Librorum Prohibitorum.[40] But this mindlessly virtuous parochialism was not troubled by Wilde's writings, written mainly in the spirit of paederasty and sexual perversity—it took a scandal to jolt them out of that base, *soi disant* rectitude for a moment.

That some writers are taking Oscar Wilde's part is understandable. Even a murderer on trial must have his defender. We can understand why these writers point out the hypocrisy of the public, English and otherwise. But it is simply a great leap from there to what *Moderní revue* (no. 8) cites as a "correct" view from the Parisian journal *La Plume*: that for one who believes in Reason alone, there is no morality, and that Wilde's "crime" is consequently "rather ridiculous and grotesque." "There is no sin except stupidity," as Oscar Wilde himself wrote.[41] *Moderní revue* goes on to add that the unbeliever in God can supposedly admit of no moral laws, since there is no authority for them. And finally, that Wilde's private life is supposedly no one else's business.

I do not presume here, in a few words, to elucidate the great problems that concern *Moderní revue*. But I will pit one opinion against another. In the first place, it seems to me that one who believes in Reason alone can never be a paederast. Paederasty is not reason, it is filth. Second, whom then are we to believe that there is only Reason? Third, it is not true that unbelievers in God do not recognize the authority of moral law: Bentham, Mill, etc., all who have been precise thinkers, even though they did not believe in God, have shown a most vigorous appreciation for ethics. Surely, however, no such man would say "one act is as good as another." If this is so, then first of all, it would follow for *Moderní revue* that the stupid and hypocritical "bourgeoisie" is likewise "rather ridiculous and grotesque," and that it would therefore be committing a mere "crime" were it simply to take Mr. Oscar Wilde and all the decadents and writers in general and drown them. "One act is as good as another." To say that private life is nobody's business! But what kind of private life is it when any writer gives his works to the public, and when at the end of the day, these works are nothing but an echo, a mirror, an outpouring of that "private" life? Some "private" life that is! A life, yes, but hardly a private one, and sexual perversion in every form is simply death. And death is not something we care to have served up to us together with Wildean green carnations.

Yet Wilde's brother in decadence, [Joris-Karl] Huysmans, took a different route.[42] He became a Trappist and converted, to the great joy of our journal *Vlast* (no. 7).[43] The news of his conversion to the Catholic Church was mentioned in Paris's *Le Figaro*; Huysmans himself confirmed it and reportedly gave the place and time when he received the holy sacraments. *Vlast* says that the news is a comfort for Catholics, for on the whole, the world's great poets are said to have been universally pious, e.g., Longfellow and Tennyson. *Vlast* seems not to remember that the two aforementioned poets were not Catholics, but that is not of primary importance here. There is something else at hand. We should be grateful to *Vlast* if it explained to us how it is that decadent and symbolist poetry originated in Paris and in Catholic countries at all. If Huysmans's conversion is truly sincere, no one will dare make light of his action. "Sincere," meaning that he did not leap headlong into monastic asceticism, and that this asceticism is not a new installment of that materialism in which everyone from Baudelaire down to Zola and Wilde has been drowning.

. . .

On May 26, the respectable German-language daily *Politik* (1862–1907), founded by politicians from the Old Czech party to promote the Czech national cause, carried a brief item by "K.-B." noting Wilde and Taylor's convictions and sentencing to two years at hard labor.[44]

. . .

Moderní revue, June 1895[45]
–A– [Arnošt Procházka], –K– [Karásek]

–A– Our remarks concerning the *affaire* of Mr. Wilde have given rise to much malice, slander, and stupidity in private. Our journals have been infected by them too. In several respects Mr. Panizza's article may serve as an explanation for them. At least on the psychophysiological side, surely. These "terrible" words: one act is as good as another—I can safely say, have been clearly set forth here. *Naše doba* states, for that matter quite astutely, that "he who believes in Reason alone will never be a paederast." That may very well be: but, we ask—where in our periodical, for goodness' sake, has there been any suggestion to the contrary? After all, to say that for believers in Reason alone there is no immorality ought not necessarily to be taken as referring to the sin stigmatized by Religion. We acknowledge that if it were up to Reason alone, there would be no such cases as Mr. Wilde's. But other factors are decisive here—a person's entire psychological and physiological nature in particular circumstances and eras. Because of this, from the standpoint of Reason, grasping this, we can hardly see any "sin" or "crime" or "unnaturalness" in the matter just the same. Finally, a "normal act" could be thought the only legitimate, "pure," "natural" one if its purpose were always kept in mind—but how often is that really the case?! But its purposefulness is hardly to be precluded or prevented... "purely" and "naturally." We understand very well that from the heterosexual person's perspective, paederasty is "filth" (*Naše doba*'s term)—but from the homosexual person's, the opposite is "filth." And is the latter wrong?! For both judgments and opinions are founded in their innermost essences, and are, in a word, inevitable and fated. Are they not? O logic! Let us not enter into a polemic against *Naše doba*'s other remarks ("whom are we then to believe that there is only Reason?"—and where the contrary has been irrefutably proven—"It is not true that men who do not believe in God do not recognize the authority of moral laws: Bentham, Mill, etc. all who have been precise thinkers, even though they did not believe in God, have shown a most vigorous appreciation for ethics"—yes, so have we, but for an individual ethic whose authority is conditioned within each person by his own truest being, not by the authority of moral laws dictated from above, wholesale, "abstract," one may say—etc.). Like *Naše doba*, we also do not presume to elucidate in a few words these great and painful mysteries. We merely state that if *Naše doba* had its way, the vast majority of great artists would be judged not by their works but by whether their lives, their private lives (and so, by implication, their books as well), were immoral: Goethe, Byron, Musset, Baudelaire, Poe, Shelley... *Čas* and *Studentský sborník* are of the same opinion. And to all of them we declare: we have not been defending Mr. Wilde—since we have no right to do so; we have not been judging him, because we have no right to do so. We have simply and merely set forth our position on the case, the position of radical individualists. We are neither impertinent enough nor narrow-minded enough nor brutal enough to judge someone for a pathological condition—should the gentlemen find such a word more palatable—to regard him as ruined and to ruin him ourselves, like the mendacious prudishness of the bourgeoisie

and its intrusive institutions, not only in England but elsewhere as well. Perhaps we have made ourselves clearer,
and we joyfully hope that the columnist from *Studentský
sborník* shall now recognize and overcome his naïve astonishment, that one can speak "favorably" of Mr. Wilde's
case without the writer himself therefore having to be—a
paederast or anything of the sort himself. He is too much
of a prankster, my boy, for anyone to be angry with him.

–K– But whatever one's opinion of the *affaire* of Mr.
Wilde may be, the particular manner in which the entire
matter was ended must fill every humane mind with infinite
disgust and loathing. I mean the punishment meted out to
Mr. Wilde for his "crime." The daily papers have made mention of it. Mr. Wilde was condemned to toil among galley
slaves, to the severe punishment of the "treadmill," intended
by the lawgivers' express intent to render the convict incapable of resuming any kind of life afterward, to exhaust his
strength, to ruin him utterly physically. And here, I beg that
our newspapers, outraged by Mr. Wilde's homosexuality
and paederasty to the extent of venting their curses—surely
only by accident and in the first flush of an unanticipated
moral distemper—and even with respect to his entire critical
and poetic oeuvre, they have likewise paused slightly and
shown no compunction about shamefully parading the brutal and bestial manner in which chaste England treats a man
who most belongs in the care of a physician and a psychologist. Psychopathologists of note such as Mr. Krafft-Ebing
(*Psychopathia sexualis*) and others have long since rightly
declared that sexual perversions should not be punished by
the lawgiver at all, just as other diseases and maladies are
not punished. Mr. Krafft-Ebing has shown the consequences
of such legal threats: that there is a caste of people who
allow themselves to be professionally abused in order then
to… exploit the criminality of the act, handed to them by the
lawgiver, and (in the true sense of the word) extort and fleece
their "victims." Not even the most well-meaning and naive

person can believe that "punishment" would "convert" someone and make a heterosexual out of a homosexual. This would be a subversion of nature, the work of a miracle, and miracles, as is well known, do not come so easily even to the most dexterous. But then what is the point of "punishment" at all?! To deter others?! Mr. Oskar Panizza has correctly set forth the complete principle of homosexuality. This means to understand and accept the entire matter without false, hypocritical, prudish pretense. Homosexuality is no modern invention; it is no mere "pernicious" fashion that can be prevented by a decree of the Lord Mayor on every corner; it has always and everywhere existed, and if it is not known and has never been known, that is only because the so-called Public has not seen fit to take cognizance of it, to sanction it, as it has taken cognizance of and sanctioned heterosexual intercourse even in its coarsest shades and forms—and that it has visited the most sovereign contempt on everything that trembled with the faintest flutter of homosexuality. And I return again to England: the barbarous punishment visited on Mr. Oscar Wilde confirms the old truth of the words of Macaulay in his essay on Byron (see Mr. Váňa's *Deliberations and Dispositions*),[46] excellently characterizing that supposed English "virtue" that so appeals to our stern Catos, as it seems to me. As for those gentlemen who have spat so upon Mr. Wilde's name, let them read this apt exposition of that much-touted English chastity, avenging itself upon the individual so that then, calmly—sin continue en masse.

. . .

Naše doba, June 10, 1895[47]
"Sursum" (Masaryk)

Moderní revue disagrees with us on the Wilde affair on two points. We return to the matter because we wish to be clear about it, if it is possible to dispense with this in so brief a discussion. Granted that *Moderní revue* has already set forth its views on the relation of art to morality and has a certain advantage over us, for we have not been over the subject as thoroughly. For the present, at any rate, it is a matter of stating opinions. *Moderní revue* cites Krafft-Ebing, according to which acknowledged authority in the field, the sexual psychopathy of sexual perversion reportedly ought not to be subject to judicial sanction—by this account, the Wilde case is at most the province of the physician and the psychologist. We are glad that *Moderní revue* cites Krafft-Ebing; for we intend to do the same, and so to dislodge this dispute from "philosophical" conjecture. In his book [*Psychopathia Sexualis*], Krafft-Ebing devotes a separate chapter to paederasty, and granted, he states that there are two kinds of perversity here: there are paederasts who are mentally ill, and these are not responsible for their actions; but "much more commonly is paederasty an ugly vice," the vice of people who are corrupted and also responsible for their actions under criminal law. According to Krafft-Ebing, every case (thus including Wilde's) ought to be examined by a physician to determine whether it is an actual disease, "lest mere immorality be excused under the cover of disease." This, then, is Krafft-Ebing's opinion, and for our part we add that, judging by Wilde's writings, his case is quite clear to us, and that Krafft-Ebing would also conclude from them that [Wilde acted] "under such cover," etc. We take the same view in assessing the article by the now famous, for being sentenced to prison, Dr. Panizza on "homosexuality":[48] to Mr. Panizza, "one act is as good as another," and there is no talking to such gentlemen. In the relationship between man and woman, Mr. Panizza sees only a physical union and therefore reaches a phenomenal conclusion: "one carnality is as good as another"—"one act is as good as another." Mr. Panizza is as good as Mr. Wilde. Of course, poor Wilde must now walk the penal treadmill—isn't it terrible? To be sure, but not only because it is Mr. Wilde treading it. He has his lordly friend, for that matter: it is a peculiar thing that not only "great" men like Mr. Wilde and Mr. Panizza have the theory of "one act is as good as another" but also "great"... bankers and financiers. Curious!

. . .

On July 24, the Brno-based German-language daily *Brünner Zeitung* reported sympathetically on the breakdown of Wilde's health at Reading Gaol from the "terrible punishment of the treadmill." It noted that he had asked for the works of Thomas Aquinas and was now engaged in the weaving of straw mats.[49]

That September, with Wilde still at Reading, the Catholic Czech publication *Čech* (1869–96, 1904–37) reported with apparent satisfaction that the "famous English poet" who was convicted for "crimes against morality" had been sent to "England's highest jail," where he labored all day "to the point of exhaustion." Although once "handsomely wealthy," the journal continued, Wilde had filed for bankruptcy with debts amounting to "400,000 of our krone."[50]

In November, *Národní listy* reported that the French prisoner "Arton," in British custody, had insistently requested not to be placed in the cell where Oscar Wilde had been incarcerated. According to the report, he was assured of placement in a cell where other Frenchmen had been held.[51]

. . .

Naše doba, October 1905[52]
1905–06, vol. 13, no. 1 (October 1905)

Ten years later, the inside front cover of *Naše doba* carries the advertisement *O dobrou četbu pro mládež* (Good Reading for Youth) that includes Wilde's *The Happy Prince*, printed by the journal's own publisher Jan Laichter. On pages 65–67 the literature column also notes two new Wilde translations into Czech (*Salome* and *The Picture of Dorian Gray*), followed by negative reviews of the works and Wilde's character.

Notes

1. Evangelista, "Oscar Wilde: European by Sympathy," 3–5.
2. Evangelista, 6.
3. For additional discussion of this Czech polemic, see Beran, "Oscar Wilde and the Czech Decadence"; and Seidl, Nozar, and Wintr, *Od žaláře k oltáři*, 79–87. For background on the period, see David-Fox, *1890s Generation*. See also the 1906 novel *Prosinec* (December) by Viktor Dyk for a fictional portrayal of multifarious and muddled ideological debate following the fall of the Badeni government in 1897.
4. *Duch času: nedělní list Svornosti* 18, no. 28, April 14, 1895, 442.
5. *Dělnické listy* 2, no. 25, April 20, 1895, 2. The paper was an arm of the International Working People's Association (IWPA, founded 1883), a revolutionary-socialist and anarchist organization.
6. *Troppauer Zeitung* 110, no. 92, April 21, 1895, 3.
7. This title has a complex history. It continued to appear until 1915 and reappears in 1920–24. For greater detail, see Databáze Národní knihovny ČR: https://aleph.nkp.cz/F/8DYEVTG8L2566JAAVBDTUAYRTECTL78BA11U2K2FC1A6IM9SD6-07763?func=short-jump&jump=000021.
8. On this subject, see Cooper, *Czech Manuscripts*.
9. Transl. from Anonymous, "Umění, věda, školství," *Čas* 9, no. 18, May 4, 1895, 276–77.
10. Vienna's liberal German-language *Die Zeit* (The World, 1894–1919) was first a journal and later a newspaper.
11. The title, as given in English in the Czech text, likely refers to Edinburgh's *The Scotsman* (weekly 1817–55; daily 1855–2004), edited 1880–1905 by Charles Alfred Cooper.

12. Lord Alfred "Bosie" Douglas, close to Karásek in age.
13. For the original English text of the letter, see Holland and Mortimer, *The Real Trial of Oscar Wilde*, 110. On his website *Famous-trials.com*, law professor Douglas O. Linder notes that "renter" was a slang term for a male prostitute; *Čas* omits this sentence and adds "for you" after "Thames." These discrepancies may have occurred in *Čas*'s source.
14. Holland and Mortimer, 110. *Čas*'s version does not identify the questioner's name or role in the trial. The bracketed portions were excluded in *Čas*'s account and possibly in its source material as well.
15. Holland and Mortimer, 207–8. In *Čas*'s version, the unidentified questioner (Carson) asks only whether Wilde kissed Grainger, to which Wilde replies, "No, he was dirty!" (*špinavý*).
16. In *Čas*'s version and perhaps in its source, this exchange is reduced to: "Was Alfonso a man of letters? Wilde: No, a creature of a pleasant sort." *Čas* does not note any laughter in the courtroom.
17. Holland and Mortimer, 145.
18. From *The Picture of Dorian Gray*: "There is no such thing as a moral or an immoral book [...]" Cf. *Lady Windermere's Fan* (1892): "It is absurd to divide people into good and bad. People are either charming or tedious."
19. Czech Romance philologist Jaroslav Fryčer found that both French Parnassians and their Czech counterparts rejected aspects of Romanticism. The French were divided into "progressives" ("politickers") who emphasized social and political engagement, and "fantasists" ("literati") who pursued art for its own sake, often setting their works in an idealized past to elevate their contents from the gray, unpoetic present. These writers increasingly rejected *pozitivistická popisnost* ("positivist descriptiveness") and alleged didacticism in art (Haman, "Prolegomena k parnasismu," 218, 219, 220–2).
20. Transl. from Procházka and Karásek, "Kritika: Časopisy," signed "–C–."
21. Karl Hugo Pruys examines the question of Goethe's sexuality in his *Die Liebkosungen des Tigers: Eine erotische Goethe-Biographie.*

22. A bimonthly journal (1889–1914) of literature and the arts, then edited by its founder, the French novelist and poet Léon Deschamps. It was supportive of the symbolist movement. For more on the French reception of Oscar Wilde and response to his trials, see Erber, "French Trials of Oscar Wilde"; Hibbitt, "The Artist as Aesthete."

23. Now considered an early gay novel.

24. *Mährisches Tagblatt* 16, no. 104, May 6, 1895, 2. This daily, German-language newspaper was based in Olomouc and ran from 1880 to 1945.

25. See Knihovna Univerzity Palackého v Olomouci, "Žalud, Augustin, 1872–1928."

26. Transl. from Žalud, "Rozhledy časopisecké" [excerpted].

27. Founded as *Pokrok* (Progress) in 1869. Lawyer and Old Czech supporter Josef Hubáček became managing editor in 1885. The journal was renamed *Hlas národa* in March 1886, continuing to 1918.

28. A financial paper (1888–1919, with a brief pause in 1893), published by Josef Lion.

29. Vrchlický's pejorative at the time for his younger literary opponents. Karásek had criticized Vrchlický in print in 1894 for his prudish translations of modern texts. The two ultimately reconciled, with Vrchlický sending Karásek a warm thank-you note (1907) for a copy of *RMM*.

30. A collection of six poems by Procházka printed in 200 copies by *Moderní revue* in December 1894. The Latin *prostibolum* ("brothel") is nearly homophonic with Czech *prostý bol* ("pure grief"). *Naše doba* reviewed the volume in its January 10, 1896 issue (pp. 449–51), where the reviewer attempts a more subtle approach than that by *Moderní revue* opponent Eliška Krásnohorská:

> Zlobit se na pana Procházku a naše dekadenty, je sice lidské, ale kritikovi lépe by slušelo, hledat příčiny toho, že dekadentství u nás tak rychle se ujalo a rozvilo. My jsme zásadní odpůrcové dekadentství; avšak sl. Krásnohorská, když už svazuje »Magdalenu« s »Prostibolem duše« (trochu maliciósnosti slečně

Krásnohorské snad sluší), mohla se stanoviska svého
vůči Macharovi dojít k vývodům docela jiným [...]
     "It is human to be angry with Mr. Procházka and
our decadents, but it would be better for the critic to
look for the reasons why decadence has taken hold and
developed so quickly in our country. We are fundamen-
tal opponents of decadence; but Miss Krásnohorská,
since she associates [the versified novel] *Magdalena*
[1894] with *Prostibolo duše* (a touch of malice perhaps
suits Miss Krásnohorská), she might have reached quite
different conclusions from her opinion of Machar [...]"

31. *The Brothers Karamazov* (1879–80) had just been published
    in Czech, translated by Jaromír Hrubý (1894).
32. This may be a paraphrase from "Essay on Moore's Life of
    Lord Byron" (1831, *Edinburgh Review*) by Baron Thomas
    Babington Macaulay, considerations on Byron's morality and
    his art.
33. Perhaps a reference to enlightened self-interest with respect for
    others, as described by English philosopher Herbert Spencer
    inter alia. Realist leader Masaryk had particular contempt for
    the utilitarianism of Jeremy Bentham and Bentham's adher-
    ents. Young Žalud's attitude may reflect this, given his ties to
    the Realist party.
34. The citation is from *Ecce Deus: Essays on the Life and
    Doctrine of Jesus Christ: with controversial notes on Ecce
    Homo* (1867, p. 162) by English Congregational preacher
    Joseph Parker: 19th-century civilization "brings society very
    much under the influence of the richest culture and refine-
    ment. The spirit of the age is æsthetic [...] Under such circum-
    stances, there is a special temptation to worship faculty, skill,
    or genius,—the attributes rather than the nature of man."
35. Transl. from Anonymous, "Umění, věda, školství. Oscar
    Wilde," *Čas* 9, no. 20, May 18, 1895, 309.
36. Nešpor, "Athenaeum (1883–1893)."
37. Nešpor, "Naše doba (1894–1949)."
38. Transl. from Masaryk [Sursum, pseud.], "Rozhledy
    časopisecké: 'Oscar Wilde'."

39. *Professional capacities.* Lit., "P.T.," *pleno titulo*, a Latin phrase often used in the Habsburg period to avoid listing all the professional and other titles ascribed to members of a group (Stach, *Kafka: The Early Years*, 150).

40. The Roman Catholic Church's list of banned books.

41. This quote appears in the Wilde essay "The Critic as Artist" (1891). English dramatist Christopher Marlowe's play *The Jew of Malta* (ca.1590) includes the similar line, "there is no sin but ignorance."

42. Wilde's prosecutor attempted to demonstrate that the defendant had referenced a "sodomistic novel" in *The Picture of Dorian Gray*. The work in question was by the French author Huysmans: *À rebours* (Against Nature, 1884), in which the hero des Esseintes has multiple homosexual encounters (Posthumus, "Oscar Wilde and Decadent Imitations," 74–76).

43. *Vlast: časopis pro poučení a zábavu* (Homeland: A Journal for Instruction and Entertainment, 1885–1934 and 1937–41), and with it the potent Vlast Cooperative (družstvo Vlast), was founded by Tomáš Škrdle, Catholic priest as well as a folklorist and early advocate of Christian socialism.

44. K.-B., "Proceß Wilde."

45. Transl. from Procházka and Karásek, "Kritika: Časopisy," signed "–A–, –K–."

46. In the 1890s, the colorful Czech textbook author, translator, and satirical poet Jan Váňa was a critic of Vrchlický and other members of the cultural elite, as well as of "art for art's sake." His collection *Úvahy a povahy* (Deliberations and Dispositions, 1892) includes essays on Macaulay and Byron. He was a specialist in English and Russian culture and language.

47. Transl. from Masaryk [Sursum, pseud.], "Rozpravy časopisecké: Ještě Oscar Wilde."

48. German psychiatrist and writer Oskar Panizza wrote the play *Das Liebeskonzil* (The Love Council, 1894), which mocked a licentious Renaissance Vatican and won its author a year in German prison on conviction of 93 counts of blasphemy (Brown, *Oskar Panizza and* The Love Council, 98–100,

126–28). *Moderní revue*'s June 1895 issue included Panizza's "Bayreuth and Homosexuality" (transl. Procházka), which Karásek considered the issue's most important article, a brave defense of homosexuality that brought the journal new subscribers (Karásek, *Vzpomínky*, 130–31); yet he also recalled the bitter opposition of rival critic F. X. Šalda, writer Růžena Svobodová, and her husband (Karásek, *Vzpomínky*, 194–200; Seidl, Nozar, and Wintr, *Od žaláře k oltáři*, 86n). Panizza also asserts that some nations and races are more inclined to homosexuality. See also Vetter, "Introduction to 'Bayreuth and Homosexuality'."

49. *Brünner Tagblatt* 1895, no. 167, July 24, 1895, 2.
50. *Čech*, "Básník a jebo život," 27, no. 220, September 25, 1895, 3. At its founding, the journal represented the Catholic faction in the Old Czech political grouping. Its frequency varied, but in 1895 it was a daily.
51. *Národní listy* 35, no. 323, November 22, 1895, 4.
52. *Naše doba* 13, no. 1, October 1905, 1b, 65.

II. A DOUBLE COMING-OUT (1901)

These letters from the start of a correspondence between Karásek and the younger writer Edvard Klas (pseudonym of Vladimíra Jedličková) reveal a side of Karásek seldom seen in public: vulnerable, disappointed, and lonely. He was tormented by an unrequited love just then. For her part, Jedličková had lost her husband in August 1901 and gave birth to their child in October; they had just married in the fall of 1901. These letters are preserved in the archives of the Památník národního písemnictví (Museum of Czech Literature) in Prague and were published in 2001. Klas's letters to Karásek do not survive.[1]

In the course of their initial exchanges, Jedličková "comes out" to Karásek as a woman writing under a male pseudonym, while Karásek comes out to her as a member of the "third sex."

December 2, 1901
[Letter sent from Smíchov to:] Mr. Edvard Klas, c/o
Mrs. V. Jedličková, 1067 Mánes Street, Royal Vinohrady

Dear Sir,

I was deeply touched by the beautiful letter that you
wrote me. I feel that although we are complete strangers, we
have much in common. This certainty remained with me as I
read your tender, sensible *Gardens in the City*, and since then
you have been my friend, though you had no inkling of this,
and I have been watching the journals for some new item
of yours. I should be very glad to meet you and would beg
that you overcome your aversion to personal contact. I am a
very simple man, and to be able to have a talk in confidence
with someone is one of my life's greatest joys. My address is
Smíchov, Palackého třída no. 406, 3rd floor. If you would
not deny me the honor of your visit (I would be at home
to you tomorrow, Tuesday, from 3 to 5 o'clock, possibly
on Thursday at the same time), I would be very happy. We
would speak of things in which we have a common interest,
and I think there would be plenty of those. In the meantime,
I am sincerely yours

Jiří Karásek

December 7, 1901
[Letter sent from Smíchov to:] Mr. Edvard Klas, c/o
Mrs. V. Jedličková, 1067 Mánes Street, Royal Vinohrady

Dear friend,

I respect your wish to avoid a personal acquaintance,
although I should be pleased to have a conversation with
you. I respect the fiction you have created—for I myself
know how reality wounds one who holds his dreams and
illusions too dear. But if someone such as I, whose dreams life
has torn from him one by one, has become so apathetic to all
slings and arrows, then believe me, solitude can be defended
even among people; one can walk among multitudes and give
voice to his dream through them without being robbed of

it. How often I sit alone in the midst of the gayest company and indulge in my dreams, even as I make small talk with those I must rub elbows with. Absolute solitude, seclusion, these are also my dream—and if I should stray into the church of the Carmelite nuns at Hradčany on certain days of the year,[2] I am renewing my desire to find myself a similar detachment from life and people. But—believe me, I have always felt the deepest solitude in the very midst of crowds, when I felt how different I was, and in solitude the opposite was true, I did not feel alone, I felt a longing for people, for their sympathy, for their friendship, even though I was aware of the fictitiousness of this longing. But—perhaps I am just such a fickle, fragmented soul, lacking the deep peace and contemplation of a true recluse.

    With sincere sympathies from your

Jiří ze Lvovic

December 11, 1901
[Letter sent from Smíchov to:] Mr. Edvard Klas, c/o Mrs. V. Jedličková, 1067 Mánes Street, Royal Vinohrady

Dear friend,

    You will forgive me for maintaining the fiction of Edvard Klas even after your last letter. I seem able to speak to him more easily and intimately. Consequently—I too am obliged to make a slight disclosure, and honesty deserves honesty. If Edvard Klas is not a man, neither am I one. I am not one, at least in the way that the world understands "manhood," and were you to say of me that I "do not love women," I beg you to understand that I do not love them as men do. But a tormented person, whoever he may be, is my brother. Your last letter, my dear, is tilled with such heartbreaking sorrow that even today, its heavy imprint lies full upon me. Life's futility— is this not the disease that has plagued me since I first began to ponder my existence? *No*, my young friend, one who can say as you do that he has known a few moments of happiness in his life (even if for but an hour, a minute), one who has ever had the opportunity to sacrifice himself (even if to no avail), has no right to say that he has lived without point or purpose. In your own words, my friend, you have come to me as a pauper to a rich man, but you will forgive my indelicacy in giving you to understand that your supposed rich man is poorer, far poorer than you, and perhaps the poorest of all—for though he has lived longer than you, his life has been nothing but austerity and indignity, and from pride alone has he assumed a mask of calm or at least of indifference, lest anyone recognize the great pointlessness of his having been born, for he finds nothing more unbearable than the pity of his fellow men. And art? I detest it, it has caused me nothing but pain. To live as a human being, even for a brief moment, as you have lived, that is everything—and that possibility was denied me at birth. I envy you, my dear, and ask you to forgive me any pain I may have caused you in momentarily laying aside the mask I have worn all my life, perhaps thus causing you some disappointment. But my frankness has had no other purpose than to tell you that I am a weak and tormented person, absolutely unfit to be the ideal for one who seeks support in strength. I hope you will not be angry with me, and in amicable esteem I remain your wholly devoted

Jiří ze Lvovic

December 16, 1901
[Letter dated in Prague and sent from Smíchov to:] Mr. Edvard Klas; c/o Mrs. Vladimíra Jedličková, 1067 Mánes Street, Royal Vinohrady

Dear friend,

Thank you for your last letter. I thought that my previous letter's candor would repel you, so willfully shattering some of your illusions about me with more brutality than is otherwise my wont. Illusions, I repeat, for I am nothing less than "great in my suffering"[3]—an emotional mimosa who trembles under reality's every coarse touch.[4] I make these confessions to you quite candidly, as if to a diary; I don't know why it is, but I feel great trust when speaking thus to the darkness, to an unknown being in whom I divine an interest in myself. These last few days I have been going through a terrible emotional crisis—may I tell you? To devote yourself entirely to one who has nothing but commonplace words for you, to one you know is so devoted to life's banality that he can have nothing but a contemptuous smile for your dreams, but to love him madly in spite of this, from spasms of hysteria to sleepless nights, from torments of jealousy to the senselessness of extreme devotion and self-sacrifice, does all this not portend the tragedy of a cursed life more terrible than any other blow dealt by fate? And just then your dear letters start coming to me. I feel so small when faced with their great confidence in me, in my powers, in my poetry, in all that is long dead to me. Thank you, my unknown friend, that your own grief has found words of comfort for my grief as well. We are kindred spirits, our kinship closer, more sisterly than you yourself suspect. And I am so glad that Fate has been so singularly kind to me, at a time when an intimate of mine has been so hurtful to me, that it has let me find sympathy in a distant soul, who is to remain forever unknown to me but whose kinship I feel in the name of a shared pain, sanctifying the greatest hardships of our present life. I thank you once again, and together I beg you, dear friend, to accept the lines above as a proof of the great confidence I have placed in you, in you who are to remain forever a precious fiction to me.

Your sincerely devoted

Jiří ze Lvovic

December 21, 1901
[Letter sent from Smíchov to:] Mr. E. Klas, c/o Mrs. Vladimíra Jedličková, 1067 Mánes Street, Royal Vinohrady

Dear friend,

Pardon the intimacy of my last letter. But I find you such an extraordinary being that I've found the courage to be confidential and confess things I most prefer to entrust to the diaries I burn. Those who know me find me so icily calm, so deadly detached; they often reproach me that I should live a little, that I am devoted only to books and not to life, but I am a different person when I leave them and enter my solitude, where alone I can be alive, where I can be my true self. It is tragic to have to spend my entire life seeming different to people than I really am, wearing a mask. For the world, I live life as if playing a role, a role utterly loathsome, unnatural to me. For myself—but can I write what I often dare not even acknowledge to myself? We may appear to be a man and yet psychically be his opposite, isn't it so? Can you make sense from this, my dear friend, of why I do not love women as other men do? So completely asexually, like the Pre-Raphaelites, so do I look upon woman, as upon a fellow creature suffering the same sorrows as myself. Sorrow has bound us together, and if we are never to become acquainted personally (the only condition of these intimacies), we shall become closer psychically than anyone else in the world. Do you accept these mutual confessions, which to anyone else would seem the outlandish correspondence of a morbid soul—but which to me will represent relief and an hour's respite from the rest of the world? Your immediate reply is not mandatory, write when you please, even in a month's time, but keep me in mind; and be assured that I am thinking of you, even if I do not respond that very instant, and think that I am afflicted by my vile hysteria, and that this keeps me from writing a single line.

You are right, this is all about a friend I am in love with. But there could be no love purer, more childlike, one of more devout adoration for his youthful manhood. At the lowest moment of my life, when I was ready to part from it violently, having taken stock of all the futility of my existence, there he was, offering me his friendship. There can be no greater contrast of natures than ours, and this causes me no end of suffering, but I never fail to return to him, however I might have tried to escape from him before; and today, today he has become a regular source of torment to me! Skeptic and hedonist, he loves and hates my psychical femininity. Just as he indulges in women, though he despises them, so does he love me, though he can only jeer at my lyricism, at my oversensitive[5] mentality. The expression of his love for me is the brutal flogging of my innermost being, and he is only good to me when he finds me so tortured that I submit to him completely. But I love him madly, and since I have known him (in fact, even before, for the mere sound of his name, when first spoken, awakened my fondness for this unknown person), he has been my only thought, my only passion. Is this a purely spiritual love, or is it a a physical one? I don't know. I love his spirit, though it has so seldom belonged to me, as well as his body, which has never belonged to me and never will. I only know that like those degenerate princes of ancient dynasties, it was never given to me, a child, to grow into a man; and that have been pierced by the ruggedness and startling brutality of his appearance, and that ever since I have loved, so childishly and so miserably, I have felt pain. My love is pain, my passion for him misery. Often there is no relief except to lose myself within the gloom of an ancient church, and to seek exhaustion in the passionate improvisations in which I can mingle Christ's name with his, so very similar. If *A Gothic Soul* was the diary of my soul before I met my friend, I am now living the sequel to this psychical tragedy. A sequel that I shall write in letters for you alone, my dearest, that I would not dare place in any indifferent hands. Will you have the patience to read it? Will your eye not grow dim from peering through a crack into the glowing flames of a psychical Inferno? Earnestly pleading for your remembrance at this moment, your devoted

Jiří ze Lvovic

Notes

1. Karásek, *Milý příteli...* The letters selected here are from pp. 11–17. Klas's biographical data come from Heczková, "Doslov," 92.
2. Klášter bosých karmelitek "U Jezulátka" (The Monastery of the Discalced Carmelites), on Prague's Hradčanské náměstí (Castle Square), features in Karásek's novel *A Gothic Soul*

(1900). It would have been reachable on foot from Smíchov. In 1939, Karásek wrote the cycle of short stories *Pražské Jezulátko* (The Prague Baby Jesus); see Bibliography. The communist regime ousted the Carmelites in 1950, shortly before Karásek's death.

3. *Great in my suffereing* (Czech *v utrpení velik*) may be a liturgical reference to Christ.

4. "Mimosa" (Czech *mimóza*; German *Mimose*) is a dated metaphor for a hypersensitive person. The *Mimosa pudica* plant is also called a touch-me-not.

5. The original Czech word *změkčilost* carries overtones of unmanliness.

III. KARÁSEK'S PREFACE TO *SODOM* (1905 EDITION)[1]

THE FIRST EDITION OF *SODOM* WAS CONFISCATED BY THE PRAGUE CENSORS IN 1895. THE CONFISCATED PARTS WERE INTERPOLATED IN THE REICHSRAT BY THE DEPUTY MR. HYBEŠ IN 1903[2] IN TERM XVII, SESSION 246, THUS MAKING THIS NEW EDITION POSSIBLE.[3]

This book has nothing in common with the run-of-the-mill erotic lyricism that extols pleasure. It expresses the *sadness of sex*, its futility and tragedy. It is one of those books whose artistic truth has become almost a destiny. It has been called a dissimulation. As though all we had of life was the mundane, for which we are least responsible, and not the dreams that pass through our fevered minds and define our being and our fate. As though only deeds that fade away were ours, and not the desires that constitute our immortality, and by which we are linked to what came before birth and to what shall be when the body is no more. And as if we could feel sorrow only over the deeds we have done, which are so small, and not for the sins we have dreamt up and that weigh so heavily upon us. For poetry should worship sin for the life that may be in it, and life for the sin in others. To ask of art that it be outwardly truthful is tantamount to asking that it be vulgar.

So only the fiction I have put into this book is truth to me, just as all that reality compels me to experience is a lie and unnatural to me. And so it seems ridiculous to me to make a so-called "sense of reality" a necessary condition of an artistic creation. If I take cognizance of reality, then the world becomes the mere application of sober, definite laws and processes for me. One may treat such "reality" as one does science, with prim politeness, but one cannot concede that it is art. At most it is perhaps even possible to be horrified at how rampant the "sense of reality" has become in recent times, and at the ferocity with which naturalism, that Sancho Panza of positivism, has thus set out to club the entire *raison d'être* of art to death. Yet it must not be forgotten that the truths of life and art are two quite different things. One can almost say that where art is true, life is almost always untrue, and that it is not the real world that tells us the sense of things, but only our dreams. The greater the divergence between an artist's life and his work, the greater the art created. Only in lesser artists do life and artwork tally. They have given nothing to their work, created for them by fortuity and a certain talent for observing minutiæ. The only real difference between an "artist" of this caliber and a non-artist is that the former is more familiar with vulgarity. But if one has the ability *not to see*, this alone qualifies him as a poet, even were no hallucinated world of fictions, colored by fire and inspiration, to exist for him. For he already stands above those who see in the ordinary way and have a mania for saying so.

So if I can be indifferent to someone I have met in life, I can never be such to someone I have come upon in my dreams. Even if I could forget faces I have seen in reality,

I cannot forget those that have come to me in my dreams; and so I see you constantly, Critobulus,[4] with your eyes that have so often looked into things beautiful and immortal, and your narrow face, pale as ivory beneath black curls of a hue nearly hyacinthine,[5] seems to smile at me. How often I seem to see you emerging from the triclinium[6] in the early morn, as dawn's first light breaks like the reflection of a silver mirror between the pillars of the silent, gloomy temple. More than others of my day have I entered your being, and more intimate have I grown with your pleasures and dreams; with greater love have I beheld the sensuous quiver of the purple on your softly curving lips, and the soft stirrings of your unsteady knees neath robe stained with spilt wine, than anyone alive. Your sorrow was my sorrow, and *your mystery my mystery*. One thing I know to be true: that *reality belongs not to art!* One must isolate one's idea from life and set every word as if in the middle of a great golden circle, to keep the mundane at bay. Far above reality and beyond it must art go, and where our dream has passed through life, it must first be purged of all that life has tainted it with before it can interest art.

Notes

1. Transl. from Karásek, *Sodoma: kniha pohanská*, 4–7.
2. Josef Hybeš—textile labor activist, editor-publicist, and politician—was something of a firebrand. In 1903, he was on his second term in the lower house of the Reichsrat in Vienna (the Imperial Council, the Habsburg parliament), representing the social democrats (SDs). When the Czechoslovak SDs split in the period around the radicalizing Second Comintern (1919–21), Hybeš went with the more doctrinaire, communist faction (Flodrová and Jordánková, "Josef Hybeš"). His three-volume memoir *Křížová cesta socialismu* (1919-20) may mention his intervention regarding *Sodom*.

3. Hybeš interpolated (asked) the prime minister about the confiscation and read the complete collection into the record from the floor. Parliamentary proceedings were not subject to censorship (Vévoda, "Dobový kontext Karáskova vystoupení," 69). Although the authorities had confiscated *Sodom* at the printer's in 1895, some copies escaped (see Figure 1 in Introduction). Hybeš had the support of 14 other deputies, including the fiery Václav Klofáč, progressive student, an editor at the liberal-patriotic *Národní listy* news daily, cofounder of breakaway Czech socialist party (1897), radical nationalist sentenced to death for treason (1915), pacifist, and first Czechoslovak defense minister.

4. Perhaps Critobulus (5th century BCE), the childhood friend of Socrates in the *Oeconomicus* by Athenian author Xenophon. Karásek also invokes the name in his poem "Příchod barbarů" (The Coming of the Barbarians) in the collection *Sexus necans* (1897).

5. A deep blue or purple color, as in similar comparisons in the *Magicians* novels.

6. A banqueting hall in ancient Rome (Czech *síň hodovní*).

IV. A PRAGUE CAFÉ'S SEMI-CLANDESTINE QUEER BACKROOM (1914)

Fin de siècle Prague, Vienna, and Budapest all had cafés and other public venues where homosexual clients might gather discreetly, often in a back room by admittance only. In Prague, Josefské náměstí (Josefsplatz or Joseph Square, today náměstí Republiky) was a space where men found each other, as noted in a 1902 report by police commissioner František Protivínský.[1] That was also the year of a media sensation over the murder of a man near the Prague Castle ramparts apparently after an assignation with another man; the weeklong police investigation found the perpetrators to be three soldiers making extra money through prostitution and theft.[2]

This feuilleton was originally written in German by *der rasende Reporter* ("The Roving Reporter") Egon Erwin Kisch. Kisch was the second of five sons in a Prague family of Sephardic Jewish heritage. His father Hermann (d. 1901) loved literature, was a friend of *Der Golem* (1915) author Gustav Meyrink, and ran a draper's shop from the ground floor of their residence.[3] During a year of voluntary military service in 1904–05, Egon Kisch first met various left-wing "freedom fanatics, anti-authoritarians, zealots for equality" and the like; his superiors considered him an anarchist.[4]

From 1906 to 1913, Kisch wrote for Prague's German-language newspaper *Bohemia*,[5] which in 1910–11 carried his regular weekly column "Prager Streifzüge" (Prague Rambles); these typically described visits to the city's underworld or places where the downtrodden congregated. The column below, written after 1911, was inspired by the Prague military administration's official list, periodically revised, of establishments forbidden to soldiers. These were often dives known for vice of one kind or another; a few tolerated a queer clientele. Kisch reported on visits to a range of these forbidden bars, among them the Artiste and Die zwei Lämmer (The Two Lambs)—included on the list dated January 26, 1912.[6]

That update to the list was promulgated while Colonel Alfred Redl (1864–1913) was chief of staff at the VIII Corps in Prague, where he served from 1910 until his death in May 1913. Redl's homosexuality was an open secret (see pp. 22–24 Introduction). Shortly after the latter's suicide, Kisch was the journalist who broke the historic story of Redl's espionage.

Egon Erwin Kisch
perhaps in *Bohemia*
ca.1912–14[7]

Our path now takes us to a small late-night café not far from Josefské náměstí.[8] We shall withhold the name and address of this establishment, for no lowlifes [in the German, *Lumpenproleten*] gather here, [not the human waste of the chaotic, arbitrary production system who endure their exclusion commendably and with cynicism and righteous hatred,] only men of a different disposition, [men who do not want to go without companionship,] and we do not wish to subject these unfortunates, who already suffer enough from official surveillance, the feelings of their passion, and the ridicule of

narrow-minded officials, to general curiosity in their hide-
away. Suffice to say that the prohibition on visiting this
venue was handed down on the same day as the one against
visiting "the Lambs." It is actually not just a café but also
a wine bar. But the space where the wine is served and the
little space for the café guests are connected by a doorway,
in spite of the fact that each has a separate entrance from
the street. The two rooms, however, are not the main part of
the establishment. A cloth curtain blocks direct access to a
large area of the café at the rear. This is the "sanctum sanc-
torum." If we head that way, a waiter will block our path
and indicate that this room is reserved for a private party.
We must try our luck again and, after entering the café, we
walk briskly up to the curtain and lift it before the waiter can
block our way. We can see inside. The rest of the place is not
that interesting, after all. The only thing of note is a massive
gramophone, the shell of its sound funnel aimed menacingly
at the serene patrons like the barrel of a cannon. When from
the mysterious realm behind the curtain the raucous sounds
of jokes and the good cheer carry too loudly into the profane
province of the café, the waiter switches on the gramophone,
the noise is drowned out, and—the guests in the front room
make their escape. Now and then carefully dressed boys
with made-up or at least powdered faces come in, as well as
older men with odd expressions on their faces. Our curiosity as to the paradisiacal delights of the separate room takes
hold, and to satisfy it we have to try again, and once inside
the café, to approach the curtain quickly and lift it before the
waiter stops us. The room is shrouded in cozy shadows, the
members of this closed society sitting at the tables, united by
warm, brotherly friendship. One is stroking another's hand,
another has laid his head on his friend's lap—it is the same
scene one sees in all [nighttime] cafés at a late hour, with the
one slight difference that there are no women here. In horror,
the evening's guests rush at the stranger who, with a criminal

hand, has lifted the veil from this painting. Despite our pretense of surprise and mutters of "Excuse me," we feel no letup in the mistrust directed at us, and we leave the room.[9]

Notes

1. Witek, "Kam se v Praze kdysi chodili muži 'bavit'." See also Antonová, *Guide*.
2. Jansová, "Léčba homosexuality byla československá specialita."
3. Christian Buckard, *Egon Erwin Kisch: Die Weltgeschichte des rasenden Reporters* (Berlin: Verlag, 2023), 34; cited in de.wikipedia.org, "Egon Erwin Kisch."
4. *Freiheitsfanatiker, Antiautoritäre, Gleichheitsschwärmer.* Egon Erwin Kisch, *Das tätowierte Porträt* (Leipzig: Verlag Philipp Reclam Jun, 1984), 400–1; cited in de.wikipedia.org, "Egon Erwin Kisch."
5. Rasmussen, "Kisch, Egon Erwin (1885–1948)."
6. Seidl, email message to author Bulkin, December 30, 2022.
7. Transl. from Seidl, Nozar, and Wintr, *Od žaláře k oltáři*, 501. First published in German (citation unidentified but likely in the German-language Prague daily *Bohemia* [1828–1938] ca.1912–14); see also Kisch, *Die Abenteuer in Prag*, 313–14; see section IV of this text on projekt-gutenberg.org. It first appeared in Czech in 1914 (Seidl, email message to author Bulkin, December 30, 2022); see Kisch, *Zapovězené lokály*; and Kisch, *Pražská dobrodružství*, 174ff. My thanks to John Wiecking for comparing my translation with the 1920 German text; any oversights are my responsibility. In brackets, I have reinserted sections absent in the Czech text. Kisch's already left-wing views were radicalized during World War I, and it is unclear whether or when he later edited his texts.
8. Instead of "not far from Josefské náměstí," the German text reads "in Elisabethstraße."
9. The 1920 German text does not include the passage that begins "In horror" and continues to the end. It may have been part of the original and then edited out by Kisch, or a flourish by the Czech translator.

V. KARÁSEK ON CREATING THE *THREE MAGICIANS* TRILOGY (1925)

The following is a column by Karásek that appeared in *Rozpravy Aventinum* (1925–34), a monthly arts journal with a literary focus. The journal was edited by the author's young supporter and Aventinum publisher Otakar Štorch-Marien and may have been intended in part to fill the market niche vacated by *Moderní revue* with Arnošt Procházka's recent passing. In 1924–25, Aventinum reissued the first two volumes of Karásek's *Three Magicians* trilogy, and it had just put out the first-ever edition of volume three, *Ganymede*.

Jiří Karásek ze Lvovic
"The Three Magicians"[1]
September 1925

With *Ganymede*, which my dear friend the publisher Dr. Štorch-Marien is just now bringing out, the trilogy of novels that I first undertook almost three decades ago is complete—although of course, the first novel came out significantly later [1907], and the third and final one came out only fifteen years after the middle novel. I did not think I would manage to complete the project, unique in Czech

novelistic writing in both concept and style. But today I am
pleased to have accomplished my task—how well, of course,
is not for me but for professional critics to judge, if not
today's, then certainly future ones, to evaluate the artistic
labors that went into, say, *Scarabæus*, concerning which, as
far as I know—in fifteen years—not a single review, however brief, has been written...[2]

The hero of the three novels is a single Magician who
appears in three forms, in three masks. *Manfred*, *Marcel*,
and *Adrian*; these are three different names for the same
type, who in each case uses his ideas and mental powers
as predatory clutches to seize and abduct, with a demonic
flourish, a character with three different names, all personi-
fications of the same submissiveness and passivity in love.
Manfred-Marcel-Adrian is drawn from reality, just like the
youths who cross his path. Don't be alarmed: I know the
world is not populated wholly by demons. It is populated
rather—alas!—wholly by ordinary mortals. But the demon
depicted in my trilogy of novels did exist; he is not a product of the imagination, nor is he taken from other books,
as assorted philistines might suppose. He came into my
life in the nineties, when through various circumstances,
I quite often found myself in Vienna, and there I fell—again
through various conincidences but by no means to the det-
riment of my artistic development—into the milieu of the
Viennese aristocracy, scented with its various "vices." Fate
enabled me to meet Manfred, from a very old family, in a
setting that could not have been more enticing in artistic
terms. And so I came to know a race that otherwise allows
no one intimate access. I also came to know a great artist of life, a brilliant German diplomat who would gather
exquisite company around himself, where all was suffused
with beauty and spirit. Reliving those nights in my imagination, those festivities of brilliant splendors and blazing
colors feel like recompense for the grey and tedious years

that followed, when art and work alone filled a life that would otherwise have been without purpose.

I then resolved to write a work in which I would capture both my Manfred-Marcel-Adrian and myself. The idea of the three novels and their three settings—Prague, Vienna, and Venice—was ripe in my soul. But it was ten years before I wrote *Manfred Macmillan*, the first part. Having been separated from my friend, who had gone far off to the Orient as a diplomat, in nostalgia for him, I wrote this novel for myself, and found an exceptional place to work on it. Deep in the autumn, in the desolate Hvězda, in the villa where Julius Zeyer had once written his *Vyšehrad* [serial 1879, book 1880], I wrote *Manfred Macmillan*'s first pages, and the desperate wind from outside, beating against the villa's lowered wooden jalousies, moaned its way into the style of the work.

I did not originally intend to publish the novel until years later, when I had completed the trilogy that I had envisioned. But the persistent Arnošt Procházka coaxed the manuscript out of me in the end. I was handsomely rewarded: Procházka was fascinated by the work and persuaded me to give him the novel for the next year's issues of *Moderní revue*. From the start, readers were equally fascinated by the novel. I received a great many enthusiastic letters. The response to the work pleased me to no end. When the novel was published separately as a book, the critics wrote very appreciatively of it, and even where they had to "cut me down," they recognized the book's artistic qualities. It sold out within a month, an unusual success.

Encouraged by *Manfred Macmillan*'s reception, I set out to write the second part of the trilogy, the novel *Scarabaeus*, right away. I went to its setting, to Venice;[3] and there I sought out the palace where Marcel lived, and I wandered in my hero's footsteps, having no idea of the tale I was going to tell... From Venice I journeyed on to Verona, and happened to be present when the police arrested a young Russian who had shot the husband of his mistress, the demoniacal Countess von Tarnów, at the Hotel Danieli in Venice.[4] The young man's beauty became so ingrained in my soul that I took a personal interest in his trial, and the Countess von Tarnów called that ingenious French poisoner Madame de Brinvilliers to mind... I acquired literature about her—and the concept for *Scarabaeus* was complete.

The novel, published in *Moderní revue*, again enjoyed success with the reading public. Once more, I was showered with expressions of enthusiasm and sympathy, but there suddenly followed a period of extreme personal adversity, during which the book was published in its entirety.[5] No one—except readers—took any notice of it, and I then found another line of work outside literature, and I thought the third volume of the trilogy would never come about...

But I hadn't counted on Arnošt Procházka. He knew of the concept for *Ganymede*, and several years later, he suddenly began to urge me so strongly to write the story, which he knew under the title of *Román o Golemovi* [The Golem Novel], that I set to work and created *Ganymede*.

When I brought him the draft, I did so with great anxiety as to whether the work succeeded as art, and I gave him leave to burn the novel if he found it worthless... My friend Arnošt read the work overnight—by then, he often could no longer sleep through the night due to his asthma—and after he went to the office the next morning, he wasted no time in calling on me in Karmelitská street, and not catching me at home, he wrote out this message in pencil on a piece of paper and dropped it into the box at the door, and I keep it as a precious memento:

Dear Jiří,

Ganymede is your finest prose. It is so compact and so mature that it is childish to worry that it shall spoil your trilogy. If you had written the novel in French, you would be famous. I advise cuts here and there. Not for my sake, not for yours, but for the sake of our conditions. There's no need to "hit people over the head." I've marked out the "trouble" spots with a colored pencil. The critics will still castigate you (if they don't completely silence you again as with *Scarabaeus*), but don't make this any easier for them.

The first part of Ganymede has already gone to the printer's. Take the rest of the manuscript back to review the cuts (but if you don't approve them, I don't mind if you print the novel as is). I'm sending part of *Ganymede* to the printer's, so you won't take it away from me in one of your moods (i.e., quirks), so this is a preventive measure. And at the same time, I ask that you give me the manuscript for my collection. I shall give you the galleys in exchange. And so, you can see how fond I am of *Ganymede* when I rank it with *Apollonius* and *Endymion*, which are my favorite works of yours.

Regards!

A. P.

So, then, that is how *Ganymede* also saw the light of day. What Procházka wanted cut, I replaced with other passages (except for three or four places), But when I later proofread the novel, I also cut much of what Procházka liked but I did not. The week before he died [on January 16, 1925], Procházka was still talking about *Ganymede*, asking me whether the book edition would be out soon. He told me: "I am glad you finished the trilogy. Don't worry about it. Writers, artists, and readers will always love it for the same reasons they love Péladan's novels."[6]

Then to come full circle, my Manfred-Marcel-Adrian has never read my novels, and is therefore unaware of the influence he has had on me in my art. Once many years later, he sent me flowers, a letter to meet him at the train station, but the letter came late, and I did not get to the station. Last year I learned—again by sheer chance—that he had been dead for three years. So he vanished for me in the same way as the mysterious Manfred Macmillan did from his friend's sight in the first volume...

Notes

1. Transl. from Karásek, "Romány tři magů."
2. Karel Sezima reviewed *Scarabæus* for the journal *Lumír* ("Z nové české belletrie").
3. The former Zeyer villa then belonged to Anna Lauermannová-Mikschová. "Although it is of no decisive importance, [her] diary [from this period] suggests that Karásek never went to Venice"; Lauermannová herself, however, knew Venice well (Lishaugen, *Speaking with a Forked Tongue*, 85–86).
4. An elegant and palatial hotel near St. Mark's Square. It is centered on the late 14th-century Palazzo Dandolo, built by a family that produced four of the republic's Doges (title of its highest public official).
5. In the 1909–12 Affair of the Anonymous Letters, Karásek was accused of sending a series of anonymous letters with scurrilous gossip; he protested vigorously against the charges.
6. Joséphin Péladan, French symbolist and occultist.

BIBLIOGRAPHY

Primary Sources

Anonymous, "Literatura." *Zvon* 2, no. 14 (1902): 194–95. https://www.digitalniknihovna.cz/mzk/view/uuid:b2c1abb0-9b2c-11e3-ad99-001018b5eb5c?page=uuid:e4f9ade0-a021-11e3-8e84-005056827e51.

Anonymous. "Umění, věda, školství. Oscar Wilde." *Čas* 9, no. 18 (May 4, 1895): 276–77. https://archiv.ucl.cas.cz/index.php?path=Cas-tydenik/9.1895/18/276.png.

Anonymous. "Umění, věda, školství. Oscar Wilde." *Čas* 9, no. 20 (May 18, 1895): 309. https://archiv.ucl.cas.cz/index.php?path=Cas-tydenik/9.1895/20/309.png.

Benešová, Božena. *Verše*. Prague: Melantrich, 1938. https://kramerius5.nkp.cz/uuid/uuid:3333eb60-8fb5-11e3-8031-001018b5eb5c.

Brünner Tagblatt. 1895, no. 167. July 24, 1895. https://kramerius5.nkp.cz/view/uuid:a0a23490-6d9f-11e4-9d98-005056825209?page=uuid:cf5e1b70-6dca-11e4-8c6e-001018b5eb5c&fulltext=oscar%20wilde.

Čech. "Básník a jeho život." 27, no. 220. September 25, 1895. https://kramerius5.nkp.cz/view/uuid:2662d300-6a1f-11e6-a9cc-005056825209?page=uuid:6bd9cf30-6a3b-11e6-9f9c-001018b5eb5c&fulltext=oscar%20wilde.

Dělnické listy. 2, no. 25. April 20, 1895. https://kramerius5.nkp.
cz/view/uuid:afbbeb9d-3fda-43c4-bf6a-30aa3254d364?page=
uuid:c49a3360-5a00-11e8-983f-005056827e51&fulltext=
oscar%20wilde.

Drápal, Florian. "Romány tří mágů." *Bibliofil: časopis pro pěknou
knihu a její úpravu* 6, no. 3 (1928–1929): 87–88. Review.
Undigitized. At Národní knihovna v Praze, signatura 54E15069.

Duch času: nedělní list Svornosti. 18, no. 28. April 14, 1895.
https://kramerius5.nkp.cz/uuid/uuid:1a2f5ed0-551f-11e9-
918e-5ef3fc9ae867.

Eisner, P. "Román z Lesbu." *Přítomnost* 5, no. 50 (December 20,
1928): 792–93. https://kramerius5.nkp.cz/uuid/uuid:89fab5ab-
35b4-4766-b0d7-8fefb714c3c2.

Jelínek, Hanuš. *Padesát let Umělecké besedy 1863–1913.* Prague:
Umělecá beseda, 1913.

Karásek ze Lvovic, Jiří. *Anonymní dopisy čili Affaira "pěti
spisovatelův."* Prague: printed by the author, 1910. https://ndk.
cz/view/uuid:d1737220-de64-11e8-a5a4-005056827e52?page=
uuid:88888830-fef2-11e8-8d10-5ef3fc9ae867.

Karásek ze Lvovic, Jiří. *Chimaerické výpravy: kritické studie.*
Critical essays (1892–1904). Prague: Hugo Kosterka, 1906.
https://kramerius5.nkp.cz/uuid/uuid:279104d0-e67e-11e3-
a012-005056825209.

Karásek ze Lvovic, Jiří. "Divadelní kronika." *Moderní revue* 11,
no. 16 (1905): 149–52. https://kramerius.cbvk.cz/view/uuid:
e1054006-435d-11dd-b505-00145e5790ea?page=uuid:ade69
798-435e-11dd-b505-00145e5790ea.

Karásek ze Lvovic, Jiří. "Feuilleton." *Nový hlas* 1, no. 2 (1932):
16–17. Cited in Lishaugen, "Speaking with a Forked Tongue."

Karásek ze Lvovic, Jiří. *Ganymedes.* Prague: Aventinum, 1925.
https://kramerius5.nkp.cz/uuid/uuid:22dbfc10-e1fb-11e3-
bb44-5ef3fc9bb22f.

Karásek ze Lvovic, Jiří. *Impresionisté a ironikové.* Prague:
Aventinum, 1926. Critical essays (1892–1902). https://babel.
hathitrust.org/cgi/pt?id=uc1.$b130553&view=1up&seq=11&
skin=2021.

Karásek ze Lvovic, Jiří. "Julius Zeyer: 'Stratonika' a jiné povídky."
Literární listy 14, no. 13 (June 16, 1893) [column dated May
31, 1893].

Karásek ze Lvovic, Jiří. "Listy z Prahy IV." *Literární listy* 15, no. 7 (1894).

Karásek ze Lvovic, Jiří. *Milý příteli... (Listy Edvardu Klasovi).* Edited and with afterword by Libuše Heczková. Prague: Thyrsus, 2001.

Karásek ze Lvovic, Jiří. "Morální záchvat Německa." *Nový hlas* 1, no. 5 (1932): 12–13.

Karásek ze Lvovic, Jiří. "O kvalitách slovenského duchu." *Elán* 1, no. 8 (1930). https://www.cesi.sk/bes/06/xi/6xikar.htm.

Karásek ze Lvovic, Jiří. *Román Manfreda Macmillena.* Prague: Neumannová, 1907. https://kramerius5.nkp.cz/uuid/uuid: 1f810350-e1d1-11e3-94ef-5ef3fc9ae867.

Karásek ze Lvovic, Jiří. "Romány tři magů" [*sic*]. *Rozpravy Aventinum* 1, no. 1 (1925): 3. https://archiv.ucl.cas.cz/index. php?path=RozAvn/1.1925-1926/1/3.png.

Karásek ze Lvovic, Jiří. *Scarabaeus.* Prague: Neumannová, 1909. https://kramerius5.nkp.cz/uuid/uuid:43dd2540-e342-11e3-bc6c-5ef3fc9ae867.

Karásek, Jiří ze Lvovic. *Sodoma: kniha pohanská.* Prague: printed by the author, 1905: 4–7. https://kramerius5.nkp.cz/ view/uuid:335d8fa0-a11d-11e3-8e84-005056827e51?page= uuid:b3f51f40-e1d0-11e3-93a3-005056825209. Original 1895 edition confiscated by Habsburg censors.

Karásek ze Lvovic, Jiří. *Tvůrcové a epigoni: kritické studie.* Prague: Aventinum, 1927. Critical essays (1900–26). https:// www.google.co.uk/books/edition/Tv%C5%AFrcov%C3%A9_ a_epigoni/Q7k_AAAAIAAJ?hl=en.

Karásek ze Lvovic, Jiří. *Upřímné pozdravy z kraje květů a zapadlých snů: dopisy adresované Marii Kalašové z let 1903–1907.* Edited and with foreword by Karel Kolařík and Jana Kirschnerová. Příbram: Pistorius & Olšanská, 2007.

Karásek ze Lvovic, Jiří. *Vzpomínky.* Prague: Thyrsus, 1994.

Karásek ze Lvovic, Jiří. "Za Arnoštem Procházkou." *Ženský svět* 29, no. 3 (1925): 25; and no. 4 (1925): 34. Interview. https:// kramerius5.nkp.cz/uuid/uuid:fb4a6500-d856-11e2-bcca-005056827e51 [registration required].

Karásek ze Lvovic, Jiří. "Za Juliem Zeyerem: vzpomínka." *Moderní revue* 12, no. 77 (February 1901): 157–60.

https://www.digitalniknihovna.cz/cbvk/view/uuid:e1000fac-435d-11dd-b505-00145e5790ea?page=uuid:ae2f393e-435e-11dd-b505-00145e5790ea.

K.-B., "Proceß Wilde," *Politik* 34, no. 144, (May 26, 1895). https://kramerius5.nkp.cz/view/uuid:f37d4e90-ef50-11dc-92f0-000d606f5dc6?page=uuid:636382e0-6621-11e8-943b-5ef3fc9ae867.

Kisch, Egon Erwin. *Die Abenteuer in Prag*. Vienna: Verlag Ed. Strache, 1920. https://www.projekt-gutenberg.org/kisch/abenprag/chap005.html.

Kisch, Egon Erwin. *Pražská dobrodružství*. Prague: Svoboda, 1968.

Kisch, Egon Erwin. *Zapovězené lokály*. Prague: Antonín Svěcený, 1914.

Kurzer Inbegriff von dem Leben und den Thaten des Joseph Balsami, oder des sogenannten Grafen Cagliostro: ein Auszug aus dem wider denselben im Jahre 1790 in Rom angestellten Untersuchungs-processe, wodurch man zugleich mit dem Geiste der Freymäurerey bekannt wird. Rome: [n.p.], 1791. https://babel.hathitrust.org/cgi/pt?id=dul1.ark:/13960/t3rv3m60b&seq=141.

Mährisches Tagblatt. 16, no. 104. May 6, 1895. https://kramerius5.nkp.cz/view/uuid:829acea0-1c15-11e1-b336-000d606f5dc6?page=uuid:d308181a-3363-4364-b794-a3ba97c29fc0&fulltext=oscar%20wilde.

Masaryk, Tomáš Garrigue [Sursum, pseud.]. "Rozpravy časopisecké: Ještě Oscar Wilde." *Naše doba* 2, no. 9 (June 10, 1895): 843–48. https://kramerius5.nkp.cz/view/uuid:21b55780-36e6-11e7-ad2f-005056827e51?page=uuid:9c182700-52bb-11e7-b6dc-001018b5eb5c.

Masaryk, Tomáš Garrigue [Sursum, pseud.]. "Rozhledy časopisecké: 'Oscar Wilde'." *Naše doba* 2, no. 8 (May 20, 1895): 752–54. https://kramerius5.nkp.cz/view/uuid:21b55780-36e6-11e7-ad2f-005056827e51?page=uuid:8131b550-52bb-11e7-b6dc-001018b5eb5c.

Mayne, Xavier. *The Intersexes: A History of Similisexualism as a Problem in Social Life*. [Rome]: printed by the author, 1908. https://en.wikisource.org/wiki/The_Intersexes:_A_History_of_Similisexualism_as_a_Problem_in_Social_Life.

Národní listy. 35, no. 323. November 22, 1895. https://krameri us5.nkp.cz/view/uuid:f3912d20-435d-11dd-b505-00145 e5790ea?page=uuid:2762e2f0-a62d-11e6-abce-005056825 209&fulltext=oscar%20wilde.

Naše doba. 13, no. 1. October 1905. https://kramerius5.nkp.cz/ view/uuid:ac390ae0-ce04-11e7-9c14-005056827e51?page= uuid:e2625890-ce24-11e7-80e7-5ef3fc9bb22f.

National Archives of the Czech Republic. Prague Police Directorate residence applications 1850–1914, box 251, folio 920. http:// digi.nacr.cz/prihlasky2/?action=link&ref=czarch:CZ-100000 010:874&karton=251&folium=920.]

Neumann, Stanislav Kostka. *Vzpomínky,* part 1. Prague: Borový, 1931. https://kramerius5.nkp.cz/uuid/uuid:59bfa720-9bad-11e8-a1e1-005056827e51.

Nordau, Max. *Entartung.* Berlin: Carl Dunder, 1892.

Procházka, Arnošt. "Scholie: Severní květy." *Moderní revue* 16 (1905): 51. https://babel.hathitrust.org/cgi/pt?id=hvd.3204403 6013217.

Procházka, Arnošt. "Význam slova 'moderní'." (1897). *Rozhovory s knihami, obrazy i lidmi.* Prague: Borovský, 1916. https://www. google.co.uk/books/edition/_/twUOAAAAIAAJ.

Procházka, Arnošt and Jiří Karásek ze Lvovic. "Kritika: Časopisy," signed "–C–." *Moderní revue* 1, no. 2 (May 1895): 48. https:// babel.hathitrust.org/cgi/pt?id=hvd.32044018698050&seq=56.

Procházka, Arnošt and Jiří Karásek ze Lvovic. "Kritika: Časopisy," signed "–A–, –K–." *Moderní revue* 1, no. 3 (June 1895): 70–72. https://babel.hathitrust.org/cgi/pt?id=hvd.32044018698050& seq=80&q1=Panizza.

Sekanina, František. "Jiří Karásek: *Román Manfreda Macmillena.*" *Národní obzor* 1, no. 48 (1907): 2–3.

Sezima, Karel. *Z mého života: Smetanovo smyčcové kvarteto e-moll: Kniha vzpomínek a nadějí,* volume 1. Prague: Vilímek, 1945. https://kramerius5.nkp.cz/uuid/uuid:ea9ef880-9862-11e2-9142-5ef3fc9bb22f.

Sezima, Karel. *Z mého života: Smetanovo smyčcové kvarteto e-moll: Kniha vzpomínek a nadějí,* volume 2. Prague: Vilímek, 1946. https://kramerius5.nkp.cz/uuid/uuid:93ced8d0-9eb6-11e3-ad99-001018b5eb5c.

Sezima, Karel. "Z nové české belletrie." *Lumír: časopis zábavný a poučný* 38, no. 11 (September 16, 1910): 481–86. https://kramerius5.nkp.cz/view/uuid:b6bd81b0-11d3-11e1-ac90-000bdb925259?page=uuid:3e574e34-9ab2-4de9-99cb-26da78e66ff1.

Troppauer Zeitung. 110, no. 92. April 21, 1895 [item dated April 19]. https://kramerius5.nkp.cz/view/uuid:99f91d20-84d4-11e3-a606-005056827e51?page=uuid:0236c970-886b-11e3-8031-001018b5eb5c&fulltext=oscar%20wilde.

Vávra, Vladimír [Vladimír Kolátor, pseud.]. "Od Hlaváčka k Nestroyovi." *Hlas* 1, no. 10 (1931): 6.

Vávra, Vladimír [Vladimír Kolátor, pseud.]. "Slovo čtenářům." *Nový hlas* 2, no. 1 (1933): 13.

Vodák, Jindřich (anonymously). "Románek infernální." *Čas* 21, no. 255 (1907): 3–4. Cited in Lishaugen, "Speaking with a Forked Tongue." AV ČR Digitální archiv has only the first half of this year online: https://archiv.ucl.cas.cz/index.php?path=Cas-denik/21.1907.

Weinfurter, Karel. "Nový román okkultní." Review of *Román Manfreda Macmillena* by Jiří Karásek ze Lvovic. In *Národní listy* 47 (1907), no. 282: 1. https://kramerius5.nkp.cz/uuid/uuid:235b02f0-2f6c-11e7-a77b-001018b5eb5c.

Žalud, Augustin. "Rozhledy časopisecké." *Studentský sborník* 2, no. 1, (May 15, 1895): 10–13. Undigitized. Held at Národní knihovna v Praze.

Zavřel, František. *Za živa pohřben.* Prague: Vlast, 1942. https://kramerius5.nkp.cz/uuid/uuid:d97475e0-ff58-11e3-a680-5ef3fc9bb22f.

Secondary Sources

Adamovič, Ivan, Ondřej Neff, and Jaroslav Olša Jr. *Slovník české literární fantastiky a science fiction.* Prague: R3, 1995.

Agnew, Hugh LeCaine. *The Czechs and the Lands of the Bohemian Crown.* Stanford: Hoover Institution Press, 2004.

Aldrich, Robert. "Homosexuality and the City: An Historical Overview." *Urban Studies* 41, no. 9 (2004): 1719–37. http://www.jstor.org/stable/43201476.

Antonová, Barbora, ed. *Queer Prague: A Guide to the LGBT History of the Czech Capital.* Translated by Katarina Mináriková and Tereza Janáčková. Brno: Černé pole, 2014.

Baer, Brian James. *Other Russias: Homosexuality and the Crisis of Post-Soviet Identity.* New York: Palgrave Macmillan, 2009.

Baer, Brian James. *Queer Theory and Translation Studies: Language, Politics, Desire.* Milton Park: Routledge, 2021.

Bassett, Richard. *For God and Kaiser: The Imperial Austrian Army, 1619–1918.* New Haven: Yale University Press, 2015.

Beller, Steven, ed. *Rethinking Vienna 1900.* New York/Oxford: Berghahn Books, 2001.

Beneš, Pavel. "Elegantní jednoplošník Rapid bratří Čiháků – první letadlo české konstrukce," Vynálezy a pokroky 1913. Bejvávalo. cz, 2018. https://www.bejvavalo.cz/clanky.php?detail=892.

Beran, Zdeněk. "Oscar Wilde and the Czech Decadence." In *The Reception of Oscar Wilde in Europe*, edited by Stefano Evangelista, 256–69. London: Bloomsbury, 2010.

Berecz, Ágoston. "The Hungarian Nationalities Act of 1868 in Operation (1868–1914)." *Slavic Review* 81, no. 4 (2022): 994–1015. https://doi.org/10.1017/slr.2023.2.

Bershtein, Evgenii. "'Next to Christ': Oscar Wilde in Russian Modernism." In *The Reception of Oscar Wilde in Europe*, edited by Stefano Evangelista: 285–300. London: Bloomsbury, 2010.

Bershtein, Evgenii. "The Discourse of Sexual Pathology in Russian Modernism." In *Reframing Russian Modernism*, edited by Irina Shevelenko, 143–71. Madison: University of Wisconsin Press, 2018.

Biedroń, Robert. "Historia homoseksualności w Polsce." In *Queer Studies: Podręcznik kursu*, edited by Marta Abramowicz, Robert Biedroń, and Jacek Kochanowski, 57–96. Warsaw: Kampania Przeciw Homofobii, 2010. https://www.kph.org.pl/publikacje/queerstudies_podrecznik.pdf.

Bláhová, Šárka. "Arthur Breisky a Oscar Wilde: kritika, maska, mystifikace." Master's thesis, Univerzita Karlova, 2017. http://hdl.handle.net/20.500.11956/90881.

Blažek, Tomáš. Comment on *Fortinbras* by František Zavřel. Databazeknih.cz. Last modified March 25, 2021. https://www.databazeknih.cz/knihy/fortinbras-305652.

Bogner-Šaban, Antonija. *Ivo Raić – hrvatski i europski glumac i redatelj*. Zagreb: Hrvatska akademija, 2017.

Břevnovský klášter. "Historia fundationis monasterii Brzewnoviensis." Last modified September 18, 2018. https://www.brevnov.cz/cs/benediktini-a-brevnovsky-klaster/historia-fundationis-monasterii-brzewnoviensis.

Brown, Peter D. G. *Oskar Panizza and* The Love Council: *A History of the Scandalous Play on Stage and in Court, with the Complete Text in English and a Biography of the Author*. Jefferson, NC: McFarland & Co., 2010.

Buben, Milan. "The Order of Malta in the Czech Lands." Order of Malta: Grand Priory of Bohemia. Last modified January 30, 2013. http://en.maltezskyrad.cz/history-of-the-grand-priory-of-bohemia/.

Burri, Michael. "Theodor Herzl and Richard von Schaukal: Self-Styled Nobility and the Sources of Bourgeois Belligerence in Prewar Vienna." In *Rethinking Vienna 1900*, edited by Steven Beller, 105–131. New York/Oxford: Berghahn Books, 2001.

Chandler, Raymond. *The Annotated Big Sleep*. Edited by Owen Hill, Pamela Jackson, and Anthony Dean Rizzuto. New York: Vintage Books, 2018.

Chew, Geoffrey, ed. and transl. *And My Head Exploded: Tales of Desire, Delirium and Decadence from Fin-De-Siècle Prague*. London: Jantar, 2018.

Compagni, Vittoria Perrone. "Heinrich Cornelius Agrippa von Nettesheim." *Stanford Encyclopedia of Philosophy* (Spring 2021 edition), edited by Edward N. Zalta. Last modified March 18, 2021. https://plato.stanford.edu/archives/spr2021/entries/agrippa-nettesheim/.

Cooper, David L. *The Czech Manuscripts: Forgery, Translation, and National Myth*. Ithaca, NY: Cornell University Press, 2023.

Crossley, Robert. *Imagining Mars: A Literary History*. Middletown, CT: Wesleyan University Press, 2012.

Crozier, Ivan, ed., Havelock Ellis, and John Addington Symonds. *Sexual Inversion: A Critical Edition*. Basingstoke: Palgrave Macmillan, 2008.

d'Adelswärd-Fersen, Jacques. *Messes noires: Lord Lyllian.* Paris: Librairie Leon Vanier, 1905. https://www.google.co.uk/books/edition/Messes_noires/iYo-AAAAYAAJ?hl=en.

David-Fox, Katherine. "The 1890s Generation: Modernism and National Identity in Czech Culture, 1890–1900." PhD diss., Yale University, 1996.

David-Fox, Katherine. "Prague-Vienna, Prague-Berlin: The Hidden Geography of Czech Modernism." *Slavic Review* 59, no. 4 (2000): 735–60. https://doi.org/10.2307/2697417.

Deák, István. *Beyond Nationalism: A Social and Political History of the Habsburg Officer Corps, 1848–1918.* New York: Oxford University Press, 1990.

Dipper, C. "Moderne (English version)." Docupedia-Zeitgeschichte. Last modified November 22, 2018. https://docupedia.de/zg/Dipper_moderne_v2_en_2018.

Du Bois, W. E. B. "Of Our Spiritual Strivings." In *The Souls of Black Folk*, 2nd edition, 1–12. Chicago: A. C. McClurg & Co., 1903. https://en.wikisource.org/wiki/The_Souls_of_Black_Folk_(2nd_ed)/Chapter_1.

Dumas *père*, Alexandre. *Celebrated Crimes.* New York: P.F. Collier, 1910. Gutenberg Project. https://www.gutenberg.org/files/2760/2760-h/2760-h.htm#id155.

Dynes, Wayne R., Warren Johansson, William Alexander Percy III, and Stephen Donaldson, eds. *Encyclopedia of Homosexuality.* New York: Garland, 1990. http://www.sexarchive.info/BIB/EOH/index.htm.

Encyclopaedia Britannica Online. "Ramon Llull: Catalan mystic." Last modified January 22, 2017. https://www.britannica.com/biography/Ramon-Llull.

Erber, Nancy. "The French Trials of Oscar Wilde." *Journal of the History of Sexuality* 6, no. 4 (April 1996): 549–88.

Evangelista, Stefano. "Oscar Wilde: European by Sympathy." In *The Reception of Oscar Wilde in Europe*, edited by Stefano Evangelista, 1–19. London: Bloomsbury, 2010.

Faulks, Philippa and Robert Cooper. *The Masonic Magician: The Life and Death of Count Cagliostro and His Egyptian Rite.* London: Watkins, 2017.

Flodrová, Milena and Hana Jordánková. "Josef Hybeš." Internetová encyklopedie dějin Brna. Last modified October 30, 2021. https://encyklopedie.brna.cz/home-mmb/?acc=profil_osobnosti&load=120.

Foucault, Michel. *The History of Sexuality. Volume 1: An Introduction.* Translated by Robert Hurley. New York: Pantheon Books, 1978.

Geffarth, Renko. "The Masonic Necromancer: Shifting Identities in the Lives of Johann Georg Schrepfer." In *Polemical Encounters: Esoteric Discourses and Its Others*, edited by Olav Hammer and Kocku von Stuckrad, 181–97. Leiden: Brill, 2007. https://doi.org/10.1163/ej.9789004162570.i-326.49.

Głuchowska, Lidia. "Munch, Przybyszewski and The Scream." *Kunst og kultur* 96, no. 4 (2013): 182–91. https://ewamaria2013texts.files.wordpress.com/2013/12/gluchowska-munch-przybyszewski.pdf.

Godsey, William D. *Aristocratic Redoubt: The Austro-Hungarian Foreign Office on the Eve of the First World War.* West Lafayette, IN: Purdue University Press, 1999. https://doi.org/10.2307/j.ctt6wq6ws.

Goodrick-Clarke, Nicholas. *The Occult Roots of Nazism: The Ariosophists of Austria and Germany, 1890–1935.* Wellingborough: Aquarian Press, 1985.

Gruen, Erich S. "Sibylline Oracles." *Oxford Classical Dictionary.* Last modified December 22, 2016. https://doi.org/10.1093/acrefore/9780199381135.013.8134.

Haman, Aleš. "Prolegomena k parnasismu." *Česká literatura* 62, no. 2 (2014): 215–37. http://www.jstor.org/stable/43322083.

Heczková, Libuše. "Doslov." In Jiří Karásek ze Lvovic, *Milý příteli... (Listy Edvardu Klasovi)*: 85–94. Prague: Thyrsus, 2001.

Hermann, Benedict. "Thomas a Jesu." *Catholic Encyclopedia, Volume 14: Simony-Tournon*, New York: Robert Appleton Company, 1913. https://www.ccel.org/ccel/herbermann/cathen14.html?term=Thomas%20a%20Jesu.

Hibbitt, Richard. "The Artist as Aesthete: The French Creation of Wilde." In *The Reception of Oscar Wilde in Europe*, edited by Stefano Evangelista, 65–107. London: Continuum, 2010.

Hillgarth, J. N. *Ramon Lull and Lullism in Fourteenth-Century France*. Oxford: Clarendon Press, 1971.

Holeček, Lukáš. "Vydávat Karáska…" Kanon. February 15, 2024. http://i-kanon.cz/2024/02/15/vydavat-karaska/.

Holland, Merlin and John Mortimer. *The Real Trial of Oscar Wilde: The First Uncensored Transcript of the Trial of Oscar Wilde vs. John Douglas, (Marquess of Queensberry), 1895.* New York: Fourth Estate, 2003.

Homolová, Květa, Mojmír Otruba, Zdeněk Pešat, eds. *Čeští spisovatelé 19. a počátku 20. století: Slovníková příručka.* Prague: Československý spisovatel, 1982. https://edicee.ucl.cas.cz/data/prirucky/obsah/CS/45.pdf.

Hora-Hořejš, Petr, ed. *Toulky českou minulostí.* Volumes 1–13. Prague: Baronet, 1985–2012. Cited in Bogner-Šaban, *Ivo Raić.*

Hoskin, Matthew. "Review: *On the Person of Christ, The Christology of Emperor Justinian.*" Review of Kenneth P. Wesche's 1997 translation of three treatises by Justinian. Last modified May 23, 2018.] https://thepocketscroll.wordpress.com/2018/05/23/review-on-the-person-of-christ-the-christology-of-emperor-justinian/.

Hudáková, Andrea. "Organizace československého spiritistického hnutí." PhD diss., Univerzita Karlova, 2012. https://docplayer.cz/30968307-Organizace-ceskoslovenskeho-spiritistickeho-hnuti.html?fbclid=IwAR1p_hnv8dsa6g4v9Rlj0y_50iggare7eVPlYINVaaqdKg7Wr7_DOx70aho.

Huss, Boaz. "Translations of the Zohar: Historical Contexts and Ideological Frameworks." *Correspondences* 4 (2016): 81–128. https://correspondencesjournal.com/ojs/ojs/index.php/home/article/download/40/40.

Hynek, Filip. "Jiří Karásek ze Lvovic." Starysmichov.cz. Last modified July 1, 2007. http://www.starysmichov.cz/view.php?cisl oclanku=2007070001.

Jablonická-Zezulová, Jana. "Matyášove práce a úvahy v Hlase sexuálni menšiny." Imrich Matyáš. Last modified 2017. https://matyas.sk/im---kapitola-4.html.

Jakubec, Jan. *Geschichte der čechischen* [sic] *Litteratur*. Leipzig: C. F. Amelang, 1913. https://kramerius5.nkp.cz/view/uuid:d4dc5dd0-d750-11ec-8aba-5ef3fc9bb22f?page=uuid:b7f11799-d69b-45fb-ac4d-16970c17d54d&fulltext=Jiř%C3%AD%20Karásek%20ze%20Lvovic.

Jansová, Petra. "Historik: Léčba homosexuality byla československá specialita." Interview with Jan Seidl. Aktualne.cz. August 11, 2014. https://magazin.aktualne.cz/historik-lecba-homosexuality-byla-ceskoslovenska-specialita/r~27580b4a17fb11e484a500259 00fea04/.

Jaworska, Władysława. "Munch i Przybyszewski." In *Totenmesse: Munch-Weiss-Przybyszewski*, edited by Łukasz Kossowski, 72–97. Warsaw: Muzeum Literatury im. Adama Mickiewicza, 1995.

Jehlička, Jakub. "Stanisław Przybyszewski: evropský modernista a česká Moderní revue v kontextu české a polské reflexe." Bachelor's thesis, Univerzita Karlova, 2010. https://dspace.cuni.cz/handle/20.500.11956/37563?show=full.

"Johann Isaac Hollandus." Second Wiki. Last modified November 26, 2020. https://second.wiki/wiki/johann_isaac_hollandus.

Judson, Pieter M. "Rethinking the Liberal Legacy." In *Rethinking Vienna 1900*, edited by Steven Beller, 57–79. New York/Oxford: Berghahn Books, 2001.

Karczewski, Kamil. "'Call Me by My Name:' A 'Strange and Incomprehensible Passion' in the Polish *Kresy* of the 1920s." *Slavic Review* 81, no. 3 (2022): 631–52. https://doi.org/10.1017/slr.2022.224.

Karczewski, Kamil. "Transnational Flows of Knowledge and the Legalisation of Homosexuality in Interwar Poland." *Contemporary European History*, 2022: 1–18. https://doi.org/10.1017/S0960777322000108.

Karlinsky, Simon. "Russia's Gay Literature and Culture: The Impact of the October Revolution." In *Hidden from History: Reclaiming the Gay and Lesbian Past*, edited by Martin B. Duberman, Martha Vicinus, and George Chauncey, Jr., 347–64. New York: New American Library, 1989. http://www.williamapercy.com/wiki/images/Russia%27s_Gay_Literature.pdf.

Karlinsky, Simon. *The Sexual Labyrinth of Nikolai Gogol.* Cambridge, MA: Harvard University Press, 1976 (republished Chicago: University of Chicago, 1992).

Kazbalová, Kateřina. "Obraz homosexuálního jedince v časopisu *Hlas.*" Master's thesis, Univerzita Karlova, 2009. https://dsp ace.cuni.cz/bitstream/handle/20.500.11956/170426/120115 558.pdf?sequence=1.

Knihovna Univerzity Palackého v Olomouci. "Žalud, Augustin, 1872–1928." Accessed December 16, 2023. https://library. upol.cz/arl-upol/cs/detail-upol_us_auth-m0211591-zalud-Augustin-18721928/.

Kolařík, Karel. "Poetika druhého básnického období Jiřího Karáska ze Lvovic." *Česká literatura* 53, no. 3 (2005): 324–60. https://www.jstor.org/stable/42687050.

Kolařík, Karel. "Raná literární tvorba Jiřího Karáska ze Lvovic." *Česká literatura* 56, no. 5 (2008): 606–34. https://www.jstor. org/stable/42687448.

Kolařík, Karel. "Věčné jinošství Jiřího Karáska ze Lvovic." PhD diss., Univerzita Karlova, 2012. https://dspace.cuni.cz/handle/ 20.500.11956/43633.

Kosofsky Sedgwick, Eve. *Between Men: English Literature and Male Homosexual Desire.* New York: Columbia University Press, 1985.

Kostková, Jana. "Kritik-básník." In *A chceš-li, vyslov jméno mé: k stému výročí narození Jiřího Karáska ze Lvovic*, edited by Jana Kostková, 15–21. Prague: Památník národního písemnictví, 1971.

Kovařík, Petr. *Literární mýty, záhady a aféry.* Prague: Nakladatelství Lidové noviny, 2003. Cited in Bogner-Šaban, *Ivo Raić.*

Kronenbitter, Günther. "Redl, Alfred." 1914–1918 Online: International Encyclopedia of the First World War. Last modified October 8, 2014. Berlin: Freie Universität. http://dx.doi. org/10.15463/ie1418.10139.

Krystýnek, Jiří. "Przybyszewski v české literatuře za války a po válce." In *Z dějin polsko-českých literárních vztahů: vlivy polské literatury a její recepce v českých zemích v letech 1914–1930*, 68–84. Brno: Universita J. E. Purkyně, 1966. http://hdl. handle.net/11222.digilib/119774.

Kubínová, Marie. "Prostory víry a transcendence: Kostel, chrám a boží muka v novodobé české literatuře." *Česká literatura* 44, no. 1 (1996): 17–49. http://www.jstor.org/stable/42686299.

Kurimay, Anita. *Queer Budapest, 1873–1961*. Chicago: University of Chicago, 2020.

Kurimay, Anita. "Sex in the 'Pearl of the Danube': The History of Queer Life, Love, and Its Regulation in Budapest, 1873–1941." PhD diss., Rutgers, State University of New Jersey, 2012. https://rucore.libraries.rutgers.edu/rutgers-lib/39124/PDF/1/play/.

Lacina, Vlastislav, ed. "Jakub Arbes." Biografický slovník českých zemí. Last modified September 21, 2019. http://biography.hiu.cas.cz/Personal/index.php/ARBES_Jakub_12.6.1840-8.4.1914.

Lang, J. P. "Josef Jiří Kolár: Pekla zplozenci." *Literární noviny* 14, no. 3 (March 1941), 71. https://archiv.ucl.cas.cz/index.php?path=LitN/14.1941/3/71.png.

Lang, Kirsten. *Sexual Politics and Feminist Science: Women Sexologists in Germany, 1900–1933*. Ithaca, NY: Cornell University Press, 2017.

Linder, Douglas O. "Letters from Oscar Wilde to Lord Alfred Douglas." Famous-trials.com. Last modified February 28, 2019. https://www.famous-trials.com/wilde/323-letters.

Lines, Richard. "The Swedenborg Society: A Very Short History." UCL Bloomsbury Project. 2010 (last modified April 14, 2011). https://www.ucl.ac.uk/bloomsbury-project/articles/articles/lines_swedenborg.pdf.

Lipša, Ineta. *LGBTI People in Latvia: A History of the Past 100 Years*. Translated by Daina Ruduša. Riga: Association of LGBT and their friends Mozaika, 2018.

Lishaugen, Roar. "Jiří Karásek ze Lvovic." *Slovo a smysl: časopis pro mezioborová bohemistická studia/Word & Sense: A Journal of Interdisciplinary Theory and Criticism in Czech Studies* 14 (2010). http://slovoasmysl.ff.cuni.cz/node/188.

Lishaugen, Roar. "Nejistá sezóna jiné literatury: Osudy časopisu *Hlas sexuální menšiny*." *Dějiny a současnost* 2007, no. 12 (2007). http://dejinyasoucasnost.cz/archiv/2007/12/nejista-sezona-jine-literatury-/.

Lishaugen, Roar. *Speaking with a Forked Tongue: Double Reading Strategies in Romány tří mágů by Jiří Karásek ze Lvovic.* Göteborg: University of Gothenburg, 2008.

Lishaugen, Roar. "'Ta pravá, ta naše literatura' (Jiří Karásek ze Lvovic jako zakladatel české homosexuální literatury)." *Souvislosti: Revue pro literaturu a kulturu* 14, no. 4 (2003): 56–69.

Lóže U Zeleného Slunce. "Společnost českých hermetiků Universalia." Last modified October 29, 2020. https://www.luzs.cz/2020/10/29/spolecnost-ceskych-hermetiku-universalia/.

Macaulay, Thomas Babington. "Essay on Moore's Life of Lord Byron." In English School Classics (series), edited by Francis Storr. London: Rivingtons, 1874. First appeared in *Edinburgh Review* (1831). https://babel.hathitrust.org/cgi/pt?id=coo.319 24013450402&view=1up&seq=16&q1=morality.

Matthias, Meg. "Gothic novel." *Encyclopedia Britannica Online.* Last modified May 12, 2020. https://www.britannica.com/art/Gothic-novel.

Mayer, Sandra. *Oscar Wilde in Vienna: Pleasing and Teasing the Audience.* Leiden: Brill, 2018.

Miller, Neil. *Out of the Past: Gay and Lesbian History from 1869 to the Present.* New York: Vintage Books, 1995.

Moran, Bruce T. "Paracelsus (1493–1541)." Encyclopedia.com. Last modified May 21, 2018. https://www.encyclopedia.com/science/encyclopedias-almanacs-transcripts-and-maps/paracelsus-1493-1541.

Murko, Matija. *Paměti.* Prague: Borový, 1949. https://kramerius5.nkp.cz/uuid/uuid:63d2a180-8129-11e7-8b50-001018b5eb5c.

Mutschlechner, Martin. "Ludwig Viktor – 'Archduke Luziwuzi'." The World of the Habsburgs. Last modified March 12, 2015. https://www.habsburger.net/en/chapter/ludwig-viktor-archd uke-luziwuzi.

Nagy, Petr. "Karáskovy Romány tří mágů." *Půlnoční expres: Listy pro odvrácenou tvář umění* 10, no. 1 (January 2013): 6–9. https://issuu.com/petrnagy/docs/pulnocni_expres_1_2013.

Neff, Ondřej. *Něco je jinak: Komentáře k české literární fantastice.* Prague: Albatros, 1981.

Nakonečný, Milan. *Lexikon magie*, 2nd edition. Prague: Kosmas, 2009.

Nakonečný, Milan. *Novodobý český hermetismus*. Prague: Vodnář, 1995.

Národní památkový ústav. "Dům U Textařů: dům U Bílého preclíku." Last modified March 19, 2016. https://pamatkovykata log.cz/dum-u-textoru-14488312.

Nešpor, Zdeněk R. "Athenaeum (1883–1893)." Sociologická encyklopedie. Last modified December 11, 2017. https://encyk lopedie.soc.cas.cz/w/Athenaeum.

Nešpor, Zdeněk R. "Naše doba (1894–1949)." Sociologická encyklopedie. Last modified December 11, 2017. https://encyk lopedie.soc.cas.cz/w/Naše_doba.

Norton, Rictor. *Mother Clap's Molly House: The Gay Subculture in England 1700–1830*. Wrecclesham: Heretic Books, 1992.

Norton, Rictor. *The Myth of the Modern Homosexual: Queer History and the Search for Cultural Unity*. London: Cassell, 1997.

Opelík, Jiří, Vladimír Forst and Luboš Merhaut, eds. "Hugo Kosterka." In *Lexikon české literatury: osobnosti, díla, instituce*. Volume 2, part 2: K–L, 872–73. Prague: Academia, 1993. Koráb–Kozák (853–904) available at https://edicee.ucl. cas.cz/images/data/prirucky/obsah/22/Kor%C3%A1b%20-%20Koz%C3%A1k%20(853-904).pdf.

Opelík, Jiří, Vladimír Forst and Luboš Merhaut, eds. "Jiří Karásek ze Lvovic." In *Lexikon české literatury: osobnosti, díla, instituce*. Volume 2, part 2: K–L: 664–67. Prague: Academia, 1993. Kancionál Franusův–Klášterský (648–99) available at https://edicee.ucl.cas.cz/images/data/prirucky/obsah/22/Kancion%C3%A1l%20Franus%C5%AFv%20-%20Kl%C3%A1%C5%A1tersk%C3%BD%20(648-699).pdf.

Opelík, Jiří, Vladimír Forst and Luboš Merhaut, eds. "Kruh českých spisovatelů." In *Lexikon české literatury: osobnosti, díla, instituce*. Volume. 2, part 2: K–L: 1007–8. Prague: Academia, 1993. Krov–Kuchař (1001–52) available at https://edicee.ucl.cas.cz/images/data/prirucky/obsah/22/Krov%20-%20Kucha%C5%99%20(1001-1052).pdf.

Ottův slovník naučný. "Jiří Karásek ze Lvovic." *Illustrovaná encyklopaedie obecných vědomostí*, volume 28: 744. Prague: J. Otto, 1909. https://kramerius5.nkp.cz/uuid/uuid:960abc70-0fc8-11e5-b0b8-5ef3fc9ae867.

Papoušek, Vladimír, ed. *Dějiny nové moderny: česká literatura v letech 1905–1923.* Prague: Academia, 2010.

Parker, N. Geoffrey. "Battle of White Mountain." *Encyclopedia Britannica Online.* Last modified November 1, 2023. https://www.britannica.com/event/Battle-of-White-Mountain.

Parker, N. Geoffrey. "Christian of Anhalt." *Encyclopedia Britannica Online.* Last modified May 7, 2023. https://www.britannica.com/biography/Christian-of-Anhalt.

Petruželková, Alena and Karel Kolařík, eds. *Knihovna Karáskovy Galerie a její světy.* Řevnice: Arbor Vitae, 2011.

Pfefferová, Radka. "Oscar Wilde a Moderní revue." Master's thesis, Univerzita Jana Evangelisty Purkyně, 2012. https://theses.cz/id/2ibljj/?fbclid=IwAR3JBIYDWfCUh10m6ZMI0UB2iNOSI8BDXYsQaVlJv_Rsk0Z3tZjYa6JlyWo.

Plass, David. "Historie Martinistického řádu v Čechách." Bachelor's thesis, Univerzita Karlova, 2014. http://hdl.handle.net/20.500.11956/70807.

Podroužek, Jaroslav. *Fragment zastřeného osudu.* Prague: Sfinx, 1945. https://books.google.com/books/about/Fragment_zastřeného_osudu.html?id=oMM_AAAAIAAJ.

Pokorná, Magdaléna. "Zeyerův fond při České akademii věd a umění." *Česká literatura* 49, no. 1 (2001): 95–103. http://www.jstor.org/stable/42686645.

Posthumus, Michaela. "'Art with Poisonous Honey Stolen from France': Oscar Wilde and Decadent Imitations between England and France." Master's thesis, University of British Columbia, 2014. https://open.library.ubc.ca/soa/cIRcle/collections/ubcthes/24/items/1.0167476.

Priani, Ernesto. "Ramon Llull." *Stanford Encyclopedia of Philosophy* (Spring 2021 edition), edited by Edward N. Zalta. Last modified February 11, 2021. https://plato.stanford.edu/archives/spr2021/entries/llull/.

Pruys, Karl Hugo. *Die Liebkosungen des Tigers: Eine erotische Goethe-Biographie.* Berlin: Edition Q, 1997.

Putna, Martin C., ed. *Dějiny homosexuality v české kultuře.* Prague: Academia, 2011.

Putna, Martin C. *Václav Havel: duchovní portrét v rámu kultury 20. století.* Prague: Knihovna Václava Havla, 2011.

Pynsent, Robert B. "Čapek-Chod and the Grotesque." In *Karel Matěj Čapek-Chod: Proceedings of a Symposium, 18–20 September 1984*, edited by Robert B. Pynsent, 181–215. London: University of London SSEES, 1985.

Pynsent, Robert B. *Julius Zeyer: The Path to Decadence.* The Hague/Paris: Moulton, 1973.

Rasmussen, Carolyn. "Kisch, Egon Erwin (1885–1948)." In *Australian Dictionary of Biography*, volume 15 (1940–1980), Kem–Pie. Melbourne: Melbourne University Press, 2000. https://adb.anu.edu.au/biography/kisch-egon-erwin-10755/text19067.

Řezníková, Lenka. "Gotická duše moderny: Gotika a gotický román v české literatuře přelomu 19. a 20. století." In *Čas moderny. Studie a materiály* edited by Dagmar Blümlová and Bohumil Jiroušek, 71–90. České Budějovice: Jihočeská univerzita, 2006. https://biblio.hiu.cas.cz/records/83c95753-b613-475f-8f69-cd0f4787b1a0?locale=en.

Rieckmann, Jens. "(Anti-)Semitism and Homoeroticism: Hofmannsthal's Reading of Bahr's Novel *Die Rotte Kohras.*" *The German Quarterly* 66, no. 2 (1993). https://www.jstor.org/stable/407469.

Ripellino, Angelo Maria. *Magic Prague.* Edited by Michael Henry Heim. Translated by David Newton Marinelli. London: Picador, 1994.

Robb, Graham. *Strangers: Homosexual Love in the Nineteenth Century.* New York: W. W. Norton & Company, 2003.

Rybička, Antonín. *Královéhradecké rodiny erbovní.* Prague: České společnosti nauk, 1873. https://kramerius5.nkp.cz/view/uuid:818d3200-21be-11dd-8ea8-000d606f5dc6?page=uuid:162e3430-e467-11e6-b333-5ef3fc9ae867.

Sabo, Anne Grethe. "William James and Friedrich Nietzsche's Revaluation of Truth and Life." Master's thesis, University of Washington, 1997. https://www.ub.uio.no/om/ansatte/humsam/ang/sabo_thesis.pdf.

Schindler, John R. "Disaster on the Drina: The Austro-Hungarian Army in Serbia, 1914." *War in History* 9, no. 2 (2002): 159–95. http://www.jstor.org/stable/26014058.

Schindler, John R. "Redl—Spy of the Century?" *International Journal of Intelligence and CounterIntelligence* 18, no. 3 (2005): 483–507. https://doi.org/10.1080/08850600590911981 [login required]

Schorske, Carl E. *Fin-de-Siècle Vienna: Politics and Culture.* New York: Vintage Books, 1981.

Schuchard, Marsha Keith. "Lord George Gordon and Cabalistic Freemasonry: Beating Jacobite Swords into Jacobin Ploughshares." In *Secret Conversions to Judaism in Early Modern Europe*, edited by Martin Mulsow and Richard H. Popkin, 183–231. Leiden: Brill, 2004. https://brill.com/view/book/edcoll/9789047401841/B9789047401841-s008.xml.

Seidl, Jan. "Legal Imbroglio in the Protectorate of Bohemia and Moravia." In *Queer in Europe During the Second World War*, edited by Régis Schlagdenhauffen, 53–62. Strasbourg: Council of Europe, 2018. https://sexualityandholocaust.files.wordpress.com/2018/10/jan.pdf.

Seidl, Jan. "Mužnost jako ctnost uvědomělého homosexuála ve třicátých letech," *Theatrum Historiae* 5 (2009): 281–92. https://theatrum.upce.cz/index.php/theatrum/article/view/202/1630.

Seidl, Jan. "'Najdu mladého přítele, přírodu milujícího?' Kulturněantropologický pohled na inzerci v meziválečném homosexuálním tisku." *Český lid* 106, no. 2 (2019): 157–78. https://www.jstor.org/stable/26774318.

Seidl, Jan. "Pokus o odtrestnění homosexuality za první republiky." Master's thesis, Masarykova univerzita, 2005. https://is.muni.cz/th/64594/ff_m/stesura_dipl._opravdu.pdf.

Seidl, Jan. "Úsilí o odtrestnění homosexuality za první republiky." PhD diss., Masarykova univerzita, 2007. https://is.muni.cz/th/yhi6p/.

Seidl, Jan, Lukáš Nozar, and Jan Wintr. *Od žaláře k oltáři: emancipace homosexuality v českých zemích od roku 1867 do současnosti.* Brno: Host, 2012.

Sledge, Justin. "Christian and Lurianic Kabbalah." Introduction to Kabbalah and Jewish Mysticism. September 28, 2021. Video series, episode 10 of 14, 1:11:26. https://www.youtube.com/watch?v=gqvcifVWjvM.

Sledge, Justin. "How Witchcraft Skepticism Produced the Lesser Key of Solomon, Modern Demonology and Psychiatry." June 9, 2023. Video, 40:57. https://youtu.be/vZLbDb8eW1c.

Sledge, Justin. "Kabbalah and the Contemporary World." Introduction to Kabbalah and Jewish Mysticism. October 26, 2021. Video series, episode 14 of 14, 1:08:47. https://www.youtube.com/watch?v=iYOBzZkngik.

Sledge, Justin. "Safedian Kabbalah." Introduction to Kabbalah and Jewish Mysticism. September 21, 2021. Video series, episode 9 of 14, 1:01:23. https://www.youtube.com/watch?v=iYOBzZkngik.

Sledge, Justin. "Sefir Yeztirah and Bahir." Introduction to Kabbalah and Jewish Mysticism. August 24, 2021. Video series, episode 5 of 14, 1:10:00. https://www.youtube.com/watch?v=c80t2F_Poao.

Sledge, Justin. "The Testament of Solomon: The Origins of Solomonic Magic, Occultism, and Demonology." June 17, 2022. Video, 28:12. https://youtu.be/BBozTcgOFGc.

Snyder, Timothy. *The Red Prince: The Secret Lives of a Habsburg Archduke*. New York: Basic Books, 2008.

Spector, Scott. "The Wrath of the 'Countess Merviola': Tabloid Exposé and the Emergence of Homosexual Subjects in Vienna in 1907." In *Sexuality in Austria* (Contemporary Austrian Studies 15), edited by Günter Bischof, Anton Pelinka, and Dagmar Herzog, 31–47. New Brunswick: Transaction Publishers, 2009.

Špiritová, Alexandra. "Spisy bývalého Poštovní muzea v Praze." *Paginae historiae* 9 (2001), 98–113.

Stach, Reiner. *Kafka: The Early Years*. Translated by Shelley Frisch. Princeton: Princeton University Press, 2016.

Stejskalová, Anna. "Italská cesta Julia Zeyera 1883–1884." *Česká literatura* 49, no. 4 (2001): 433–40. http://www.jstor.org/stable/42686694.

Štorch-Marien, Otakar. *Sladko je žít: paměti nakladatele I*. Prague: Aventinum, 1992.

Swedenborg, Emanuel. *True Christianity*, Portable New Century Edition. Volume 1. Translated by Jonathan S. Rose. West Chester: Swedenborg Foundation, 2010. https://swedenborg. com/wp-content/uploads/2017/06/NCE_TrueChristianity1_ portable.pdf.

Szott, Randall. "Lebenskünstler: What might it mean?" Randallszott.org. Last modified April 26, 2011. https://randa llszott.org/lebenskunstler/.

Tardieu, Auguste Ambroise. *Question médico-légale de l'identité dans ses rapports avec les vices de conformation des organes sexuels. Souvenirs et impressions d'un individu dont le sexe avait été méconnu.* Paris: J.-B. Baillière et fils, 1874. https:// wellcomecollection.org/works/v9cdq3n2/items?canvas= 7&page=2.

Thuleen, Nancy. "*Dichterstreit*: Homoeroticism in the Conflict between Stefan George and Hugo von Hofmannsthal." Last modified May 17, 1995. http://www.nthuleen.com/papers/ 711George.html.

Tobin, Robert Deam. *Peripheral Desires: The German Discovery of Sex*. Philadelphia: University of Pennsylvania Press, 2015.

Trevor-Roper, Hugh. *The Crisis of the Seventeenth Century: Religion, the Reformation, and Social Change.* Indianapolis: Liberty Fund, 1967. https://oll.libertyfund.org/title/roper-the-crisis-of-the-seventeenth-century.

Ulrichs, Karl Heinrich. *Incubus: Urningsliebe und Blutgier: Eine Erörterung über krankhafte Gemüthsaffection und Zurechnungsfähigkeit, veranlasst durch den Berliner Criminalfall v. Zastrow; Mit 15 Fällen verwandter Natur; Als Fortsetzung der Schriften von Numa Numantius.* Leipzig: Serbe, 1869. https:// archive.org/details/bub_gb__IHp0oDd2moC.

van Gijsen, Annelies. "Isaac Hollandus Revisited." In *Chymia: Science and Nature in Medieval and Early Modern Europe*, edited by Miguel López Pérez, Didier Kahn, and Mar Rey-Bueno, 310–30. Newcastle: Cambridge Scholars Publishing, 2010. https://chg.kncv.nl/l/library/download/ urn:uuid:79ba7f09-3f05-460f-9901-ed9e5be407fc/chymia_ vangijsen.pdf.

Váňa, Jan. *Úvahy a povahy*. Prague: V. Řezníček, 1892. https://kramerius5.nkp.cz/view/uuid:76309c00-4d81-11dd-add8-000d606f5dc6?page=uuid:b3b26da0-f3b7-11e8-9984-00505 6825209.

Vetter, Isolde. "An Introduction to Oskar Panizza's 'Bayreuth and Homosexuality' (1895): 'Checkmate,' or, 'A Heavenly Tragedy' and its Earthly Consequences." *The Opera Quarterly* 22, no. 2 (spring 2006): 321–23. https://doi.org/10.1093/oq/kbl011.

Vévoda, Rudolf. "Dobový kontext Karáskova vystoupení." *Neon* 1999, no. –2 (1999): 64–69. http://martinreiner.cz/public/neon/3.pdf.

Vojtěch, Daniel. "Polemičnost a strategie: k proměně české literární kritiky po roce 1900." *Česká literatura* 50, no. 2 (2002): 149–73. http://www.jstor.org/stable/42686748.

Volavková, Hana. *Pražská musea*. Prague: Orbis, 1949. https://kramerius5.nkp.cz/view/uuid:162c1400-cdf1-11e8-bc37-00505 6827e51?page=uuid:9d2a05a0-50cf-11e9-b3de-5ef3fc9bb 22f&fulltext=Jiř%C3%AD%20Karásek%20ze%20Lvovic.

von Bülau, Friedrich. *Geheime Geschichten und rätselhafte Menschen*. Vienna/Leipzig/Olten: Bernina-Verlag Ges. m.b.H., 1937. https://www.projekt-gutenberg.org/buelau/geheim/chap 014.html.

Wagener, Mary L. "Fashion and Feminism in 'Fin de Siècle' Vienna." *Woman's Art Journal* 10, no. 2 (1989): 29–33. https://doi.org/10.2307/1358209.

Wilde, Oscar. *The Complete Works of Oscar Wilde, with Oscar Wilde Biography and Criticism*. Golgotha Press, 2011.

Witek, Jan. "Kam se v Praze kdysi chodili muži 'bavit' aneb Historie pražského cruisingu." *LUI*. February 14, 2018. https://www.lui.cz/co-se-deje/item/12585-kam-se-v-praze-kdysi-chod ili-muzi-bavit-aneb-historie-prazskeho-cruisingu.

Young, Michael B. "James VI and I: Time for a Reconsideration?" *Journal of British Studies* 51, no. 3 (2012): 540–67. http://www.jstor.org/stable/23265594.

Zach, Aleš. "Gemini." *Slovník českých nakladatelů 1849–1949*. Last modified May 14, 2017. https://www.slovnik-nakladatels tvi.cz/nakladatelstvi/gemini.html.

Zach, Aleš. *Nakladatelská pouť Jiřího Karáska ze Lvovic.* Prague: Thyrsus, 1994.

Zach, Aleš. "Thyrsus." Slovník českých nakladatelů 1849–1949. Last modified January 24, 2021. https://slovnik-nakladatelstvi. cz/naklavelikdatelstvi/thyrsus.html.

Karásek Bibliography

The purpose of this bibliography is to give some sense of the range of Karásek's publications by type and over time. He was no one-book wonder. Karásek was a prolific author who often issued his works in small bibliophilic editions. For a study of Karásek's publication history, see Zach, *Nakladatelská pouť Jiřího Karáska ze Lvovic*; for a mapping of Karásek's early publications, see Kolařík, "Raná literární tvorba Jiřího Karáska ze Lvovic." For an overview of Karásek's development as an author, see Lishaugen, "Jiří Karásek ze Lvovic"; for a discussion of Karásek's poetics in his middle period (1909–12), see Kolařík, "Poetika druhého básnického období Jiřího Karáska ze Lvovic."

A complete, single-source Karásek bibliography does not seem to exist yet. The following is based on titles in the unified Czech National Library catalog and on the website Databazeknih.cz. *Lexikon české literatury* broadly outlines the publications Karásek contributed to and when, but I have not attempted to trace every article and review here, or to include juvenilia that may be attested in the sources but does not survive. Works are listed under the first known year of publication, and works are alphabetized within each year.

In listing each work's editions, I have used these abbreviations:

AH = Alois Hynek
Av = Aventinum
HK = Hugo Kosterka
KN = Kamilla Neumannová
MKP = Městská knihovna v Praze
MR = *Moderní revue*
ŠF = Šašek a Frgal (Velké Meziříčí, Moravia)

Sp = self-published, often distributed by a particular bookseller.

All publishers were based in Prague unless otherwise noted here.

c = number of copies
n.f.i. = no further information (most likely individual poems)
n.i.n. = no issue number(s)
n.p. = no place
p = number of pages

Example: MR 1895 [34 p] = Prague: *Moderní revue*, 1895 [34 pages].

Additional descriptions or synopses of a given work may be available in Czech at Databazeknih.cz. The terms *povídka* (short story), *novela* (novella), and *romaneto* (romanetto, an Arbes coinage) overlap in usage.

See further below to locate individual Karásek poems anthologized in English, and for known translations of Karásek's prose works.

1890

"Vondra Pláteník" (short story). *Obzor: List pro poučení a zábavu* 12, n.i.n. (November), 314–17, 326–29.

1891

"A přece se našli…" (short story, They Were Found After All, a Neruda-inspired humoresque of Prague's Malá Strana) *Vesna* 10, n.i.n,, 312–15, 328–31.

"Dle slov Kristových…" (n.f.i., In Christ's Words) *Vesna* 10, n.i.n., 280.

Emil (novel) serial *Jitřenka* 10, n.i.n., 23–27, 27–29, 33–36, 45–47, 53–56, 64–66, 72–74, 80–82, 88–90, 96–98, 105–06, 112–14, 120–22, 129–30, 136–38, 144–46. ŠF 1891,[1] Antikvariát Křenek 2019 [60 p, 250 c]. See 2023 *Preludia*.

"Fiakrista" (n.f.i., Fiacre Coachman) *Moravské orlice* 20, no. 26 (February 1), 1.

"Kávová společnost" (n.f.i., Company over Coffee) *Jitřenka* 10, n.i.n., 181.

"Malostranský pensista" (n.f.i., Malá Strana Pensioner) *Vesna* 10, n.i.n., 338.

"Necudná idylka" (n.f.i., An Unchaste Idyll). *Máj* (Jaroměřice) 2, n.i.n., 240.

"Pobožná klepna" (n.f.i., The Pious Gossip) *Jitřenka* 10, n.i.n., 181.

"Pokažená idyla" (short story, A Spoiled Idyll; a Malá Strana humoresque) *Vesna* 10, 190–94, 206–8.

"Poprvé v kanceláři" (n.f.i., First Time in the Office) *Vesna* 10, n.i.n., 338.

"Zasněženo..." (n.f.i., Covered in Snow) *Jitřenka* 10, n.i.n., 181.

1892

"Bez viny" (n.f.i., Without Blame) *Vesna* 11, n.i.n., 86–87, 107–9.

Bezcestí: Pražský román (A Roadless Place: A Prague Novel), serial *Moderní revue* 14 (1892–93),[2] ŠF 1893 [312 p]. See 2023 *Preludia.*

"Děcku na fialkách" (n.f.i., To the Child on the Violets) *Máj* 3, n.i.n., 433–34.

"Hřbitovní meditace" (n.f.i., A Graveyard Meditation) *Máj* 3, n.i.n., 299–300.

"John Greenleaf Whittier" (n.f.i.) *Literární listy* 13, n.i.n., 420.

"Nezapomněla" (n.f.i., She Did Not Forget) *Máj* 3, n.i.n., 417–18.

"Pan baron Specht" (short story, Baron Specht; a Malá Strana humoresque) *Máj* 3, n.i.n., 297–300, 327–32.

"Poslední podpora" (n.f.i., The Last Support) *Vesna* 11, n.i.n., 298–300, 311–13.

"Rudohorské krajky" (n.f.i., Lace from Rudá Hora) *Vesna* 11, n.i.n., 253.

"Slepý" (n.f.i., Blind) *Vesna* 11, n.i.n., 253.

"Za půl roku" (n.f.i., In Half a Year) *Obzor* 15, n.i.n., 242–43.

"Ze života" (n.f.i., From Life) *Vesna* 11, n.i.n., 13.

1893

"Albatros" (poem, Albatross; translation from Baudelaire) *Vesna* 12, n.i.n., 176.

"Do bahna" (n.f.i., Into the Mud) *Vesna* 12, n.i.n., 9–11.

"Jaroslavu Vrchlickému v den čtyřicátých narozenin" (poem, To Jaroslav Vrchlický on His Fortieth Birthday)[3] *Niva* 3, n.i.n., 81.

"Julius Zeyer: 'Stratonika' a jiné povídky" (article, "Stratonika" and Other Stories) *Literární listy* 14, no. 13 (June 16) [column dated May 31].

"Noční nálada" (n.f.i., Night Mood) *Jitřenka* 12, n.i.n., 68.

"Oběť" (n.f.i., Victim, or Sacrifice) *Jitřenka* 12, n.i.n., 20.

"Písaři" (n.f.i., The Scribes) *Niva* 3, n.i.n., 173–74.

"Václavu Jansovi na poděkovanou za nakreslený portrét" (sonnet, To Václav Jans in Appreciation for a Sketched Portrait).[4]

1894

"Listy z Prahy IV" (article, Letters from Prague 4) *Literární listy* 15, no. 7.

Mimo život (prose, Outside Life) serial *Vesna* 14 (1894–95),[5] ŠF 1898 [274 p].

"Octovství" (n.f.i., Fatherhood) *Niva* 4, 69.

"Psychosa" (short prose, Psychosis) *Rozhledy* 3, n.i.n., 24–5. See 2023 *Preludia*.

Stojaté vody (novella, Stagnant Waters) serial *Vesna* 1894,[6] ŠF 1894. MR 1895 [34 p]. See 2023 *Preludia*.

"Ukřižovanému Kristu" (poem, To the Crucified Christ; translation from Teresa of Avila) *Vesna* 13, n.i.n., 143.[7]

Zazděná okna (poetry, Walled-Up Windows) ŠF 1894 [66 p]. KN 1912 [107 p]. Av 1921 [80 p].

1895

with Arnošt Procházka: "Kritika: Časopisy" (Criticism: Journals) *Moderní revue* 1, no. 2 (May): 48.

with Arnošt Procházka: "Kritika: Časopisy" *Moderní revue* 1, no. 3 (June): 70–72.

Sodoma (poetry, Sodom). Printed on August 28, 1895 by Emanuel Stivín at V jichářích 146, Nové Město, Prague; court approved confiscation in fall 1895. MR, 1895 [45 p, 220 c]. Sp 1905 [69 p; modified from original]. KN 1909 [73 p]. Av 1921 [85 p]. Mladá fronta 2002 [96 p]. MKP 2022 [ebook].

1896

Kniha aristokratická (poetry, The Aristocratic Book) MR [29 p, 199 c].
"Legenda o melancholickém princi" (prose, Legend of a Melancholy Prince).[8] See also 1904 *Lásky absurdní.*

1897

Sexus necans: pohanská kniha (poetry, Sexus Necans: A Pagan Book) MR 1897 [59 p, 212 c]. Av 1921. See also 1932 "Vyhnancům lásky" (excerpted poem).

1899

Hořící duše: tragédie o třech aktech (play, The Burning Soul: A Tragedy in Three Acts) MR [92 p].

1900

Foreword to Emanuel Lešehrad, *Paní Modrovouska,* E. Weinfurter.
Gotická duše (novel, A Gothic Soul) MR 1900 [170 p]. KN 1905 [89 p] [https://archive.org/details/gotickdueromnji00l vovgoog/page/n10/mode/2up]. Av 1921 [100 p]. Vyšehrad 1991 (including 11 short stories, 248 p). Torst 2021 [90 p]. For original version, see also 2023 *Preludia.*
Ideje zítřku: Henrik Ibsen – Walt Whitman, 1894–1898 (critical essays, The Idea of Tomorrow) HK [84 p].

1901

"Za Juliem Zeyerem: vzpomínka" (Julius Zeyer: A Recollection) *Moderní revue* 12, no. 77 (February): 157–60.

1902

"Nad obrazem Marie Magdaleny v Hradčanské Loretě" (poem, On a Painting of Mary Magdalene in Hradčany) Sp 1902 (leaflet); confiscated and destroyed by the censors (Databazeknih.cz). Jiří Weyr [n.p.] 1925 [20 p, 30 c].

Renaissanční touhy v umění: kritické studie (critical essays 1894–1900, Renaissance Longings in Art) HK 1902 [167 p]. Av 1926 [184 p].

1903

Cesare Borgia (play in verse) HK 1903 [113 p]. KN 1908.

Impressionisté a ironikové, dokumenty k psychologii literární generace let devadesátých (critical essays 1892–1902, Impressionists and Ironists) HK 1903 [183 p] [https://arch ive.org/details/impressionistai02lvovgoog/page/n6/mode/ 2up]. Av 1926 [132 p].

1904

Háj Mylittin (short prose) Arno Sáňka[9] (České Budějovice?) 1926 [51 c]. Ina Fürstová [n.p.] 1930 [15 p, 30 c]. (First issue date per Databazeknih.cz.)

Hovory se smrtí (poetry, Conversations with Death) Sp 1904. KN 1909. Av 1922 [84 p].

Lásky absurdné: "Vánoce v Grecciu," "Háj Mylittin" [1904], "Legenda o melancholickém princi" [1897] (short stories, Absurd Loves) Sp 1904 [125 p]. KN 1909 [126 p]. Av 1929 [123 p].

1905

Apollonius z Tyany (play in verse, Apollonius of Tyana) Sp (distributed by Hejda & Tuček) 1905 [38 p]. KN 1909 [40 p].

"Divadelní kronika" (review of Ivo Raić's performance as Pierrot, Theater Chronicle) *Moderní revue* 16 (1905): 150. One of many theatrical reviews by Karásek.

1906

Chimaerické výpravy: kritické studie (critical essays 1892–1904, Chimerical Expeditions) HK 1906 [230 p]. Av 1927 [172 p].

Umění jako kritika života: kritická studie (critical essays 1892–1902, Art as a Critique of Life) HK 1906 [154 p]. Av 1927 [124 p].

1907

"Charles Baudelaire" (study) In *Rakety mé srdce obnažené: denníky Charlesa Baudelairea*. *Přeložil Jarmil Krejcar z růžokvětu se studií o Ch. Baudelaireovi od Jiřího Karáska ze Lvovic*: v–ix. Moderní bibliotéka, vol. 5, book 8. Král. Vinohrady [Prague]: F. Adámek (April).

Román Manfreda Macmillena (novel, Manfred Macmillan's Novel) (serial May–September 1907, book July 1907) KN 1907 and 1909 [154 p]. Av 1924 [136 p]. Antonín Pokorný [Prague] 1996 [174 p]. See also 2012 *Romány tří mágů*.

Sen o říši krásy: čínská pohádka o dvou dějstvích (play in verse, Dream of the Realm of Beauty: A Chinese Fairy Tale in Two Acts) HK 1907 [63 p]. Josef Hladký [n.p.] 1932 [54 p, 200 c]. Anthologized in *Pohádkové drama* (prose, A Short-Story Drama) Lidové noviny, 1999. See also 2001 Karásek collection by same name.

1908

Scarabaeus (novel, Scarabæus) (serial May 1908–August 1909, book 1909) KN 1908 [256 p]. Av 1925 [212 p]. See also 2012 *Romány tří mágů*.

1909

Endymion (poetry) KN 1909 and 1913 [60 p], 1922 [55 p]. See also 1929 *Čtyři sonety*.

1910

Anonymní dopisy čili Affaira pěti spisovatelův (essay, The Anonymous Letters or The Affair of the Five Writers) Sp [27 p].

Foreword to Artur Breisky, *Triumf zla: essaie a evokace* (The Triumph of Evil: Essays and Evocations) František Adamec.

Jan Neruda: kritická studie (study) AH [78 p].

"Otakar Březina" (foreword to *Výbor básní Otakara Březiny*, a selection of Březina's poems) AH: 3–16.

1911

"Genenda" (prose) In collection *Posvátné ohně* 1911, 4–46 (see below). Karel Dyrynk (Prague?) 1928 [first issue date per Databazeknih.cz.] Republished in 1984 *Ocúny noci*.

Král růží paní Hussonové (novel; from 1887 novella *Le rosier de Madame Husson* by Guy de Maupassant, translated by Jiří Karásek ze Lvovic and A. Veselý) Prague: Vilímek, 1911.

Posvátné ohně (short stories, Holy Fires) František Adámek 1911. R. Šimek 1921. Reissued in 1921 as *Vytvořit vlastní seznam*. Contains "Genenda" (prose), "Smrt Salomina" (prose, The Death of Salome), "Večeře svaté Kláry" (prose, St. Clare's Supper), "Legenda o kouzelníku Šimonovi" (prose, The Legend of Simon Magus), and "Růže svatého Šebestiána" (prose, The Roses of St. Sebastian).

1912

Ostrov vyhnanců: básně (poetry, Island of Exiles) KN 1912 [86 p]. Av 1922 [88 p].

Památce K. H. Máchy (critical essays, one by Karásek, on the Czech Romantic poet Karel Hynek Mácha, 1810–1836). Jednota umělců výtvarných [16 p].

1914

Dafnino hoře (short story, Daphne's Grief) In Moderní revue 1914. František Kobliha [32 p, 55 c].

1916

Král Rudolf: drama (play, King Rudolf) Thyrsus [70 p].

1919

Obrácení Raymunda Lulla: novella (novella, The Conversion of Ramon Llull) A. Srdce [48 p].

Zlatý triptych (short stories, A Golden Triptych) A. Srdce [36 p].

1920

Legenda o Sodomovi (short story, A Legend of Sodom) Ludvík Bradáč [36 p].

1921

Sebrané spisy (collected works, 1921–32, 19 volumes).
Vytvořit vlastní seznam (five short stories) Rudolf Šimek [190 pp.] (Reissue of 1911's *Posvátné ohně*.)

1922

Barokové oltáře (short stories) Karel Janský [77 p, 615 c].
Básnické spisy Jiřího Karáska ze Lvovic (poetic works) Aventinum [452 p]. (Contains: *Zazděná okna*; *Sodoma*; *Sexus necans*; *Hovory se smrtí*; *Endymion*; *Ostrov vyhnanců*.)
Legenda o ctihodné Marii Elektě z Ježíše (prose, The Legend of the Venerable Mary Electa of Jesus) Ladislav Kuncíř [92 p].

1923

Zastřený obraz (novel, A Veiled Painting) Av [80 p].

1925

Ganymedes (novel, Ganymede) (serial October 1922–June 1923, October 1923–June 1924, book 1925) Av 1925. See also 2012 *Romány tří mágů*.
Interview in *Ženský svět* 29, no. 3, 25; and no. 4, 34
"Romány tři magů" [*sic*] (article, The Three Magicians Novels) *Rozpravy Aventinum* 1, no. 1: 3.

1926

"Úvod" (Introduction). In *Dopisy Karla Hlaváčka Marii Balounové*. Kladno: [Svatopluk Klír] [200 c].

1927

Tvůrcové a epigoni (critical essays 1900–1925, Creators and Epigones) Av [202 p].

1928

Boží převozník: legenda (prose, The Godly Ferryman: A Legend) Svatopluk Klír [40 p, 120 c].

In memoriam Karel Hlaváček (as editor) Kladno: Svatopluk Klír.

Žena a bůh: dramatická báseň o 1 dějství (one-act opera, The Woman and the God) Adapted from 1905 Apollonius z Tyany, score by Karel Boleslav Jirák (op. 3, 1910–13) and first staged in Brno in 1928. Hudební matice Umělecké besedy [28 p].

1929

Čtyři sonety ze sbírky Endymion (poetry, Four Sonnets from the Collection Endymion) Illustrated by Jan Konůpek. Jaroslav Picka [n.p.] 1929 [7 p]. See 1909 *Endymion*.

foreword to *Postupímský zločin* (A Potsdam Crime) by Edmond Rostand (original French title unidentified) Karel Reichel (bibliophilia).

introductory sonnet to *Rudé kamélie* by Tereza Dubrovská. Illustrated by T. F. Šimon. Prokop Toman ml. (bibliophilia).

1930

foreword to "Jules Barbey d'Aurevilly: *Ženatý kněz*" (from 1865 novella *Un prêtre marié* by Jules Amédee Barbey d'Aurevilly, translated by Arnošt Procházka) Ladislav Kuncíř, 1–4.

"O kvalitách slovenského duchu" (interview, On the Qualities of the Slovak Soul) *Elán* 1, no. 1.

Písně tulákovy o životě a smrti (poetry 1929–30, A Vagabond's Songs of Life and Death) Av [92 p].

Tryzna za básníkem Karlem Hlaváčkem [assembled by Jiří Karásek ze Lvovic]. Kvasnička & Hampl, 1930 [16 p]. Excerpted or anthologized in 1984 *Ocúny noci*.

1932

"Feuilleton" *Nový hlas* 1, no. 2, 16–17.

"Morální záchvat Německa" (article, Germany's Moral Paroxysm) *Nový hlas* 1, no. 5, 12–13.

Cesta mystická: iniciály a iluminace (critical essays, The Mystic Path; often fragmentary, considering various Slavic artists and writers; Dostoevsky pp. 81–82, Mickiewicz pp. 83–85) Av [107 p].

Vyhnancům lásky (poem from *Sexus necans*) František Bartoš [19 p].

1933

"J. Arbes" (foreword to *Ukřižovaná, Akrobati: romanetta* by Jakub Arbes; *Ukřižovaná* is from 1876, *Akrobati* from 1878) Sdružení pro vydání spisů J. Arbesa: 5–6.

"Malostranský bibliofil" (short story with essayistic elements, The Malá Strana Bibliophile) Sdružení českých umělců grafiků Hollar, 1933 [11 p].

1934

J. S. Machar – přednáška k sedmdesátinám básníkovým v sále Slovanského ostrova 8. března 1934 (lecture given March 8, 1934 on the poet J. S. Machar's 70th birthday) [Prague or Kroměříž]: Čech [private edition] [17 p].

1935

Dílo Františka Bílka (lecture given for Prague Radio in November 1932 on Art Nouveau sculptor and architect František Bílek, 1872–1941) Kroužek přátel díla Bílkova [9 p, 240 c].

1936

Platon Dějev (profile of artist and author Platon Dějev, with Jan Linhart; Dějev wrote *Výtvarníci-legionáři*, a 1937 book on WWI Czech legionnaire-artists) [n.p.]: [publisher unknown] [14 p, 300 c] (Databazeknih.cz).

1938

Ztracený ráj (novel, Paradise Lost; with autobiographical elements) Pražská akciová tiskárna, 1938 [340 p]. Melantrich, 1977 [284 p] (with note by Jarmila Víšková, afterword by Miloš Pohorský). Městská knihovna v Praze, 2022 [ebook: MOBI, PDF].

1939

Hvězdy nad Prahou (poetry, Stars over Prague) Josef Portman, 1939. See 1946 Aventinum reissue.

Pražské Jezulátko (short story cycle, The Prague Baby Jesus) E. Beaufort [81 p, 1100 c].

1940

foreword to Jakub Arbes, *Štrajchpudlíci.* Evropský literární klub.

foreword to Josef Jiří Kolár, *Zplozenci pekla.* Also editor. Beaufort.

1941

foreword to Karel Hynek Mácha, *Máj* [first critical edition]. Kropáč a Kucharský.

1943

Loretánské meditace. Vojtěch Kubašta. Pět původních kolorovaných grafik na loretánské thema. [Five color graphics of the Loreta church at the Prague Castle, evidently by Kubašta; available cataloging lists Karásek as the "author"] See Library of Congress catalog at https://catalog.loc.gov/vwebv/holdingsInfo?bibId=10309065.

1946

Poslední vinobraní; Hvězdy nad Prahou, Bludné kořeny; básně (poetry, The Last Vintage: Stars over Prague, Wayward Roots: Poems) Av.

1947

Zlověstná madona: staroměstské romaneto (short story, The Ominous Madonna) Zodiak, 1947 [32 p]. Republished in 1984 *Ocúny noci.*

1962

"Vzpomínky na Jana Štursu a jeho rod." In *Jan Štursa* (memorial collection, Memory of Jan Štursa), 122–23. Štursa was a Czech sculptor, 1880–1925.

1967

Z dáli dýchla vůně cyklamen (selected correspondence, From Afar the Scent of Cyclamens) Lumír Kuchař [16 p, 100 c] (bibliophilia).

1969

Sbírka korespondence a rukopisů Karáskovy galerie (correspondence, A Collection of Correspondence and Manuscripts from the Karásek Gallery). Edited by Jana Kirschnerová. Literární archív Památníku národního písemnictví.

1970

"Smrt Salomina (Nubijský apokryf)." In *Čas a smrt* [short-story anthology], edited by Jan Dvořák. Hradec Králové: Kruh.

1984

Ocúny noci (anthology, Colchicums of the Night; edited by Jaroslav Med) Odeon [192 p, 3000 c].

1988

Polské umění XIX. a XX. století ze sbírky Jiřího Karáska ze Lvovic: výstava, 1988, Muzeum literatury Adama Mickiewicze, Varšava, červen–srpen, Společnost přátel krásných umění, Krakov, Palác umění, září–říjen (catalog from exhibition of 19th- and 20th-century Polish art from the Jiří Karásek collection; edited by Antonín Boháč) Památník národního písemnictví.

1989

Vteřiny duše (short story anthology, Seconds of the Soul) Odeon [310 p, 5000 c].

1994

Vzpomínky (Memoirs) Thyrsus [278 p, 2000 c].

1999

Tři vzpomínkové portréty (Karásek's recollections of three figures from 1890s Czech culture) Thyrsus [40 p].

2001

Milý příteli… (Listy Edvardu Klasovi) (correspondence between Karásek and Vladimíra Jedličková). Edited and with afterword by Libuše Heczková. Thyrsus [86 p, 600 c].
Sen o říši krásy (collection of Karásek pieces). Edited by Jan Nepomuk Assmann et al., Obecní dům (Prague), Tigris.

2003

"Chimérické výpravy" *Literární noviny* 14, no. 50, 1.

2007

Upřímné pozdravy z kraje květů a zapadlých snů: dopisy adresované Marii Kalašové z Jiřího Karáska ze Lvovic z let 1903–1907 (correspondence between Karásek and Marie Kalašova, Heartfelt Greetings from the Land of Flowers and Fallen Dreams). Edited by and with afterword by Karel Kolařík. Příbram: Pistorius & Olšanská [88 p].

2012

Romány tří mágů. Volvox Globator [480 p].

2023

Preludia (anthology of early works): *Emil* (1891); *Bezcestí* (1893); first version of *Gotická duše* (1900); and two shorter works: *Psychosa* (1894), previously unpublished, and *Stojaté vody* (1894). Dybbuk.

A partial index of Karásek stories. The collections can be found in the list above:

"Františkánská legenda" *Barokové oltáře* 1922
"Genenda" *Posvátné ohně* 1911
"Košíček Dorotein" *Zlatý triptych* 1919
"Legenda o kouzelníku Šimonovi" *Posvátné ohně* 1911
"Pokání svaté Pelagie" *Barokové oltáře* 1922
"Růže svatého Šebestiána" *Posvátné ohně* 1911
"Sen Lutgardin" *Barokové oltáře* 1922
"Smrt sábské královny" *Zlatý triptych* 1919
"Smrt Salomina" *Posvátné ohně* 1911
"Tříkrálová legenda" *Zlatý triptych* 1919
"Večeře svaté Kláry" *Posvátné ohně* 1911

Karásek Poetry in English Translation

The Karásek poems listed here, translated into English, have been sorted by the name of their original Czech collection, and those collections have been listed in order of publication.

Zazděná okna (Walled-Up Windows, 1894)

Záchvěje mrtva… "Wafts of Dead Air" (Lodge: 36)
V barvách chorobných "In Sickly Colors" (Lodge: 33)
Touha samoty "The Longing for Solitude" (Lodge: 39)
Tuberosy "Tuberoses" (Lodge: 27)
Somnambula "Sleepwalker" (Lodge: 29)
Příšerná loď "The Spectral Ship" (Selver 1929: 235; Selver 1946: 183; French: 348–49, revised)
Miserere "Miserere" (Lodge: 23)
Spleen [Den za dnem…] (Lodge: 25)
Nálada zmrtvělá [Dlouho je tomu, dlouho již…] "Deathly Mood" (Lodge: 28)
Kalný západ [Jak trosky zčernalé ze spaleného vraku] "Mired West" (Pinkava)

Sodoma (Sodom, 1895)

Jsem dítě Sodomy... "I Am Sodom's Child" (Volková and Cloutier: 26–27)

Sodoma "Opening Poem of the Collection *Sodom*" (Lodge: 40)

Io triumphe! "Io triumphe!" (Lodge: 45)

Metempsychosa "Metempsychosis" (Lodge: 32)

Kniha aristokratická (The Aristocratic Book, 1896)

Spleen [Vše horkem umdlévá pod tíhou neviděnou] (Lodge: 42)

Sen "The Dream" (Selver 1919: 244; Selver 1929: 236)

Beethoven [Ó smutku zhořklý...] "Beethoven" (Selver 1919: 246; Selver 1929: 237; Selver 1946: 185)

Růže hřbitovů "Cemetery Roses" (Volková and Cloutier: 30–31)

In memoriam "In Memoriam" (Lodge: 30)

Přátelství duší "Friendship of the Soul" (Lodge: 43)

Sexus necans: kniha pohanská (Sexus Necans: A Pagan Book, 1897)

Venus masculinus "Venus Masculinus" (Lodge: 41)

Incubus "The Incubus" (Lodge: 38)

Smutek těla "The Sorrow of Flesh" (Lodge: 47)

Pozdní okamžik "Late Moment" (Lodge: 46)

Setkání "The Meeting" (Salmonson, *Fantasy & Terror* 14 (1992): 11–12)

Rozklad "Decomposition" (Lodge: 31)

Narkosy "Narcosis" (Lodge: 26)

Poznání "Knowledge" (Lodge: 34)

Hovory se smrtí (Conversations with Death, 1904)

Whitman epigram: *Není smrti, a kdyby byla náhodou, / byl by v ní zárodek života.* (From *Song of Myself*, "The smallest sprout shows there is really no death; / And if ever there was, it led forward life, and does not wait at the end to arrest it, / And ceas'd the moment life appear'd.")

Beethoven "Beethoven" (Selver 1919: 246; Selver 1929: 237; Selver 1946: 185)

Endymion (1909)

Tíha věčnosti "The Weight of Eternity" (Volková and Cloutier: 28–29)

Sources Cited

French, Alfred, ed. *A Bilingual Anthology of Czech Poetry*. Ann Arbor: Czechoslovak Society of Arts and Sciences in America/ University of Michigan, 1973.

Lodge, Kirsten, ed. and transl. *Solitude, Vanity, Night: An Anthology of Czech Decadent Poetry*. Prague: Univerzita Karlova, 2008.

Pinkava, Václav Z. J., transl. "Jiří Karásek ze Lvovic." Life and Legends. Last modified December 29, 2014. http://lifeandlege nds.com/jiri-karasek-ze-lvovic-translation-pinkava/.

Salmonson, Jessica Amanda, ed. *Fantasy & Terror*. Seattle: Violet Books, 1984–92.

Selver, Paul, ed. and transl. *A Century of Czech and Slovak Poetry*. [London]: New Europe Publishing Co. Ltd., 1946.

Selver, Paul, ed. and transl. *An Anthology of Czechoslovak Literature*. London: Kegan Paul, Trench, Trubner, 1929.

Selver, Paul, ed. and transl. *Anthology of Modern Slavonic Literature in Prose and Verse*. London: Kegan Paul, Trench, Trubner; New York: E. P. Dutton, 1919.

Volková, Bronislava and Clarice Cloutier. *Up the Devil's Back: A Bilingual Anthology of 20th-Century Czech Poetry*. Bloomington: Slavica, 2008.

Karásek Prose in Translation

"La conversión de Raimundo Lulio" (Obrácení Raymunda Lulla, 1919). Novella. Palma de Mallorca: Universidad de Barcelona, 1971.

"The Death of Salome (A Nubian Apocryphon)" (Smrt Salomina [Nubijský apokryf], 1970 text). Short story. From *Posvátné ohně*, 1911. Translated by Cyril Simsa. In *Fantasy Macabre* 16 (1994): 32–35; and by Kirsten Lodge. Issuu (Twisted Spoon Press). Last modified March 16, 2012. https://issuu. com/twistedspoon/docs/death_of_salome.

Dream of the Empire of Beauty (Sen o říši krásy: Čínská pohádka o dvou dějstvích, 1907). The title is the name of a play by Karásek. Translated by Barbara Day. Prague: Obecní dům, 2001.

A Gothic Soul (Gotická duše, 1900). Novel. Translated by Kirsten Lodge. Prague: Twisted Spoon Press, 2015.

"The Legend of Simon Magus" (Legenda o kouzelníku Šimonovi, 1911). Short story. From *Posvátné ohně*, 1911. Translated by Geoffrey Chew. In *And My Head Exploded*. London: Jantar, 2018: 149–63.

"Legende von der ehrwürdigen Maria Electa von Jesus" (Legenda o ctihodné Marii Elektě z Ježíše, 1922). Novella. In German publication *Fin de siècle* (2004).

Il romanzo di Manfred Macmillen (Román Manfreda Macmillena, 1907). Novel. Translated and introduced by Růžena Hálová. Bergamo: Moretti & Vitali, 2017.

"The Roses of St. Sebastian" (Růže svatého Šebestiána, 1911). Short story. From *Posvátné ohně*, 1911. Translated by Kirsten Lodge. In *Slovo a smysl/Word & Sense* 7, no. 14 (2010). http://slovoasmysl.ff.cuni.cz/node/228.

"Stagnant Waters" (Stojaté vody, 1895). Short story. Translated by Kirsten Lodge. Issuu.com (Twisted Spoon Press). Last modified March 16, 2012. https://issuu.com/twistedspoon/docs/stagnant_waters.

Notes

1. *Jitřenka* was a Moravian monthly (1882–1948). See Holeček, "Vydávat Karáska..."

2. Holeček, "Vydávat Karáska..." Per Kolařík, "Raná literární tvorba Jiřího Karáska ze Lvovic," 607, this same title was also serialized in *Jitřenka* in 1892–93 under the title *Zmařené žití* (Thwarted Living).

3. Part of an improvised almanac produced by the Mahábhárata circle (q.v. note 125 in Introduction). Kolařík, "Raná literární tvorba Jiřího Karáska ze Lvovic," 607.

4. Dated February 28, 1893. Unpublished. See Introduction, n124 for description. Kolařík, "Raná literární tvorba Jiřího Karáska ze Lvovic," 607.

5. Under the title *Neschopnost žití* per Holeček, "Vydávat Karáska..."

6. Holeček, "Vydávat Karáska..."

7. Later included in the first two editions of Karásek's poetry collection *Hovory se smrtí* (1904) and among the various texts in *Cesta mystická* (1932). Kolařík, "Raná literární tvorba Jiřího Karáska ze Lvovic," 608.

8. First published in 1896 per Kolařík, "Raná literární tvorba," 608.

9. Zach, "Gemini."

ABOUT THE AUTHORS

Carleton Bulkin is an independent scholar and translator who holds a master's degree in Slavic languages and literatures from Indiana University. He has lived in Prague, Havana, Moscow, Budapest, Kabul, Rabat, Jeddah, and the Washington, DC area. Among his publications is the first bidirectional Dari–English/English–Dari dictionary. He currently resides in Seattle.

Brian James Baer is professor of Russian and translation studies at Kent State University. His recent publications include *Queer Theory and Translation Studies: Language, Politics, Desire*. He is founding editor of the journal *Translation and Interpreting Studies*, and coeditor of book series on translation studies for Bloomsbury and Routledge.